Always the Bridesmaid

Always the Bridesmaid

Sarah Webb

AVON
TRADE

An Imprint of HarperCollinsPublishers

This book was originally published in 2001 in the UK by Poolbeg Press Ltd.

HarperCollins books may be purchased for education, business, or sales promotional use. For information please write: Special Markets Department, HarperCollins Publishers Inc., 10 East 53rd Street, New York, NY 10022.

FIRST EDITION

Designed by Elizabeth M. Glover

Library of Congress Cataloging-in-Publication Data

Webb, Sarah.
    Always the bridesmaid / by Sarah Webb.
        p. cm.
    ISBN 0-06-057166-7 (alk. paper)
    1. Single women—Fiction. 2. Weddings—Fiction. 3. Ireland—Fiction. I. Title.

PR6123.E23A79 2004
823'.92—dc22   2003058258

04   05   06   07   08   JTC/RRD   10   9   8   7   6   5   4   3   2   1

To Tanya,
who loved this one so much

Acknowledgments

Due to my tendency to "gush" at this point, I would advise any readers, with weak stomachs to skip this bit and go straight to chapter one where Amy is waiting patiently for your full attention!

There would have been no book without many, many people— My Thanks . . .

As always to my wonderful family—Mum, Dad, Kate, Emma, Peter, Luan, Richard—for all their help, love and babysitting. And thanks for the illustrations, Kate.

To Sam for being a great son and for making me smile every day.

To Ben—my very own "Steve" and one of the kindest men on the planet.

To Andrew, Tanya and Nikki—my "youngest" old friends. Andrew for his wonderful taste in best men, Tanya for all the tireless manuscript reading, and for the "Italian" bits and Nikki for never failing to make me laugh.

To Emma and Peter for letting me blatantly pilfer "wedding" details. I would like to point out that the Aussie best man, Luke, is in no based way on Justin, who is an upstanding young man of good character and has never, to my knowledge, had anything to do with bridesmaids' legs!

To Niamh for the introduction to the heady world of wedding fairs.

To the McDonald family for their kind and loving care of Sam, especially Muireann.

To Michael, bookseller extraordinaire. His "Exchange" bookshop in Dalkey is an Aladdin's cave for any bibliophile.

To Mary and the staff at Dalkey library for their good-humored help with all my unusual book requests.

To Margaret and Sinead from Loreto Dalkey School—keep reading! And to Treasa, Pauline and the girls in St. Kevin's in Kilnamanagh, my favorite school.

To Socky, Joe, Geri and Sharon for all the "research"! RTE are lucky to have you—true professionals who make work fun.

To the latest additions—Lia, Lara, Molly, Daniel, Ian, Rory and Isaac.

To all at Poolbeg, especially Gaye, Paula, Helen, Lucy, Kieran, Conor and last, but certainly not least, Suzanne. For your combined patience, enthusiasm and for making the whole "book experience" run so smoothly.

Once again, to all the booksellers around the country who tirelessly promote books and reading, especially the constantly tidying children's ones!

To the gang at Eason's who have been so kind and supportive about my work. Special thanks to Tom, Adrian, Alan, David, Sally, Caron, Monica, Catherine, Maria and "The Reps," Bernard (and Katie), Caroline, Adele and Mary for all their enthusiasm.

To all the extended family and friends who have been there for me and Sam over the years, especially June, Marty and Pam.

And almost finally, to all my friends whose weddings I've ever attended—they were all inspirational! To the "newly-weds" amongst you—Sally and Ciaran, Dave and Sarah, Jamie and Shirley, and Paul and Dee—may you all live in wedded bliss!

And last but not least, to you, the reader, for parting with your hard-earned cash—I hope you enjoy this book as much as I enjoyed writing it!

Life is like a wild tiger. You can either lie down and let it lay its paw on your head—or sit on its back and ride it.

A Guide for the Advanced Soul,
Susan Hayward

Chapter 1

The paranoia all started to kick in when my "baby" sister Suzi came home from Australia last December at the tender age of twenty-four, with the Golden Delicious rugby-playing Matt in tow. I thought things couldn't get any worse.

I was wrong.

"Suzi, have you told Mum and Dad?" I asked as we were loading my Golf with the bags in the airport car park. Matt had kindly offered to get rid of the baggage trolley.

"About what?" she asked quickly.

"About Matt," I replied. "Do they know he's come to live in Dublin?" She certainly hadn't told me and I'd got rather a shock when I'd seen the whole hunky six-foot-something of him coming through the arrivals gate with his arm draped over my sister's shoulders. Although I must admit that I'd thoroughly enjoyed the firm, muscular hug his brown arms had generously given me.

"Not exactly," she said nervously, "but they'll love him and there's loads of room in the house and . . ."

"The house?" I interrupted, trying to keep my voice level. "You and Matt are planning to live at home?"

"Well, we want to save for a house and I'm sure Mum and Dad won't mind."

"Right," I muttered darkly. First me, now Suzi—it wasn't as if we were Italian. Surely we were supposed to have our own homes at our age.

"Do you think it'll be a problem?" Suzi bit her lip.

"No," I lied. "They're so excited about having you home, I'm sure they won't mind."

Suzi nudged me. Matt was smiling at her across the car's roof.

"Let's go," Suzi said.

"You're very quiet," I said to Suzi who was sitting in the back with Matt as I drove down the motorway. Matt was looking anxiously out the back window at the driving rain and the dark gray sky. She leaned forward and popped her head through the space between the two front seats.

"I'm a bit worried about Mum and Dad. You're right. I should have told them. I just thought I'd surprise them, you know."

"I shouldn't have said anything," I said. I felt bad—I should have kept my mouth firmly shut. I was always putting my Yeti-sized in it.

"Can we go for a drink before going home?" Suzi asked. She turned her head. "Matt, how are you feeling?"

"Fine," he stated. "Did you say drink?"

"Yes."

"Sounds cool."

"How about Johnnie Fox's?" I asked. "Show Matt a bit of real Ireland."

"Tourist Ireland, you mean," Suzi giggled. "Good idea."

As we drove up the steep, almost vertical, road toward the pub, I thought about the "lovebirds" and where they would sleep. Although neither of the parents are priests or vicars (unless they secretly belong to some strange sect who only practice early on Saturday and Sunday mornings when normal mortals, myself included, are dead to the world), we live beside the local church, which gives the term "what will the neighbors think?" new meaning. And directly opposite the house lives Father Lucas. So you can see why Suzi and Matt "living in sin" might not appeal to Mum and Dad.

When the church sold off some of its land and buildings to pay for a new roof, Dad and Mum bought a run-down, cut-stone Victorian house, originally the rectory. It was described as being "full of charm and old-world character." Bloody cold is what it really was.

There was no central heating, no hot water as the immersion was on the blink, cold stone-tiled floors on the ground floor and bare pitch-black floorboards in the bedrooms and bathroom upstairs.

At the time we didn't give a monkey's about "the original Victorian iron fireplaces," or "the hand-glazed stained-glass window panels" or "the ancient white claw-footed bath with brass taps." We were freezing our tits off and destined to be woken every Sunday morning in the wee small hours (well, ten o'clock is very early if you've had one too many the night before) by the deafening clanging peal of the "original" Victorian church bells!

Mum and Dad had, to give them credit, turned the cold *Psycho*-house on the hill into—as an estate agent would say—"a delightful residence full of original character and untouched by the scourge of rabid modernization." But it had taken over twelve years and a lot of trips to house auctions, antique shops, not to mention rummages in skips and derelict houses. Dad always claimed they were completely derelict but we often wondered. Suzi and I had learned to spot old pine, original cast porcelain tiles, brass fenders and other weird and wonderful Victorian "housey bits" at a tender age.

Several years ago Dad opted for early retirement from his job as an architect with the Civil Service and set up The Architectural Salvage Company. A few weeks into the work and he was as happy as Larry and wondering why he hadn't packed in the office job years ago. He was dead right, if you ask me. Life's short and if you're going to spend years of your life working you may as well pick something you like. I should have taken my own advice . . . Anyway, as I said, he loved the work and soon filled the garage and back garden with his "finds," much to Mum's disgust. Mum used to be an air hostess for Aer Lingus, and she's still always perfectly coiffured and immaculately dressed. She'd look glamorous in a polyester house-coat! I don't know what happened to the rest of the family. Neither does she for that matter.

Mum and Dad make an interesting couple, chalk and cheese really. Dad is never out of his jeans, which are usually covered in rust or mud or paint, his hair is usually in need of a drastic cut and he insists on wearing an old pair of black army boots, although Mum bought him a trendy pair of beige Timberland boots, which live in their box under the bed.

It's funny. Dad stopped working on our own house as soon as he got into the "business." I kind of miss helping him painting, giving furniture the distressed look and painting terracotta pots with yoghurt to make them "mold" and look ancient more quickly.

I used to help my friend Jodie sometimes when she needed a hand. She's an interior designer—the type who will come in and rip your house apart before even starting! So I helped her some weekends when I wasn't in the bookshop—The Wonderland Children's Bookshop in Blackrock.

I really wanted to be . . . it was kind of embarrassing really. I'd never said it out loud to anyone and I knew it would never happen . . . but I really wanted to present children's programs. On *Den 2*. The girls and guys they have on *Den 2* looked like they were having so much fun. They got to wear cool clothes in really bright colors and act like kids. I used to watch all the time—research, you understand—and they were making little eggshell men, filling eggshells with earth and putting mustard and cress seeds on top. And they had one they'd made earlier—how I longed to say that— "Here's one I made earlier, boys and girls!" Anyway Damien, the cute dark-haired one, watered his little eggshell man and left him to grow in studio. And as I watched I just wanted to be him. Imagine making eggshell men and introducing cartoons every day— heaven!

"Me ears are popping, mate," Matt exclaimed as we pulled into the car park.

Suzi laughed and nibbled one of his earlobes. I watched them in the rear-view mirror, trying not to let the green-eyed monster grip my heart and squeeze. Suzi's legs were draped over Matt's firm thighs. She curled his hair around her tanned fingers and gazed at him longingly. A black Range Rover blared its horn at my Golf which had wandered, with my mind, onto the wrong side of the road. I waved, mouthed a "sorry" and pulled the car into an empty space beside the pub's front door. Beside us was a large bus whose signs proclaimed it to be the servant of the Clontarf Rugby Club.

Matt's eyes lit up as soon as he spotted the word "rugby." His generous mouth broke into a wide smile, showing two gleaming layers of perfect teeth, honed from years of carnivorous tearing of meat in a rugged, manly way no doubt. Attractive crinkles formed at the sides of his eyes and I gazed, smitten—he was only gorgeous. Suzi glared at me dangerously.

"Amy," she hissed, "stop staring."

"Sorry," I mumbled. But Matt hadn't noticed—his head was full of hookers, oddly shaped balls and tries. I'd always thought rugby was a bizarre sport.

We got out of the car and Matt threw his manly arm around Suzi's petite frame and propelled her through the door. She's five-foot-nothing, with a mane of long silky blond hair, bright blue eyes and clear peachy skin—your average nightmare! It wouldn't take much to propel her anywhere as she's so tiny. And of course she wears the obligatory "cute girl" clothes to boot—well, wouldn't you? Belly tops, skin-tight trousers or short leather skirts. I feel like a heffalump beside her. I'm an average sort of size twelve to fourteen, depending on the day and the label. With shortish blond hair that has to be helped quite considerably to stay blond, depending on the time of the year. But beside Suzi everyone looks huge. The worst thing is that she eats like a horse, honestly. And I just have to think about chocolate and I put on pounds—it's so unfair!

As we walked through the door our eyes adjusted to the darkened room. Loud cheers were coming from the back, where a group of larger-than-average men had gathered. Matt gazed over longingly. He loped over to the bar to fetch the drinks while Suzi and I flopped onto the huge sofa beside the open fire.

"Bliss," Suzi said as she flipped off her navy Converse sandals and curled her dainty feet under her. Although it was December, her legs and feet were bare.

"Are you not cold?" I asked. She was wearing a purple cotton dress which just skimmed her knees and a white hooded fleece.

"I am a bit," she admitted. "I hope Matt's OK. He's not used to the cold."

"It's not that cold today," I warned. "You're lucky."

"Thanks for collecting us." Suzi smiled and placed her hand on my knee. "It was really good of you."

"Not at all," I replied. "It was nice to get out of the house for a while."

Suzi looked at me carefully. "Are you all right? I was sorry to hear about . . . you know."

"About Jack," I stated firmly. "It's OK, Suzi. I don't mind talking about it."

"It was just so sudden," Suzi continued. "We all thought you two were perfect together. What happened?"

I smiled. Suzi had a habit of coming straight to the point. But it was refreshing in a way. Everyone had spent the last few weeks pussyfooting around me and avoiding asking any direct questions. I guess they all thought that Jack had instigated the "broken engagement."

Jack and I had been living together for three years and had begun skirting around the whole marriage thing. Jack seemed to think it was the way forward but I wasn't so sure. Things hadn't been right for ages. I knew I couldn't marry him in the foreseeable future—it just wouldn't be right if I wasn't 100% sure.

"I don't know where to start, Suze. There was this work party and . . ." I began.

"Here you are, girls," Matt interrupted, plonking the glasses of Guinness down on the table in front of us. "Met a guy from Clontarf Rugby Club. Plays wing like me. OK if I join him for a scoop, love?" he asked Suzi.

"No worries," she replied.

"Great," he grinned. "See you Sheilas later." In a matter of seconds Matt was demonstrating the haka with a rapt audience of adoring Irish and American men and women.

"That's my man," Suzi proclaimed proudly as she watched him waggle his tongue around and slap his thighs.

"I thought it was New Zealand players who did the haka? And I thought Australians hated New Zealanders?" I asked, a little confused.

"It is," Suzi confirmed. "And they do normally. But Matt's special, I guess." She smiled widely. "No one could dislike him. He played for a club in Auckland for a while—that's where he learned it. Matt's really good, played for his country on the Under-21 reserve team."

"Of course he did," I muttered darkly. "Friend of Jonah's, is he?" He probably had a bloody doctorate in aeronautics too! A right Mr. Perfect.

"Sorry?" Suzi asked.

"Nothing. Don't mind me."

Suzi smiled. "Tell me about Jack. What were you saying?"

I took a sip of my drink and stared into the fire. My cheeks were beginning to glow in the warmth and I cast my mind back to that evening, only weeks before.

"I guess the doubts began to set in when Jack's architectural firm had a work party for some of their big clients. They wanted to show how they could use modern technology—Autocad—stuff like that. Anyway before the party each of the established architects was given a "team" and each team had to produce a design using computer technology. Jack's lot had to design a church using natural materials." I paused and looked at my sister. "Are you sure you want to hear all this?"

Suzi smiled kindly. "Yes. I really do. Go on."

"OK. Jack had been working really hard on this design. I barely saw him at all. When he wasn't in the office he was working on the computer at home."

"That was hard on you," Suzi said.

"That didn't bother me at all, to tell the truth," I said. "I liked it in a way—seeing him so involved in work and so into something. He'd been moaning about being underutilized and this gave him a chance to show what he could do." I took another sip of my Guinness. It was so good to have Suzi back. I needed to talk to someone about Jack. Beth was busy with Tony, and Jodie . . . I loved her dearly but she wasn't the most sympathetic of people at the best of times.

"The night before the presentation he was up to ninety, the design was nearly finished and his team had gone home. He rang me from the office to tell me he'd be late as he was going to try to finish it by himself." I stared at the fire again, watching the flames lick around the red-hot coals. "I heard Jack's car roar into the drive hours later. I was asleep at the time and I remember thinking it was strange as he was usually so careful not to wake me up. He slammed the car door and he made loads of noise stomping up the stairs and fell in the bedroom door." I looked at Suzi and sighed. "He'd been drinking, Suze. I could smell it off his breath. He sat down on the bed and began to talk to me. Asking why I hadn't waited up and ranting about how I never supported him and his work."

"Why?" Suzi asked. "I don't understand. What was wrong?"

"After a while he told me that something had happened to the computer system and he hadn't saved his work properly. Jack went and lost the whole file, Suze. The design his team had been working on so hard for that presentation."

"Jesus!" Suzi said. "Poor man. But why was he annoyed with *you*? It was hardly your fault."

"Because I was there. Because he was annoyed at himself, I guess. And maybe I wasn't as sympathetic as I could have been. I think I told him that it was only work and not to overreact. Something like that anyway." I wondered what exactly I *had* said. I couldn't really remember—I'd been half-asleep at the time and not exactly delighted to be woken up in the middle of the night.

"Did he calm down?" Suzi asked with concern.

"Eventually. And the following day one of the women in the office managed to retrieve the file from the hard drive so it was OK in the end. And to be honest it wasn't even his behavior that got me thinking."

"What was it?" Suzi asked.

"At the presentation the next evening I was sitting with a group of his colleagues and I just didn't want to be there. The people were nice but I felt so tired and fed up. And as I sat there watching the presentation and listening to Jack's speech, I realized I didn't want to be with him anymore. The strange thing is that I couldn't quite put my finger on why—the whole relationship simply felt wrong. It's hard to explain." I stared into space.

"Go on," Suzi urged.

"That's pretty much it, really," I sighed. "The next day I got up early and packed some stuff while he was still asleep. He woke up halfway through."

"What did he say?" Suzi asked.

"He asked me what I was doing," I explained in hushed tones. "I told him I didn't want to be with him anymore and that I was really unhappy and that I was moving back home."

"Just like that?" Suzi asked, her eyes wide open in astonishment.

"Yes," I replied firmly. "I knew, given a few days, he'd talk me out of it. You know how strongly he can put things."

Suzi murmured assent. She remembered Jack's "strong words" at many a family dinner. His was usually the only raised voice at the table as the O'Sullivan family wasn't one for arguments.

"That was the strange thing," I said. "He just sat there and looked at me for ages. I started crying and I think I said I was sorry." I started to cry. Suzi put her arms around me. She silently stroked the back of my head.

I took a big gulp of air. "Then he said that I was right, that he'd felt the same way for ages. I couldn't believe it! He didn't want me anymore!"

"But, Amy," Suzi said quietly, "you were leaving him. Did you not stop to think that he was only protecting himself? You know what male egos are like. And anyway, why did you care? You were about to walk out on him!"

"I don't know," I said truthfully. "I suppose I wanted him to be still in love with me. For some reason that would have made it easier."

"In the short term, maybe," Suzi said thoughtfully. "But you did the right thing. I know it must have been difficult. Have you spoken to him since?"

"A few times," I grimaced. "To organize picking up my things and to cancel our joint account—that kind of thing."

"But you've never talked about your feelings," she asked, "like how you've both coped with the split?"

"No," I whispered. "Jack did suggest meeting up but I didn't feel strong enough. I knew I'd just cry in front of him and make myself miserable."

"I'm sure Jack has seen you cry before," Suzi smiled gently.

"Um," I murmured. Jack had asked to see me several times in fact but I'd stubbornly refused. I sighed. "I don't know. I'm beginning to think I was a little hasty. Maybe I should give it another chance. Sometimes I think I'm being unrealistic, expecting things to be perfect. Maybe I should have married him and be done with it."

"What are you talking about?"

"Oh, I don't know. I'm a bit down at the moment, I suppose. I'm feeling my age—I'll be thirty in a few months and it's getting to me."

Suzi snorted. "Jeez, girl, would you get a grip! Thirty is hardly the end of the world."

"I know, I know. But I thought I'd be, well . . . married at this stage. With two children and a nice house and a husband."

"I think you need one of those to be married all right!" Suzi laughed.

I smiled. "I'm serious. I had it all planned. Married at twenty-six, a baby girl at twenty-seven and a baby boy at twenty-nine. And what do I have—nothing!"

Suzi laughed. "Amy, I think you're blowing things well out of proportion. Hitting thirty is no reason to get married. Especially to someone you're not in love with."

"Who says I'm not in love with Jack?" I asked quietly.

Suzi looked at me carefully.

"That's the problem," I continued, tears welling up in my eyes. "I do love him. I just can't stand being with him."

Suzi gave me a hug. "Oh, Amy. I'm sorry. Don't cry. It'll be OK. You'll feel better soon, I promise. You did the right thing."

Chapter 2

"Amy, I know it sounds like a cliché, but it will get easier," Suzi said after coming back from the bar with a pint of Guinness for me and an orange juice for herself. Suzi had decided that she'd drive home as I needed to drink more than she did. Suzi is nice like that—most of the time. She's not bad as sisters go. Although she's a crap driver and I was putting my life in her hands letting her behind the wheel. Still, I did appreciate it.

"Matt's in heaven," she continued, taking off her hoody and draping it over the back of the sofa. "I brought him over a pint but he had three already in front of him. The whole back row were buying him drinks. They already have him persuaded to join their club."

I tried to smile. It wasn't fair on Suzi landing her with all this on her first day back. "Do you have any cigarettes?" I asked hopefully. I didn't really smoke, but now and again, mainly in the pub or in times of dire need, I scabbed one off my friend Beth. Or if things were really bad I bought a pack myself. I always felt guilty buying cigarettes in the shop. And drink too for that matter. It's ironic, I suppose—I'm twenty-nine for heaven's sake and I still worry about being asked my age in the pub. I wish! The last time I was asked for ID was when I put my hair in plaits (very trendy) for Suzi's twenty-first. And that was several years ago.

"Yup, but it's my last pack. I'm giving up. I can't afford to smoke now what with the . . . ."

"The what?" I asked.

"Um, the lack of a job," Suzi smiled. "I'm nipping out to the loo. The smokes are in my fleece." She jumped up and walked behind the bar to the toilets, followed by the admiring male eyes of the bar staff. I guess she did look well and a tan was unusual in December. I unzipped her pocket and found the cigarettes and gold Zippo lighter, my fingers grazing something cold. I pulled out the offending object. It was a small metal box. Being a nosy cow I opened it—in it, slipped into the lush red velvet interior, was a ring. Why did Suzi have a ring in her pocket? It looked kind of valuable, the stone sparkled in the dim light almost like a . . . I studied it carefully. It *was* a bloody diamond! Nothing else sparkled like that.

Suzi slipped onto the sofa beside me. "Are you OK?" she asked. "You took kind of pale?"

I held the ring up in front of her face. She blushed a deep scarlet, visible even under her even golden tan.

"Well?" I asked. "Is this what I think it is?"

Suzi sighed. "I'm sorry. Terrible timing I know, what with Jack and . . ."

I stared at her in amazement. "You mean this *is* an engagement ring?"

"Yes," she whispered. "I was going to wait a few weeks to tell you—when you felt a bit better. I'm sorry."

I felt really bad. Poor Suzi had been listening to me drone on about Jack Daly when she had news of her own. Huge news, the news of the year. The century even.

"Suzi," I leaned over and gave her a hug, "I'm the one who should be sorry." Tears welled up in my eyes and I'm embarrassed to admit they were a mixture of tears of happiness for her and tears of regret for me. I was her big sister after all—it was supposed to be me getting hitched first. I tried to stop feeling sorry for myself. It wasn't every day your sister got engaged.

"Oh, Suzi, how exciting! I'm so happy for you." I wiped away a genuine "happy for you" tear. "I don't know what to say."

"Thanks, sis," Suzi beamed back. She took the ring out of my hand and slipped it onto her ring finger.

"Amy?" she asked smiling at me. "Will you be my bridesmaid?"

"Of course, I'd love to," I lied. I mean what could I say? She was my sister. I'd only been bridesmaid once before when I was eleven at my cousin John's wedding. I'd worn a dark pink raw-silk dress with tiny pale pink rosebuds sewn onto the puff sleeves. I still cringed when I looked at the photos. Doing my duty once more wouldn't kill me. At least that's what I thought at the time.

Suzi spent the rest of the evening trying not to talk about her wedding. After a while I could see it was killing her not to discuss the plans. She mentioned a wedding dress and then quickly changed the subject.

"It's all right," I lied for the second time. "I'd love to hear your dress ideas."

"If you're sure," she said. "I'm just so excited. I can't believe it— me—getting married!"

I smiled. It was going to be a long evening. Maybe we could join Matt and his new friends. I tried to tune in to what Suzi was saying.

"I was thinking of ivory or even pale pink. I saw this amazing dress in *Vogue*. It was a real fairytale affair with loads of pink net and tiny daisies embroidered all over it. Or maybe tartan, but no, it's not a winter wedding. Or what about light-blue or sky-blue? Maybe not. I think classic white or cream. What do you think?"

"Um, yes," I replied smiling. I hoped it was the right answer. I kept thinking about Jack. I could be planning my wedding now instead of Suzi. And I knew exactly what I wanted. Small wedding— just family and close friends in the local church, big party the following night for the rest of my family, and friends. I'd mapped it all out years ago and refined the details until it was perfect. Trendy and fun but classy. I'd decorate the church and the tables myself. With my own vows and my own readings . . .

"Amy? Pink and yellow?" Suzi asked.

"Sorry?"

"About the flowers. Pink and yellow or lilies. Or daisies."

"Wow, I'm not sure, Suzi. It would depend on the dress, I suppose."

She smiled beatifically. "Yes, of course, you're right."

Bingo! Right answer.

"I think Matt is waving at us," I said hopefully. He wasn't, but it was enough to distract Suzi.

"We have been a bit antisocial, I guess," she said anxiously.

I picked up our drinks and stood up. "We should join him. Rude not to," I stated before she had a chance to think about it.

Matt was in the middle of recounting an Australian rules joke as we shoved our way through the crowds toward him.

"Here she is, my beautiful Irish Sheila. All right, Suzi?"

"Hi, Matt," Suzi beamed, wiggling her way to his side. He threw his arm over her shoulder and held her to his chest.

"Hi, babe," he said, kissing the top of her head.

"I told Amy," she bubbled, unable to keep it in for one second longer.

"We're getting married!" Matt informed the whole bar in booming tones, delighted that he didn't have to keep it in any longer. "And you're all invited!"

Suzi dug him in the ribs. "Matt, this is Ireland. You can't say things like that."

I laughed. "She's right, you know. They might all turn up at the wedding!" I kissed my prospective brother-in-law on the cheek. "Congratulations, Matt."

"Thanks, Amy," he grinned. "I'm a lucky man."

"I'm the lucky one," Suzi trilled.

And I'm the unlucky one, I thought to myself darkly.

Suzi drove us all home at half past ten. We'd meant to leave earlier but the Clontarf boys kept buying us drinks. They'd already installed Matt on the seconds and written his training times and first game on a napkin for him. Suzi was half-delighted and half-dismayed.

"I don't want him to turn into one of those rugby husbands who sees his wife and kids whenever the lads let him," she moaned.

"Kids?" I smiled. The last round—champagne—was beginning to go to my head.

Suzi blushed. "Maybe, eventually." She smiled. "Stop slagging me."

"Wouldn't dream of it." I laughed. It really was good to have Suzi back.

We drove back slowly. Suzi was a bit nervous on the road, not that either Matt or I would have noticed what side of the road my car was on. I hoped Mum and Dad would understand.

"Matt?" I asked as we drove past Foxrock Church. "Do your folks know about the wedding?"

No answer. I looked into the back seat. Matt was fast asleep, head resting against the side window, his warm breath misting up the glass.

"Yes," Suzi answered for him. "They were thrilled. Molly and Dan are great, you'll like them. A little mad but good fun. Matt has a very cute little brother too, Luke."

"Oh, don't you start," I complained.

"What did I say?"

"Sorry, I didn't mean to snap. It's just people."

"What are you talking about, Amy?" My poor sister was confused. But I guess I wasn't making much sense—to anyone other than myself that is. I tried to explain.

"People keep trying to set me up with any old man and I'm sick of it," I said eventually. It wasn't exactly what I meant but it was near enough. "I'm not a basket case. Don't treat me like one."

"A what?" Suzi asked.

"You know—mad. I can get my own men, thank you very much. I don't need help."

"I didn't mean . . ."

I was being hard on Suzi and it wasn't fair. I felt bad—again.

"Matt, Matt, we're here," Suzi got out of the car, opened the side door and started shaking him.

"High tackle. Run the ball, run the ball," Matt muttered, waking up. He opened his eyes. "Hi, Suzi," he hiccuped, eyes crinkling as he beamed up at her.

"Come on, love. We're here now," Suzi cajoled. She tried to pull him out of the car. I stood beside her, watching the scene. "Give us a hand, will you, Amy?" Suzi asked in desperation. Matt was a hulking sixteen stone or so and there was no way us puny, not to mention unfit (on my part!), lightweights would be able to shift him.

"Matt, if you come inside I'll make you a sandwich," I coaxed. Surely a man that size must like his food. I was right.

"What kinda sandwich?" he asked with interest.

"Meat," Suzi whispered. "Any kind of meat."

"Um, beef," I lied. I knew there was some old, curling-at-the-edges ham in the fridge as I'd thought about eating a slice for lunch before thinking better of it. But he was hardly likely to notice in the state he was in.

"OK," he stated. "Where's the kitchen?"

Suzi and I giggled as he lumbered out of the car and stood up straight.

"He's not used to champagne," Suzi whispered.

The light went on in the hall as we helped Matt toward the door.

"Shit," Suzi said.

Mum opened the door, Dad standing just behind her. The doorstep was bathed in golden light and Matt and I squinted at it from behind Suzi's back. I was trying to appear sober by fixing my eyes on the red and blue stained-glass side-panels on the door. It seemed to stop the swaying anyway.

"Suzi, my darling," Mum gushed, putting her arms around her and giving her a warm hug. Then she noticed Matt who was cowering behind Suzi. He could sense an awkward situation when he saw one. She unwrapped her arms from Suzi and looked at me with a dangerous glint in her eye. "Amy! Tonight of all nights. Have you no sense of decorum?"

"He's not mine!" I wailed before I could help myself.

Suzi smiled sheepishly. "Mum, Dad, this is Matt. My fiancé."

Chapter 3

Matt and I sat at the kitchen table tucking into two huge sandwiches—cheese and tomato for me, and ham and everything I could find in the fridge for him. He had some appetite—he was making proverbial mincemeat of the sandwich and sloshing down a pint of milk which left a cute ring around his manly mouth. I couldn't help myself—I noticed these things even when half-cut. I really had to stop.

I could hear raised voices coming from the living room where Suzi, Mum and Dad were ensconced. Mum had nearly fainted on the doorstep when Suzi had broken the news. Luckily Dad was behind her to steady her. He had brought her into the living room and sat her down on the sofa while we all followed behind anxiously. Otherwise she would have come a cropper on the hard tiled floor of the hall. I could just see it now as a headline in *The Star*—"Mother Struck Dead by Daughter's Confession." I was trying not to laugh. I have a terrible habit of giggling when I'm nervous. Matt didn't seem to know what was going on, poor lamb.

As soon as Mum was settled on the sofa, Dad took matters into his own hands. "Amy, bring Matthew into the kitchen and make your mother a cup of tea with lots of sugar." He smiled at Suzi who was quivering in her Converse. "Don't worry, pet. You just gave your Mum a bit of a shock. She'll be grand. Now where's my hug?"

I directed Matt down the three steps into the kitchen. He gave his head a bit of a bang on the doorframe, which is a little low. But he didn't seem to notice.

"Who were they?" he asked in confusion as I pulled two plates out of the wooden drainer above the sink.

I smiled. "Your future parents-in-law."

As we were eating Dad came in. "Is your Mum's tea ready?" he asked.

"Sorry, Dad. I forgot."

"Don't worry," he replied. "I'll do it." He flicked on the kettle and waited while it boiled.

"How's Mum?" I asked.

"Fine. Suzi just gave her a bit of a fright. She explained about Johnnie Fox's and the Clontarf rugby team buying you champagne. I'm not surprised you two are feeling a little under the weather." He smiled at Matt. "Sorry. It wasn't the warmest of welcomes, mate." Dad held out his hand. "I'm Frank O'Sullivan. And you've met my wife, Denise."

Matt wiped his mayonnaise-covered fingers on his jeans before taking Dad's hand. "Matt Street. Pleasure's all mine."

Dad sat down at the table and began to talk to Matt. "Suzi tells us you're a bit of a rugby player. Used to play myself . . ." And they were off. The usual male-bonding session focusing on sport, sport and more sport. I made Mum's tea and brought it up to her.

The door of the living room was ajar and I stopped for a moment outside. I didn't want to interrupt anything, you understand. They were talking about weddings. It hadn't taken long!

"We'll have to ask Father Lucas about the garden, Suzi. You may have to get officially married in a church or a registry office. But he might give a blessing in the garden."

The garden! She hadn't told me about the garden bit. "Suzi, are you getting married in the garden?" I asked, walking carefully toward the conspiring pair on the sofa, trying to keep the tea in the mug and off the floorboards.

"Maybe, or St. Martin's. I did tell you. You mustn't have been listening."

I smiled sheepishly at her. She was probably right.

"Here's your tea, Mum." I handed over the mug.

"Isn't it wonderful news?" Mum glowed. "Suzi and Matt. Who would have thought? I'd heard about the wonderful Matt in Suzi's letters, of course. But finally—a wedding. And this summer. Isn't it exciting?"

I murmured assent under my breath. I was beginning to feel a bit left out if the truth be told. I decided to go to bed and to leave them all to it. I gave Suzi a kiss and said goodnight.

"You're not going already?" Mum asked and then added gently, "Oh my God, Amy, I'm so sorry. I'd forgotten . . . what with all the excitement . . ."

"It's fine. I'm fine. I'm just tired. I have to work tomorrow," I stated quickly. Then it dawned on me. I really did have to work tomorrow. I had to don my Story Princess hat and tell stories to little hyperactive brats for two hours in the bookshop. A nightmare at the best of times, but with a hangover—pure hell!

I staggered up the stairs to my bedroom. As I walked in the door I felt miserable. I was thirty in a few months and I was still living at home, in the same bedroom I'd slept in since I was a child. It had the same yellow walls, Victorian iron-framed bed and huge mahogany chest of drawers. Nothing was different except the bedcovers. Instead of a Garfield duvet cover I now had a plain white one with tiny yellow daisies embroidered on it. It was from the single bed in the guest room of our old house—mine and Jack's. I started crying. I couldn't help it. I pulled off my clothes and crawled into bed in my underwear. I didn't care about my still made-up face. Blocked pores were the least of my worries at this stage. I remembered to set my alarm and then fell soundly asleep as soon as my head hit the pillow.

I walked into the kitchen in my white toweling dressing-gown the next morning wincing my eyes. My head was throbbing and I felt like death. Mum was chopping tomatoes at the counter, dressed in a perfectly laundered light-blue tracksuit and sparkling white runners. Why did my tracksuit never look like that?

"Morning, love," she said cheerfully. "I'm just cooking Matthew an Irish breakfast. Would you like one?"

My stomach lurched. I wasn't quite sure if it was indicating re-
pulsion to food or hunger. I decided to risk it. I needed sustenance
to cope with work. "Thanks, Mum, that would be great. Can I
help?"

She smiled. "No, it's all under control. And how are you feeling
this morning?"

"A little ropey," I admitted. "Are Suzi and Matt up yet?"

"Matt's out running and Suzi's in the bath."

Running! Was he mad? You can't run with a hangover. It's
masochistic.

"Isn't he a nice young man?" Mum asked. "So easygoing and so
polite." I couldn't help but feel that she was having a dig at Jack but
I decided to ignore it.

"He's lovely," I replied.

"Suzi's a lucky young lady," Mum continued. "He'll make a wonderful husband."

"Um," I replied, opening the Review supplement of *The Sunday
Tribune.* You'd want to have rhino-thick skin to live in this house, I
thought to myself. I began reading an interesting article on a new
children's book.

Suzi walked into the room a few minutes later and sat down at the
table. "Amy?" she asked tentatively. "Could we borrow your car
today? We're going to look at houses near Clontarf."

"If you drop me into work on your way. I don't have the energy
to walk this morning."

"Fine," she agreed.

An hour later we were driving toward Dublin city. Suzi was at the
wheel with Matt beside her and I was in the back. It was quite interesting sitting in the back. I'd never sat there before. I noticed new
things about my car, and I even found my pink hairbrush lodged between the upholstery and the side. As we drove past Blackrock College rugby pitches Suzi told Matt about Landsdowne Road and
promised to show him the stadium another day. Amazing how
sports stadiums could bring out the child in any man, I mused. Jack
was into soccer in a big way—Man United were his idols and he had

never stopped boring me about the red-jumpered team. It all went in one ear and out the other, of course. At least I wouldn't have to pretend to listen to any of it anymore.

I tried to push Jack out of my mind but it was proving difficult. Everything reminded me of him, from music on the radio to certain smells. Especially smells, in fact. Jack had a lemony, clean, boyish smell. It was very attractive and I couldn't get enough of it at one stage. I used to smell the pillows when he'd gone to work and when he was away. I had to stop torturing myself. It was all for the best.

Suzi pulled up outside the bookshop and I hopped out.

"Thanks, Suze," I said. "See you both later." I watched the car drive off. I was trying not to be jealous of my sister but it was hard.

Lynn, the owner and manager, had put the Story Princess board outside the door of the shop. "Today between two and three the Story Princess will read from *Alice's Adventures in Wonderland* by Lewis Carroll. All welcome."

I smiled. *Alice* was Lynn's favorite book. Maybe today wouldn't be so bad after all. I mean, reading children stories was hardly "work," was it? I took a deep breath and smiled again. The shop's window looked wonderful. Lynn had put the Christmas decorations in. A small, real Christmas tree twinkled with white lights. A glorious array of glossy hardback gift-books were displayed against a dark red velvet backdrop. Tiny gold bows adorned each book and handcrafted wooden Christmas decorations hung from the branches of the tree. It looked enchanting.

Lynn was originally from New York, a vibrant and infectiously enthusiastic lady in her early sixties. She wore bright, stylish clothes and always reminded me of a ballet teacher I'd once had when I was in primary school in the way she moved—elegantly and fluidly—with her head held high and her neck and back poker-straight. Good posture you'd call it, I suppose. She had moved to Ireland with her husband, but was now a widow.

I loved working for Lynn. I'd worked for her part-time during college—Arts in UCD—and when I'd graduated she'd offered me a "proper" job. I hadn't a clue what I wanted to do so I took it. And I'd been there ever since.

As I stepped in the door the bronze bell tinkled. Lynn looked up from the desk where she was reading a new picture-book edition of *The Wizard of Oz*. Perched on her nose were special glasses with green lenses which made the pages glow green, like the Emerald City in the story.

"My, my, you look just like an alien," Lynn smiled. She removed the glasses. "That's better. How are you this good morning?"

I smiled. It was impossible to be in a bad mood with Lynn around. "Grand, thanks. I had a bit of a late night in the end though, so you'll have to go easy on me today."

"And how's Suzi?" she asked warmly. "Happy to be home?"

"Yes," I said. "And wait till I tell you . . ."

"Stop!" Lynn commanded. "Let's get some coffee and you can unravel the whole story."

Soon I had "unraveled" the whole story as Lynn put it. Matt, Mum and Dad—the whole enchilada.

"It's hard on you, honey. After the whole Jack thing." I had told Lynn some of the Jack tale. She was a good listener, more like a big sister than a boss.

"I'm fine," I replied. And I would be fine—eventually. "And Suzi's so excited."

The bell tinkled. A man walked in, a large bag over his shoulder and a small, dark-haired girl following closely behind. I stopped talking and went over to help him with the door.

"Thanks," he said as I held the door open for him.

"I'm looking for some books for Zoe," the man said.

"I'm Zoe," the little girl ventured, staring at me intently. She was quite stunning—pale, with huge dark-brown eyes and long black hair which hung in two thin plaits down her back. She was wearing a denim dress, pink woolly tights and tiny red Doc Marten·boots.

"Hi, Zoe," I said. "It's very nice to meet you. Now what type of books do you like?"

Silence. Zoe held what I assumed was her Father's hand tightly. He looked at me and smiled warmly.

"She's a little shy today. I think we'll just have a look around for a bit if that's all right." He had a lovely smile. Blond hair, tightly cropped, bright-blue eyes, dressed in black from top to toe like a movie star. He was in his late twenties or early thirties, it was hard to tell, and he had a Southern English accent, soft and attractive.

"Of course," I smiled, trying to concentrate. Things were bad when I started sizing up Fathers! Although he wasn't wearing a wedding ring—I sneaked a look at his ring finger.

Zoe stared at me again. "Are you the Story Princess?" she asked quietly.

"I am," I replied.

"I'd like a princess book, I think," she whispered.

"Let's see what I can find," I smiled. The bell rang as Siobhan Molloy, and her three girls, regular Sunday customers, walked in the door. Lynn greeted them and the girls, all dedicated readers, made their way under the golden arch and into the fiction room at the back of the shop. Lynn had designed and decorated the shop herself and it was a child's heaven, full of nooks and crannies, cloud-painted ceilings and specially crafted bookshelves in the shapes of dragons, the Children of Lir, Matilda and other favorite children's book characters.

I flicked through the picture-books with Zoe by my side.

"Princesses," I murmured. "Let's see. *The Little Princess* by Frances Hodgson Burnett." I pulled out an illustrated edition of the children's classic. "I love this story. It's all about a little girl who's a princess but she has to stay at this boarding-school while her father is away."

Zoe frowned. "Is she a real princess?"

"She is," I replied, trying not to smile. "Or here's another one— *The Thistle Princess* by Vivian French." I opened the book and flicked through the pages. "Look at the pictures—beautiful, aren't they?"

Zoe smiled. "I like the colors. Pink's my favorite, you know."

Her Dad was standing behind us, listening.

"Would you like me to read to you, Zoe?" he asked.

The little girl nodded firmly. Soon their heads were buried in *The Thistle Princess.*

I looked at them and sighed. I loved seeing Dads and their kids but it always made me feel jealous. I could hear my biological clock ticking away at times as loudly as the hands on my ancient bronze alarm clock. It's not that I wanted kids, well, not right then. But I would have liked the option. Jack was never big into children at all. He hadn't much time for them really. It was different for him I supposed. He didn't have fermenting eggs in him. I mused on the unfairness of it all for a few minutes.

"Amy, are you OK?" Lynn joined me at the counter where I was staring listlessly at the computer screen. "You've been staring at that thing for ages. It's not healthy."

I tore my eyes away.

"Sorry, I was in another world."

"Are you ready for the story session? If you're not up to it, I'll do it." Lynn smiled. She really was very kind. But I knew she had Internet orders to process.

"I'm fine, honestly," I tried to appear enthusiastic. "I'm looking forward to *Alice*. I'm going to read the Cheshire Cat chapter."

"Good choice," Lynn enthused. "I'll leave you to get ready."

Lynn sat down on the stool behind the counter and accessed our e-mail to collect the on-line orders. As we were a small specialist shop the Internet was important to our business. We had customers from all over the world, Japan to North America, many of whom relied on Lynn's expertise. She had a doctorate on children's book illustration and was especially keen on the work of the young Irish illustrator P. J. Lynch who was a personal friend of hers. She was quite a woman!

I fetched the Story Princess hat from the back room and set the little wooden chairs and bean bags in a circle at the back of the shop, beside the Enchanted Castle shelves which held the Irish picturebooks. The shop was beginning to fill up. Siobhan's daughters sat down at the front, gazing up at me expectantly. Although they were well able to read themselves they still loved to hear stories told aloud. Zoe and her father sat down behind them, followed by two small boys and several other children.

I began. "I'm the Story Princess and today I'm going to read to you from *Alice's Adventures in Wonderland* by Lewis Carroll." The shop went quiet as all eyes were on me. It was a strange feeling but I liked it.

When I first started the story-telling sessions I felt self-conscious and nervous, but Lynn made me stick with it and I began to look forward to them. Children were an unforgiving audience but an honest one. You had to work hard to hold their attention. "Alice is lost in the woods and she spots a strange cat sitting in a tree above her head. And now I'll begin. 'Cheshire Puss,' Alice began rather timidly. 'Would you tell me, please, which way I ought to go from here?' 'That depends a good deal on where you want to get to,' said the Cat . . ."

After the story my audience clapped and Clara, Siobhan's eldest daughter, a serious girl of eleven, bought a copy of the book to read to her sisters at home.

"Thanks, we really enjoyed that," Zoe's father shook my hand warmly. "Can I buy these?" He handed me a pile of hardback picture-books, including the ones I'd chosen earlier for Zoe.

"Of course, come over to the desk and I'll wrap them for you." I placed the pile on the desk and began to put them through the till. "Oh, I love this one," I smiled as I noticed the cover of *Where the Wild Things Are.*

"It's for me," he smiled. "I love it too. I'm Steve by the way and you've met Zoe."

"I'm Amy," I faltered, blushing. I just couldn't help it. He was so damn nice. Why did they always have to be married?

I bagged his books and gave him his credit card back. And of course I read the name. Stephen J Jones. There had to be some good things about working in a shop after all.

"Goodbye, Steve. And Zoe. See you again." Zoe put her small hand out and Steve grasped it firmly. He smiled. "I hope so."

I gazed out the window after they had left.

"So do I," I whispered. So what if he was married? I could always dream. And maybe he had a nice brother or a friend—who knew? I liked to keep the options open.

Lynn sidled over to me. "Cute, isn't he?" Typical, caught in the act. "You know who he is, of course?"

I stared at her, feigning indifference. "Who?"

"Don't play the innocent with me, young lady," she laughed.

"OK, OK," I sighed. " I admit it, he was nice. So put me out of my misery. Who is he then?"

"Stevie J."

"*The* Stevie J?"

"Yep!"

"The Stevie J who writes those amazing fantasy books?"

"The very same." Stevie J was an English writer and one of the most famous children's book personalities in the world. His books, based on the adventures of a young wizard called Henry, had sold in their millions and Spielberg was filming the first one.

"And," she grinned mischievously, "he's single and living in Dublin. The little girl is his niece."

"And how do you know that exactly?" I asked amazed. Maybe there was a God.

"Female intuition," she laughed. "And his website!"

Chapter 4

I smiled to myself as I walked down Seapoint Road toward Jodie's flat. Stevie J. I intended to tell Jodie all about my encounter. Not that she would have a clue who he was. But she was always interested in cute guys, no matter who they were. She was pretty much permanently single, by choice and not by design. She'd had one or two "boyfriends" but they never lasted long. Jodie had unbelievably high standards and wouldn't take any shit from a guy. Which made relationships almost impossible. After all, men and trouble go together hand in glove.

It was nice to think about another guy. I knew I'd probably never see Stevie J again and if he did happen to come into the shop again nothing would happen. What was I going to do—ask him out while he was paying for a book?

"That's ten pounds, please. And by the way how about dinner tonight?" I didn't think so. Not after the waiter episode. Never, ever again.

"Of course you can ask guys out," Jodie had stated one Sunday in June. "They love it. Remember Liam from Club 92? I asked him out."

"Jodie, he'd already bought you three drinks and you'd been dancing with him all night. And I thought you said he dropped hints all night, like 'What do you do at the weekends?' "

Jodie smiled. "OK, you're right. But I still made the arrangement, didn't I?"

"Um, I suppose," I muttered. Everything was always so black and white in Jodie's world. Life seemed to be so much easier for her than for me. She knew exactly what she wanted and stuck to it no matter what. I was a bit more of a "gray" sort of person. I didn't find life all that simple or easy at all. In fact some days I found it downright hard to get out of bed. "Moody," my mother called me. I guess sometimes I thought about things too much. I've always found it hard not to. Made for many a sleepless night as three in the morning seemed my brain's favorite time to think about things. Three in the morning until six in the morning. Then I always fell into a comatose sleep and felt really groggy and crap at seven when I had to get up.

There was this really nice waiter in the Café Java in Blackrock and whenever we went in he always chatted to us and smiled over when he was serving other people. Jodie and I got talking to him one day when the café was quiet. He told us he was a student. After a few weeks he began to sit down at our table and chew the fat for a few minutes. He was really interested in interiors and found Jodie's work fascinating. Jodie reckoned he fancied me. I reckoned he was lonely and liked a natter.

So one day, while Jodie excused herself to go the loo (planned of course!) I mortified myself.

"Um, Joel, I was wondering . . . um, if perhaps you'd, um . . ."

Joel had looked up from his mug of hot chocolate with interest. "Yes?"

I could feel myself blushing. But I couldn't stop now.

"I was wondering if you'd like to go out for a drink sometime?"

Joel seemed very surprised. He gazed at me intently. "You and me?"

I was wringing my hands under the table in embarrassment. "Um, yes."

He had smiled nervously. "That's really nice of you but I guess I should come clean. I'm still in school and . . ."

"What?" I exclaimed, turning heads. I tried to ignore their interested stares.

He continued unabashed. "But if that doesn't bother you . . . I like older women and . . ."

I interrupted him right there. "What age are you exactly?" I emphasized the word "exactly."

"Seventeen."

"I see," I cringed. "I'm sorry. I should have realized. You just look so much older. Stupid of me. Forget it."

He looked disappointed. But I guess to most seventeen-year-olds the whole Mrs. Robinson thing is dead exciting. Teenagers have too many bloody hormones for their own good.

"Pity," he shrugged his shoulders. "But if you ever change your mind . . . Shit, the boss is staring over. I'd better get back to work."

When Jodie returned I was almost crawling under the table. I had both my hands over my by-now-scarlet face.

"Well?" she asked, sitting down. "Did you ask him?"

"Jodie, can we go now? You pay and I'll settle up with you later." I jumped up and grabbed my bag from under the table. Luckily, Joel seemed to be in the kitchen.

Before she could answer I was out the door. When she found me outside I was still cringing.

"Are you OK?" she asked gently. "What happened?"

"He's seventeen," I whispered.

"Sorry?" she spluttered.

"I've just made a bloody fool of myself!"

She started laughing. "I'm sorry, Amy. I can't help it. I know you like younger men but seventeen . . ."

"He told us he was a student! I assumed he was in college, not school." I stated strongly, "I blame you. You shouldn't have encouraged me."

Jodie was holding her hand over her mouth and trying not to laugh.

Luckily for her I began to see the funny side and began laughing myself. In seconds we were creased up on the pavement, holding our sides.

"I can't believe it," I gasped. "He's so cute."

"Maybe his dad's available," Jodie said, taking a deep gulp of air to get her breath back.

We didn't go back to Café Java for a few weeks. I couldn't face it although Jodie kept telling me not to be so stupid. And when we did go back Joel had left. Pity really—he was a nice guy regardless of his ineligibility.

I vowed never to ask another guy out for a drink in my whole entire life. So that was out. Stevie J was just a nice distraction, something to think about. I liked having someone on my mind, a cute guy to dream about. I liked to lie in bed and imagine my perfect wedding and it was easier if I had a real face on the bridegroom. Somehow it made it a little spooky if I didn't. Like a black and white horror film—*The Faceless Bridegroom*. I wondered if everyone did this—visualize their future wedding in their head for years and years? Maybe they did. So now Stevie J could take Jack's place in my daydream.

As I approached Jodie's place I noticed a dark green MG parked in the drive. Jack has the same car, I thought. Damn, I kept being reminded of him.

Jodie lived in this amazing basement flat in an old house that belonged to her granny. Granny O'Connell lived on the ground and first floors. She had given her eldest grandchild the basement floor in a "living will" six years ago. It all sounded a little morbid if you ask me but I guess it made sense. Jodie had knocked down a lot of the interior walls—except the load-bearing ones, and stripped some of the walls and hefty supporting pillars right back to the bare stone. She created two large bedrooms, a huge bathroom, a study and a massive open plan living room-cum-kitchen. The whole flat was painted white, with some terracotta on selected walls. Gigantic wall-to-wall mirrors, elaborate floor-standing candelabras and halogen spotlighting gave the living room a dramatic Gothic look.

In each bedroom Jodie had created a "four-poster bed" by draping white muslin over self-constructed curving metal hoops which were attached to the ceiling with chain. The wardrobes and dressingtables were old pieces which Dad had recovered from a Georgian house on Merrion Road. Jodie had stripped them down to the bare wood and given them a "distressed" look with light-green paint and furniture wax.

At the time she was working in an interiors shop in Blackrock. After the flat was finished she had a house-warming party and everyone was blown away by what she had done to the place. One friend of her mum's, the wife of a "Captain of Industry," asked her to redesign and decorate her house from top to bottom. Jodie transformed the place and it soon became the talk of the town and was featured in *Image Interiors* magazine. Soon Jodie had more work than she knew what to do with. She packed in her day-job and formed Dream House, her own interior-design company. Jodie had a natural talent but she also worked bloody hard in the first few years. We were dead proud of her, me and Beth.

Jodie would ring me in a desperate state some evenings or weekends. "Amy, I need you! Bring Beth." And Beth and I would be handed a stubby paint-brush and a stencil or a paint-stripper and set to work. It was fun though. Now Jodie had three full-time employees and a secretary. She'd done well. Put myself and Beth to shame really. Beth works as a PA to Louise Keily, the designer. Sounds glamorous but it's not. She likes it though.

I crossed the road and stood at the top of Jodie's steps. I stared at the MG which was parked beside Jodie's Range Rover on the gravel to the right of the house. It was a 2000 reg, just like Jack's. In fact it had a similar number plate—with three sixes. We used to joke that it was the "devil's car." Suddenly something clicked in my head. It was Jack's number plate! 00–D–29666. Bloody hell. What was Jack doing in Jodie's place? He was hardly visiting Granny O'Connell. They must be talking about me, I thought. I walked over to the car to make sure. It was Jack's all right. His gray fleece jacket was still on the back ledge just where it had been weeks ago.

Just then I heard Granny O'Connell's voice call down from her doorstep.

"Hello, Amy, how are you?" She came down the steps with Laddy, her old black Labrador, sloping along beside her.

"Fine thanks, Mrs. O'Connell. And you?"

"Grand. I'm just taking Laddy for a walk." She looked at the MG. "Nice, isn't it? It's been here since yesterday evening. Jodie's new man. She was making him a fine dinner last night. Lucky fellow."

My heart jumped and I suddenly felt sick. I could feel the blood draining from my face.

"Are you all right?" Mrs. O'Connell asked. "You look like you've seen a ghost."

Jodie and Jack. Jack and Jodie. She was my friend. How could she do this to me?

"I'm fine," I muttered. "Just tired. Been working. Have to go now." I scuttled off quickly. It was rude I know but I didn't know what else to do. I didn't want to break down crying in front of Jodie's Granny. I just wanted to be on my own. I ran down the side road which led to the Martello tower. When I felt safely away from Mrs. O'Connell I sat down on a wooden bench and gazed out at the sea. My eyes filled with tears and soon I was sobbing my heart out.

Thoughts went rushing through my head. How long had it been going on? While Jack and I were still together? Was she going to tell me? They were probably both laughing at me right now. How could I have been so stupid? He never loved me, he was just trying to get close to Jodie.

I pulled out my mobile phone and rang Beth.

"Beth?"

"Amy, is that you? Are you all right?"

"Nooo," I wailed.

"Where are you?" she asked. "At home?"

"Nooo."

"Are you crying?"

"Yesss."

"Amy," Beth said gently, "tell me where you are."

I tried to talk, but it was hard. I'd been crying so hard that there was a huge lump in my throat and my breath was out of synch. I gulped.

"Take a deep breath, love. You'll be OK. Just tell me where you are."

"The tower . . . in Blackrock."

"The tower?" she asked a little confused. Then it came to her. We often walked along the seafront and she knew I liked the Martello tower. "The Martello tower?"

"Yes."

"Stay right there. I'll be two minutes. OK?"

"OK." I held the phone in my two hands on my knee like a safety blanket. I felt calmer now I knew that Beth was coming. She was brilliant when I was upset. She always knew how to make me feel better. Now and again my bad moods would last days, weeks even, and she accepted that. Sometimes more than a bad mood, a touch of depression really. But only Beth and my family knew that. Jack had never really understood and I could never explain to him properly. I just put a brave face on things and hoped the blackness would go away. The doctor suggested pills at one stage but I was loath to take them. Somehow if I dealt with it myself, without medication, it seemed less serious to me—something I could deal with on my own. And a while back, when I'd been really bad, I'd gone for a few sessions of counseling with a friend of Mum's called Dr. Shiels and that had seemed to help.

When we were kids Beth had lived across the road from me. We'd known each other since we were seven. We'd grown up together and knew each other back to front and inside out. She now lived in Dun Laoghaire with Tony, a computer programer from Sutton. I'd first met Jack through him—they were old college friends.

Beth was the kindest and the strongest person I knew. And I needed her right now.

I kept my head down until I heard her gentle voice beside me.

"Amy?" She sat down on the bench and put her two arms around me. "That's it, love. Cry if you want to. Let it all out." She held me as huge sobs racked my body.

I wanted to tell her about Jack and Jodie. About what they'd done to me. But I was crying too much.

When I'd stopped enough to talk I lifted my head and tried to explain.

"It's Jack. And Jodie. They're . . . together."

Beth looked at me carefully. "What?"

"I saw his car and Granny O'Connell said he'd stayed and she'd made him dinner. Dinner!"

Beth was confused. "Granny O'Connell made Jack dinner?"

"No," I wailed. "Jodie."

"Jodie made Jack dinner?"

"Yes!"

"Are you sure?"

I looked at her and she could see the answer in my heartbroken eyes.

Beth was quiet for a second. "I don't know what to say. I'm so sorry, love." She held me close again and sighed. "Let's go back to my place and I'll make you something to eat."

Food was the last thing on my mind but it would be some distraction, I supposed. "OK," I mumbled.

Beth stood up and keeping her arm around me walked me to her car. It was warm inside and we drove in silence toward her house. Beth avoided going past Jodie's house which was probably for the best. In my state I don't think I could have taken any more and seeing Jack's car still outside would have sent me over the edge.

Chapter 5

"Here we are," Beth smiled as she pulled up outside her small redbrick townhouse across the road from Dun Laoghaire library. She and Tony had bought it together a couple of years ago, before the property market had gone mental.

"Tony's playing on the Internet at Jed's house so we have the place to ourselves." Jed was another computer programmer, a lanky South Park fan who I'd never paid much attention to.

I tried to smile but my mouth wouldn't cooperate. "Thanks."

I opened the car door and pulled myself out of Beth's Honda Civic. Why were they built so bloody low on the ground? I muttered to myself, cursing Beth's choice of car ungraciously. I felt exhausted and my head throbbed, but at least I'd stopped crying.

Beth locked the car and smiled hopefully at me again.

"Are you OK?" she asked kindly. I grunted.

I felt terrible for being such an old bag. Beth was being so nice to me and I was being a pain in the ass. The worst thing was that I knew it. I knew how painful and childish I could be when I was in this kind of irrational mood, but I couldn't help it. Luckily, patience was one of Beth's many virtues. She put her arm around me and I tried to shrug it off. But she was having none of it.

"Amy," she stared at me, her brown eyes betraying her concern. "I'm trying to help you. Don't shut me out."

She was right. I was being obtuse and unreasonable. It wasn't her fault I hurt so badly that I wanted to curl up and die.

"Sorry," I mumbled and began to cry again.

"Let's get you inside," she said brightly, "and I'll make you a cup of tea."

"Tea," I spat, glaring at her. "I don't want tea."

Beth sighed. It was going to be a long evening. She opened the yellow front door and stood back.

"In you go," Beth commanded in her headmistress voice. She followed behind me, switching on the tiny halogen lights which were set into the ceiling in the small, narrow hall. She opened the door to the living room and placed a hand on the small of my back. The room was warm and inviting. Beth flicked on the uplighter in the corner, illuminating the terracotta-painted room with a soft, gentle glow.

"Lie down on the sofa and I'll get you a duvet."

"Don't be thick," I wailed. "I'm not sick."

Beth smiled. "You sound like one of your Dr. Seuss books. Don't be thick, I'm not sick. Don't be slow, go, go, go."

I wasn't amused. I glared at her again.

"No," Beth hesitated, "you're not sick. But you are in shock and you need to rest. I'll be back in a second."

I looked around the room from my now bolt-upright position. Beth had changed the curtains, I noticed in my distracted state. They used to be a busy pink floral design which had come with the house. But now heavy cream linen curtains hung in their place. I scowled. Beth should have told me about the new curtains, I thought irritably. Why hadn't she told me? I bet she'd told Jodie. Bloody Jodie . . .

Anyway I was damned if I was going to be treated like a child! I didn't need to lie down. I needed to . . . and in a blinding flash I knew what I needed to do. I needed to hurt Jodie. Physically or mentally—either would do. I needed to smack her smug little face from here to kingdom come. Or tell her what a bitch she was, what a lying, conniving, Cruella de Ville of a traitor. Of course, I thought hysterically. I'll ring her. I pulled my mobile out of my jacket pocket and punched in Jodie's name.

"Hello? Amy?" Jodie asked uncertainly. For a moment I was

caught off guard—I'd forgotten that her mobile would recognize mine instantly. I gulped. I was so angry that speech evaded me.

"Amy? Are you there?"

I wiped away my tears with the back of my hand and sniffed loudly.

"Oh Jesus, Amy," Jodie whispered, the penny dropping with a resounding clunk. "Gran said you called by . . . she said you'd seen . . . I'm so sorry . . . I . . ."

"*Fuck you,*" I screamed down the phone. "*You bitch, you fucking bitch . . .*"

Beth lashed down the stairs, dropping the duvet she was carrying on the floor of the hall and pounced on me, pulling the phone out of my shaking hand. She clicked it off and focused on my tear-stained face.

"What are you doing?" she asked, sitting down beside me and taking my hands in hers. "That's not going to make you feel any better. You're in no state to talk to anyone, especially to Jodie." She stroked my hands gently.

I erupted into huge, racking sobs which thundered through my entire body. She was right again.

"Lie down," she commanded in a steely voice and I assented—I was too tired not to. Beth reclaimed the duvet from the hall floorboards and placed it over me, tucking it around my body. She placed a cushion under my head and sat on the floor beside me stroking my hair.

"It will be all right, Amy," she crooned over and over again. "I'm here now, love. You'll be OK."

Later I woke up and opened my swollen eyes. My head throbbed and my body felt like it had been through ten rounds with Muhammad Ali. Although I'd recently seen *Once We Were Kings,* the documentary about the American boxer and I didn't think he'd rate me as much of an opponent. "Fly like a butterfly, sting like a bee." I chanted Muhammad's catch phrase over and over like a mantra. He'd had his fair share of troubles, had poor old Muhammad. Yes, I really was losing it.

"Amy?" Beth interrupted my rambling thoughts. She was standing in the doorway with my mobile in her hand. "You should ring your mum. It's getting late and she'll be worried about you."

I sat up gingerly, trying not to move my head too much. I felt strangely hollow, all cried out. I gave Beth a stilted half-smile.

"OK," I nodded.

She eyeballed me carefully. "Jodie rang your mobile a couple of times earlier. I just thought you should know."

My eyes narrowed and I could feel a fiery ball of rage entering my heart once more.

"Amy, leave it," Beth advised. "Talk to her tomorrow. I didn't answer so she has no idea you're here. Why don't you stay the night? Things will seem clearer in the morning."

I glared at her. "Things are crystal clear to me right now, thank you very much," I said, trying to stay calm and giving her a withering look.

"Um," Beth gulped and continued bravely, "ring your mum."

I took the phone from her and thought about screaming abuse at Jodie again. I was sorely tempted but I knew it would disappoint Beth. Although at this stage she had probably despaired of me already.

"Hi, Suzi."

"Amy, where are you? You missed dinner."

I pushed back my sleeve and stared at my pink Baby G watch. Shit, it was almost nine o'clock. I'd been asleep for nearly three hours!

"Oh, yeah," I said vaguely, "I lost track of the time, sorry."

"Jodie was looking for you," Suzi said. "She rang a couple of times and she called in. Is something up?"

Suzi wasn't stupid.

"No," I said without hesitation. "Tell Mum I'm staying at . . . at a friend's house."

I could almost hear Suzi smile. She presumed that there was a man involved, of course. I wish.

"A friend? Sounds interesting. Anyone I know? Is he cute?" she bubbled.

I wasn't in the mood. I sighed. "Bye, see you tomorrow."

"Wait, Amy," Suzi interjected. "What will I tell Jodie if she rings? She said your mobile didn't seem to be working. Will I tell her you'll ring her?"

"No!" I stated emphatically, raising my voice to a dangerous level. "You can tell her to go fuck herself!"

"Oh," Suzi whispered, shocked.

I suddenly felt bad. It wasn't her fault that Jodie had betrayed me. "I'm sorry," I apologized. "Forget I said that. I'm sorry." I started to cry again.

"What's wrong?" Suzi asked with concern. "Where are you, Amy? Will I come and get you?"

"I'm fine," I sobbed. "I'm at Beth's, but don't tell Jodie."

"OK," Suzi promised. "But I'm worried about you. I'm here if you need me."

"Thanks," I whispered.

Beth left me alone for a little bit while she cooked. She came back into the living room carrying a large tray.

"Dinner," she stated. "And I'm making you eat it whether you like it or not."

I stared at the tray which she placed on the low pine coffee table in front of me. Lasagne and chips and a large tub of cookies and cream Häagen-Dazs.

I smiled. Comfort food at its very finest. "There goes the waist-line," I hiccuped, my tears abating.

Beth handed me a calorific plateful and a knife and fork. "I ran up to the video shop while you were asleep," she smiled, kneeling beside the video with a pile of tapes beside her. "You can choose— *Children of the Corn Part 5, Scream 4* or *Nightmare on Elm Street Returns.*"

"Beth!" I yelled. "Are you trying to kill me?" She knew I hated horror films, especially big-budget ones with no plot.

"I'm only joking," she grinned. "*Rear Window* or *Casablanca*?"

I smiled. Beth was such a sweetie. She'd be much happier watching bad television but she knew I couldn't stand it.

"Beth?" I asked sheepishly. "Do you still have my *Field of Dreams* tape?" I'd lent it to her months ago when she was off work with the flu and bored out of her skull.

"Oops, sorry, I thought I'd given it back to you," she said uncertainly, flicking through the tapes piled neatly in a stack at the bottom of the bookshelf. "Yes, here it is."

She popped it into the video and rewound it to the beginning.

"Do you mind watching it again?" I asked.

"No, I was out of it on Night Nurse the last time I watched it. And anyway," she added, "Kevin Costner looks great in those tight Levis."

I smiled. "Thanks. Thanks for everything. Sorry for being, well you know . . . difficult earlier."

"It's fine," she said kindly. "That's what friends are for." She sat down on the sofa beside me and we munched away contentedly. I didn't much feel like talking and Beth seemed to understand.

Now *Field of Dreams* is hardly a Hollywood classic but I've always loved it. It's basically the story of a farmer from Iowa (Kevin Costner) who hears a voice in his cornfield. And this voice tells him to plow up his corn and build a baseball field on the land in front of his house. Crazy behavior as he stands to lose his farm—but he does it! I like the film because it says—follow your dreams, do crazy things, don't worry about what other people think even if they call you mad.

We spent the evening on the sofa, eating and watching dreams come true.

At half past eleven Beth started to yawn which set me off too.

"Bedtime, I think," she said, stretching her arms above her head.

"Where's Tony?" I asked.

"He's staying at Jed's tonight," Beth replied. "He'll get a lift into work with him in the morning. He had no idea about Jack and—you know. He said to say he's very sorry."

I was touched. Tony was a decent guy.

"I don't have to be in work till lunchtime, so we can hang out until then. Louise is away and Holly can hold the fort." Holly was one of Louise's young designers.

"Are you sure?" Beth knew I had tomorrow off. I was relieved. I didn't want to be on my own—my brain would conjure up all sorts of conspiracy plots and elaborate revenge plans.

"I'm sure," she smiled.

"Thanks," I said again. "And Beth?"

"Yes?"

"Were you talking to Jodie?" I couldn't help it, I had to know.

"I left the phone off the hook and my mobile off," she said, looking decidedly embarrassed. "I don't want to talk to her right at the moment."

"Me neither," I said. My spirits lifted considerably. Beth was definitely on my side, I thought to myself childishly. Although I'd known them both for years and years I'd always felt closer to Beth. She was more like a second sister than a friend. Jodie liked to think she was my closest friend but if push came to shove I'd save Beth first from a sinking ship any day. And now . . . who needed a traitor for a friend?

I lay in bed in Beth's spare room staring at the ceiling. It had been a long day and I was exhausted. A thin shaft of light pierced the darkness, a streetlamp outside shining through the gap in the curtains. Outside all was still except for the faint rattle of diesel freight-trains clicking over the nearby tracks.

When we were younger someone had told us that the very same night-trains carried deadly chemicals and nuclear waste and if one crashed that it would wipe out the whole population of Dublin city. Funny, the things you believe when you are kids. Maybe it's true, I mused. I tried to focus on things less depressing than mass destruction. But I couldn't think of any.

Chapter 6

I must have fallen asleep eventually because the following morning Beth shook me gently and opened the curtains, letting the gray winter's day into the room.

"Amy," she said quietly, "Suzi is here."

I pulled my weary eyes open and winced in the daylight. My head felt groggy and my whole body ached. Then I remembered and it shot through my whole being like a bad dose of the flu. Jodie and Jack, Jack and Jodie.

"Amy? Amy?" I heard Suzi's voice beside me and I sat up gingerly. Suzi was sitting on the end of the bed, smiling at me warily. "How are you feeling? Beth said you were a bit under the weather."

I tried to smile but my mouth didn't seem to want to cooperate.

"Hi, Suzi. I'm fine, thanks. What are you doing here?"

"I was worried about you. Beth rang me this morning and told me you weren't feeling too well and that you'd had a fight with Jodie. And I wanted to see how you were."

I grimaced. Good old Beth—at least I didn't have to tell Suzi about Jack and Jodie yet. I didn't much feel like going over it all.

"Anyway, you look fine," Suzi continued when she realized I wasn't going to say anything. "I was hoping you'd come shopping with me this afternoon. I have none of my Christmas presents and I was to get something really special for Matt. I see Beth is as organized as usual." Suzi nodded over at the corner of the room. I looked over. Heaps of Christmas presents covered the surface of the dressingtable. Beth's "theme" this year seemed to be pink and silver and each present was carefully wrapped in metallic paper and adorned with a large pink satin ribbon and bow.

I groaned. I hadn't bought a single present either and it was less than ten days till Christmas! Maybe a good bout of retail therapy would take my mind off things.

"Sounds good," I smiled, properly this time.

"Beth's making us lunch, so I'll go down and give her a hand and you can have a shower."

"Fine."

Suzi walked out of the room and I swung my legs over the side of the bed and onto the cream-carpeted floor. Beth had left a pile of clean clothes on the chair under the window, together with a towel. Tears pricked my eyes. She was so good to me—I didn't deserve it. I promised myself that I'd buy her something really special for Christmas to say thank you.

When I was clean and dressed in a pair of Beth's soft denim dungarees and her red hoody fleece—real comfort clothes—I made my way into the kitchen. Delicious cooking smells were emanating from the hob where Beth was standing. Suzi was sitting at the white pine Habitat table and flicking through the latest issue of *Image* magazine.

"Hi," Beth beamed. "You look great. Fancy some lunch?"

"What's cooking?" I asked, mouth watering. I was starving. "Smells divine."

"Chicken breasts in a cream and Dalkey mustard sauce. And Suzi knocked together a salad."

"It's more Brutus, I'm afraid, than Caesar," Suzi laughed. "I threw in whatever I could find, and I may have gone a little heavy on the dressing. But it should taste nice."

"You guys," I drawled in a heavy American accent, "you just kill me. I love ya."

Suzi giggled. "Who are you supposed to be?"

I threw my eyes up to the heavens. "Joey from *Friends*, of course."

"Ah," Suzi grinned. "I see."

"I hear you two are off shopping, lucky things," Beth said with disappointment trickling off her voice and dropping on the wooden floor. There was nothing Beth loved more than shopping. "They need me in work this afternoon—there's a big consignment of Italian fabrics coming into the warehouse."

I smiled at her sympathetically. "That's a shame. But I promise—the next time you want a spending partner—I'm your woman!"

"Deal!" Beth said emphatically, scooping the chicken breasts onto some crusty French bread and stirring the cream and mustard seed into the frying pan. She poured the rich sauce over the chicken pieces and placed the plates on the table.

"That smells delicious." Suzi licked her lips and helped herself to some salad. "Thanks, Beth." She munched happily on her salad, popping a piece of crisp iceberg lettuce into her mouth with her tanned fingers.

"How are you feeling this morning?" Beth asked me after she had sat down at the table. She tried to keep her voice light and breezy but I knew that she was genuinely concerned.

I took a sip of freshly squeezed orange juice and attempted a "normal" smile.

"Better, thanks. You were right. Things don't seem as dark and hopeless as they did yesterday." I winced, still feeling sick to my stomach thinking about Jack and Jodie.

"Amy," Beth said softly, reading my mind. Sometimes she knew me far too well. "Try not to dwell on it. Focus on this afternoon's shopping, OK?"

"I'll try." I pushed some salad around my plate, spearing a cube of cucumber despondently. I'd been ravenous a few minutes ago but now a lump had formed in my throat, making swallowing difficult.

"This chicken is delicious," Suzi purred, dipping a finger into the rich sauce and licking it with relish. She glanced over at my plate. "You can't go shopping on an empty stomach," she stated resolutely. "It's against the rules—eat!"

I jabbed a sliver of chicken onto my fork and popped it into my mouth. Suzi was right—it was delicious. I managed to chew and swallow methodically. Beth and Suzi chatted amicably about Australia while I listened. I didn't much feel like joining in. The more I ate the easier it became and soon, much to my surprise, I'd cleared the plate and was crunching on a deliriously cool red apple from Beth's fridge. I felt a little more alive and was even beginning to look forward to the afternoon's retail blitz.

After coffee Suzi skipped off to ring Matt, leaving Beth and me sitting at the table. I stood up and reached over to gather up the sunny yellow plates.

"Leave them," Beth admonished. "I'll tackle them this evening."

"Are you sure?" I asked suspiciously.

Beth looked me straight in the eye. "Yes!" she smiled warmly. "I'm sure. Sit down and relax."

"Beth," I hesitated. She waited expectantly, her brown eyes full of compassion. I blinked back tears. I didn't deserve such a good and kind friend.

"I'm sorry . . . about last night . . . I was . . ."

"I understand," Beth interrupted. "You don't need to say anything else." She reached over the table and placed her hands on mine and held them tight.

"I don't want to feel like this," I continued wretchedly. "I just do."

Beth sighed and squeezed my hands. "I know, love. But you have to move on, leave the past behind. These things happen for a reason. Jack wasn't good for you and some day the right man will come along and everything will click into place."

"My knight in shining armor on his white steed," I muttered, my words dripping with sarcasm.

Beth was a determined romantic and believed wholeheartedly in fate. I wasn't so sure. But at this stage clutching at straws had become second nature.

"Look at myself and Tony," Beth continued, hammering her point home. "Before I met him I'd never had a boyfriend for more than three weeks!"

"I know," I sighed.

"I'm not really helping, am I?" Beth asked resignedly.

I smiled. "You are. I'm just not the easiest of people to help."

"You can say that again!" Beth laughed.

"What are you two giggling about?" Suzi asked as she walked back into the kitchen.

"Nothing," Beth assured her. "How's lover-boy?"

"Grand. He's helping his hooker paint a bedroom today."

Beth and I started laughing again. "Sounds interesting," Beth giggled. "As his fiancée, would his dealings with Dublin's seedy underworld not bother you?"

"Would you two stop?" Suzi insisted, trying to keep a straight face. "The hooker, which for your information is a position in a rugby team, is called Bruce Gorman and he's a painter."

"I'd keep a beady eye on Matt just in case," I hiccuped, holding my stomach which hurt from laughing so much.

Beth continued. "He'll be window-dressing or set-designing with the prop next."

"That makes no sense," Suzi said in exasperation. "Is it supposed to be funny?"

Beth could hardly force the words out. She was in convulsions.

"You know—rugby prop, stage prop."

"That's brutal," Suzi smiled in spite of herself.

"I know," Beth gasped. "I know."

Half an hour later we were on the northbound Dart.

"I wish I was going with you," Beth grumbled as the train drew into Blackrock station.

I kissed her on the cheek and stood up. "I'll ring you later and tell you all about our purchases," I grinned mischievously.

"Don't you dare go into Khan without me," she said dangerously.

"Bye, Beth," I smiled.

Suzi and I waved as the train pulled away from the platform. Ducking a hanging basket full of ivy and bright purple heather, we chatted companionably as we sauntered toward Blackrock main street. The road outside the station was being resurfaced and there was a heady smell of hot tar lingering in the air. The new tarmacadam steamed and hissed as it was flattened into place by the slowly moving roller.

"Hiya, ladies!" a young man shouted as we walked by. "Nice day, thank God."

"He's cute." Suzi whispered. "He looks like the guy from the Diet Coke ad."

"In your dreams," I smiled. "You've been in Australia too long."

As we crossed the busy main street to the Blackrock shopping center I remembered the last time I'd been here—a few months ago with Jack. We'd been looking for a wedding present for Chris, one of the partners in his firm. Chris was marrying an English girl and the wedding, the second for him, was in Sussex so we weren't actually going. But Jack had wanted to make a good impression.

He had settled on an original glass piece by a young Irish artist, from a small gallery on the main street. It was a vase, a glorious celebration of form and fluidity in the palest green glass—classy yet unusual. Afterwards we had sat in the Californian Coffee Dock sipping cappuccinos, the carefully wrapped vase by Jack's feet.

"What type of wedding do you want?" he'd asked out of the blue, after he had filled me in on the latest Formula 1 controversy.

I hesitated awkwardly. "I'm not sure. I've never really thought about it," I lied. "It would depend on who I'm marrying, I suppose." I smiled.

He looked at me carefully. "What do you mean by that?"

I stiffened. I felt like a deer caught in the headlights of an oncoming vehicle—a pick-up truck with those brutish "cow-bars" at that.

"Nothing," I said lightly. "I was joking. What were you saying about Eddie Jordan's team?"

"Don't try to change the subject," Jack continued, a serious look on his face. "You have considered . . . us . . . you know . . ."

"Our wedding?" I asked.

"Yes," he said sheepishly, playing with a packet of sugar, turning the small rectangle over and over in his fingers.

"I've thought about it," I replied honestly.

"And," Jack prompted.

"I'm just not ready to make that sort of commitment," I sighed. "It's a lot of work—setting dates and thinking about dresses and flowers and things."

"I'm the one who's supposed to have problems with the C word," he smiled, trying to lighten the mood. For once he wasn't going to start an argument. "People have been asking when we're giving them a day out, that's all. We have been engaged a while now."

"I know," I said, trying not to sigh. "And when I'm ready I'll tell you, I promise."

"Don't leave it too long," he said ominously. Little did he know. "Anyway, it's no big deal." He opened *The Irish Times* on the table at the listings page. "Let's see what's on in Stillorgan. How about the new Bruce Willis thriller? Or there's a romantic comedy with Julia Roberts. You'd like that. Amy, Amy?"

I was miles away wondering why I didn't want to set a date for our wedding. It suddenly dawned on me that maybe I didn't want to marry Jack. Maybe I wasn't nervous of getting married, maybe I was nervous of getting married to him.

That was before the arguments and the tears. And before I finally realized that Jack wasn't who I wanted him to be.

"Amy?" Suzi interrupted my musings and pulled me by the arm into Crowley's Chemists. The chrome, glass and ash-wood interior sparkled under the bright shop lights. Towers of glittering gift boxes were stacked beside the door—bright pink Clinique ones and Gold and Silver Lancôme ones. Every inch of the glass countertops was covered with boxes and bottles of all shapes, sizes and descriptions— all holding wonderfully smelling treats for the senses.

"This is perfect for Mum," Suzi said animatedly, her blue eyes dancing. She held up an Estée Lauder make-up tray. The tortoise-shell tray was filled with all kinds of products, from Re-Nutriv All Day lipsticks to nail-polishes and eye-shadows.

"Oooh," she squealed next, "Matt would love this!" She sprayed a fine mist of Hugo Boss for men into the air and sniffed it appreciatively.

I smiled. It was hard to be in a bad mood with Suzi around. We headed toward the perfume counter and covered our wrists with lots of different scents.

"This is nice. It says it's light and fresh with a flowery bouquet." Suzi sprayed some Anaïs Anaïs on her left wrist. "What do you think?"

"It suits you," I smiled.

She beamed back. "What about you, Amy? Which one do you like?"

"I'm still a Chanel No. 5 girl, like Marilyn Monroe," I admitted. I'd worn the fragrance for as long as I could remember.

We left Crowley's laden with plastic shopping-bags. Suzi had bought presents for Mum and Matt and I had bought myself a new Clinique lipstick called Tenderheart—I reckoned I needed a bit of pampering. I bought Dad his obligatory bottle of Old Spice. It always made me feel safe and secure, the smell of Old Spice. It reminded me of Dad so much. I tried to make Jack wear it once but he was having none of it.

"No way!" he'd stated emphatically one morning in the very same chemist's. "It's a corduroy and Labrador man's aftershave. My Dad wears it, Amy."

"So does mine," I'd said softly.

"Sorry?" he'd asked.

"Nothing," I'd mumbled.

In the end Jack had bought Eternity for men—he was always a sucker for clever advertising.

As we walked past Kiddi Kutz on the way up the stairs, *Rugrats* blaring from their bright yellow televisions, I heard a familiar voice behind me.

"Amy? Is that you?"

I turned and came face to face with a real blast from the past— Sheena Morris. Sheena had been in my class at St. Peter's—head girl, captain of the First XI hockey team, prize-winning debater, A student—you know the type. And she was slim and pretty to boot, with a halo of softly curling brown hair, a generous mouth and a perfect set of *Beverly Hills 91210* even white teeth. Your average nightmare.

"Hi, Sheena," I said, forcing myself to smile. "How are you?"

"Wonderful," she gushed. "I'm married." She thrust her ring-finger into my face. "I'm Sheena Goodyear now. And I have two little angels. They're both in getting their hair trimmed and I just popped into the newsagent's to get the new copy of *VIP*. There's a photo of us in it." She flicked through the glossy pages and planted a long, ruby-red talon on the tiny photograph of a "glamorous charity media ball." "Isn't that gas!" she shrieked. "Me, famous."

I studied the photo carefully. For the first time since meeting her I smiled genuinely. Her husband, Terry Goodyear, was a pig, bless him. He looked about forty-five, with lank gray hair and thick-rimmed, black glasses.

Suzi peered over our shoulders at the magazine. "Is that your husband beside you?" she asked curiously, peering over our shoulders.

"Sorry, Suzi. I'm being rude. This is Sheena, she was in my class at St. Peter's. Sheena, this is Suzi, my sister."

"Suzi," Sheena gushed. "Of course I remember you. Always a pretty little thing. Actually the man beside me in the picture is my brother-in-law, Terry. My husband is in the next picture with Pat Kenny."

Of course he was. Drop-dead gorgeous too, with a full head of glossy blond hair, sallow skin and a muscular, athletic build. He looked familiar. I'd seen him on a couple of current affairs programs on RTE.

"Tasty!" Suzi said, sizing him up from the picture.

"Oh, stop!" Sheena giggled, obviously delighted. "He's in TV so he has to look good. Come and see my little ones, Hannah and Dan." She dragged us over to the window of the hairdresser's where two white-blond-haired children were staring at *Barney* crooning a version of a Frank Sinatra song. Surreal!

"They're beautiful," I said honestly. They really were exceptionally attractive youngsters and perfectly turned out in little matching Osh Kosh denim outfits, dungarees for the boy and a pinafore for the girl.

"Thank you," Sheena cooed. "Hannah's just turned six and Dan's four. "Are you married?" she asked, turning her attention back toward me.

"No, I'm too busy for that!" I lied. "But Suzi's getting married in May."

"How lovely," Sheena said. "Congratulations."

"Thanks," Suzi replied graciously.

"We must fly now, I'm afraid. Shopping to do, you know . . ." I began. "It was nice bumping into you." I wanted to make a swift exit before the embarrassment of swapping numbers, promising to keep in touch and having no real intention of doing so. Too late. She pressed an elegant, cream business card into my hand.

"Give me a ring sometime and we can catch up properly. Lovely to see you!" She kissed both of my cheeks.

"You too," I said evenly.

"Bye," Suzi said.

Sheena joined her home-made genetic success stories and Suzi and I walked toward the escalator in silence.

"Is that the Sheena who was caught in the showers with the rugby captain?" Suzi asked eventually.

"God, no," I laughed. "That was Sheena Connolly. Sheena Morris was Miss Goody-Two-Shoes."

"Must have done it at least twice though," Suzi smiled. She paused for a second. "Makes you think though, doesn't it. "Married with two kids and she's only your age."

"From her card it seems that she also edits a specialist food and wine magazine," I said looking dejectedly at her business card.

"Of course," Suzi said, grinning. "And I bet she holds amazing dinner parties for twenty people that would put Darina Allen to shame, is an expert on New World wines, has an immaculate garden and runs the PTA in her daughter's school.".

"Obviously," I joined in. "And she buys all her clothes from a little boutique in New York, darling, and only holidays in the most obscure and exotic places."

"Makes you feel a bit inadequate though, doesn't it?" Suzi asked resignedly.

"Humm, I suppose," I replied. "But you know something?" I grinned wickedly.

"What?" Suzi asked.

"Her feet stank in school. We used to make her leave her runners outside the changing rooms on her way out. They were that bad."

"Well, that's OK so!" Suzi laughed. "At least she's not perfect." She linked my arm. "Let's try on some clothes in Khan. I saw an adorable pink Whistles cardigan in *U* magazine and I think they stock it."

"You're on!" I grinned, trying to push all thoughts of wedded bliss, successful classmates and perfect children out of my mind. As if things weren't bad enough.

We crossed the road and gazed at the glittering beaded black and deep-red evening dresses in the window before going in.

"I'd never be able to wear that," I moaned, pointing at a tiny black slip dress with delicate spaghetti straps and a dramatically low-cut back. "It would show up all my lumps and bumps."

"Don't be ridiculous," Suzi stated. "At least you have the figure to fill it. I have so little chest that it wouldn't stay up."

"Rubbish," I snorted. "You're perfectly proportioned. Don't give me that."

We walked in the door and squeezed our way to the back of the shop to look at the dresses. The small shop was packed with women of all ages—from tall, gangly teenagers with their mothers to im-maculately dressed matrons.

"Feel this," Suzi commanded, handing me a dark bottle-green velvet dress with a dramatically boned bodice.

The skirt material was soft and light, and Suzi held it against me with delight.

"Amy, you have to try it on."

I looked at the price tag and smiled. "In your dreams, sis. It's one of Louise's designs and it's three hundred pounds."

"The woman Beth works for?"

"The very same."

"Try it on anyway," Suzi cajoled. "Just to see what it's like on."

"Maybe," I said, hoping she'd forget about it. The way I saw it, there was no point trying on something that you knew you couldn't afford.

Suzi slung it over her arm and moved toward the coats. I followed her, squeezing past a nymph-like teenager who was parading a wickedly tight pink sheath dress for her adoring mother.

"Darling," the older woman purred, "it's just perfect for Aspen. You must have it."

Suzi glanced at me and raised her eyes to heaven. "Hardly much use for skiing," she whispered in exasperation. I smiled.

Suzi found two glorious full-length padded silk coats by Fenn, Wright and Manson, one in metallic gray and one in copper, and whisked them off their hangers. She also found the coveted Whistles cardigan. We made our way back to the changing area and waited to use the tiny, curtained-off cubicle.

Suzi became impatient and pulled off her bulky jacket and jumper in the queue, revealing her tiny white vest top and deliciously tanned and well-toned shoulders and arms. I noticed with delight the teenage girl surveying her, eyes flicking green with envy. Suzi had a figure that money couldn't buy.

She looked divine in the cardigan which clung in all the right places, wrapping around her body in an unusual manner and tying at the front with pink ribbon.

"What do you think?" she spun around, almost hitting the woman behind us in the mouth with her shoulder.

"Lovely," I said firmly. "The color is great on you."

"I have absolutely no clothes to wear over Christmas and I want to look nice when I . . . when we announce the engagement." Suzi's eyes glistened with happiness. "You know what some of the rellies can be like. They'll have me and Matt under the microscope. So I want to look well."

I smiled. She was right—the relatives would be all over herself and Matt like a rash at the parents' annual drinks party and a particular nasty scarlet-fever rash at that.

"I could buy a black skirt in Dunnes and I have a pair of strappy sandals somewhere that never made it to Oz, so they should be still in one piece."

Suzi stared at the price tag hanging from the left sleeve and bit her lip.

"It's a little expensive," she winced, "but it can be my Christmas present from Matt and from Mum and Dad."

"And I'll buy you a skirt," I added.

"Perfect," Suzi beamed, kissing me on the cheek. "You're a star."

The changing room was now free and Suzi pushed me into the brightly lit compartment and thrust the green dress into my arms.

"I'll try on the coats out here," she smiled.

"But . . ." I protested, but Suzi simply closed the heavy linen curtain and ignored me.

I struggled with my fleece and T-shirt, dragging them over my head, and I removed Beth's supremely comfortable dungarees. What am I doing? I asked myself as I carefully guided the luxurious material over my hips. It was easier than I thought it would be—sometimes dresses got caught midway. Thighs were a terrible curse. Mine were white with tiny areas of mottled red veins in places which resembled a London tube map. I spent most of the summer with fake tan on my legs and other selected parts of my body—depending on the weather. I was one of those people who turned lobster with a mere whiff of the sun, so fake tan had been something of a revelation to me. It gave me some confidence to wear skimpy summer clothes which I wouldn't previously have considered. Jodie had introduced fake tan to me, she swore by it and even added a drop to her moisturizer over the winter to give herself a healthy glow. Bloody Jodie . . .

"Amy," Suzi interrupted my thoughts, "how does it look?"

I finished fastening the tiny hooks at the side of the dress and stared in the mirror. I was surprised. The bodice fitted my curves perfectly, giving me a pronounced cleavage and slimming my waist and my hips deceptively. The cleverly cut flowing skirt hung in shimmering folds, lightly grazing my thighs and falling to my ankles.

I twitched back the curtain nervously.

Suzi drew in her breath. "Amy, it's stunning. You're a vision."

A tall, elegantly dressed shop assistant smiled at me.

"It's a joy to wear, isn't it? The color is perfect on you."

I blushed. I wasn't used to compliments.

"That's an amazing coat," I said, changing the subject. Suzi ran her fingers longingly over the padded silk.

"One day," she said dreamily. She shrugged the coat off her shoulders and handed it to the assistant. "Take it away," she grinned.

I retreated back into the safety of the linen sanctuary and reluctantly glided the dress back over my body. It was beautiful but there was no way I could afford it—not on my salary! Stepping out of the cubicle I joined Suzi who was paying for her cardigan at the cash desk with her credit card.

"I hope I'm not over my limit," she whispered to me surreptitiously. "That would be embarrassing."

The card went through and soon we were walking down the main street toward the tiny jeweller's near The Wonderland Bookshop. I wanted to buy Beth something special for Christmas as a thank-you for being there for me.

Suzi swung her black and white Khan bag jauntily by her side. I decided to check my messages as the phone had been switched off since my psychotic "Jodie" episode yesterday. The familiar voice told me I had five new messages.

Message one. "Hi, Amy, this is Jodie . . . um, ring me."

I grimaced.

Message two. "Hi Amy, this is Jodie again . . . please ring me. We should talk."

Message three. "Amy, please ring me back. I feel terrible. I really need to speak to you. Um, it's Monday morning. Ring me, please."

Message four. "It's Mum. Will you pick up some Christmas wrapping-paper for me in Blackrock? Thanks. See you later."

Message five. "It's me again—Jodie. I'm so sorry. I know you're annoyed with me . . . and you have every right to be. But it just happened. We didn't mean it to, honestly. You've got to understand . . . oh, Amy, please ring. I never meant to hurt you. Ring me."

Tears welled up in my eyes. Bollocks it just happened. Jodie could have stopped it happening. I stopped on the street and took a deep breath. Suzi turned toward me and gave me a hug.

"Amy, let's sit down for a second." She gestured toward a wooden bench outside The Coffee Bean and we made our way there and sat down.

"What is it, love? Do you want to talk about it?"

I sniffed and looked at her through blurred eyes. I wiped the tears away with the back of my hand and sniffed again.

"Jodie and Jack are . . ."

"Together?" she asked gently, disbelief on her face.

I nodded.

"Jeez," she whispered.

We sat in silence for a few minutes.

"How do you know?" she asked after a little while. I explained about the car and Jodie's Granny. Her eyes widened in astonishment.

"You poor thing. You must have got a real shock."

"I just feel so stupid. I feel as if they're laughing at me behind my back. And I can't believe Jodie would do such a thing. She's supposed to be my best friend." I raced through my words, barely taking a breath.

"It's all right," Suzi crooned. "Calm down. Let's have some coffee before we do any more shopping."

She led me into The Coffee Bean and we both had a caffè latte, mine laced with oceans of sugar. After I'd taken a few gulps of the strong hot liquid I began to relax.

"You're still in shock," Suzi stated firmly. "You've got to take things easy and give yourself some time." She looked at me carefully. "I think you should talk to Jodie."

"No way," I hissed. "I'm never going to talk to her again."

"I think you should hear what she has to say," Suzi continued bravely, ignoring my dagger looks. "It may make you feel better and it might put things in perspective. Tell me you'll think about it anyway."

I muttered "right" sarcastically under my breath.

"I'll take that as a yes," Suzi continued. "I'll drop the subject now. But if you want to talk about it I'm here, OK?"

I felt horribly guilty. Suzi didn't deserve my spleen any more than Beth had last night. I was a terrible and ungrateful person and I hated myself for it.

"Thanks," I stapled a smile onto my face. "I appreciate it."

"I know," Suzi smiled. "You mad thing." She punched me playfully on the arm.

Chapter 7

Later that afternoon I sat on my bed fingering the delicate silver Alan Arnduff necklace I'd bought for Beth. A gleaming chain supported a tiny open-fronted embossed silver box in which a heart was suspended. The tiny heart moved from side to side as the wearer moved. I hung the chain over my fingers and watched as the heart swung hypnotically.

It was simple yet beautiful; I knew Beth would love it.

I flicked off my runners and lay back against the Wombles pillow. My head throbbed and I felt tired and achy. Maybe I was coming down with something—flu perhaps. But I knew in my heart of hearts that it was psychosomatic. Maybe Suzi was right. Maybe I should give Jodie a ring.

"Amy," Mum's powerful voice clattered up the stairs and through my bedroom door. "Jodie's here. Will I send her up?"

"Shit," I muttered. OK, so I'd considered ringing her—but seeing her face to face, well that was another matter. I tried to think of a decent excuse but failed miserably. I jumped up and locked my door. I could hear footsteps climbing the stairs. They stopped outside my door.

"Amy?" Jodie knocked gently on my door. "Can I come in?"

I didn't answer. I didn't trust myself not to swear blindly at her so I just stayed stumm.

Jodie tried the door. "Can you unlock the door? Please? I really want to talk to you."

I sat on my bed, bolt upright and eyes focused on the doorknob. It turned once more.

Jodie coughed theatrically. "I'm still here. Open the door, will you? I feel stupid."

"Stupid!" I spat, unable to help myself. "How do you think I feel? Go fuck yourself!"

There was shocked silence for a second before Jodie whispered. "Amy, I'm going now. I'm so sorry . . ."

I listened transfixed as Jodie made her way downstairs. I could hear Mum and her talking in the hall before the heavy front door clunked shut. I expected a telling-off from Mum for being so rude but it was several minutes before anyone ventured up the stairs.

"Amy?" Suzi had been sent to calm the stormy waters. I turned the old iron key in the lock and let her in. As I looked at her concerned face I began to cry.

"Ah, love," she put her arms around me. We sat down on the bed and she held me in her arms, stroking my head.

The next morning I left early for work. I'd managed to avoid any social interaction the previous evening by staying in my room all night and feigning a headache. Mum was a little concerned but Suzi had smoothed everything over. I assumed she'd explained about Jodie and Jack as Mum was being extra nice to me. She'd brought me some comfort food on a tray—Heinz tomato soup and toast fingers—and the latest Cathy Kelly novel to keep my mind off things.

Work was going to be mental all week. Recommending books for "brilliant" seven-year-olds—of course they were always "brilliant," never average or normal. Grandparents were the worst— "My little Nikki, he's quite brilliant, you know. Reads all by himself. He's very advanced for his age. I want something to stretch him—maybe Dickens or *Treasure Island*." Poor kids, all they really wanted was *Buffy the Vampire Slayer* and *Goosebumps* and *Harry Potter*. I usually tried to come to some sort of compromise but there was no pleasing some customers. Still, it would take my mind off things.

*   *   *

The next few days flew by in a haze of Christmas wrapping-paper and "brilliant" children. All the regulars had been in—Siobhan had spent a small fortune on beautiful hardback books for her girls. I was wistfully half-hoping that the lovely Stevie J would be in again, but of course he wasn't. Before I knew it Christmas Eve had snuck up and thumped me on the head. From eight in the morning (we opened early to get the shop straightened up before the stampede) the place was hopping.

As the afternoon drew in things began to get a little heated and frantic.

"Miss, Miss." Bony fingers clicked in my face. Someone was "summoning" me.

"Where is the latest Larry O'Loughlin?" a tall woman in a voluminous red coat demanded. "I must have it for my niece. It was reviewed on the radio."

"I'm afraid it's sold out," I said politely. "But we have some of Larry's other books."

"What do you mean sold out?" the woman replied with contempt. "It was reviewed in *The Sunday Tribune,* for goodness sake. You must have it!"

"We had it this morning," I continued, losing patience. "But I'm afraid it's a very popular book and we sold the last copy at lunchtime. Maybe you could try the bookshop in the shopping center."

She looked at me with disdain. "Ring them and see!"

"Excuse me?" I asked lifting my eyebrows. I'd had quite enough of this rude woman. It was hardly my fault that she'd left her Christmas shopping until now.

"I said ring them!" she repeated, glaring at me.

I looked her straight in the eye. "I presume you mean 'Would you please ring them for me'?" I asked, staring pointedly at the silver mobile phone clutched in her hand.

Her cheeks began to coordinate with her coat and she opened her mouth to respond. Luckily Lynn had noticed the altercation and stepped in, grinning broadly.

"Can I help? I'm afraid Amy is needed at the picture-books." She pushed me toward the back of the shop.

When the customer from hell had left, Lynn squeezed her way to the desk where I was Christmas-wrapping some books.

"What a dragon!" she exclaimed.

I smiled. "Thanks for taking over. I was about to thump her. Wait till we try to close the shop—then the real loonies will come out of the woodwork!"

Lynn opened a bottle of red wine and poured two large glasses.

"We'd better fortify ourselves, so," she grinned, lifting her glass and clinking it gently against mine. "Cheers!"

After we had herded the last straggling customers out of the shop and locked up I walked into Blackrock to meet the gang in Fitzgerald's. My feet ached and I had a sharp pain in my arms and shoulders— repetitive strain injury of the Christmas book-wrapping genre. Lynn had been in flying form—it was the shop's best Christmas yet and she was delighted. She'd even decided not to open until December the twenty-eighth, giving us both an extra day's holiday. Excellent!

I knew Jodie would be in the pub—it was traditional for the three of us—Beth, Jodie and me to meet up every year before the rest of the gang came in. I'd kind of resigned myself to the fact that she would be present; it was Christmas after all. But I didn't want to talk about Jack, and I was doggedly determined to keep off the subject, no matter what. But as I walked in the door and was blasted with hot, deliciously mulled-wine-scented air I spotted Beth sitting alone at a table in the corner, her coat, scarf and bag draped over other seats in a desperate attempt to keep seats.

"Hiya," I smiled, pulling off my coat and hat and flopping down beside her. "Where's Jodie?"

"She didn't want to come."

"Why not?"

Beth looked at me carefully. "She didn't want to ruin the evening for you."

I felt slightly guilty. I knew how much she loved our Christmas Eve drinks. I sniffed. "I suppose she's staying in with Jack so?"

"No," Beth said. "He's going to his family drinks thingy and she's staying at home."

"Oh," I said. If I was a nice, gregarious person I would have rung her and told her not to be so stupid and to get her butt down there. But I wasn't. I was glad she had to stay in on her own. OK, so I felt a little guilty but not enough to spoil my night!

"What are you having?" I asked, changing the subject.

"Mulled wine," Beth smiled.

"Sounds great." I spotted a young lounge boy and ordered four glasses of mulled wine.

"He's cute," I murmured, watching his pert, tight behind moving away in the shiny black trousers.

"Get a grip," Beth giggled. "He's probably still in school. I'm sure those are his uniform trousers."

"I like them young," I smiled. "I dare you to wink at him when he comes back."

"You're in good form," Beth replied. "If I wink at him you have to tell him he looks like Brad Pitt."

"You're on."

The boy walked toward us and nearly spilt the tray on Beth's lap when she winked at him lasciviously.

"Um, who are these drinks for?" he asked nervously, gesturing at the third and fourth glass balanced on his precarious tray.

"They're the standby drinks. For when these run out," I explained. "You can put them down here. Has anyone ever told you you're the split of Brad Pitt?"

The boy reddened from the tips of his ears to his bum-fluffed cheeks. He smiled broadly.

"Jeez, are yer serious? Tanks." He looked me up and down, his brown eyes lingering a little too long on my chest for comfort. "Listen, I'm off early tonight—want to meet me outside later?"

Beth spluttered her drink all down her top. Luckily it was black so the dark red wine didn't show.

"We'll see," I laughed.

"He was well able for you," Beth giggled after he had left to serve another table. "You're not really going to meet him, are you?"

I stared at her in mock amazement. "I'm not that hard up," I insisted. "But it'll make getting drinks easier if he thinks he's in with a chance."

"You're a wicked woman."

"That's the nicest thing anyone's said to me in a long time." I smiled.

"You pair look well stuck in." Tony approached the table, gave Beth a kiss on the cheek and squeezed in beside her. His friend Jed stood awkwardly beside us. "Jed, get some pints in, will you?" Tony asked. "How's it going, Amy?"

"Grand, thanks, Tony." I knew he knew all about the fall-out with Jodie but he had the decency not to mention it.

"Amy's found herself a toyboy," Beth said.

"Some of my mates from work are calling in later. Does this mean they'll have some competition?" Tony asked smiling.

"I can handle them all," I replied confidently.

"What's that you can handle?" Jed asked, placing two dark velvety pints on the table.

"Don't ask!" Tony said. "Cheers! Here's to a good night and a great Christmas!"

"Cheers!" We all clunked glasses. Maybe it wasn't going to be so bad after all.

"Amy, wake up," Suzi was sitting on my bed and shaking me hard.

"Wha?" I muttered. "It's early. Get off."

"Mum has breakfast all ready and she wants the whole family downstairs."

"Tell her to bugger off," I said darkly.

Suzi laughed. "I don't think she'd appreciate that on Christmas Day. How's the head?"

"Not good," I admitted.

"I'm not surprised with the amount of drinks you threw back last night. When we arrived you'd already started on a round of tequilas with some of Tony's lot. You drank Jed under the table. Matt was well impressed."

"I didn't do anything stupid, did I?" I asked slowly.

"Well . . . not really."

I sat up gingerly and stared at Suzi. "Go on, tell me."

"You know the bar guy? Brad you were calling him?"

"Yes?"

"You pulled him under the mistletoe and kissed him."

"Really?"

"Yup," Suzi continued smiling. "But the funniest thing was that his girlfriend gave him a belt with her handbag. She was sitting at the bar waiting for him to get off work."

I groaned.

"It was brilliant! I haven't laughed so much for years. Matt and Jed practically carried you home but we were all laughing so much it took forever."

"Jed?" I asked.

"Yes, nice guy. He's not as quiet when he's had a few drinks in him. Single too." Suzi looked at me with a funny expression.

"What are you staring at?" I demanded. "Stop the matchmaking. Leave me alone, for heaven's sake."

"Only if you promise to get up."

"Fine."

I pulled myself out of bed and opened the curtains. It was a manky gray, dull, listless day—an Irish special. No doubt it would start raining later to make it even "better." I sighed. As it was Christmas Day I supposed I'd better make some sort of effort to look half-decent. I staggered across to my door, yanked my white toweling robe off its hook and wrapped it around last night's underwear. At least I'd managed to undress before hitting the sack. Yesterday's discarded clothes were straggling inside-out on my wooden floor.

I made it to the shower and soon sharp warm darts were piercing my lethargy. I let the water pummel my body and tried not to think about the headache which was building in my temples. My stomach felt amazingly settled considering the tequila. I was a demon for the dangerous Mexican drink. In college Jodie and I consumed a whole bottle between the two of us one wet, cold afternoon. I can't remember why. Anyway, after hallucinating wildly for several hours, dancing to our own bad singing and dressing up in each other's clothes, getting very confused as to our "real identities," we passed out and slept until the following day. I'll never, ever forget the hangover. It was the mother of all hangovers—hot sweats, spasming stomachs, jack-hammers in our heads, shaking hands—the works. I've never had a hangover quite like it since—thank goodness!

I stepped out of the shower and grabbed a towel. While drying myself I remembered that I hadn't used any shampoo or soap, so I had to get back into the shower! Eventually I walked back to my room, feeling much more alive, and pulled on a pair of black trousers and a dark red polo-neck. I layered on the make-up, finishing off with some "Hell Red" lipstick and I was ready to face the world.

Breakfast was already well under way when I entered the kitchen.

"Morning, Amy. Nice of you to join us," Mum said, smiling.

"Late night, was it?" Dad asked while spearing half a sausage on his fork and dipping it into his fried egg.

"Would you like a fry?" Mum asked.

I thought for a second. My stomach seemed OK, so why not? "Thanks, Mum, that'd be great. No pudding though."

Suzi and Matt were holding hands over the table and feeding each other pieces of toast.

"Look what Matt bought me," Suzi exclaimed, pulling up her new pink cardigan and revealing a sexy purple lacy bra. "There's matching knickers too." She stood up to show me.

Dad coughed. "I don't think you need to show us, thanks, Suzi. I'm sure they're lovely."

I laughed. Suzi was great. Matt looked a little embarrassed.

"What did Suzi get you, Matt?" I asked kindly, trying to change the subject.

"Some aftershave," he beamed. "And a season ticket for Lansdowne Road. She's a star."

Dad's ears pricked up. "How did you manage that, Suzi?" he asked. "They're impossible to get."

Suzi smiled. "My new boss."

We all looked at her in amazement. I didn't know Suzi had even been looking for a job.

Mum smiled knowingly as she placed a sizzling breakfast in front of me.

Dad looked at her in amazement. "Is someone going to tell me what's going on?"

"And me," I added, a little miffed that Suzi hadn't said anything to me.

Suzi giggled. "I wanted to tell you all but I didn't want to say anything until I was sure. Matt's coach in Clontarf was looking for a nanny urgently for his brother and Matt suggested me."

"Go on," I urged impatiently.

"Well, I went to meet the family and the kids were great. Katie is five and Simon is seven. So I start in January."

"Tell them who their Dad is," Matt cajoled.

"Oops, I nearly forgot. Their Dad is Brian Lowan."

"No!" Dad exclaimed. "Not *the* Brian Lowan?"

"The rugby guy?" I asked. "The captain of the Irish team?"

"The very same," Suzi replied. "He's a really nice guy and his wife, Julie, is a pet. And I'll get to fly all over the place as he likes his family to travel with him."

"Wow," I exclaimed. I was delighted for Suzi but a little jealous. Everyone seemed to be falling on their feet except for me these days.

Mum kissed Suzi on the head. "We're very proud of you, love. And the Lowans are very lucky."

"They sure are," Matt agreed.

Jesus, I thought. My family has turned into the bloody Waltons. It was going to be a long day.

"Eva's dying to hear all about your wedding plans," Mum continued. "Judy too." Eva and Judy were relatives of some sort—cousins of Dad's or something.

"I can show her my wedding folder," Suzi piped up, delighted.

"Your what?" I asked incredulously.

"Amy, don't be like that," Suzi scolded playfully. "I knew you'd take the piss so I haven't shown you yet."

"Language, please!" Mum exclaimed.

"Oops, sorry, Mum. Anyway, it's a folder of ideas for our wedding." Suzi gazed adoringly at Matt. "You know, color schemes, dresses, flowers, menus, that sort of thing."

"Um," I muttered. It really was going to be a brutally long day.

Chapter 8

Mum and Dad left for church, followed by two drinks parties, leaving myself and Suzi to begin the Christmas dinner. Matt went for a run, more to keep out of our way I think than from any real desire to pound the local crazy paving that masquerades as pavement.

"I think we're supposed to put the turkey in now," Suzi said in confusion. "But I'm not sure. Dad said it's a twelve-pound bird and according to Mum it needs fifteen minutes per pound—does three hours sound right?"

"I'm not sure," I said nervously. "To be honest I don't have a clue. But I think it went in for longer last year and it was a smaller turkey."

"I'll stuff it anyway. Will you look up one of Mum's cookery books or something? I don't want to poison everyone."

"I'll ring Beth," I decided. "She'll know. She's cooking for her family at her house."

I picked up the phone in the hall and dialed Beth's number.

"Hello?" Beth answered uncertainly.

"Hi, Beth, happy Christmas! How are you this morning?"

"Not too bad considering. And yourself?"

"Getting there. Listen, I need your help urgently." I explained about the twelve-pound uncooked turkey.

"Right, do you have the oven pre-heated?" she asked anxiously—she knew what I was like in the kitchen.

"I think so," I said, trying not to sound as scared as I felt. What if I struck the whole family down with salmonella. On second thoughts . . .

Beth sighed. "Maybe you'd better write this down. Pre-heat the oven high."

"What's high?"

"You have gas, so mark seven. Have you done the stuffing?"

"Suzi's doing that now."

"Fine. Then after she's finished, wrap the turkey in tinfoil and cook it on high for half an hour."

"Right."

"Then turn down the heat to mark three and cook for three hours."

"Three hours! Are you sure?" I asked. "It seems like a long time."

Beth laughed. "Believe me, I'm sure. I've been doing the Christmas dinner for years. Then turn up the heat again and cook for another twenty minutes. And don't forget to baste the thing. OK?"

I breathed a sigh of relief. I hadn't a clue what basting was but I didn't want to appear a total ignoramus. "Thanks, Beth. You've saved our lives—literally. We might have poisoned the family otherwise. Although that might not be such a bad thing," I added darkly.

"No problem. Is it OK if I call in around seven? I want to give you your present."

"Perfect. I'll see you then."

Suzi looked up from the backside of the turkey as I entered the kitchen. "Well?"

"I have it all here," I said, waving the piece of paper in the air.

"Excellent," Suzi replied, wincing as she shoved more chestnut and apple stuffing into the bird. "Right, he's well filled now." She washed her hands in the sink

"What's basting?" I asked her as we lifted the heavy bird into the oven.

Suzi smiled. "I'm not sure. Is it a trick question? Is it something to do with sex?"

I laughed. "No! It's something to do with cooking a turkey. You have a one-track mind."

I pulled Delia Smith's *Complete Cookery Course* off the bookshelf and studied the index. Nothing on basting.

"Beth?"

"Oh, hi, Amy."

"Sorry to ring again, but what's basting?"

Suzi and I cheered as we heard the front door slamming. Excellent, I thought—Mum was back to take over the cooking. We were sprawled at the kitchen table, exhausted from peeling the spuds for the roast potatoes.

Matt stuck his head around the kitchen door.

"Damn," I exclaimed. "I thought you were Mum."

"Sorry to disappoint you," Matt grinned. "I'm off to have a shower."

"Come here," Suzi said, a wicked smile on her face. She stood up and kissed Matt firmly on the lips. "I love sweaty men." She licked Mail's dripping left temple.

"That's disgusting," I shrieked.

"Yum, salty," she smiled as Matt lumbered out of the kitchen.

"You are revolting," I said, swatting her with a tea-towel. "I suppose we'd better baste the turkey."

The front door slammed again and this time it was Mum and Dad.

"Hallelujah," Suzi shouted. "Mum, we need you urgently."

Mum came into the kitchen, her face flushed. "Hi, girls. How are you getting on?"

"Fine, but we need a break."

"Right, me and your Dad will take over now. Frank!" she called.

We left them to it and retired to the sitting room, glasses of chilled white wine in hand. Dad had kindly handed us the whole bottle.

"You keep Eva and Judy occupied and we'll finish the dinner."

"Deal," I agreed.

Several hours later the whole ensemble were seated around the dining-room table tucking into the turkey.

"Beautifully cooked," Judy enthused, cutting her turkey into small, evenly sized pieces.

"Perfect," Eva agreed, piling more cranberry sauce onto her already loaded fork.

"Now tell me all about your wedding plans, Suzi," Judy asked expectantly. "I want to hear all about them."

"Every little detail," Eva agreed. "We're dying to hear everything."

I groaned inwardly. Just what I needed, more bloody wedding talk.

"Might put a fire under your Jack," Judy continued. "It's about time he made an honest woman out of you."

Dad coughed and tried to change the subject "Um, more turkey anyone?"

I sighed and decided to bite the bullet. "Jack and I broke up, Judy. We won't be getting married, not now, not ever."

There was an awkward silence.

"I'm sorry, Amy," Judy said quietly. "I had no idea . . ."

"It's fine. You weren't to know," I lied breezily. "It's for the best anyway. Has Suzi told you about her wedding folder?"

Suzi glanced at me and smiled kindly. We were quite used to playing talk-tag to get our parents and relations off a difficult subject.

"I've collected all kinds of things in a folder, Judy. Dress designs, flowers, menus, the works. I'll show it to you after dinner."

"What fun!" Judy exclaimed before launching into a lengthy tale about her own wedding over sixty years ago. Her husband was dead now and they'd never had any children so Suzi and I were kind of her surrogate children. I couldn't concentrate on what she was saying though. My mind kept drifting back to Jack. What had I done? Of course I should have married him. But he was with Jodie now and I'd lost a boyfriend and a best friend all rolled into one. I'd never find anyone else now—I was nearly thirty, for heaven's sake. Who'd want a thirty-year-old with a track record of broken relationships, who had a crappy job and lived at home? No one in their right mind . . .

"Amy?"

The whole table was staring at me.

"Yes?"

"Eva just asked you about work."

"I'm sorry, I . . ." My eyes filled with tears. "Excuse me . . ." I abruptly left the table and thundered up the stairs to my room. I flopped on the bed, tears spilling all over my pillow. Damn, I thought I was fine today.

"Amy?" Suzi was standing over me. "Are you all right??"

"No," I cried. "But I will be." I sniffed. Suzi handed me a tissue. "I'm sorry. It's Christmas Day and I'm spoiling everything."

"Don't be daft," Suzi said gently. "Come down and finish dinner."

"I don't know if I can."

Suzi looked at me sternly. "Don't let Jack-fecking-Daly spoil everything. He's not worth it. In a few months' time you'll have forgotten all about him."

"Maybe," I murmured unconvinced. But I knew Suzi was right. If I could just get through the next few months . . .

"You don't want to miss opening your presents, do you? The bet's still on this year, I presume?"

I smiled. Every year we placed bets on Judy's and Eva's presents. They were creatures of habit but I was convinced that one year they would surprise us both.

"Twenty quid on Judy giving us both BodyShop baskets and Eva giving us Marks & Spencer's vouchers." Suzi was going for the safe bet.

"Fine," I agreed. "Anything else and I win, deal?" I'd lost money every Christmas for the last few years. Maybe my luck would change this year, although it was highly unlikely.

Everyone behaved normally as I returned to the table which was twilight zonish but blissfully easy to deal with. I had no desire to explain the twists and turns of my emotions, especially not on Christmas Day.

"Christmas pudding, Amy?" Mum asked kindly as I gingerly

wiggled my chair under the ancient mahogany table, trying to avoid the strut which I'd crucified my knees on more than once.

"Thanks, Mum," I smiled. Dad refilled my wine glass and stroked my head gently as he walked behind me. The unexpected tenderness made my eyes well up again but I managed to control myself. The rest of the dinner went past in a blur of animated small talk.

"You'll never guess who that singer is stepping out with . . . Simon Strummer," Eve stated with a glint in her eye. She was a great woman for celebrity gossip and lived for her doses of *VIP* and *Hello* magazines.

"Isn't he married?" Mum asked in a disapproving voice.

"Men!" Suzi declared. "Too many hormones for their own good. Except Matt, of course." She gazed at Matt who seemed more than a little overwhelmed by the way that the afternoon had gone. I'm sure my emotional display hadn't helped. He was knocking back the wine like there was no tomorrow.

"I'm sure Matt is full of hormones, aren't you, Matt?" I asked.

Matt turned puce. He had no idea what to say.

Dad took pity on him. "Pay no attention to those two," he said, leaning toward Matt. "I shouldn't have given them so much wine!"

After dinner we brought our drinks into the sitting room. The fire was roaring in the grate and the tree's white lights sparkled, making the delicate colored glass baubles glisten. Dad and Matt settled on the sofa beside the fire and began a conversation on Ireland's chances in the Rugby World Cup. It was nice for Dad to have another male in the company. Although last year he'd had Jack to talk to . . . I shivered. I wanted to stop thinking about Jack but it was so damn hard.

"Present time," Mum said, sitting down on the other sofa between Eva and Judy. "Will you do the honors, girls?"

Suzi and I began to distribute the wrapped presents to their owners. Soon the room was filled with oohs, ahhs and shrieks of laughter.

We had various relations who still sent us presents—like Marty, Mum's sister in London, who Suzi and I adored. Every year she treated us to trendy tights, scarves and jewelry she'd picked up in Covent Garden Market. And "The Canadians"—Dad's brother, the computer nerd and his perfect cheerleader wife and three perfect children, who always sent us perfect presents, professionally wrapped in tissue paper and divine, luxurious gold paper with bows and ribbons—the works.

Chapter 9

This year Marty had sent Suzi a silver silk boa and me a pair of bright pink fishnets—cool! She really was the bee's knees.

"What are those?" Matt had asked from the sofa, his interest suddenly captured by the offending tights which I was pulling out of their plastic packaging.

"Matt!" Suzi exclaimed.

"I was only asking," he muttered sheepishly, deciding to keep his mouth firmly shut in future. He couldn't win.

"The Canadians" had given Mum and Dad a small plastic box and a spiral-bound book. It was called *The Magnetic Poetry Set*.

"It's like Scrabble," Dad exclaimed animatedly. He had a passion for Scrabble. Poor man, he didn't get out much. He scattered the small white rectangular pieces on the coffee table and began to make sentences. "You make up poems and stick them on the fridge." That was him sorted for the evening. Matt seemed a little lost now that his sofa buddy had been swept away to the land of academia. Poetry wasn't really Matt's thing. Although he did like Purple Ronnie—the guy who wrote those funny, stick-people cards.

Mum wasn't so thrilled. She had hoped for something useful. Fat lot of good some old poems were going to do.

"What the hell is this?" I pulled the gold paper off my "Canadian" present and wrinkled my nose in disdain.

Suzi giggled. "Looks like a willy warmer!"

"Suzi," Mum spluttered, trying not to laugh.

"Well, it does," she protested.

I held the bright yellow tubular neoprene object in the air. "What do you think Matt? Does it look like a willy-warmer to you?"

"Girls," Mum said in exasperation, "what age are you? What will Eva and Judy think?"

"Don't worry," Judy laughed. "We're not as sheltered as you think. Are we, Eva?"

"Certainly not," Eva agreed. "In fact, we could both teach you a thing or two, I'm sure. And Amy, I think you'll find that you are holding a can-cooler in your hand. And if you've seen willies that size, you're a lucky woman!"

I grinned, delighted.

Dad had chosen to ignore the conversation—he knew when he was outnumbered. Matt was sitting mouth open in amazement.

Suzi jumped up and planted a fat kiss on his mouth. After a few seconds I could tell that there was some serious tongue action going on there so I tried to keep the attention on the presents.

"This is for you, Judy." I handed her the neatly wrapped (by Suzi) present.

She tore off the Christmas paper like a small child, eyes twinkling, and held up a tiny silver-covered pencil which hung on a delicate silver chain. Her eyes watered. "Girls, it's just beautiful. You remembered."

I sat down on the edge of the armchair. "Of course." Last Christmas Eve Judy had lost an identical necklace at the Concert Hall. It was her favorite necklace, given to her by her late husband.

"Where did you find it?" Judy asked, running her age-spotted fingers affectionately over the tiny pencil and smiling.

"My boss, Lynn, has a friend who owns an antique shop and I asked her to keep her eyes open."

"Thank you," Judy whispered.

"It's a pleasure," I beamed.

Suzi tore herself away from Matt, surreptitiously wiping her glistening mouth on her sleeve.

"Isn't Amy clever?" she asked. "Open yours, Eva."

Eva pulled back a tiny piece of the Christmas paper on her present and then another. A smile came to her coral pink lips. "Is this what I think it is?"

I turned toward Suzi and smiled. She had found the most exquisite natural pearl hairband in Australia for Eva.

"Like in that photograph," Suzi said gently, "with Albert." Albert was Eva's childhood sweetheart and she had shown us old black and white photographs of the pair of them attending a Midsummer's Ball in the Tennis Club. She had worn a cream silk full-length dress that fitted her like a glove and a delicate pearl hairband in her glossy raven black hair.

Eva placed the hairband in her silver hair and closed her eyes. "I can remember that night like it was only yesterday."

It was a surreal moment. The wrinkles on her face disappeared and she looked in complete bliss. There was silence for a few seconds. I looked at Suzi and smiled. For two brain-dead and batty females it was pretty impressive! As Eamon Dunphy would say—*the girls done good!* She winked at me and smiled back.

"This is for you, Suzi," Eva handed her a red envelope. "And for you, Amy." We didn't have to look inside, but we did anyway—rude not to. Yep, M & S vouchers again. Suzi was delighted—she was on her way to winning some drinking money.

"Thanks, just what I need. New underwear, here I come! They have a new Wild West range—I fancy the pink basque, or maybe the bra and string set . . ." Suzi was lost in knicker heaven. Matt's eyes lit up again.

He was lovely. I could see what Suzi liked about him—he was solid and cuddly. Like a huge big affectionate puppy. But I wasn't sure if I could deal with the predictability.

"Thanks, Eva," I said, plastering a smile on my face.

Judy presented us both with—do I have to say it?—two BodyShop baskets. Not the tiny little cheap ones, mind. Huge, hulking ones, filled to the brim with all kinds of sweet-smelling bubbles, lotions and soaps. And it's a superb present, don't get me wrong. It's just that I hadn't washed my way through last year's basket yet. And it meant I lost the fecking bet—typical. It was obviously going to be another crappy year! The omens were bad enough.

And then Beth arrived.

Chapter 10

"Beth, what do you think of this one?" Dad was kneeling at the coffee table, composing "poems" when Beth entered the room. *"I tell the four corners of the world about you, my love rose."*

Beth smiled. Luckily, she was well used to my Dad. Matt, on the other hand, was still looking a little shell-shocked. Judy and Eva had decided to "take him under their wing," which was a polite and unconfrontational way of saying they were checking out his bloodlines. Suzi was helping Mum in the kitchen, talking weddings no doubt.

"That's clever, Frank. Read me another," Beth encouraged, kindly. Great—encouragement was definitely not what he needed right at that moment.

"How about this—*You ear desire like a poison dart within your heart.* That should be wear but I can't find a 'w.' "

"Can I do one?" Beth asked foolishly.

Soon Beth and my Dad were moving the little rectangles over the table like two of the bloody Romantic poets—that Browning lady and Lord Byron. Or like something out of *American Beauty.* You know, where the Dad fancies the girl's best friend. OK, so maybe I was being a little unfair but Beth was my mate and I wanted her all to myself. I wanted to bore her with the details of my weepy episode and I wanted her to analyze it and tell me it would be all right . . . selfish, wasn't I? On Christmas Day too.

"So what did Tony get you this year?" Dad asked, in between

poems. Beth was very proud of her *Fireflies glimmer in the garden like my love for you.* Yuck!

Beth blushed and sat up. This was interesting. Maybe Tony had given her some sort of sex toy or something. You couldn't exactly tell your friend's parents that, could you? On second thoughts, maybe Suzi could but not Beth.

"This." She beamed and pulled a tiny blue box out of her pocket. My heart plummeted. Please, no. Not another one. I couldn't deal with it.

Beth got up and sat down beside me on the sofa. She opened the box. In it sat the most beautiful engagement ring I'd ever seen. A large single diamond was held in a solid platinum band, like a tiny suspension bridge.

"Beth, it's lovely," I whispered. "Put it on."

She took the ring out of the box and slid it onto her ring. It sparkled in the light and seemed to illuminate her face with its brightness. That was pure happiness of course, not the ring. But it always amazed me how an engagement ring could make even the most nail-bitten or spatula-fingered hands attractive. A monster green dart of jealousy shot through my heart. I tried to swallow it. Tears came to my eyes. And I'm ashamed to say they were not tears of happiness for Beth. I was feeling sorry for myself again. But Beth has such a good heart this wouldn't occur to her and I was relieved that she assumed that they were for her and Tony.

"It's wonderful news," I lied. It was a good day for lies. They were tripping off my tongue like water off the rocks at Powerscourt Waterfall. Pity you can only get away with lying to yourself for a little while.

"How exciting," Dad said. "When's the big day?"

"The first week in May—on the third hopefully if the church is free that day. And if my bridesmaid is free." Beth turned her big, brown eyes on me—what could I do? Say "no, sorry, I'm busy that week"?

"Of course I'm free!" I gushed. "I wouldn't miss it for the world!"

"Wouldn't miss what?" Suzi asked, coming in the door.

"My wedding," Beth grinned.

"Oh, Beth," Suzi hugged Beth and kissed her on the cheek. "That's excellent. I've just set my date too."

"Two weddings in one summer," I said, attempting a happy, light tone. "Isn't that great?"

"When's yours, Suzi?" Beth asked.

"I haven't told Matt yet." She waved over at her fiancé who was reading a *Calvin and Hobbes* cartoon book. Judy and Eva had completed their interrogation and were now discussing Dolly and genetic engineering. Although it involved sheep, Matt had no interest in their conversation. So Judy had kindly handed him the comic book, one of his presents from my good self. Excellent choice in everything but men.

Matt looked up and smiled. "I'd marry you tomorrow, my love." Jesus, Dad's poetry kit was making everyone barmy, rugby players included. "You just name the date."

Suzi sighed. "Isn't he sweet . . . where was I? Oh, yes, Mum and I set the date—May the third."

Suzi's announcement was met with an icy silence. "What have I said?" she asked with concern.

This was a bit more like it. Things going wrong for people who were not me! I know, I know.

Beth coughed and looked around the room nervously. "That's the date myself and Tony have chosen." She gulped. "But I suppose in the circumstances we can change it. What with Amy being bridesmaid and all . . ."

Typical, I thought to myself. That's right, blame me. I stepped in quickly. "You could always ask someone else, Beth. I wouldn't mind." Please ask someone else, I begged under my breath. I really, really, really don't mind.

"No," Beth stated firmly. "You're my best friend, Amy. I want you. I'll change the date. It's no big deal. The following week would be fine." She looked doubtful for a second. "I think." She bit her lip.

Suzi was delighted. She slipped over to Matt and threw her arms around him. "Hear that, love. May the third it is." Matt was stuck for words (what's new?) so he just smiled. God, he really did have the most lovely teeth, white and even.

I was beginning to feel like the Ugly Sister at this stage. Unfair, I know, to begrudge the two people who were closest to me in the whole world but hey . . .

Soon the whole room was buzzing with wedding talk. After a respectable interval I snuck off into the kitchen to find more wine. It was dark but I was too lazy to find the light switch. I felt my way to the fridge and opened the door. The light cast a bright yellow shaft over the kitchen table where Suzi's wedding folder lay open. Pictures of wedding dresses insulted my eyes. Pieces of material danced in the dark, silks and organzas flirting on the brown table top.

I pulled a bottle of Australian Chardonnay (in Matt's honor no doubt) out of the fridge and opened it. Pouring myself a large glass, I sat down at the table and looked at the paraphernalia, the open fridge sending an icy chill down my spine. Or was it the fridge? The thought suddenly came to me that maybe Tony had asked Jack to be his best man.

"Amy?" Beth whispered in the gloom. She flicked on the lights. "Are you all right?"

I looked up.

"Not really," I said, attempting to pull my lips into some sort of smile. I failed. "Is Jack Tony's best man?"

"No," Beth said. "Tony asked him, it was only right, but Jack said that in the circumstances he'd have to say no."

I let out a sigh of relief.

"I'm sorry . . ." Beth began. "About the news. The wedding and everything. But I wanted you to be one of the first to know. I didn't mean to upset you."

Dear, sweet Beth. One of the happiest days of her life and I was being a real killjoy.

"No, I'm sorry. It's brilliant news. Tony's a lucky guy." I stood up and held her close.

"Thanks, Amy." We heard a cough behind us and moved apart. Matt was standing in the doorway, blushing.

"Sorry, Matt," I quipped. "Just having a bit of a snog with Beth here. Bit of an Irish tradition if your mate gets engaged." Beth giggled.

Matt looked more than a little worried.

"Only joking," I smiled. "Although I've always had a bit of a thing for her." I winked at Beth suggestively and licked my lips.

This was too much for Matt who backed away toward the hall. A few minutes later Suzi burst in the door.

"What have you been saying to Matt? Dad sent him down to get the champagne from the fridge and he said he'd interrupted you both. He looked mortified."

"He'd better get used to us," I laughed. "He ain't seen nothing yet!"

"No kidding," Beth agreed.

Suzi looked at us both and sighed. She swung the bottle of champagne out of the fridge and tucked it under her arm. "Are you two coming back up?" she asked suspiciously.

"In a minute," I said. "There's something I have to give Beth first." In all the excitement I'd forgotten to give Beth her Christmas present. I told you I was selfish!

"Here, this is for you," I handed Beth the tiny black suede drawstring bag which had been keeping warm in my pocket.

Beth smiled. "Thanks, Amy. I'll just nip to the car and fetch yours and then we can open them together."

I waited in the kitchen for Beth to come back. I could hear the humming of the fridge, the ticking of the red Habitat clock on the wall and the sound of laughter and glasses tinkling in the sitting room. Once again I felt achingly alone.

Beth bustled into the room, clutching a large black bin-bag which dwarfed her small frame. "Here you go."

"What is this?" I exclaimed.

"Open it and see," she laughed.

I took the bag from her and ripped open the plastic.

"Jeez, you're such a child." Beth smiled at my impatience.

In astonishment I pulled out a giant bag of multicolored pompoms, red and yellow ping-pong balls, a packet of colored pipe-cleaners, some cardboard insides of toilet rolls, paper glue and craft glue and three plastic tubs filled with glitter, tiny gold stars and tiny red hearts respectively.

I grinned. "What are you like, Beth? What am I supposed to do with this lot?"

"If you want to be a children's presenter you have to start practicing. I want to see a whole menagerie of pipe-cleaner animals and loo-roll people the next time I'm around."

"You're joking?" I spluttered.

"No," Beth looked at me straight in the eye. "Amy, if this is something you really want to do you have to take fate into your own hands. No one is going to walk into your shop and offer you a starring role on *Den 2,* you know."

"I know," I muttered. Beth was being a little freaky.

"You've got to take control of your own life. I think you should visit some schools, offer to talk to the kids about books, do some art with them, anything. Get some experience."

"And?" I asked doubtfully.

"And tape yourself interacting with the kids and send it into RTE."

I was silent for a second. She had a point. And maybe it would take my mind off things to do something different, something a little mad. It couldn't be any worse than being the bloody Story Princess, could it?

"I'll see," I said finally.

"Promise?" Beth asked gently.

"Yes, now open your present."

Beth opened the drawstrings and poured the tissue-covered present onto her open palm. She unwrapped the tissue and gasped.

"Oh, Amy, it's beautiful!" She held the necklace up and watched the tiny heart sway in its silver casing. "You shouldn't have!"

"You've been so good to me," I began, tears welling up in my eyes. "I wanted to get you something special."

Beth put her arms around me and kissed me tenderly on the cheek. "Thank you."

We heard a noise behind us and turned around, but the interrupter had gone back to the sitting room.

"I hope it wasn't Matt," I laughed.

Beth giggled. "God love him."

Later that evening I sat on my bed in the dark and listened to the sounds of laughter coming from downstairs. I had smiled long enough so I'd excused myself and was now regretting it. Feeling sorry for yourself isn't much fun, especially when you recognize it as just that. Beth had gone home—to Tony. Suzi was sticking her tongue down Matt's throat in the kitchen, and Mum and Dad, Eva and Judy were finishing off the champagne and playing with Dad's poetry thingy.

I felt like shite. It was my first single Christmas in a long time and I wasn't impressed. Last year I'd had Jack to cuddle up to, and to peel and feed me mandarin segments. And now I had no one. It was all most unfair.

And to top it all I had to go back to work on the twenty-eighth. But maybe it was just as well—it would keep my mind off things. Beth had made me promise to go to her engagement party on New Year's Eve before she'd left. Which was something to look forward to, I supposed. It was fancy dress for some reason—namely that Beth loved fancy dress. At least it was giving me something to think about. The theme was Heroes and Heroines.

After two hours of deliberation I'd decided to go as either Kermit the Frog or Ms. Indiana Jones.

Chapter 11

"How was work?" Beth asked, opening her front door to me on New Year's Eve.

"Don't ask," I muttered darkly, walking into the hall. I really was in flying form these days. "Stupid people trying to exchange books they bought somewhere else and hoards of bored children looking for the Story Princess."

Beth smiled. "Was the Story Princess available?"

"Yes," I said. "But she read *Struwwelpeter*."

Beth looked confused. "Sorry?"

"They're German cautionary tales about bad children and the things that happen to them."

Beth looked a little shocked. "I think I remember my Granny reading them to me. Was there some boy who had his thumbs cut off 'cos he sucked them? And some girl who burnt the house down with matches?"

"That's the one."

"Are you serious?" Beth asked with concern.

"No," I admitted. "It was *The Secret Garden* this time. But I should have gone with the *Struwwelpeter*."

"Um," Beth murmured doubtfully. "Anyway, you're here now so make yourself useful."

We moved into the kitchen. The table was covered with dishes, bowls and plastic bags of shopping. Long sticks of French bread poked out of one of the bags and I spotted trays of fresh herbs in another. Beth loved throwing parties and never did things by half measures.

"Garlic bread and dips," I said, pulling the shopping out of the bags and placing it on the table. "And lasagne."

"Correct," Beth beamed from the counter where she was making two cups of tea. "You know me so well."

"Hey, isn't that a really bad song?" I laughed. " 'I Know Him So Well'?"

Beth began to sing. She had a nice voice, did Beth. Shame about the song.

I joined in.

"Lovely singing, girls," Tony smiled as he walked into the kitchen. Jed followed in his wake, looking embarrassed.

"Hi, Amy," Jed said nervously.

"Hi," I smiled. He was male, wasn't he? With a pulse. And he wasn't all that bad-looking in a computer-geeky sort of way. And if you remember—single. Which is usually all the encouragement I need. "Looking forward to tonight, Jed?" I said, gazing into his eyes and tucking my hair behind my ears. When I had long hair I used to flick it, but, now it was short, tucking seemed to do the trick.

He blushed—bingo!

"Yes," he managed. "Yes, I am."

Tony looked at me strangely. Was he frowning? "We're off to buy the booze. Anything you want in particular?"

Beth squiggled up her nose. She always did this when she was thinking—it make her look like a rabbit but it was cute. Kind of.

"Tequila," I interjected. "And Red Bull."

"No way," Beth exclaimed. "Not after Christmas Eve. No more tequila for you, Amy."

"Ah, go on," I cajoled. "It's only New Year's once a year. What harm can it do?"

Tony looked at Beth and raised his eyebrows. She sighed. "OK, but only one bottle, mind."

I rubbed my hands together. "Excellent. Now where's the garlic? Not that I'll be having any, of course," I reassured the room, looking Jed straight in the eye.

Tony pushed a lobster-faced Jed out the door.

"Look what you did to that poor bloke," Beth scolded as the front door slammed shut. "You'll eat him for dinner."

"I was hoping it might be the other way around."

Beth looked confused.

"I wouldn't mind a bit of nibbling and licking, in the right places of course."

"Amy, you're disgusting!" Beth wrinkled her nose.

"I aim to please."

Beth handed me the garlic-crusher. "Garlic, now!"

"Yes, master."

"Excellent party," Jed whispered in my ear. "Good call on the tequila."

I had spent the last two hours pouring it down his neck and it seemed to have had the desired effect. We were sitting on the sofa beside the stereo and Jed was stroking my leg—which was clad in dramatic leopard-skin hold-ups—enthusiastically. I was hoping he wouldn't create some sort of static electrical charge and burn my lips when we kissed—but I guess you have to take your chances.

"Have some more," I purred, topping up his glass. We'd slugged our way through nearly the whole bottle which was quite an achievement as it was only ten o'clock. I was kind of tipsy but my mind was still sharp—well, sharp-ish. I was mildly enjoying playing with Jed, but it was all a little too easy.

And then Branigan walked in the door.

Branigan was the coolest and hippest guy any of us knew. He ran a club in town, designed his own range of handbags of all things and was at every movie, book or fashion launch in Dublin. And he was drop-dead gorgeous and knew it. Tonight he was wearing skin-tight red plastic trousers, a black T-shirt which clung to his toned torso and outlined his pecs and a black leather jacket. This outfit on any-one else would have looked plain stupid but on Branigan it looked deadly. Well, I assumed he was dressed up as some sort of New Ro-mantic from the 80's, but come to think of it maybe he had just come as himself—I'd seen him in a similar outfit before.

He strode into the room with a pout on his full lips. His short dark hair glistened in the subdued lights. And, sad to say, my stomach lurched. He looked like sex on legs and had a reputation to match. And, praise the Lord, he was alone.

I stood up and tried not to stagger as I sashayed toward him. He looked bemused.

"Amy, how are you, darling?" He kissed both cheeks flamboyantly. "Delighted to hear about Jack. You're far too good for him."

I winced. Obviously the Blackrock old boys' grapevine had kicked in. Unbelievably, Jack and Branigan had been in the same class. I think they had even been some sort of friends at one stage. I could never picture it, they were so different, but maybe they had appreciated each other's selfish streaks.

"Hi, Branigan. How's tricks? Like the outfit—very Simon Le Bon." I should explain that Branigan was Branigan's name. First name that is. Branigan Luce. And it was always said with a drawling emphasis on the "b." Bbbbbrrranigan. Like that.

"Thanks. But I dressed up as me. And you look . . ." His eyes wandered languidly over my body, lingering on my legs and chest. "Grrrr." He growled.

I should probably explain at this stage that I'd gone for the Ms. Indiana Jones costume—complete with the aforementioned leopardskin hold-ups, short fake snakeskin skirt, brown leather top with tiny shoe-string straps and long black whip (made out of a stick of bamboo painted black with string attached). I'd nicked my father's fishing hat—an Indiana Jones leather affair—and I'd attached fake spiders, bugs and rats to every available surface.

When he growled my legs nearly went from under me. Honestly, I have too many hormones—I should be kept away from men like Branigan.

Jed appeared beside me. "Amy, would you like another drink? The tequila's gone but I've found a bottle of vodka."

I smiled at Jed. He looked at me hopefully. "Thanks, Jed." I turned to Branigan. "Would you like a vodka and Red Bull?" Branigan nodded curtly. "Make that two, Jed."

God, I'm horrible sometimes. When Jed returned from the

kitchen Branigan and I were sitting on the sofa which had been nicely warmed up by Jed and me. Like he was the supporting act and Branigan was the main attraction. When Jed saw us his face dropped. He handed us the drinks in silence and sloped off into the hall.

Ten minutes later Branigan and I were playing tonsil-hockey on the same sofa. His tongue was sucking and nipping my eager lips, tantalizing my senses. One hand was firmly guiding my head and the other was snaking its way up my leg. Branigan was forceful, manly and, God, I wanted him.

"Hey, babe, I'm on fire for you. Let's go upstairs!"

I peeled my lips from Branigan's earlobe which I had been flicking with my tongue. "Good idea," I whispered.

He stood up immediately and pulled me up off the sofa in one swift, forceful move. I gasped as he held me against him and gyrated his pelvis against mine.

"I need action and I need it now," he said, grinning broadly.

I bit his upper lip—gently, mind, I didn't want to draw blood—and we made our way into the hall.

"Follow me," I said, starting to walk up the stairs.

Branigan followed behind, his hands holding my snakeskinned behind firmly and squeezing now and again. We fell into Beth's room where the coats were piled on the bed. The curtains were open and the streetlamps were lighting the room.

I began to search for my coat, throwing a leather jacket and a long black coat off the pile. But Branigan had other ideas. He launched himself on top of me, kissing the back of my neck and resting his weight on my body. His hands reached forward and encircled my body, resting on my breasts and kneading gently.

I pulled one of his hands toward my mouth and began to lick his forefinger, popping it in and out of my mouth and caressing it with my tongue.

Branigan was breathing heavily at this stage. He lifted his weight off me and turned me around. He lifted my top, negotiated my bra, unclipping it skillfully with one hand, and kissed my breasts. I began to sigh.

I pulled his head toward me and began to kiss him passionately. His hands moved down my body, pushing up my skirt. He moaned as he caressed the bare thigh at the top of my hold-ups. He slid one of his hands slowly toward my stomach and began moving it down.

I froze. Even in my drunken state it felt wrong. I didn't really know Branigan, not properly. And I was damned if I was going to have meaningless, drunken sex with him just for the sake of it.

"Easy, Branigan," I whispered, placing my hand on his firmly and guiding it onto safer territory. We kissed for a few more minutes before I felt woozy and rolled off him.

I was woken by the sound of Branigan's voice. He was on his mobile.

"Yeah, babe, ten minutes, I promise. I'm on my way."

"Branigan," I smiled.

"Hi, gorgeous," he stroked my cheek. "I'm sorry. I have to go now. I'll ring you, OK?"

I sat up and pulled my skirt down. "Do you have to?" I asked. It wasn't that late.

"Yes, I really do. Bye, princess." He leaned over and kissed me on the lips. "Enjoy the rest of the party."

"I'll put my mobile number on your phone," I said desperately, sad person that I am.

"Um, whatever, sure," Branigan muttered, looking a little uneasy. He handed me his chrome mobile.

I punched in my number slowly and carefully. And after watching his back disappear through the door, I lay down on the coats and fell fast asleep.

"Amy, Amy, wake up." Beth was standing over me with a worried expression on her face. "I wondered where you'd got to."

"Hi," I said, dozily. "What time is it?"

"Just before twelve."

"Shit," I exclaimed. "I'm sorry, I must have been asleep for a while."

"Branigan left about an hour ago. Apparently Elena was looking for him."

"Elena?" I asked, puzzled.

"His girlfriend."

"Oh, feck."

"What's wrong?" Beth looked at my face and raised her eyebrows. "You didn't?"

Now I was on the defensive. "No, I didn't. We just kissed a bit. And he didn't tell me about "Elena." It's not my fault. Anyway he said he'd ring me. Maybe they're on the way out."

Beth took my hand in hers and held it firmly. We heard shouts and cheers from downstairs. "Happy New Year," she whispered, giving me a hug.

"You should be downstairs with Tony," I said guiltily.

"Don't worry," Beth replied kindly. "He won't mind."

"Is Jed still downstairs?" I asked hopefully. I know, I have no shame. I just didn't want to be on my own right at that minute.

Beth frowned at me and ignored my question. "Listen, it's still early. Why don't you come downstairs and get something to eat."

Shit, with all the drinking and carousing with Jed and Branigan I'd forgotten to eat. No wonder I was out of sorts. I put my arm around Beth. "Sounds good, thanks."

"I kept you a plate of lasagne and some salad, just in case."

Tears pricked my eyes. "You're too good to me."

"I know," Beth smiled.

Tony gave me a dirty look as I walked into the kitchen. He was sitting at the table with Jack and Jodie. Feck it—that was all I needed. My heart lurched as I saw the "loving couple." It was the first time I'd seen them together and it cut through my heart like a hot knife through butter.

"Hi, Amy," Jodie said awkwardly.

"Hi," Jack said, his cheeks reddening. "How are you?"

Bloody awful, I felt like screaming. And it's all your fault. But I stood staring at them for a few seconds before deciding to be a mature, together adult. Yeah, right.

"Hi, Tony," I said firmly and ignored the other two completely. I didn't trust myself to speak to them. They didn't deserve my forgiveness and I was damned if I was going to pretend that everything was all right when it very clearly was not.

"Amy . . ." Jack began.

"Fuck off," I finally muttered.

Beth quickly intervened, handing me a plate and ushering me into the hall. I felt like a zombie.

"I'm sorry. I had to invite them," Beth apologized. "I didn't think they'd come. Are you OK? You must have got a shock."

I sighed deeply. We sat down on the stairs. "It hasn't been a good night for me," I whispered. The plate of food sat on my knee getting cold but I had no appetite for it now.

Chapter 12

Fuck you, Branigan. Why haven't you rung?

It was seven o'clock on New Year's Day and I'd waited in all afternoon in case he'd call. I checked my mobile for the umpteenth time. It was working all right.

I was lying on my sofa at home, channel-hopping with the remote control. Mum and Dad had gone on a monster walk, and Suzi and Matt were depressingly (for me) in bed where they had been since they had heard the parentals' car drive away.

Nothing on the box seemed to hold my attention for more than a couple of minutes. I was very, very angsty.

In my heart of hearts I knew Branigan wasn't going to ring. But I was hung-over to shit, feeling very sorry for myself and holding onto the glimmer of hope that someone, anyone liked me.

"Beth?"

"Amy! Hang on a sec," Beth's voice sounded groggy. "Where did you get to this morning? I went in to wake you and you'd gone."

"I walked home," I explained. "I thought some fresh air might do me good."

"You must have turned some heads in your outfit," Beth giggled.

I laughed. "I did get the odd strange look all right. Listen, what are you doing today?"

"Well . . ." Beth went quiet for a moment. "Why don't you call over this evening?"

I heard Tony groan in the background. They were clearly still in bed. He yelped after his groan—Beth had obviously kicked or el-bowed him. I heard her whispering to him. I could make out the words "depressed" and "selfish."

I was mortified. I didn't want to cause trouble for Beth. And I most certainly didn't want to be a burden.

"Actually, we have a family dinner thing, but thanks for asking."

"Are you sure?" Beth asked, sounding relieved. "You could call over after."

"No. I have to work tomorrow but I'll give you a ring."

"Amy, are you OK?"

"Yes, why wouldn't I be?"

"It must have been a shock for you seeing Jodie and Jack. And that business with Branigan . . ."

I winced. "Branigan, who's Branigan?" I asked lightly.

"Amy, you completely ignored Jack and Jodie. That was a bit rude. I know you're upset but . . ."

I took a deep breath. I didn't give a flying fuck about Jack and Jodie. They had ruined my life. In fact, I was never going to speak to either of them again.

"Beth, I don't want to talk about it. I'll ring you tomorrow."

"Listen, they're going away in a few days—why don't you ring Jodie? You don't have to say much . . ."

"No," I interrupted, grumpily. I could be very stubborn when I wanted to. "I suppose you're watering the plants?" It used to be me who watered Jodie's prize rubber plants. Before the betrayal.

"Yes, I am," Beth admitted. "Please. Talk to Jodie. Otherwise you'll lose her as a friend."

"Friend," I spat. "Some friend. There's no way I'm ringing her, ever."

Beth sighed. "I think you're making a mistake."

"I don't care," I said, tears pricking my eyes. "I have to go. I'll talk to you tomorrow."

I put down the phone. I felt bad—it wasn't Beth's fault that my life was in the doldrums at the moment. In fact, if I was honest with myself I'd have to admit that it wasn't really anyone's fault except my own. But it was easier to blame Jack and Jodie. I retreated up the stairs to my bedroom, lay down on my bed and began to cry.

The following day I woke up feeling a little cheerier. A little. I was back to work which wasn't a bad thing—at least it kept my mind off my crappy life.

"Hi, Amy. How was New Year's?" Lynn was sitting in the window of the bookshop, surrounded by sheets of multicolored perspex, a staple gun in her right hand.

"Great, thanks," I lied. "You look busy, what are you doing?"

"Putting in a new *Wizard of Oz* window. I thought I'd go with an Emerald City theme. I'm covering the lights with green perspex and building a castle with these different *Wizard of Oz* books." She pointed to the pile of large picture-books at her feet.

I smiled. Lynn could make any day brighter. "Sounds great. Can I help?"

"I'm going to be busy here for a while. But the books on the table are from the previous window. Maybe you could find a home for them and keep an eye on the till."

"No problem." I dumped my bag behind the till and stuffed my fleece into one of the large drawers under the computer. The blackboard was leaning against the back wall and I wiped it down and pulled out the box of colored chalks.

"What story are you reading today?" Lynn asked with interest.

"I'm not sure," I said thoughtfully. I walked over to the picture-books and began to look through them. I pulled out a hardback edition of *Winnie the Pooh*. Pooh always made me smile and I could do with all the smiles I could get at this stage.

"Would you like some help?" Lynn asked from the window. She was brilliant at calligraphy and always made the blackboard look very professional. My efforts on the other hand always looked like a six-year-old's. I could draw all right but lettering was a completely different ball game.

While Lynn wrote the Story Princess details on the board and placed it outside the door I sat down on one of the small wooden children's chairs, my adult bum squishing over the sides unbecomingly, and began to read. I was lost in the story about Piglet meeting the Heffalumps when I heard a discreet cough beside me. I looked up. I recognized the big brown eyes and neat pigtails. It was Zoe, my young pre-Christmas customer.

"Hello, Zoe," I smiled. "Did you have a nice Christmas?"

"Yes, thank you," she said politely. "Mum says I can choose a bedtime book. We've just finished *My Naughty Little Sister.*"

"What type of book would you like?" I asked kindly.

"One about a little girl," she began thoughtfully. "With animals in it."

I walked over to the fiction shelves and pulled off an illustrated copy of *Charlotte's Web.* "I think you'd like this one," I began, handing the book to her. "It's about a little girl called Fern and a pig called Wilbur. They make friends with a spider who saves Wilbur's life. It's very funny."

"*Charlotte's Web*—that was one of my favorite books when I was your age, Zoe. I'd forgotten all about it." A tall blond woman in black leather trousers and a dark-brown padded jacket pulled one of Zoe's pigtails playfully. "Hi, I'm Rita, Zoe's mum." She held out her hand.

I shook it, smiling. "Amy. Nice to meet you."

"Ah, the Story Princess. Zoe and Steve told me all about their last trip here. It sounded wonderful so I thought we'd visit ourselves. We haven't been in the area long but I can't believe we've missed this place. It's lovely," she gushed in a soft English accent.

"Thanks," I smiled. "It is kind of special."

"Mum," Zoe interrupted, "can we buy this?" She held up *Charlotte's Web.*

"Of course," Rita replied. "And would you like to come back to hear Amy's story later?"

"Yes, please," Zoe looked up at her mother. "We should bring Uncle Steve. He said the Story Princess was one of the most beautiful princesses he'd ever met."

I blushed.

"Did he now?" Rita grinned.

"Yes, and he said he'd bring me here any time I wanted."

Rita laughed. "You seem to have made quite an impression on my brother. We're meeting him for lunch so he may join us here for the story session from the sounds of things."

"Um, how nice," I murmured, my face on fire. I was mortified. Now she was going to tell her brother I fancied him. I just knew it. And I'd be all over the place and I wouldn't be able to read. Disaster. That was all I needed.

Zoe was waiting patiently at the till. She pulled out a small pink purse and counted out seven pound coins onto the counter.

"I think I have a customer." Rita followed me over to the till. I gave Zoe her change and placed the book in the small, brown bag with pink ribbon handles.

"Great bags!" Rita exclaimed. "We'll see you later, Amy."

I walked them over to the door. "Bye, Zoe. Bye, Rita. See you later."

"Bye, Story Princess."

Lynn popped her head over the side of the bookshelf beside the window. "Another satisfied customer," she beamed.

"Yes," I replied, thinking about Stevie J and how embarrassed I would be if they really did bring him.

I walked back to the till and sat down on the stool. I picked at the skin around my right thumb. The bell over the door tinkled. Customers. I tried to keep my mind on the job.

Chapter 13

At three o'clock the reading area of the shop was crammed with children. Their parents stood behind, waiting expectantly for their respective wards to be amused. No sign of Stevie J, thank goodness. I donned my princess hat and stood in front of my audience.

"I'm the Story Princess and today I'm going to read you a story about a bear called Winnie the Pooh. *Once upon a time, a long time ago . . .*"

I was so lost in the story that I didn't notice Zoe edging her way to the front until I'd finished the tale of Pooh and his elaborate plans to steal honey from the bees. As the crowd clapped and began to disperse she came up to me.

"Thank you. That was good," she said quietly.

Then I felt him beside me. Stevie J. You know, when you can just feel someone's presence. Like a fly without the buzz. Not that I was equating him with a fly, but you know what I mean.

"Hi, Amy," he smiled. "I enjoyed that. Pooh is one of my favorite philosophers."

I forced myself to look him in the eye. And, of course, I blushed. He really was cute. But he was a man and men ruined lives. Well, mine anyway.

"Hi." I didn't know what to say. I hardly knew him.

I heard Rita call Zoe over.

Stevie smiled again. "I was wondering if you'd like to go for a coffee with me sometime. I'd love to talk to you about children's books."

"Oh really?" I arched an eyebrow. I wasn't in the mood to be flirted with, even if he was cute and, according to Lynn, single. And rich . . . "Is this your usual chat-up line? Let's talk about how rich and famous I am?"

He looked a little confused. "No, I really do want to talk to you. I've written a picture-book and I'm looking for an illustrator. I'd like to use an Irish one if possible. Fresh talent. Someone young and exciting. I thought you might be able to help. I don't really know anyone in Dublin and I thought . . ." he stopped awkwardly.

Now I was mortified. He hadn't been asking me out at all. He really did want to talk about children's books. Now things really couldn't get any worse. I reached up and took my Story Princess hat off.

"It's Lynn you should talk to then. She's an expert on Irish children's illustration. Lynn!" I called her over.

"Lynn, this is Stevie J and he'd like some advice. I think you could help him." I walked toward the till and left them to it. I couldn't help glancing over toward them though. They were sitting on children's chairs beside the Irish published books. Lynn was showing him different young Irish illustrators. He was gazing at the vibrant colors in a Mary Murphy book and nodding his head sagely.

I sighed. Now I'd really made a complete fool of myself. What was happening to me at all?

"Amy?" Rita was standing beside the counter. "Can I buy this, please?" She handed me a copy of Steve's latest book, *Henry and the Master Wizard*.

"Sorry," I mumbled. "I was miles away."

"I noticed," Rita smiled.

"Your brother's latest," I said, dropping the book into a bag.

"Oh, don't worry about a bag, I'll pop it in with *Charlotte's Web*. I want to get Steve to sign it for one of Zoe's friends. He hates signing books. He says he feels foolish. He's very modest. I don't think he realizes how well he writes."

"But he must," I exclaimed. "He's won the Carnegie and the Smarties . . ."

Rita sighed. "I know. But he's . . . I probably shouldn't say this but . . ."

"Are you talking about me?" Steve squeezed his sister's arm affectionately.

"No, of course not." Rita was flustered.

He smiled. "Lynn was really helpful. I think I may have found my illustrator." He handed me a copy of *Little Penguin* by Mary Murphy. "Look at those vibrant colors, and the black outlines and the movement of the figures—wonderful."

I turned the pages as he talked. He was so enthusiastic about the artwork. I wished I hadn't made such a fool of myself earlier. I would have enjoyed talking to him about children's books. It was so rare to find someone who had any interest and he was a renowned writer to boot.

Lynn joined us beside the till. "Steve has very kindly agreed to a signing session of his new book the weekend after next."

Steve looked a little embarrassed. "I don't usually do many signings, but Lynn has been so kind . . ."

"That's great!" I enthused. "The kids will be delighted. Wait till I tell Siobhan's girls. They love your books."

Steve smiled and his eyes crinkled at the edges. "I'll see you both in two weeks then."

Rita and Zoe said their goodbyes and Lynn saw the group to the door.

"A Stevie J signing, think of it, Amy," Lynn said in rapture. "I'll advertise in the local paper and send flyers out to the local schools. How exciting!"

"We'll be mobbed," I smiled. "I wonder how many *Henry* books we'll sell."

"Hundreds, I hope," Lynn sparkled. "No, honey, thousands! Reach for the stars."

"Amy, this is Jodie. Are you OK? I'm worried about you. Please ring me back. We're off to Galway later today and I'd love to talk to you before we go."

I grimaced, listening to the familiar voice on my mobile. I was sitting in Lynn's kitchen having a chicken sandwich and some carrot and orange soup. Lynn lived over the shop and always made us both lunch, although we could never eat it together—one of us always had to man the shop floor. She used to close at lunch-time but these days a lot of our adult customers shopped in their lunch hour and we had to stay open to accommodate them.

I didn't mind eating on my own. It gave me some time out from the bustle and noise of the shop. And it meant I had a few minutes to sit and think. Although the way my mind was at present, sitting and thinking was the last thing I needed. I'd remembered the frozen shrimps this morning, stolen from the freezer at home. And the screwdriver. I just wasn't sure if I was going to go through with my master plan. Hearing Jodie's voice, however, pushed me over the edge. What did she mean "Are you OK? I'm worried about you"? How dare she? Bitch. I'd felt reasonably all right earlier but now I was slipping into a black mood again. I'd get through the afternoon by throwing myself into some menial tasks.

I had to attend the Wedding Fair in the RDS at the weekend with Suzi and Beth and to say I wasn't looking forward to it was a huge understatement.

I walked back down the narrow stairs, brushing past Lynn's original Niamh Sharkey drawing and making it swing alarmingly from side to side. I put my hand out to steady it. Pity I couldn't steady my mind as easily.

Lynn looked up from a pile of returns. "How was your lunch?"

"Lovely as always," I smiled. She really was very kind. "The soup was delicious—did you make it yourself?"

"Yup, I like making soup. It's very therapeutic—chopping and blending. I have something for you by the way. Wait there." She jumped up and bounded up the stairs. I wished that I had her energy— she was like a teenager. I, on the other hand, felt like an old Granny at the moment. She handed me a white tube. "It's excellent stuff. I used it for the first time a few weeks ago. It's the most soothing mask I've ever had the good luck to find."

"Clinique Deep Cleansing Emergency Mask," I read aloud. "For skin under stress." Tears welled up in my eyes, but I really couldn't help it. Lynne was so kind, I didn't deserve such a nice boss. "Thank you," I murmured, holding the cool tube in my hot hands.

Lynn put her arm around me and gave me a hug. "Amy, I know you're going through a tough time but it will get better, I promise."

"I'm sorry," I began. "Is it that obvious?" I sighed. "It's just . . ."

"You don't have to explain today," Lynn said kindly. "After I've had lunch, why don't you go home? Get some rest. And I'll see you tomorrow."

"That would be great," I said appreciatively. "If you don't mind."

"Of course not."

While Lynn was upstairs I threw myself into taking old price-stickers off the books which we were returning to the publishers. I even managed to avoid any paper cuts which was quite an achievement.

"Off you go now," Lynn said firmly on her return. "See you tomorrow."

I skipped out the door, slinging my bag over my shoulder. I felt like a kid ditching school. It was barely three o'clock and I knew exactly where I was headed.

I lifted the flowerpot to the right of Jodie's door and smiled. She still kept the spare key in the same place. And Granny O'Connell always went to Jodie's aunts in Cork for a week after New Year's so I let myself in, safe in the knowledge that no one would know I was there. Because there was something I had to do.

Jodie's place looked immaculate as always. The curtains were all drawn, giving the basement an eerie, gothic look. A chink in one of the curtains let in a dart of light, allowing me to make my way to Jodie's bathroom.

I clicked on the switch and walked over to the windowsill where Jodie kept her make-up and potions. I picked up her large bottle of Oil of Olay moisturiser. Jodie, as I had hoped, had been ultra-organized as usual. She always decanted her moisturiser, shampoo and conditioner into small travel bottles when she was going away, leaving the larger versions here—mine for the doctoring.

I put my bag down on the floor and removed my tube of Vichy self-tanning gel. I squirted half the Oil of Olay down the sink and replaced it with the gel. It had a slightly sweeter smell but I hoped the Oil of Olay would drown it out. Then I unscrewed her L'Oreal shampoo bottle, poured half of it down the sink and filled it with Sun-In hair bleach. Just to be on the safe side I did the same with the conditioner. Because let's face it—Jodie was worth it!

I smiled as I thought of her looking in the mirror. Looking back at her would be a brown-streaked face and orange/white streaked hair. As she had a pale complexion and long black hair I thought the effect would be quite stunning!

I put the bottles back where I had found them and washed my hands carefully. I didn't want incriminating brown streaks on my own hands.

Then I went into Jodie's bedroom. My stomach lurched as my eyes fell upon one of Jack's fleeces, draped over the back of Jodie's dressingtable chair. I opened her cupboard. No sign of Jack there, thank goodness. I checked the back of the door. As I thought—two Polo shirts, pink and dark green. I was tempted to cover them in Sun-In and tanning lotion too but that would have been too obvious. And I didn't want to be obvious. God forbid.

I looked at her curtain-rod. Excellent—I was right—it was brass and hopefully hollow. I pulled the chair over to the window and stood on it. Jack's fleece was under my foot, treatment that was too good for it by half. I examined the end of the rod. It was covered by a brass fitting which looked like a pine cone. I hopped down and took a screwdriver and a plastic bag of now wet and soggy defrosted shrimps out of my bag. I placed the shrimps on the chair beside my feet. The bronze pine cone popped out of its socket after a couple of levers and digs with the screwdriver and fell onto the floor with a bang. I stood still for a few seconds, nervous that the neighbors might have heard me. They hadn't. I reached down and picked up the bag of shrimps. And I began to slowly and carefully feed each shrimp into the curtain-rod.

"Amy, what the hell are you doing?"

Chapter 14

I fell off the chair and crashed onto Jodie's bed, splattering shrimps all over myself and the antique white lace bedspread.

Beth stormed over. "What the hell are you doing? What are these?" She held up a limp pink shrimp in disgust.

It was lucky I'd fallen onto the bed and not onto the floor. "Look what you made me do," I shouted, sitting up and rubbing my leg which had hit the side of the brass bed. "I could have killed myself."

Beth stared at me in amazement, picking the screwdriver off the floor. "What are you doing here? What's this for?" She held up the screwdriver and waved it in my face.

I looked at the curtain-rod guiltily.

"Oh, I get it. You've been listening to too much Gerry Ryan. You were putting those pink things which I assume are prawns . . ."

"Shrimps," I interjected stroppily.

"Shrimps. You were putting shrimps into Jodie's curtain-rod. Amy, how could you?"

I looked at her and winced. "Was it really on Gerry Ryan? I wondered where I'd heard it."

Beth stood in front of me, a fierce look on her face. "Show me your bag."

"Why?"

"Just show me."

"OK, OK," I agreed. I had nothing to lose now.

I handed her my bag. She pulled out the mustard and cress seeds. "You were about to plant these on the carpets, I presume?"

I nodded, blushing furiously.

"And what are these for?" She held up the Sun-In and self-tanning gel.

I smiled. I couldn't help it. "For her moisturizer and shampoo."

Beth stifled a smile herself. "Now that wasn't on the Gerry Ryan show. How original." She looked at me and began to laugh despite herself. "Amy, you're nuts."

"I know," I said, pulling a shrimp off my fleece.

Beth made me buy Jodie new shampoo and moisturizer. And she made me remove all the shrimp from the curtain-rod. It took hours—some of the little buggers didn't seem to want to leave. I had to pull some of the pink squishy bits out with tweezers. It was revolting. It was late before I got home.

Beth saw me to the door. "I've removed Jodie's spare key and I'm going to tell her that it's not safe to leave it there because of burglars. So don't go near the house, understand?"

I hadn't said much all afternoon. I felt ridiculous, to be honest. But it had seemed like a good idea at the time. I didn't like Beth being so disapproving of me. So maybe it was a bit mad and to be honest I was kind of glad in a way that Beth caught me. I didn't want to be labeled as a "bunny boiler" for the rest of my life.

"Say something, Amy."

"I'm sorry," I muttered.

"What would have happened if I hadn't come along?"

"I probably would have changed my mind anyway," I said brightly, "and taken out the shrimps myself."

"Um," Beth muttered darkly. She didn't seem convinced. "We'll talk about it tomorrow. I don't have the energy right now. Are you still on for the Wedding Fair this weekend? You don't have to come, you know."

"I'm coming," I said firmly. I was in a sadomasochistic mood. I might as well make myself even more miserable. Hell, Jodie and Jack might even be there. Now wouldn't that be nice?

* * *

That evening I curled up on the sofa and watched *Runaway Bride* with Suzi and Matt. It was that or *Muriel's Wedding* or *Four Weddings and a Funeral* again. Worryingly all Matt's choices. But I'm sure he was just trying to get on Suzi's good side. Not that he needed to bother—if he hadn't worked out that she was a sure thing by now he needed his brain tested.

At least things weren't exactly going to plan for Julia Roberts on the wedding front. She wasn't called "the Runaway Bride" for nothing. Pity about the ending though. Why did they have to ruin a perfectly acceptable film about marital evasion by slapping on a happy ending? I won't tell you what happens because you may want to watch it at some time in the future—I'm not that mean. But it wouldn't take a genius to work out that it's saccharinely happy.

The next two days of work dragged along at a pedestrian pace—a ninety-year-old pedestrian. Lynn was very kind. She let me avoid most of the customers by setting me stockroom tasks and sending me into town to collect art and craft supplies for our new window. Stevie J hadn't seen the completed work of art—when he'd been in all that was in place was a background of purple material, crepe paper and lights—he was in for a surprise. Beth hadn't rung since the shrimp incident and to be honest I didn't blame her. And I was too embarrassed to ring her myself. I hoped that she'd forget all about it and never mention it again. Hell, a girl can dream, can't she?

Suzi bounded into my room on Saturday morning and sat down on my bed. Tigger from *Winnie the Pooh* had nothing on her. Her dogged optimism and good humor were beginning to annoy me. What right had she to be in such damned fine form? It was raining outside, she was stony-broke and . . . and . . . actually, come to think of it, things were pretty rosy for Suzi at the moment. She had a man who loved her to death and who would fight lions for her, an impending marriage to same said man and a size-eight body which was still on the Australian side of white. And regular sex. Let's not underestimate the power of regular sex.

"Hey, Amy, are you ready? Beth's downstairs," she said, smiling.

I groaned inwardly. Now I remembered—this was the Wedding Fair day.

"Do I look fucking ready?" I muttered from beneath my warm, snuggly duvet.

"Don't be like that," Suzi frowned. "I'll bring you breakfast in bed. How about that?"

My ears pricked up. "Sausages?" I muttered.

"OK, I'll cook you sausages. I'll even make you a banana smoothie."

I looked at Suzi and tried not to smile. It was very difficult to be annoyed with her. She was too nice.

"Right, you stay here and have a doze. And I'll bring up breakfast when it's ready." Suzi flitted out the door and down the stairs. I rolled over and clamped my eyes tight shut.

A few minutes later I heard footsteps on the stairs. That was quick, I thought to myself. I hope she didn't microwave my bloody sausages, I liked them grilled or fried, not bloody microwaved.

"Amy?"

Shit, it was Beth. I wasn't in the mood. I pretended to be asleep.

"I know you're awake." She sat down on my bed, squashing my arm into the bargain.

"Ow," I yelped.

She jumped. "Sorry, I didn't see your arm there."

"Yeah, right," I muttered, my eyes still closed.

"I don't suppose you're in the mood to discuss the other day?" she asked quietly.

"No."

"Look at me, Amy."

I opened my eyes slowly. Beth's concerned face peered down at me. Sympathy. I hated it.

"I think you should talk to someone about all this. What about that nice lady you went to before—Dr. Shield?"

"Dr. Shiels," I corrected her.

"Well?"

I winced. Dr. Shiels had been very kind to me. I'd gone to her before when things had been a little out of control. But that was when I was having panic attacks, for goodness sake, not revenge attacks. Highly provoked revenge attacks, I might add.

"Amy?"

"What?"

"Will you go to Dr. Shiels again?"

It would have been easy to say yes, of course, I will, Beth. You're right. I need help. I can't cope with how I feel about Jack and Jodie. I am behaving in an inappropriate manner and I recognize that. I'll make an appointment first thing Monday morning.

But I didn't. "Fuck off. There's nothing wrong with me. Stop being such a moan!" Nice, Amy. Swear at your best friend who's only trying to help.

Luckily Beth had a very thick skin. "Amy. You leave me no choice then. I'm going to talk to your mum."

She knew she had me now. The last thing I wanted was for Mum to get involved. I'd be watched morning, noon and night. She'd have a diet and exercise plan made out for me before I could say boo. And to top it all Dr. Shiels was a friend of hers so they'd have "casual" deep discussions while I was in the room. Morag Shiels would never betray her Hippocratic Oath, of course, but when she was calling in to Mum for coffee I was fair game.

"Amy, tell your mum what you told me about your fear of being alone," Dr. Shiels would say. Or "Amy, ask your mum about that incident when the boy next door locked you in the toy-cupboard . . ."

No. There was no way I wanted Mum involved this time. I was perfectly capable of dealing with this myself. I'd talk myself out of my bad mood and into a good mood. It was January after all. And come to think of it, I hadn't even made my New Year's Resolutions yet. No wonder I had no sense of direction these days. This afternoon I'd sit down and write out my resolutions starting with 1) fuck up Jack and Jodie's life.

"Amy?" Beth interjected, breaking into my racing thoughts. "Are you listening to me? I'd said I'd have to talk to your mother."

"I heard you." I took the easy way out this time. "I know you're worried, Beth. And I don't blame you. But I recognize I have a problem and I'm going to deal with it. I promise. So you don't have to worry anymore."

Beth looked at me carefully. "Does this mean you're going to go back to Dr. Shiels?"

"Yes," I lied.

"Promise?"

I crossed my fingers under the duvet. "Promise."

Just then Suzi, bless her little heart, pushed open the door with her shoulder and came in.

"Breakfast," she said, smiling, "for my favorite grumpy sister. Matt made you some scrambled eggs with salmon, just how you like them."

I had to smile. "Thanks," I said gratefully. God, I was being such a ratty bitch. I didn't deserve such kindness. I sat up straight and Suzi placed the tray on my lap. She pulled over a chair and sat down beside the bed.

"So, are we all set for the Fair?" she asked. "It's going to be such a laugh."

"You think?" I asked incredulously, mouth full of sausage.

"What was that?" Beth asked. Luckily neither of them could understand my garbled question.

"I said you're right," I lied.

Beth smiled and patted my leg. "I'm dying to see the wedding dresses. And I want to find a gold silk waistcoat for Tony."

"Ooh, I saw some great waistcoats in one of my wedding magazines. I'll run down and get it for you." Suzi bolted out the door.

Beth and I sat in silence waiting for her. I munched my way half-heartedly through my breakfast. Sometimes, when I was emotional and not feeling myself, eating went out the window. Food just didn't taste of anything and I found it hard to swallow. It was better when someone was with me—to encourage me along.

Beth was twisting her engagement ring around and around her finger. She seemed deep in thought.

I swigged the last piece of sausage down with some orange juice. "Beth," I asked, "are you all right?"

"I just worry about you, that all. You're overreacting to things. The business with the shrimps . . ."

"Do we have to talk about the bloody shrimps again?"

"What about shrimps? Are you talking about wedding starters?" Suzi asked as she came in the door laden down with an armful of glossy wedding magazines.

"Not exactly," Beth replied looking at me darkly. "Now, show me these waistcoats."

Soon the two affianced women were discussing color schemes for grooms' clothes and I slipped discreetly out to have a shower.

Standing under the warm darts of water I tried to block all negative thought out of my head. Focus on the positive, I told myself. Count your blessings. But the only "blessing" that I could come up with was that I wasn't dead yet.

We took the Dart to the RDS. Beth quite sensibly pointed out that it would be a nightmare to find parking. I moaned a bit as I liked being driven around—but I knew I was being stupid.

As we approached the RDS the area outside the main entrance was heaving with people. There was a queue snaking back toward the gates and well-dressed women and bored-looking men stared apprehensively at the body-jammed doorway.

"We'll be queuing for hours," Suzi said in dismay.

Beth smiled and waved three blue tickets in front of our noses. "I don't work for one of Ireland's top designers for nothing," she stated, walking confidently toward the top of the queue. We were ushered in immediately. Things were looking up.

But as we walked in the door, all my worst nightmares became real.

Chapter 15

The RDS was wall-to-wall shiny, happy wedding people. I'd never seen so many engagement rings in one place in my life. Beaming brides-to-be, excitement oozing out of every pore. A large catwalk ran down the center of the hall. To either side, stalls of every size, shape and description were pushing their particular nuptial wares. We gazed around in awe.

"It's huge," Suzi exclaimed. "Where are we going to start?"

Beth, Little Miss Organized, had a plan as usual. "I've studied the hall layout and pinpointed stalls that I thought might be worth visiting." She pulled a catalog of the Fair out of her bag. "I've highlighted those in pink." She certainly had. The map of the hall was dotted with pink splodges. And blue and yellow ones too. "The blue stalls are ones Suzi might be interested in. They specialize in home weddings—marquees, table hire, that sort of thing. And the yellow are Amy's ones."

I stared at her in bemusement. "Sorry?"

"Bridesmaid dresses."

"Ah," I decided not to question this. I'd rather fancied a Karen Millen number or something from French Connection. There was no way either of them were getting me into a traditional bridesmaid full-length flowery thing. No way!

"I thought you could wear fuchsia pink," Beth smiled. "Something quite classic, off-the-shoulder maybe. With turquoise shoes and silk flowers in your hair."

I realized that I didn't have much choice in the matter. It was her wedding after all. And at Beth's wedding Tony's sister, Stella, was also a bridesmaid. Stella was nearly six foot, with flowing dark hair all the way down to her bum and clear sallow skin. Your average nightmare. She was seventeen and still in school. And she had a stunning boyfriend of twenty-seven who ran a successful computer magazine called *Online News*. I'd look like one of the Ugly Sisters from Cinderella beside her. I hated her already.

"Stella said she was happy with whatever we picked."

"She'd look good in a bin-liner," I pointed out gloomily.

"No," Beth replied calmly. "She tried wearing one at her Christmas party. Didn't suit her. Black isn't really her color."

I smiled despite myself.

"I thought you could wear pink at mine too!" Suzi said excitedly. "Light pink though, baby pink."

I tried not to wince.

Suzi continued. "You know how much I like pink. I was thinking of something long and slinky. Maybe with a scooped neck and a little diamante tiara. Or a ballerina skirt thing, you know, like a tutu."

My sister was mad. Quite, quite mad. I'd look ridiculous.

"What do you think?" she asked.

"Um," I said, noncommittally.

Beth brandished her multicolored map. "Let's start on the right-hand wall and work over to the left. There's a wedding-dress fashion show on at two—that should be good."

"Can't wait," I muttered.

Beth dug me in the ribs. "Stop that," she said admonitorially. "As bridesmaid to both of us, you could at least be a little enthusiastic. If it was the other way around and you were getting married I'd be Miss Enthusiasm."

"Fat chance of that," I said, trying to hide my bitterness. "But you're right. Roll out the bridesmaids' dresses. I'm ready." She had a point, I was being a pain in the rear. I decided to try a lot harder. I pasted a smile on my face and determined to keep it there all day.

Beth took matters into her own capable hands. "Why don't we stick together to start off with?" she asked.

Suzi nodded. "Suits me. I really want to find a wedding dress. Can we look at those first?"

"Of course," Beth agreed. "My plan exactly. I saw a Lynn Carr dress I really liked in *Brides Today* magazine and I want to check it out in the flesh."

"I'll just tag along for the laugh, will I?" I asked, biting my lip as soon as the words had snuck out of my mouth. "Sorry," I smiled, trying to make it look genuine. "I'm only joking, I'd love to look at wedding dresses. Pay no attention to me."

We began walking down the left side of the hall. I tried to feel like I belonged here, not like some sort of leper.

We made our way from stand to stand—The Bridal Suite, Loreto Brides, Bridal Beauties, Brides of Ireland, Wedding Belles, Pronuptia. That name always made me smile—Pronuptia—it reminded me of sex? Sad really, isn't it. You know—Pronuptia, prenuptial, wedding night.

Soon I became convinced that everyone was glancing at my wedding finger and pitying me for not having a ring. Eventually I slipped my plain silver ring onto my wedding finger. I thought it might make me feel less conspicuously unmarried. Didn't really work though. I remembered that I could have had a real engagement ring on my finger if I hadn't been so damn fussy. OK, so Jack wasn't perfect, but he was male and breathing. I tried not to think about him. But this wasn't exactly the ideal atmosphere to forget about boyfriends and weddings.

There were wedding dresses everywhere—white puffy ones, gray satin ones, slinky ones, ones that looked like nighties and lacy ones. But none of them seemed quite right for either Suzi or Beth. They both saw shoes they liked though. Suzi's were little satin ballet pumps with a pinkish shimmer and light-pink satin ribbons. Beth's were more traditional, open-toed sling-backs in cream satin with tiny cream flowers along the straps and a kitten heel.

And Suzi found a tiara—a gorgeously frothy affair in silver wire inlaid with tiny pink beads. Like a fairytale crown. It suited her perfectly. But still no dresses.

"How about this?" Beth asked doubtfully, fingering a linen dress with corset type lacing down the back.

"For you or me?" Suzi asked in confusion.

"Oh, you. Definitely." Beth replied, smiling.

"I don't think so," Suzi said. "It looks like some kind of old-fashioned underwear."

"What type of dresses are you both looking for?" I asked, trying to be helpful.

But it wasn't that simple it seemed.

"I'm not sure," Suzi answered. "Something romantic. White, I guess. With lace. I'll know it when I see it."

"And I want something very classy. In silk or satin. Flowy," Beth added.

"Sorry?" I asked.

"You know, flowing."

"Right." God, I was bored at this stage. We'd been window-shopping, or stand-shopping should I say, for nearly an hour now and neither of them had seen a dress that they were remotely interested in.

Suddenly Suzi gave a little gasp. "That's it," she whispered. "That's my dress."

Beth and I followed Suzi eyes and gazed at the lace, net and satin creation before us on the Sharon Hoey stand. And it was beautiful.

"Try it on," I suggested. An immaculately made-up sales assistant swarmed over to Suzi.

"Can I help you?" she asked in a clipped South Dublin accent.

"Can I try on this dress, please?" Suzi asked politely.

"Certainly, madam," the assistant replied. She looked Suzi up and down appraisingly. "I think you may find it a little on the large side though. It's a size twelve. I'll get some pins."

She ushered Suzi into the makeshift changing cubicle and took a plastic box of dressmakers' pins from a table top in readiness.

Less than a minute later Suzi stepped out.

This time it was my turn to gasp. She looked quite amazing. Tears pricked my eyes. My baby sister was really getting married. Although the dress was far too big and swam on Suzi's tiny hips, she still looked a million dollars. The long net skirt floated just above the floor. The lace bodice had tiny cap sleeves and white satin flowers cascaded over the surface, each flower's center embellished with a small light-pink sequin. The overall effect was quite breathtaking.

"It's just lovely," Beth gushed. "It's perfect on you."

The sales assistant buzzed around, taking in tucks of material around Suzi's hips and pinning them down. Eventually she stood back to admire her work.

"It's called the 'Daisy.' A classic ballerina skirt with a modern lace bodice. For a fresh, young look," she pitched.

Suzi gave a twirl and the skirt followed her movement effortlessly. "How much?" she asked gingerly.

"Nine hundred and fifty pounds. With fittings, of course," the assistant replied.

Suzi bit her lip. "It's a lot more than we'd budgeted for," she said disappointedly. "Sorry."

I intervened. "Suzi, it's the dress for you. I just know it. What's a few hundred pounds anyway? You won't find anything else you like as much."

"I know, but it's so expensive. Maybe I could get something similar made . . ." she added hopefully.

Beth smiled and put her hand on Suzi's shoulder. "Amy's right. It's gorgeous on you. But go home and think about it. Take your Mum to see it. Don't make any rush decisions."

Suzi beamed. "Of course, you're right." She turned to the assistant. "Can you give me your shop details, please? I'll be back."

"Great," I smiled. "Now you're turning into Arnie Schwarzenegger, that's all we need."

Suzi smiled and skipped back into the changing cubicle. Beth and I waited, flicking through the rails of dresses.

"She's going to make a beautiful bride," Beth said.

"So will you," I said, smiling. I could be nice when I wanted to, after all. I was relieved.

"Thanks," she replied, squeezing my hand.

Beth found the Lynn Carr dress she had seen on the very next stand. It was very "Beth." It also turned out to be the dress Melanie in *Eastenders* wore at her marriage to Ian Beale. I hoped Beth's marriage would last longer than the ill-fated soap one—Melanie did a scarper after a mere eighteen minutes!

The dress was called the "Olivia." It had a long, flowing satin chiffon skirt and a satin fitted bodice. Beth tried it on and it suited her down to the ground.

"What do you think?" she asked as she twisted her body to survey her bum in the full-length mirror. "You don't think it makes my bum stick out?"

"No way," Suzi enthused. "You look slim and elegant."

"Right answer," Beth grinned gratefully. "I'll have to go on a diet though," she added wistfully. Beth, like me, liked her food.

"Me too," Suzi piped up. "I'm going on this protein diet. It's not supposed to be very good for you, but it's the one the *Friends* girls use apparently. And your one, the lawyer from *Ally McBeal*."

Within seconds Beth and Suzi were discussing the merits of different diets—the Cabbage diet, Food Combining, the Dine Out Lose Weight diet (now that one had possibilities) . . . if Suzi was any skinnier she'd fall down a drain—honestly the girl didn't have a pick of fat on her. Beth shouldn't have been encouraging her.

Jack used to drop hints about diets to me now and again. He wasn't exactly the most tactful of men. Bloody Jack! I really didn't want to think about him, or him and Jodie. I tried to shut him out of my mind. Jodie wasn't exactly slim. She was at least a size fourteen, for goodness sake. I wondered if he dropped hints to her about the gym and cutting out fat in your diet. I doubted it. She wouldn't stand for that kind of nonsense.

Beth went back into the cubicle to change and Suzi and I leaned against the back of the stand waiting for her in silence. I was exhausted. If I saw another wedding dress in my life again it would be too soon.

My thoughts were interrupted by the tannoy.

"Ladies and gentlemen, the Wedding Fair Fashion Show will commence on the main runway at three o'clock. A large selection of wedding dresses and bridesmaid dresses will be shown by some of Ireland's top models including the current Miss Ireland, Celia Davitt. Men's wedding attire will also be featured. Thank you."

"Come on, girls," Beth grabbed my arm and pulled me reluctantly along. Suzi followed behind us. "It's show-time."

Brilliant, I thought to myself murderously. Bloody brilliant!

Chapter 16:

After half an hour of white, cream, gray, gold and more white my eyes were accosted by bright pink. Two tall, leggy blond freaks of nature were modeling the most in-your-face bridesmaids' dresses I'd ever seen. The bodices were raspberry-pink, with tiny shoe-string straps. And the skirts, well the skirts wouldn't have looked out of place in a circus. Acres and acres of light pink net were layered on top of each other. And the worst thing was I just knew what Suzi was going to say. And I was right.

"How pretty! Amy, you would look darling in that," Suzi trilled.

I sighed. It was her wedding after all. Who was I to upset the apple-cart? To be honest I was beyond caring at this stage. My feet hurt and I could feel a headache coming on. If I said yes at least it would mean I wouldn't have to look at any more dresses. I mean there's only so much even I can take.

Beth glanced at me questioningly. I shrugged.

"If you like it, Suze, that's good enough for me," I said graciously.

"Excellent. Beth, can you jot down the details?"

Beth wrote down the name of the Dublin shop, Beautiful Brides (even the name sent shivers down my spine), on the side of the program.

We watched some hunky men parade down the catwalk in an assortment of suits, black tie and morning dress. Both Suzi and Beth decided then and there to put their men in morning suits. Suzi was adamant that she wanted Matt in cream, to set off his tan. Beth was thinking along more traditional lines, surprise, surprise—dark jacket, pinstripe trousers and gold waistcoat.

I wondered what Jack would have looked best in—something classic with a modern twist. Being an architect he would have gone for a wacky waistcoat or a red velvet jacket or the like.

"Amy," Beth asked. "What's up? You're miles away."

"Sorry," I mumbled. "Just thinking about something."

"The show's over. We were going to have a look at the wedding stationery. Are you coming?"

"Um," I replied. "Yes, I mean."

Suzi powered on ahead toward the right side of the hall.

"Where does she get her energy?" Beth asked.

"I don't know," I replied, "but she has Matt worn out too!"

"Amy!"

"Well, it's true," I insisted. "He doesn't seem to mind though," I added.

"I'm sure he doesn't," Beth smiled. "Do you really like that pink dress?"

I scrunched up my face. "What do you think?"

Beth stared at me. "Why don't you tell Suzi? It's not too late, you know."

I sighed. "I don't really mind what I wear, to tell the truth. So if it makes her happy . . ." I shrugged again.

Beth smiled. "You and Stella can choose what you'd like to wear at my wedding. The decision will be up to both of you."

"Thanks," I said gratefully. Beth was the kindest girl in the universe. "And I'll make sure we choose elegant and flowy dresses."

"Are you making fun of me?" Beth asked with a twinkle in her eye.

I raised my eyebrows. "Would I?"

Two hours later we had chosen Suzi's wedding stationery—delightfully wacky cream cards with tiny cartoon characters of a bride and groom, designed by an Irish company called Big Leap Designs. Beth had found a website which helped you organize your big day—www.weddingsireland.com. And we were all fit to drop.

We dragged ourselves out of the RDS into the dying daylight.

"God, I'm knackered," Suzi complained, rubbing her shoulders as we made our way to the Dart station.

"Think of what we achieved though," Beth stated in her own inimitably positive manner. "We got a hell of a lot of the more difficult things done. And loads of ideas for other things."

We arrived at the Dart station, put our return tickets through the machine and made our way to the southbound platform. We sat down on a wooden bench.

Beth pulled out an A4 sheet and a pen and began ticking things off on a list.

"What are you doing?" Suzi asked curiously.

"This is my wedding checklist. I'm seeing what I still have to arrange."

I peered over her shoulder with interest. "I didn't realize weddings were such a hassle," I said.

"Only if you're not organized," Beth scolded. "I still have to arrange flowers, music, your dress, Stella's dress, lingerie, veil if I want one—I haven't decided yet, my wedding style . . ."

"Your what?" I asked incredulously.

"You know, what type of decoration and color schemes we want—for example, Suzi's style, and correct me if I'm wrong, Suzi, would be young and fun, the flowers would be spring flowers in pinks, yellows and blues, freesias for example, and the wedding color would be pink."

Suzi beamed. "You're right. Although I think I'll go for daisies instead of spring flowers. I'm impressed."

Beth continued. "And my style is elegant . . ."

"And flowy," I added with a wink.

"Amy, I'm being serious," Beth chided.

"Sorry," I mumbled.

"My style," Beth resumed, "is elegant and traditional. My flowers will be lilies and roses."

"And your color is cream," Suzi added.

"Precisely," Beth said.

"I get you," I nodded. "Very interesting." Yeah right!

Just then the crossing gates over the tracks lowered with a clatter and our train approached. We stepped on and fell into the green seats.

"I'll sleep well this evening," I said.

"We all will," Beth agreed.

"Thanks for coming with us, Amy," Suzi said. "It can't have been much fun for you."

"It's OK," I smiled. "Anything for my two favorite brides-to-be. It was a laugh." And the strange thing was that it was kind of fun in a way. A giant shopping trip. And miraculously, I was starting to feel better.

The following Thursday evening Suzi dragged me into town for her first dress fitting. She'd tentatively shown Dad the picture of the "Daisy" dress the evening before and told him how much she loved it and how happy it would make her to wear it and how it would make her big day just perfect.

Dad had smiled and asked "How much?," winced and given in.

"If it would make you that happy . . ." he'd trailed off lamely. Mum was less enthusiastic, asking could Suzi not shop around and consider some other dresses but at the end of the day it was Dad's checkbook that was paying the deposit and her sensible words fell on deaf ears. Dad was a bit of a pushover at the best of times, especially when it came to his little princess Suzi, or so it always seemed to me. As I'd expected, Mum and Dad generously (as they were paying for it!) conceded that a wedding was a once-in-a-lifetime experience and that they might as well get used to the idea that the whole thing was going to cost them a king's ransom.

As we walked down the steps to the Sharon Hoey showroom Suzi grabbed my arm.

"This is so exciting," she gushed. "It's all really happening. Thanks for coming with me, Amy."

"Not a problem," I said. "It'll be . . ." I fished for the right phrase but words escaped me, "interesting."

The assistants in the showroom were lovely. Kind and patient. They clucked over Suzi like mother hens, taking her measurements, showing her tiaras, shoes and underwear that would suitably accompany her dress.

"You've made the right choice, love," the older woman who had identified herself as "Bronagh" said. "The Daisy is perfect for you."

Suzi smiled appreciatively. "Thanks."

It took nearly an hour for me to drag Suzi out. She was caught up in trying other dresses on—just to reinforce how "right" the Daisy was for her. I blamed Bronagh, she was definitely encouraging her. The woman seemed to love her job a little too much for my liking. In fact she was positively wedding-obsessed. I guess it was probably hard not to be in that line of business.

Finally Suzi made another appointment. I hadn't realized the dress would entail so much work. I presumed that they'd measure you, make the thing and Bob's your uncle, it was all yours. But, oh no, it wasn't as simple as that. It would take six fittings or more! Seemed like a bit of a waste of time to me, but I supposed if you were shelling out nearly a grand for one dress you'd want it to fit all right!

I rang Beth on Friday evening. There was a film I wanted to see in the multi-screen in Dun Laoghaire, a bodice-ripping costume drama. I knew it would be just Beth's cup of tea as Hugh Grant was playing the lead and she had an inexplicably large (and very sad) crush on him. I'd already asked Suzi to go but "we," otherwise known as herself and Matt, were "staying in." Mum and Dad had been invited to a book launch by an author friend of theirs. It was sad when your parents' social life was more exciting than your own. Embarrassing really.

"Hi, Amy," Beth answered, sounding a little flustered.

"Are you in the middle of something?" I asked.

I could hear Beth sigh. "We're having a discussion. Hang on a sec. Tony, Tony . . . come back, don't be like that . . . Tony . . ." I heard a door slam and Beth came back to the phone. "Sorry about that." She sounded more than a little shaken.

"Is everything OK?" I asked carefully.

"It's just the whole wedding thing. I think it's begun to get to him. He's refusing to wear a morning suit. He says he'll look like a ponce."

I tried not to laugh. It sounded like the sort of thing Tony would say all right. "He'll come around," I assured her. "Once he's tried one on and seen how handsome he looks."

Beth sighed again. "I hope you're right."

"I don't suppose you want to come to the cinema tonight?" I asked hopefully. "The new Hugh Grant has just been released."

"I'd better wait for Tony to come back. Sorry. We're supposed to be sorting out the guest list tonight."

"That's OK," I replied, trying not to sound too disappointed.

I put down the receiver and stared at the phone. I couldn't think of anyone else to ring except Jodie and there was no way I was ringing her. All my friends were living in wedded or cohabitual bliss. I'd given up on most of them, especially the ones with babies who never, ever seemed to go out.

Everyone I knew seemed to be a "we" and not a "me." I sat down on the stairs and stared at the front door. I suppose I could have gone to the film on my own but I would be dead embarrassed if anyone saw me. They'd think I was Billy No Friends, and the sad thing is that they'd be right! I could feel tears pricking my eyes and I began to feel very sorry for myself. I could hear Suzi giggling in the living room. Matt seemed to spend his life making her laugh. Lucky cow.

I retreated into the kitchen, piled a tray full of crackers, two packets of Tayto cheese and onion crisps, a huge packet of dry roasted peanuts, a tub of Philadelphia cream cheese (with chives), a tub of garlic and lemon mayonnaise dip, two Diet Cokes and half a tube of Pringles and headed up the stairs. After all, I reasoned, I needed extra salt to replace all the salt lost in my tears.

Chapter 17

I sat down on my bed and started to eat. I piled a cracker high with cream cheese and bit down hard. Crumbs scattered all over my bed. I munched away, trying to take my mind off my sad and lonely life as a spinster. My eyes rested on a bright blue book which was lying on my bed. I picked it up and read the title—*The Power Is Within You* by Louise L. Hay. I figured Mum had left it there for me—she was mad into popular psychology books. Her favorite was called *Happiness Is a Choice* by some American guy. She was a firm believer that you could make yourself happy or unhappy depending on your state of mind. Followed logically, this means that she believed that I made myself miserable. Which I think is a bit insulting and over-simplistic myself. When I was feeling crappy and down I didn't need her leaving bright-pink sticky notes on my door saying "Embrace your fear" or "Life is a journey. Travel light." Or her reading positive affirmations to me over breakfast—"Love yourself. You are a child of the universe," "Be free to be yourself," "Every day in every way I am stronger and stronger."

As I had nothing else to do I picked up the book and began flicking through it while shovelling peanuts down my throat. I nearly choked when I read "Stuffing food into our bodies is another way to hide our love . . . often we use food and diets to punish ourselves and create obesity." I snapped the book shut and opened a packet of Taytos.

Half an hour later, after demolishing most of the food on the tray

I began to feel a bit sick. I put the tray on the floor and lay back on my bed.

I woke up later and groggily looked at the clock beside my bed. It was ten past three. I wrapped the duvet over me and went back to sleep. Another exciting Friday night.

Work flew by on Saturday. We were inundated with calls, e-mails and faxes about Stevie J's signing session the following weekend. Children and parents alike were madly excited to be meeting their hero. RTE's *Den 2* were sending a roving reporter to cover the event and the newspapers were also sending out interested signals, which was very unusual in itself. Usually the papers couldn't give two hoots about children's books except at Christmas, or so it seemed to Lynn and me—we were always trying to get them to cover children's events in our shop.

We took reservations for over three hundred signed books over the phone from places as far away as North America. Stevie fans had found details of the event from our website and were anxious to secure a rare signed copy. Not to mention the fact that Stevie's signature alone tripled the value of the book instantly.

Luckily he'd agreed to come in both days—Saturday and Sunday. I wondered if he'd stamp the books with a custom-made rubber signature block, like I'd seen some lazy authors do. Or just produce an illegible squiggle?

I hoped he'd forgotten my rude rebuff the last time I'd seen him. I was such an idiot.

After work I staggered home. My feet were killing me from rushing about all day and I had a throbbing headache. At least I had Sunday off. Beth had taken pity on me and postponed bridesmaid-dress shopping for two weeks, until Stella had finished some sort of weekend web design course. Of course, Stella's some sort of computer genius, as well as being young, gorgeous and in happy coupledom with Mr. Rich and Successful.

I had dinner with Suzi and Matt. Mum and Dad were off at some friend's housewarming party. I never saw them at the weekends—they were always doing something. I retreated to the living room when Suzi started spoon-feeding Matt ice cream. I watched crap television for a while—some sad people pretending to be even sadder "famous" people, and some couples fighting after expensive sun holidays had been wasted on them.

What was I doing with my life? I should be out having fun with my huge gang of trendy and fun mates, not stuck in on my own—again.

I'd spoken to Beth earlier and she and Tony had made up. Which was good but it also meant that they were going out to dinner tonight, just the two of them. Which left me alone.

Uncharacteristically for me, I decided to do something positive—to tidy my room. Since I'd moved back from Jack's house I still hadn't unpacked the black bin-bags that contained many of my prized possessions. In fact some of my favorite clothes were still lurking in a suitcase under my bed. I pulled myself off the sofa and plodded upstairs.

As I fished the suitcase from under the bed, I also pulled out another slightly dusty black bin-sack. I peered inside and smiled. It was the craft materials that Beth had given me for Christmas. Funny old Beth. She really thought I could do something with them.

I pulled out the multicolored pipe-cleaners and started playing with them. The bright green ones reminded me of Kermit the Frog and I began to twist the furry wires into a frog shape. It was quite good fun and very—therapeutic, I suppose. An hour later I had made a yellow duck, a black cat and three tiny white mice.

Beth had supplied some "goggly eyes"—you know, the ones that move when you shake them. The bag contained "over a hundred eyes for all your craft needs"! They looked very strange in the plastic bag—disembodied eyes caught in all kinds of weird expressions—but made my animals really come alive. Beth, bless her, had thought of everything—glue, glitter, felt, foam, pompoms, colored feathers—you name it. A veritable treasure-trove of materials. I began to run my fingers over the feathers and think about what I could do with them.

"Amy," I jumped as Suzi bounded through the door, "what are you doing?"

She looked at the bed where I'd lined up my little pipe-cleaner menagerie.

"They're brilliant. How did you make those?" she asked. "I like the rats." She picked up one of the white and pink mice and popped it onto her palm.

"They're mice," I smiled. "Do you really like them?"

"Of course. They're excellent. You know me—if they were crap I'd tell you."

I laughed. "I guess you would."

"You used to make things all the time. Your room used to be covered in things—clay people, candles, weird pasta jewelry, remember? And you used to make up stories and embroider pictures on cloth with feathers and bits of material, remember?"

I ran a bright purple feather over the cat's back. "I always liked making things."

"You should have been an art teacher or something," Suzi said. "Anyway we're about to put on a video. Do you want to come and watch it with us?"

"No, thanks," I replied. "There's something I have to do."

"Was someone up in the attic?" Dad asked the following evening during dinner. The whole family were gathered around the kitchen table, enjoying Mum's lasagne. "The hatch hasn't been closed properly."

"Sorry," I explained. "That was me."

Dad looked at me with interest. "What were you looking for?"

"Just some old things, nothing in particular." I didn't feel like telling them all I was looking for my old clay figures and little cloth books for some reason. It would trigger too many questions and I wasn't in the mood. "What evening are we doing the bridesmaid dress thing?" I asked Suzi, blatantly changing the subject.

"Thursday, if that suits. They're open late. Maybe Mum would like to come." Mum had missed the Sharon Hoey expedition.

"I'd love to," Mum assented.

"Thursday's fine," I said. "I'm sure Lynn will let me off early as I'll be working all weekend."

"That Stevie J guy is in your shop, isn't he?" Dad asked. "*The Irish Times* had something about it in the books section last weekend."

"That's right. He's signing all weekend. It'll be mobbed," I sighed.

"Is he cute?" Suzi asked. Typical Suzi.

I tried not to blush. I supposed he was kind of cute. "I guess so," I replied. "He wouldn't be my type though," I added, just to cover myself.

"I think I'll call in on Sunday," Suzi smiled.

Matt glared at her from across the table. "I like his work," she assured him. "And Simon loves his books, I've been reading them to him. Kate listens too, but I'm not sure how much she understands— she's only five after all."

Matt grunted. "I'll come with you."

Suzi grinned at him. "That would be great. You can look after Kate while I bring Simon to meet Stevie J." Matt frowned. That wasn't exactly what he'd planned for his weekend.

"How's work going?" I asked Suzi. She'd been with the Lowan family for a couple of weeks now.

"Great," she enthused. "Julie still models part-time, so she's out a lot. Kate and Simon are both little dotes, no trouble at all."

"And is Brian around much?" Dad asked. Brian Lowan was one of his rugby heroes. The charismatic Irish captain had been widely credited for turning the team around. Ireland was now one of the most highly respected teams in the world, and one of the youngest. Brian had been responsible for encouraging and nurturing talented young players, some still in school.

"Sometimes," Suzi replied. "He's mad busy though. But he's brilliant with the kids, and when he is around he plays with them non-stop. I don't know where he gets his energy."

Matt smiled. "Suzi's asked Kate to be flower girl and Simon to be pageboy at the wedding."

"Will Kate be wearing pink too?" I asked cautiously. I wasn't sure I liked the idea at all.

"No," Suzi said. I breathed a sigh of relief. "I saw a darling little dress in Monsoon, plain white cotton with little pink flowers embroidered on the bodice."

"Sounds lovely," Mum beamed. "It's no time away now, only fifteen weeks."

Dad caught my eye. "Thank goodness," he mouthed.

I smiled at him. At least I wasn't the only one bored with the wedding already. Roll on, May.

I looked in the mirror. I expected to see a large light pink meringue, but I was surprised. My bridesmaid's dress didn't look too bad really. I'd expected to look really ridiculous and I only looked a little ridiculous. And the way my life was going these days I could live with a little ridiculous.

The assistants in Beautiful Brides were nice enough. They helpfully suggested some foundation underwear to "smooth out the lines," a tactful way to say "to lessen that pot belly." The size fourteen dress fitted almost perfectly. They just had to take in the bodice a little and shorten the skirt—which was depressing as I'd previously been living in a size-twelve fantasy world. In recent weeks I'd had to wear a belt on my jeans as the button wouldn't do up, but I thought that was just post-Christmas tummy and would magically melt away in January. No such luck. I reluctantly decided I'd better go on some kind of diet. I felt sorry for Suzi too—I'm sure she wanted a slim and attractive bridesmaid. She probably felt like she had to ask me as I was her sister. Suzi stood beside me and smoothed down the top layer of net. "It's lovely, Amy," she smiled. "Really lovely."

"Thanks," I said, trying to hold in my stomach.

When I woke up on Saturday morning I was a bundle of nerves. I'd spent most of the second half of the week making Valentine's cards to decorate the shop. Although Valentine's Day was weeks away Lynn wanted to make the shop as interesting as possible. So as well as Stevie J's posters, cardboard cut-outs and mobiles, we had "love" shelves in each of the different book areas.

In the picture-book corner I'd made giant pink and silver cards with pompoms. Copies of *Guess How Much I Love You?* with its cute hares nestled among the oversized cards. In the fiction area I'd made huge cardboard hearts and covered them with multicolored feathers. And in the Irish section I'd made a huge mobile of red foam hearts sprinkled with gold glitter which moved gently, twinkling in the lights. Beth's goody-bag was proving very useful.

I managed to eat a slice of toast before walking into work. It was a mild enough day for January and the sky was clear for once. The odd cloud puffed by but otherwise it looked like it wasn't going to rain.

As I reached the top of Blackrock Road I gasped. Outside The Wonderland there was a whopping great queue. As I drew closer I stared in amazement at the crowd which was increasing right before my eyes. The queue snaked along the path, against the windows of the neighboring shops and houses.

Lynn had placed the blackboard outside the shop and as I walked toward the door a little girl pulled my fleece.

"It's not open yet. We were here at seven o'clock this morning," she said quietly.

Her mother smiled at me. "We drove up from Cork last night. She's a huge Stevie fan."

"I work here," I explained levelly. "I'm not skipping the queue."

"That's OK then," the little girl said.

Lynn came to the door and opened it just enough to let me in.

"Hi, Amy," she said when I was safely inside. "Am I glad to see you! Isn't it crazy out there?"

"You're not kidding!" I replied. "And it's not even nine yet. Heaven knows what it will be like later."

"Jess is coming in to help and she's bringing three friends from college." Jess was a student who was training to be a primary school teacher.

"Great, we should be fine then. I hope Steve doesn't get mobbed on the way in."

Lynn grinned. "I've already rung him. He's going to drive up the back lane and come in the delivery door."

"Good thinking," I said. "I'll just go and dump my stuff upstairs."

When I came back down Jess and her friends Frank, Paul and Lucy had arrived. Frank and Paul were nice and tall and Lynn immediately assigned them to crowd control, Frank outside and Paul inside. Jess would be in charge of the door with Lucy, leaving Lynn and me to man the signing.

The PR woman, Rachel, from Steve's publishers arrived next with the Dublin sales rep. They offered to help sell the books.

Steve arrived at ten to nine. He seemed a little shell-shocked.

"Mate, did you see the kids outside?" he asked me as he stepped over the boxes in the goods-in room. "Must be hundreds of them."

"Popular guy," I smiled. "I hope your hand is up to it."

"I'm wondering that myself," he smiled back. He really was very cute. Then it occurred to me that he was highly unlikely to be interested in me—I'd made a right wally of myself the last time we'd met. In fact, I'd been downright rude. He was being dead nice though— maybe he'd forgotten all about it.

"Can I get you a coffee or anything?" I asked.

"You mean now or are you asking me out?" he laughed.

Shit! He hadn't forgotten. I could feel my face getting redder and redder. I didn't know what to say.

"I'm sorry," Steve said. "I didn't mean to embarrass you. I just couldn't resist it."

"It's OK," I mumbled.

At that moment Lynn bustled in, saving me from further mortification.

"Steve, I'm delighted to see you. I presume you saw your fans outside?"

"Sure did, mate," he replied. "Scary stuff. I hope you have lots of books."

"Absolutely!" Lynn assured him. "I'll show you your signing desk. Can I get you a coffee?"

Steve smiled. "Amy's already kindly offered."

I looked at him and smiled. "Milk and sugar?" I asked.

"Black," he replied. "One sugar. Thanks."

The morning flew by. From the first little Cork girl, Steve was the epitome of charm. He signed each book with a smile, often writing a special dedication. He chatted to the children, answered their every question and also talked to the parents. Mid-morning, I spotted Siobhan and Clara making their way to Steve's desk, ably shepherded by Paul and Jess.

"Hi, Amy," Siobhan smiled when she spotted me over the sea of heads and squeezed over. "How's it going?"

"Brilliantly," I said enthusiastically. "Steve's a star. I've never seen anyone write so quickly."

Clara moved forward, toward Steve and passed him her book. I moved behind him with Siobhan.

"I've seen you before," Steve said to Clara, kindly. "At one of Amy's Story Princess sessions."

"That's right," Clara replied, delighted that he'd remembered her. "Amy's cool. We love her."

At that moment I nearly cried. I could honestly feel tears prick the back of my eyes. It was the nicest thing anyone had said about me for a long, long time. And when I heard Steve's reply . . . I couldn't remember feeling so happy.

"She is, isn't she?" Steve smiled at Clara. "And don't tell her, but I think she's really pretty."

Clara giggled. "I won't," she promised, "but she's right behind you."

"Ah," he turned his head and smiled at me. "Hi, Amy."

I laughed. "Hi, Steve. You're all right. I didn't hear anything."

"That's OK then," he smiled again.

I spent the rest of the day walking on air.

At lunchtime I went upstairs to grab a bit of lunch. Lynn had made sandwiches and wraps for everyone and they were delicious. Steve had taken a ten-minute break, thrown some food and coffee down himself and gone back to the fray. Brave man! He figured he'd have to get stuck in if he was going to meet every child. And as some of them had traveled long distances to meet him, he didn't want to disappoint anyone.

Jess popped her head around the kitchen door as I had just bitten into a chicken tikka wrap.

"Amy, there's a woman from RTE who wants to talk to you. Can I bring her up?"

"Sure," I nodded. Lynn had nominated me as the Wonderland press person. Only because she didn't want to do it—I was famous for my lack of tact so it was an odd choice.

Jess returned with a tall, slim woman with cropped black hair. She looked really young and trendy and I was intimidated already.

She bounced toward me on shiny, red DKNY trainers. "Hi, I'm Helen. I work for *Den 2*. I just wanted to find out who did the Valentine's cards downstairs?"

I winced. She obviously thought some child had done them. How embarrassing. I bit the bullet.

"Hi, I'm Amy." I thought about offering my hand but decided against it. She looked too cool to be into handshaking. And anyway, I had tikka sauce on mine. I wiped them on my jeans just in case. "I made the cards."

"No way," she gushed. "They're so cooool! So original. I love them."

I was taken aback. She wasn't here to slag my feeble craft attempts. She really liked them.

"Um, thanks," I mumbled.

"I'm putting together the Valentine's set at the moment for *Den 2*. Would you be interested in making some more for me?"

I nearly fainted. Me? Make things for television—and *Den 2* no less? Was she kidding?

"Of course," I spluttered. "If you really think . . ."

"They'll need to be even bigger but I love the colors and the styles. So if you could make six for me, poster size?"

"Two of each style, A0 size?" I asked, wanting to get it right.

"Exactly!" she exclaimed. "And we'll cover all your expenses and give you a design fee. I'm afraid we don't pay that much, but how does one hundred pounds sound?"

Like music to my ears, I thought.

"That sounds fine," I said.

"Cool!" She pulled a gleaming black personal organizer out of her jacket pocket and began to play with it. "I'll need them by the end of next week. Delivered to the television center, if that's all right."

"No problem," I said in a daze. "I'll have them done by Friday."

"Cool! Friday afternoon is perfect. Give me a ring when you get to reception. Great to meet you," Helen held out her hand and shook mine firmly. "I look forward to seeing your hearts." With that she bounded back down the stairs, leaving me staring in her wake.

Amazing, I thought to myself. Quite amazing. I immediately began to worry—what if I can't do it, what if they turn out crap, what if I catch some disease and I'm in bed all week . . .

Jess called up the stairs, interrupting my musings. "Amy, are you finished? Paul and I are dying for a cigarette."

"Just coming," I yelled down, slurping down some orange juice and rinsing my hands under the tap.

Chapter 18

The afternoon was a little less frantic. The queue outside had abated—it was now only twenty or thirty children long. Steve was exhausted by the end of the day.

"Blimey, mate," he said as we shut the door behind the final customer at half past six, "I thought I'd be here all night. I can't believe I have to do this again tomorrow."

Lynn smiled. "We've sold over six hundred books today alone, not including the mail orders. That's incredible!"

Steve whistled. "That's a lot of books all right." He chatted to his publishers while Lynn and I cashed up the till. Jess and her friends were straightening up the shop, which looked like a bomb had hit it.

"We'd like to take you and your staff out for drinks and dinner tonight, if everyone's free," Rachel said, walking across the room toward us. "Where's good around here?"

"The Italian on the main street is nice," Lynn said. "Or there's a couple of places in Dun Laoghaire and Dalkey."

"How about Coconut Street?" I suggested. "It does Caribbean food and it's always a good laugh."

"Sounds perfect," Steve said, joining us.

"Coconut Street it is," Rachel pronounced. "How many can come? Lynn, Amy, Jess?"

"Count me in," Lynn smiled.

"I can't," Jess replied, "and Lucy's baby-sitting but Paul and Frank might be able to—how about it, boys? Free for dinner tonight?"

The boys nodded enthusiastically.

"How about you, Amy?" Rachel asked. I tried my damnedest not to look at Steve. But it was no use. He smiled at me.

"You have to come, Amy," he encouraged. "It wouldn't be the same without you."

"OK," I agreed. "I'd love to. Right, who's on for pints before-hand?"

"Good idea," Steve said.

We made our way to the Purty Kitchen. Steve was adamant that he wanted to walk. He said he needed some air to clear his head after the day's session. I kindly offered to walk with him. Anne, the sales rep, took Lynn and Paul, and Rachel insisted on giving Frank a lift in her car, a rather nifty-looking red two-seater BMW. The PR woman seemed to have taken a shine to Frank, although I'm sure he was at least ten years younger than her.

"It's not a bad evening," Steve commented.

"No, it's grand," I replied. I thought it was a little chilly myself, to tell the truth. But after his gracious comments about me to Clara earlier I was willing to brave the sub-zero temperatures of the Arc-tic for him.

"Thanks for walking with me," he continued. "I need some fresh air before tonight's session."

"That's OK," I smiled. "Me too."

As we walked past Jodie's house I shivered. I hadn't thought about Jack or Jodie all day, we'd been so busy.

"Are you cold?" Steve asked kindly. He started to take off his leather jacket.

"I'm fine. Please, put your jacket back on. You'd freeze in your shirt. Someone just walked over my grave, that's all."

"Ghosts?" he asked gently.

"Sorry?" I asked, confused.

"Ghosts of the past?"

"Something like that."

"Want to talk about it?" he asked.

I hesitated. I would have loved to talk about Jack and Jodie and how hurt and alone I felt but I didn't want to put him off. I was starting to really like him. "No, thanks though."

He stopped suddenly and wheeled around to face me head on. "There's something I wanted to tell you. I think I was asking you out that time. I was just afraid you'd say no. Which you did." He paused. "It's funny," he continued. "When I'm writing, words come out so easily and I have no trouble expressing anything. But when I'm with real people it's a different story."

"You're doing fine," I reassured him. "But what are you trying to say?"

"That I like you. That I want to get to know you," he said honestly. He looked at me intently.

"OK," I said.

"OK, yes," he asked, "or OK, no?"

"What are you asking exactly?"

He blushed. "I guess I'm asking do you like *me*?" He blushed even more furiously.

I was delighted—that blushing was something other people did and not just me, that he liked me and most of all that he wanted to get to know me.

"Yes," I said, "I like you." I tried not to giggle. I felt like a teenager.

He blew out a breath. "Phew, that wasn't so bad. Now let's go drinking. I could murder a pint of Guinness."

We began walking again and he put his arm around my shoulders. I could feel the side of his body moving against mine beneath his jacket. He smelled warm and male, a mixture of faded aftershave and leather.

We chatted amicably about the signing—the noise and mayhem of the morning, the delighted children, the unbearably pushy parents. As we passed the Martello tower at Monkstown I remembered the day, not that long ago, when I had cried my heart out on a bench beside the tower. I could still feel the hurt like it was yesterday.

"Amy," Steve said, "I asked you a question. You're miles away."

"Sorry," I mumbled. "What did you ask me?"

"About Dun Laoghaire pier. How old is it?"

I tried to keep my mind from wandering. "I'm not sure exactly. I know the rock used came from Dalkey Quarry. They used to bring it on tracks down a pathway called The Metals from the top of Dalkey Hill. You can still see the tracks in some places."

"Is the quarry still there?" he asked.

"Yes, but it hasn't been used for a long time. It's popular for rock climbing these days. There's The Purty." We rounded the corner and the cream building came clearly into view—you couldn't miss it.

"Just one thing before we go in," Steve stopped in his tracks and put both his arms around me. My stomach gave a little lurch and I closed my eyes. I was disappointed when I felt a soft kiss on my forehead.

When we walked in the door we spotted Anne, Lynn and Paul at the bar starting into their drinks.

"What are you having, guys?" Anne asked. "The night is on your publishers, Steve, so drink away."

"In that case I'll have a bottle of champagne and a Guinness to start with," Steve grinned.

"Is the champagne just for you or can anyone join in?" I asked. He patted me on the head.

"Don't be such a muppet. It's for everyone," he smiled.

"I'll have champagne, so. And what the hell is a muppet?"

Steve began to explain. While he was talking Lynn grabbed my shoulder and pulled me toward her.

"What's going on between you two?" she whispered, nodding toward Steve. "You look very chummy."

I smiled conspiratorially. "That would be telling."

"Dinner is booked for eight," Anne reminded us all. "So don't get too cozy."

"Where's Rachel?" Steve asked with a mischievous grin.

"Good question," Anne replied.

Rachel and Frank appeared at seven. Frank's hair was tousled and his cheeks were flushed. Rachel was in high spirits. She draped her camel cashmere coat over the back of Steve's chair. She had changed out of her black trouser suit into a black dress. Her make-up had been immaculately re-applied, her blood-red lips standing out on her pale face. In fact, she looked just like a Billy girl from *Ally McBeal*.

"Sorry, darling," she gushed, kissing Steve dramatically on both cheeks and leaving striking red lip-marks. "We got caught up." She looked at Frank pointedly. He smiled sheepishly, blushed and looked at the ground. "Excellent, champers. Another bottle, please," she called to the barman, waving the empty bottle in front of his face. "Actually, make that two."

At eight o'clock we made our way toward Coconut Street. The Irish among us—myself, Frank and Paul—insisted that eight meant eightish and that we had time for another bottle of champagne, but we were outnumbered by punctual foreigners.

"Honestly, they won't be expecting us on time," I told Steve as we staggered toward the restaurant. Luckily it was only a few minutes walk. The cold air was making me feel quite tipsy.

Rachel and Frank, who had been flirting quite shamelessly for the last hour, were walking in front of us. Rachel's hand was planted firmly in Frank's back jeans pocket and she was whispering in his ear. Actually it looked more like nibbling than whispering. Paul, Anne and Lynn were enjoying a good discussion about the marginalization of children's books in the Irish media. Paul was an English Literature student in Maynooth and was writing his thesis on the famine books by Marita Conlon-McKenna, a popular Irish children's writer. The conversation sounded way too serious for me.

"Are you working tomorrow?" Steve asked me.

"Yes, unfortunately. We'll all be the worse for wear, I'd say."

"Good," he smiled, squeezing my shoulder. His arm was around me again. "That means I get to see you again."

The outside of the restaurant was lit by huge orange lanterns. As we walked in the door a waft of warm, spicy air hit us. As we waited to be seated I looked around. The walls were a warm orange, decorated with large, bright modern paintings. The lighting was subdued and every table was packed with people. The place was humming.

Our table was in the back of the large main room. It was already laden with dips and home-made breads which we laid into without ceremony.

"Good choice, Amy," Rachel said approvingly. "Great place. I hope they do champagne."

We all laughed. A young American waiter took our drinks order—red and white wine and two bottles of champagne—and left us to decide on our food. Soon we were all busy chatting and laughing. The poor waiter had to come back several times before we'd all even looked at the menu. He was very good-tempered about it though.

"I don't know what to have," Lynn said. "It all sounds wonderful. What are you having, Amy?"

"Jerk chicken, I think. Or Calypso chicken. And yam sticks to start with."

Finally we placed our orders. The food came swiftly and we were soon tucking into our starters. Steve was sitting beside me. Rachel and Frank were opposite us. Rachel's hand kept disappearing under the table. Frank didn't seem to mind though.

"Where do you live, Rachel?" Lynn asked, oblivious.

"West London," Rachel replied. "I have an apartment. I'm not there much though. There's always some launch or function on."

"Do you have to travel to Ireland much?" Frank asked hopefully. At twenty, his libido was the foremost thing on his mind.

"Yes, lots," she replied. "I'm over here a lot and in Edinburgh, Bologna for the Children's Book Fair, Frankfurt, that kind of thing."

"Sounds very glamorous," I said enviously.

Rachel smiled. "It can be, I suppose. But sometimes I'd just like to be at home, curled up on the sofa with a video and some ice cream. Launches can be a bore."

"Remind me not to invite you to any of mine," Steve laughed.

"Yours are never boring, honey," Rachel smiled.

Soon our main courses arrived. I'd decided on the Jerk chicken, a deliciously spicy dish.

"What are you doing later?" Steve asked.

I smiled lazily. This was more like it. "That depends."

"Would you like to share a taxi?"

I'd like to share a lot more than a taxi, I thought. But I decided I'd better not scare him off.

"Sounds good, thanks," I said graciously.

After dessert—deep-fried fruit fritters with cream all around—it was time for Irish coffees and flaming sambucas. Even Lynn had a sambuca.

"How are you feeling?" I asked Steve, putting my hand on his leg under the table and leaning toward him.

"Drunk and very, very full. And you?"

"The same."

He put his hand on mine, lifted it toward his lips and planted a kiss on it. "I've had a great evening. You're good company, Amy."

"Thanks," I smiled. I wished it was just the two of us at that moment. It was difficult to be romantic at a table full of people. Although Rachel and Frank seemed to be managing it. Frank was nuzzling Rachel's neck with his lips.

Rachel stood up. "Bedtime for me, I'm afraid. Early start in the morning. My hotel is just around the corner so Frank is walking me back."

We all smiled knowingly and said our goodbyes.

"Don't do anything I wouldn't do," Paul told Frank with a wink.

Frank grinned back. "See you tomorrow."

Anne, Lynn and Paul left next, sharing a taxi, leaving myself and Steve alone. This was more like it.

Unfortunately the waiter signaled over to tell us our taxi had arrived.

"My lady," Steve said, helping me on with my fleece jacket, "our carriage awaits." We climbed into the taxi.

"Monkstown and . . ." Steve looked at me expectantly.

"Oh, Blackrock," I said. When he said he'd take me home I presumed he meant to his house and not literally. I was disappointed. Maybe he didn't like me at all. Maybe he'd gone off me during the evening. Luckily I wasn't too drunk, otherwise I probably would have lunged at him in the taxi. I tended to do that when I was feeling insecure and needy.

I told the taxi driver my address and sat back in the seat. Steve held my hand. We sat silently until we reached my house. It was terrible—I couldn't think of anything to say.

"This is me," I said. I fumbled in my pocket for some money.

"I'll get it," Steve said. He leaned over and kissed me on the cheek. "See you tomorrow." He let go of my hand.

I stepped out of the taxi and walked toward my front door. The car waited until I'd opened the door and then drove away. It was after one and I was exhausted and faintly disappointed. It had been quite a day.

Chapter 19

The next morning my alarm trilled, waking me out of my dead sleep. I'd had the foresight to set my alarm last night, proving that I couldn't have been too drunk. I pulled open my eyes. It was ten o'clock. Luckily the shop didn't open until eleven on Sundays. I lay in bed for a few minutes thinking about Steve. If he really liked me, in a romantic way, last night would have been different. He obviously liked me but wasn't attracted to me—typical!

I showered and pulled on some clothes. Sitting at the breakfast table I contemplated my hangover. I had a pain in the back of my neck and my head throbbed. I'd been poisoned by drink again and I had no one but myself to blame.

As I pulled the car out of the drive the rain pummelled down. It was a miserable day, dark and cold as well as wet. It matched my mood. The roads were completely clear and I arrived at work well before eleven. There were no crowds outside today—the rain had put them off no doubt. Lynn was piling *Henry and the Master Wizard* behind the signing table.

Steve arrived next, by the front door this time, followed by Rachel and Frank. Frank had yesterday's clothes on which Jess, Lucy and Paul took delight in pointing out as soon as they arrived.

"Your shirt could do with an iron," Lucy laughed. "It looks like it spent the night on the floor."

"Maybe it did," Paul said. "Where did you sleep last night, Frank? Care to tell us."

Luckily Lynn and Rachel were in the kitchen at the time, making coffee.

"Shut up," he blushed. "You're just jealous."

"Damn right," Paul said. "Rachel's a fine-looking woman."

"No way!" Jess exclaimed. "She's ancient."

Charming, I thought to myself. Rachel was a year older than me. I left them to it and began to check the new e-mails. Steve stood at the desk watching me.

"Anything interesting?" he asked.

"There's a message here for you," I smiled. I decided I'd try to keep my distance with Steve today. After all, I wasn't sure what was going on or if he liked me.

He stood beside me and read the e-mail over my shoulder. It was from a young boy in Cork who was sick and couldn't make the signing. But he wanted to ask Steve what his favorite football team was.

"May I?" Steve asked. I nodded. He leaned over the keyboard and typed in a reply.

"My favorite team is Manchester United. Thanks for asking. I hope you get better soon. Keep reading, Stevie J."

As soon as he'd finished I got back to work. He stayed beside me.

"Amy? Are you OK?"

I looked up from the screen. "Sorry?"

"You're ignoring me."

"I'm not ignoring you. I'm just busy," I explained.

"Have I done something wrong?" he asked.

"No," I said, trying to make my voice come out evenly. I wasn't in the best of moods and I wanted to be left alone. "I told you. I'm just busy."

"I'll go and sit at my table then."

"Here." I handed him the sheet of e-mail requests for signed books. He took it from me in silence.

The day went slowly. We were all nursing hangovers and a shop full of excited children and associated adult hangers-on didn't help. Frank and Rachel disappeared for a long lunch at two. Lucy and Jess were a godsend. They took over much of the work, helped by Paul, whose hangover didn't seem as bad as us "ancient" people's.

At four Suzi, Matt, Simon and Kate arrived. Kate was sitting on Matt's shoulders and had to duck to come in the door. Luckily The Wonderland had a very high ceiling.

"Hi, Amy," Suzi called as they spotted me behind the till. Simon joined the queue to meet Steve, and Matt was directed toward the picture-books by Kate. He whisked her off his shoulders and plonked her on the floor. Kate handed him a copy of *Can't You Sleep, Little Bear?* and Matt, looking a little startled at first, began to read.

"He's a natural," Suzi laughed, watching her fiancé. "Kate has really taken to him and Simon adores him."

"Sweet," I said darkly.

"You're in a good mood," Suzi said.

"Sorry," I mumbled.

"What's up?" she asked.

"Nothing," I muttered. "I'm woefully hungover."

Suzi put her hand on my shoulder. I shrugged it off. "I'm in later," she said. "If you feel like talking."

I felt bad. I was being irrational again, I knew the signs. I just couldn't help it.

"Stevie J's lovely," she said, running her eyes over him appreciatively. "Nice shirt too." He was wearing a dark-blue shirt which I had to admit really suited him.

"Um," I grunted noncommittally.

"He's about to sign Simon's book now so I'll just go and say hello," she squeezed into the queue beside her ward.

I watched as she smiled at Steve and asked him a question. He smiled and nodded and looked over at me. Suzi said something else and he beamed. What the hell were they talking about? I stared at the screen in front of me.

Finally it was six o'clock and we ushered the last remaining customers out of the shop. Steve sat back in his chair and sighed.

"I'm glad that's over, I'm exhausted."

"Me too," Rachel said.

Paul guffawed in the background. Frank threw him a dagger look.

"That went brilliantly," Lynn said. "I can't thank you enough, Steve."

"It was a pleasure," he replied graciously.

I went upstairs to collect my jacket. I heard footsteps on the stairs behind me. It was Steve.

"Amy, would you like to do something tonight? Maybe the cinema or a drink?"

"No, thanks," I said stiffly. His face fell. God, I could be such a bitch sometimes. He was just being nice. "Maybe some other time."

"OK," he smiled. "I'm sure you're tired. Can I ring you?"

What's the point? I thought to myself. "Whatever," I said, trying not to catch his eye.

There was silence for a second. "Right," he said, making his way back down the stairs. "Whatever."

I stood at the top of the stairs. I'd upset him. I knew it, but I didn't care.

That evening I was lying on my bed staring at the ceiling. Suzi came into my room.

"Thanks for knocking," I muttered.

She sat down on my bed and ignored my comment.

"You didn't come down for dinner."

"I wasn't hungry," I said. It was the truth—I really wasn't hungry. I hadn't really felt like eating at lunchtime either. I had managed half a cheese and salad roll but the food had tasted of cardboard.

"I brought you up a mug of soup—it's tomato."

I sat up slowly. "Thanks." I took the mug from her and placed it on my bedside table. I could always pour it down the sink later.

"Steve seemed nice. He's quite taken with you," Suzi smiled.

"What do you mean?" I asked suspiciously.

"I told him I was your sister and he said he hoped he'd be seeing more of me in the future," she explained.

"Did he?" I asked in amazement. Then I remembered how rude I'd been to him after that. "It's unlikely you'll ever see him again," I stated baldly.

"Why?" Suzi asked gently. She could sense that I wanted to talk but she didn't want to push me. Closing up like a clam was one of my specialities.

"Just because," I couldn't be bothered to explain, and anyway I didn't understand it myself.

"But he seemed really keen. What's going on?"

I sighed. I thought I might as well tell her so she'd get off my back. "We were getting on really well last night and then he dropped me home. So I guess he just wants to be friends."

"Amy, not everyone jumps into bed on the first night. Some people like to get to know each other first."

I reddened. "That's not it!" I lied. "I didn't mean I wanted to . . . you know. I just don't think he was interested in me in that way. He barely kissed me."

"Was he being affectionate?" Suzi asked thoughtfully.

"He held my hand and put his arm around me, that sort of thing," I admitted.

"But he didn't kiss you?"

"No. Only on the hand and the cheek which hardly counts."

Suzi began to giggle.

"What are you laughing at?" I asked angrily.

"You!" she exclaimed. "You've met a decent guy who likes you and you're annoyed because he didn't hop on your bones."

"That's not true," I said defensively.

"Really?" Suzi asked.

"Well, maybe it's a bit true," I admitted painfully. "But I blew it anyway so there's no point dwelling on it."

"What happened?" she asked.

I told her about my "whatever" remark. She frowned and bit her lip. "He might still ring," she said, trying to sound hopeful.

"Yeah, whatever," I muttered.

The following week was unbearable. The usual waiting for the phone to ring lark. Steve was no different from any other man, I decided. Allergic to the phone. But I figured I'd scared him off with my Jekyll and Hyde impersonation.

Lynn sensed something was up and she went easy on me at work. Luckily I had my *Den 2* hearts to keep me occupied in the evenings. I threw myself into it—cutting, coloring and gluing like billy-oh and trying to keep my mind off Steve. Steve, Jodie, Jack, weddings—the whole damn lot.

And my thirtieth birthday was creeping up on me with alarming speed. Not that it mattered anyway—I had no one to celebrate it with (although I think commiserate would be more the thing). Even Suzi and Beth had forgotten—they were too tied up in their bloody weddings to think about me.

I delivered my hearts to Helen in RTE the following Friday. She bounced into the reception area down the sweeping stairs with the energy of a young puppy.

"Hey, Amy, these are amazing," she enthused. "Perfect. Can you give me a hand up with them to the set?"

"Of course," I smiled. I was feeling a little better, less hormonal and mad, thank goodness.

We made our way through the narrow corridors and up the stairs toward the *Den 2* studio. The room was much smaller than I'd imagined. There were all kinds of props all over the floor and walls—toys, books, huge toothbrushes, giant Pokemon figures—the works. The set had been covered in swathes of pink and purple net material which reminded me of my bridesmaid's dress.

"This is the Valentine's Day set," Helen explained. "Or Valentine's week I should say. What do you think?"

I looked at the set carefully. It was, well, it was boring. I could see why they needed my hearts to jazz it up. "It's nice and bright," I said finally.

"Missing something, isn't it?" Helen asked. "Hopefully your hearts will liven it up a little. I'm going to put them up now."

"Would you like me to give you a hand?" I asked.

"Are you sure?" she asked. I nodded. "If you're not doing anything, that would be fabbo, thanks."

It turned out to be a more difficult job than Helen had anticipated. The hearts were quite heavy and were threatening to pull the material off the walls. So I suggested suspending them from the ceiling. Finally we had all the hearts in place. I'd found some silver and gold spray in the corner of the studio and gave the pink net a metallic layer which made it shimmer in the strong studio lights.

Finally, after almost two hours we had finished. The set now looked amazing, like a romantic pink wonderland. The hearts spun slowly on their suspending wires, catching the light.

We went outside to look at the set on the television screen. Helen introduced me to Mary, the producer, and a tall young man. I blushed as I realized it was Damien, the presenter from *Den 2*. I felt like I knew him from watching the program so much but he was much better-looking in real life.

"Hiya," he said, smiling broadly. "Like what you've done with the set."

"Thanks," I murmured nervously.

"He's right," Mary added. "It looks brilliant. Helen, you must get Amy in to help with the Paddy's Day set."

"Good idea," Helen agreed. She turned toward me. "I'll see you out. It's a bit of a rabbit warren in here."

As we walked back through the corridors Helen showed me the offices of the various departments.

"Listen, I'm sorry it took so long to fix up the set," she said. "We'll pay you for your time, of course."

"It's no trouble. It was fun," I smiled.

"I'll give you a ring in two weeks or so about the Paddy's Day set. I can get you at The Wonderland, right?"

"Yes," I beamed. Maybe things were finally looking up.

Chapter 20

I tried to push Steve out of my mind but I was finding it nigh impossible. Working in The Wonderland didn't help. There were vivid reminders of him in every nook and cranny. Huge posters of his smiling face hung on the walls, there was a constant barrage of e-mails thanking us for bringing him to the shop and his books were selling like proverbial hot cakes. We were finding it hard to keep them in stock. The latest—*Henry and the Master Wizard*—was now out on CD. The full unabridged story was available to play in our shop and boy did it play—over and over again. And guess who was reading this fine recording? Yes, none other than Steve himself. So not only were my eyes assaulted with his image, I had to listen to his calm, hypnotic and sensual voice as well. It was all driving me crazy. And it all meant that I couldn't forget him even if I wanted to.

Suzi asked about him one evening and I bit her head off, so she didn't mention it again. Beth had been lying very low. In fact I'd only had very brief conversations with her over the last two weeks. I hadn't even filled her in on the whole Steve thing, not really. She claimed she and Tony were up to their tonsils organizing the wedding, but I'm sure she was simply fed up with me and all my complaints. Who wouldn't be?

However, Beth did deign to call over on Wednesday evening, just when I was getting settled into an episode of *Dawson's Creek*. I'd become quite addicted to this American teenage soap as the characters in it had even more problems than I did. Although they were all un-realistically good-looking and eloquent. Far too philosophical too, especially that Joey one. I also identified with Andie, the kooky blond one who suffered from depression and found life a trial.

"Hi, Amy," Beth smiled as Suzi led her into the sitting room.

"Hang on," I said, jumping off the sofa and grabbing a blank video tape off the shelf. I placed it in the recorder and pressed record. I didn't want to miss the end.

"What are you watching?" Beth asked in amusement. "It's not *Dawson's Creek,* is it? Stella loves it. She has a big crush on the Pacey guy."

"I'm not surprised," I smiled. "He's very cute. More her age than mine unfortunately."

"I feel like I haven't seen you for ages," Beth said.

"You haven't," I replied, trying not to sound bitter or accusing.

"I know, and I'm sorry. It's just all this wedding stuff. And, to be honest, Tony and I, I guess we're feeling the strain a little. We've been having arguments. And you know how much I hate argu-ments."

I felt terrible. It hadn't occurred to me that Beth might be having problems of her own.

"I'm sorry," I said gently. "I had no idea. Do you want to talk about it?" I asked.

"I'm being stupid. It'll all be fine. There are just so many things to arrange and organize. We never seem to have time to ourselves. And then Tony gets moody and storms over to Jed's and they spend all evening playing with the bloody Internet. They've decided to start up their own website design company and I'm so worried. We could lose the house if it doesn't work out. And I'm so tired all the time. I think I may be sick." Tears pricked Beth's eyes.

I gave Beth a hug and sighed. She was always so strong and to-gether. It was strange to see her like this. But it made me feel a little better. At least I wasn't the only one who couldn't cope at times. And maybe this time I could stop feeling sorry for myself and help someone else.

"Beth, there's no point worrying about things that may or may not happen. Tony and Jed have been in the computer business for long enough now to know the risks. And they work so hard—you're always telling me so. I'm sure they'll be sensible about the whole thing. When are they thinking of leaving their jobs?"

"Next September."

"And they'll be able to bring some of their clients with them, I presume?" I asked.

"I think so," Beth said thoughtfully.

"And will they be running an office?"

"No, they'll be using Jed's house to start with."

"Beth, I really don't think you have to be concerned. They are starting off small and their overheads will be tiny if they're not running an office. Trust them."

Beth smiled. "You're right. I should stop worrying, but it's hard."

"I know. And you're probably just tired because of all the stress. You've been running about like a blue-assed fly getting everything ready. And worrying takes a lot of energy too. Believe me, I know all about it." I gave her another hug. "And you and Tony will be fine, you're made for each other. It will all slot into place, you'll see."

"Thanks, Amy. I feel a bit better now. Sorry for unloading all this on you."

I laughed. "Don't be ridiculous. It's usually you listening to me. It's the least I can do. And Beth, if you're really worried about your health, why don't you ask your GP to do some tests, just so you can be sure. You should probably have a check-up before your wedding anyway."

"That's a good idea."

"And maybe you should try to get away for a few days before the wedding. For the weekend or something. To relax."

"Amy, that's another good idea, thanks. I'll talk to Tony about it later."

"I aim to please," I smiled.

Beth smiled back. "Now, rewind that *Dawson's Creek* and let's have a look at this Pacey guy! I want to find out what kind of taste in men Stella has."

*   *   *

Later that evening Beth rang me.

"Amy, I was talking to Tony and he had an idea. He and Jed are taking a week off work next month to finalize their business plan and he'll be pretty tied up. He suggested that I take a week's holiday then."

"Sounds great!" I enthused. "Where will you go?"

"I'm sure you thought I'd forgotten but I haven't."

"Forgotten what?" I asked in confusion.

"Your birthday. The big three—o."

"I was trying to forget," I grimaced. "But what has that got to do with your holiday?"

Beth was silent for a brief moment. "I want to take you to Rome for your birthday. I know you've always wanted to go."

I gasped. I'd dreamt about going to Rome ever since I was a highly impressionable child and I'd heard all about the fountains and the architecture from Mum. It was her favorite city, and she and Dad had honeymooned there. But I couldn't let Beth pay for me—with the wedding coming up she couldn't possibly afford it.

"Amy, what do you say?"

"It's a lovely idea but . . . Beth, I couldn't let you pay and I'm afraid I can't afford it at the moment," I said, disappointed.

"Amy, I insist. And it won't cost that much. Louise has given me a holiday voucher as a wedding present. With Tony and Jed's business starting up we can't really go away for long. So that will cover the flights. And Mum and Dad have friends in Rome we can stay with. Remember Lucia?"

"Your Italian au pair?" I giggled. "Vaguely, we were quite young at the time."

"She now lives in Rome with her husband and daughter and she's always saying how much she'd love us to come over. Her husband's Irish—remember Pat?"

"The son of your next-door neighbors. I'd forgotten they'd got married. And Olivia is their daughter." Olivia had stayed with Beth's family one summer to improve her English.

"Exactly. She's seventeen now and she e-mails me sometimes. She'd love to show us around."

I gave in. It all sounded so perfect. Rome in the spring with my best friend. What could be nicer?

"Beth, it sounds perfect. When are we going?"

Valentine's Day loomed closer. I was in much better form now that I had a holiday to look forward to. We had settled on the third week in March and I couldn't wait. Helen from *The Den* had rung and we'd talked about large green shamrocks and huge, dancing leprechauns for the St. Patrick's Day set. I was going to make the shamrocks out of lots of different materials—tissue paper, feathers, glitter, card and foam. I had two weeks to finish everything and I was getting stuck in already.

The girls in the arts and craft shop in Dun Laoghaire shopping center were very helpful. I'm sure they wondered why I needed a large bag of green feathers but I'm sure they were used to unusual requests.

I was sitting at the desk at work on Monday morning, thinking about the best glue to attach feathers to foam, when a familiar voice startled me.

"Hi, Amy."

I looked up. It was Steve. He had a strange expression on his face. I couldn't quite make it out. Hard, I suppose you'd call it, businesslike.

"Is Lynn here?"

"No, it's very quiet so she's gone to the bank. She'll be back in a few minutes."

"Right, I'll call back later then."

"Stay," I said suddenly, surprising myself. "I'll make you some coffee."

He looked at me carefully. "I don't think so, Amy."

"Is something wrong?" I asked blithely. I knew damn well there was.

He looked at me again. "You and me and . . . *coffee* . . . let's just leave it."

"What are you talking about?" I asked defensively.

"I don't really want to have this conversation." He started walking toward the door. Luckily there were no customers in the shop to overhear.

I jumped up and followed him. "Why? What are you talking about?"

"Are you being smart?" he asked. I flinched. I'd obviously really hurt him. I was ashamed of my previous behavior. His hand reached out to open the door.

"I'm sorry," I began, putting my back against the door.

"Amy, can you stand back please, I'm trying to leave."

"And I'm trying to apologize," I said agitated. "And . . . and . . . you never rang. You said you'd ring!"

"What?" he asked, raising his voice. "I asked could I ring you and you said 'whatever.' Remember? You acted like you couldn't care less about me. You were bloody rude to tell the truth. We spent a really nice evening together and I thought . . . let's just forget it."

And then I started to cry. I couldn't help it. I threw my hands to my face and ran toward the stairs.

"Amy?" I heard Steve's voice after a few minutes. I presumed he'd gone. I was sitting in the middle of the stairs, trying to compose myself. How embarrassing, I thought. He must think I'm a right idiot.

He sat on the step below me. "Don't cry. For heaven's sake, I didn't mean to upset you."

"It's not you," I hiccuped. "It's me. I always fuck things up."

I looked down at him. He was smiling.

"It's not funny," I stated. And then I began to laugh. I guess it was a little funny.

We sat on the stairs for a few minutes while I caught my breath.

"Hell, the shop," I stood up when I'd stopped crying.

"I locked the door and put the closed sign on it," Steve said.

"Thanks," I said. I was now feeling very, very stupid. I had no idea what to say.

"Amy," Steve said gently, "how about we start again?"

"Sorry?" I asked.

"You and me."

I smiled and sniffed. "OK."

"Amy, can we go out for coffee sometime? I'd really like to get to know you."

I smiled again. "That would be nice. How about Friday afternoon? It's my day off."

"Friday is perfect. Can I ring you?"

"Yes," I nodded. "I'd like that."

Chapter 21

Mum had been videoing *Den 2* with my set on it for the last week. I kept trying to explain that it was unlikely to change but she insisted on getting a shot of it every day. Beth had rung during the week about it. I was quite proud of myself really—it looked very striking and professional. Not bad for a rank amateur.

Suzi asked me to visit the Montessori where Kate went to make things with the kids. It sounded like fun and it would be good practice for my future television career. Right! Like they'd ever in a million years want me in front of the camera. I'd probably break the lens. But a girl could dream.

I decided to make Valentine's cards with them as Saturday was Valentine's Day. The class were all four and five, junior infants, so I decided to do lots of collage—cutting and sticking. Not all little ones could draw or write and I wanted them all to feel involved.

Wee Place Montessori School was in Blackrock, near our house. At ten o'clock on Friday morning I knocked on the bright yellow door and waited. The windows of the school were framed with the pupils' work. Outside there was a fenced-in playing area with a wooden climbing-frame and a slide painted red.

A large, gray-haired woman opened the door. She looked familiar. She was wearing a raspberry pink velour track suit and a wide smile.

"Hi, you must be Amy. I'm Nancy. Welcome." Nancy held out her hand. I balanced the cardboard box I was carrying on my hip and shook her hand.

"Let me help you with that," she said kindly.

"There's another box in the car," I said, handing her the box. I fetched the other box and she showed me into the front room. Lots of tiny, round faces stared up at me expectantly.

"Boys and girls, this is Amy. Say hello to Amy," Nancy said loudly.

"Hello, Amy," chorused the children.

"Now, playtime for ten minutes while Amy gets ready. Una, will you bring them outside?"

"No problem," said a tall young woman who was standing at the back of the room. "Coats on, everyone. Line up. No pushing, Luke."

We watched as the children snaked outside.

"Now you'll have a little peace and quiet for ten minutes," Nancy laughed. "Can I get you tea or coffee?"

"No, I'm fine, thanks," I replied. I looked around the room. The walls were covered with art work of all kinds. Mobiles hung from the ceiling and there was a large nature table under the window. Low bookshelves held hundreds of books of all shapes and sizes. Posters displaying the alphabet and numbers adorned the walls.

"This is a lovely room," I said.

"Thanks," Nancy smiled. "It used to be the dining room and the sitting room. Suzi tells me you work at The Wonderland."

"That's right," I nodded.

"I love that bookshop. We get a lot of our books there. Picture-books especially. You have an amazing range."

"I knew I recognized you from somewhere," I smiled. "I think I helped you order some Richard Scarry books from the States last year."

"That's right," Nancy smiled. "You were very helpful and the kids love the books, especially *Busy, Busy World*."

"I'm glad," I smiled.

"Would you like to use this desk?" Nancy asked kindly. "I'm sure you'd like to set up now, before the little monsters come back inside."

"Great," I said, putting down one of the boxes on the desk. Nancy put the other box down beside it.

"You're very good to come in," Nancy began. "Suzi didn't mention your fee. I hope this covers it." She handed me a check.

"I wasn't expecting anything . . ." I said lamely.

"Take it," Nancy smiled. "Please. I know how much art materials cost, believe me!"

"Thanks." I put the check in my pocket.

I began to lay out the materials—large sheets of colored card, glitter, pipe-cleaners, feathers and tissue paper.

Una and Nancy brought the children back in and they sat down excitedly at their desks.

"Hi, I'm Amy," I began tentatively. "And I'm here to make Valentine's Day cards with you. Now who would like to tell me who you'll give your cards to?"

A sea of tiny hands were raised in the air. I smiled at Kate who was waving her arm around in front of my face.

"Kate, who will you send your card to?" I asked.

"My Mummy, my Daddy and my Suzi," she said sweetly.

"I guess you'll have to make three cards then," I smiled. "In that case we'd better get started. "I'll hand around the colored card first and then I'll show you the different cards you can make."

I spent a happy hour with the children. Once they were engrossed in making their cards they were mercifully quiet.

"They seem to be enjoying themselves," I said to Nancy as she helped me dole out feathers to the children.

"You're very good at explaining things," she said. "You have great patience. Some people take it for granted that they will understand everything. You made sure that every child knew what to do before you went on."

"Thanks," I smiled. "My sister Suzi often brings Kate to our house, so I guess I'm used to five-year-olds."

"Suzi tells me you made the wonderful hearts on the *Den 2* set. I was watching it yesterday afternoon with my son."

"Miss, did you meet Dustin and Socky?" a little boy with sandy blond hair asked.

"Were you eavesdropping, Kevin?" Nancy asked, trying not to laugh.

"Sorry, Mrs. Carver," he said contritely. "But did you, Miss?"

"Amy," I smiled. "Call me Amy. And no, I didn't. But maybe I will next time."

"You're so lucky," another little girl said. "I'd love to meet Damien and Geri May. They're so cool."

"Yes, I am lucky," I agreed.

That afternoon I walked into Blackrock village to meet Steve. He'd rung the previous day to arrange the "date." I was tired after the morning's session in Wee Place but I'd really enjoyed it. I was looking forward to meeting him but I was also very nervous. What if he didn't like me when he got to know me? I knew it was pointless worrying but it was hard not to.

As I walked into Angel Café he was already there, sitting at a table by the window writing into a small spiral-bound notebook.

"Hi," I said, walking toward him.

He stood up and gave me a kiss on the cheek. "Hi, Amy. Nice to see you."

Steve looked great. His blond hair had been freshly cut and was now very short, giving him a young, boyish look. He was wearing a white, long-sleeved T-shirt and dark blue denims. His leather jacket hung from the back of his chair. I felt dowdy and uninteresting in comparison in jeans and a pink fleece.

"Writing your next masterpiece," I smiled, looking at his notebook.

"I wish," he grinned. "List of things I have to do, I'm afraid—find a tiler, choose a color for the hall, buy a new notice-board. Boring really."

I ordered a cappuccino from the waitress.

"When do you write?" I asked with interest. I'd always wondered how it worked.

"Depends on the day really," Steve said thoughtfully. "Sometimes I write from ten to four, with a break for lunch. Sometimes I write all day and all night until I'm tired out. At the moment I'm taking a break."

"A break?" I asked.

"Yes. I'm on book six in the Henry series and I find it takes over my life sometimes. So I've told my publishers that there won't be another book until the year after next. I want to do other things, picture-books maybe. Or even something totally different. I'm not sure."

"How long have you been in Dublin?" I asked. I realized that I knew nothing about his "real life."

"Not long, nearly four months now. My sister Rita, you've met her, she's married to an Irish guy and she loves it here. I needed a change and I thought it would be a nice place to live. And, once I'm a resident, I don't have to pay any tax in Ireland," he grinned.

"Are you serious?" I asked.

"Yes, artists' exemption."

"I knew I should have been an artist," I joked. "And do you like it here?"

"I miss my friends in London." Steve rubbed his chin. "And it's not that easy to meet people really. But things are looking up." He looked at me and smiled.

"And was there anyone special in London?" I asked before I could stop myself.

Steve was silent for a few seconds.

"I'm sorry I'm being too nosy," I said. "Ignore me."

"No, it's all right," he said. "There was someone. Ella. We lived together for a few years but we broke up last year. We decided that we weren't going to get married. We were just too different and we wanted different things in the end. It was for the best. But it's hard."

"I know," I said quietly. I told him about Jack and Jodie. And it felt so good to talk to someone who had been in a similar situation. He understood how you could still love someone even though you couldn't live with them. And he was a bloody good listener.

The light outside was fading by the time we looked at our watches. The staff had begun to clear up around us.

"Time to go," Steve smiled. "I hadn't realized how late it was." It was well past six.

"Thanks for the coffee," I said, standing up. We walked outside.

"I'm this way," I smiled. "I'll . . . ." Steve interrupted me with a kiss. And this time it was on the lips. A gentle yet firm kiss.

"Come home with me," he said. "I'll cook you dinner."

"I'm not sure. I have to . . ."

He kissed me again.

"Please, Amy. I'd really like you to."

"OK," I smiled. "If you insist."

That evening, over plates of pasta in Steve's kitchen, we talked like old friends who had known each other since birth. He was easy to be with. We had so much in common and seemed to have the same warped sense of humor. There was just one thing holding me back. And that was myself.

"You can't like *Goodnight Moon*," I screamed during dessert— strawberry ice cream.

"What's wrong with *Goodnight Moon*?" Steve asked, laughing. "It's a damn fine picture-book, bright, modern illustrations, simple text . . ."

"Exactly," I interrupted. "The text is far too simple. In fact it's downright sleep-inducing."

"No, it's not," he argued. "I think I have to warn you that my own picture-book is pretty simple. I hope it won't put you to sleep too. And anyway—that's the point of *Goodnight Moon*. It's supposed to put little kids into a relaxed state. It's a bedtime book."

He had a point. "Fine," I smiled. "You win. Can I read your book?"

"After what you've just said I'm not so sure." He stood up, picked up the empty dessert bowls and put them in the sink.

"Please," I begged. "I'll be nice. I promise."

"I'll only let you read it if you're honest, not nice," he said seriously.

"Deal."

I stood up and followed him into the hall. Steve's apartment was on the first floor of a large Georgian house. It was set back off the road and had a garden full of mature trees and rose bushes. It reminded me of Jodie's Granny's house.

"Sorry about the mess," Steve said as we climbed over a pile of paperbacks which had fallen and spilled all over the floor of the living room. "I haven't really done much to the place since I bought it. The walls need to be repainted and I've no curtains anywhere."

"I doesn't matter," I said honestly. "It's beautiful. I love the high ceilings and the space."

"That's the main reason I bought it," Steve explained. "I wanted somewhere that wasn't too big but that still had a sense of space."

In the window bay of the sitting room was a large glass-topped table on which stood a black computer screen and keyboard. On either side of the table were waist-high wooden bookshelves where copies of Steve's books nuzzled against dictionaries, a book of quotations, a pocket encyclopedia and books on ancient Greek and Roman mythology. To the right was a notice-board on which photographs, illustrations, letters and all kinds of newspaper and magazine cuttings were pinned. I spotted a feature about The Wonderland signings from *The Sunday Tribune*.

"This is where I work," Steve said. He sat down at the desk and switched on the computer. "I'll print out a copy of the picture-book text for you to read, if you're still keen."

"I'd love to read it," I smiled. "Really." I sat down on the cream sofa and watched him. After a few minutes he handed me the freshly printed story.

"It's about a little mouse who is adopted into a cat family," Steve explained, sitting down beside me. "I wanted to explain racism to children without being too heavy-handed or preachy. It's about accepting differences and loving each other."

"Sounds good," I smiled.

"I'll go and make some coffee while you read." Steve stood up and I pored over the printed pages.

A few minutes later he came back in.

"Well?" he asked nervously.

"It's good," I stated firmly. "In fact, it's better than good. It's great."

He smiled. "Thanks."

"It has just the right mix of seriousness and fun. The mouse, Ernie, is a lovely character and I think kids will have no problem identifying with him. Who are you getting to illustrate it?"

Steve sighed. "I'm not sure. Lynn had suggested Mary Murphy but I contacted her through her publishers and she wouldn't be able to do it for about two years. She's really busy with her penguin and koala books. So any suggestions would be gratefully received."

We talked about illustrators for a while. Steve than asked about my *Den 2* work—Lynn had told him about it when he'd rung for me.

"So do you draw?" he asked slowly.

"Sorry?" I asked.

"You're obviously very artistic. I've seen your work in the shop—the embroidered banners over the picture books are yours, aren't they?"

I was nervous as to where this was heading. "Yes, I guess they are. I don't draw but I sew and I used to make things all the time . . . but not anymore."

He looked at me carefully. "How about trying some embroidery illustrations for my book? I think they'd work with the text."

I laughed. "There's no way I'd be good enough to illustrate a Stevie J book!" I laughed. "Are you mad?"

"How do you know if you haven't tried?" he asked. "I tell you what—I won't even look at them. We'll send them to the publishers and see what they have to say. How about that?"

"Are you serious?" I asked.

"Deadly," he grinned.

I thought about it for a second. He was right—I had nothing to lose. The worst that could happen is that they would get rejected. The fact that he suggested it at all gave me confidence. "You're on. Give me your story and I'll have a go."

"Excellent! I'll drop a copy of the manuscript into the shop—I've a few changes still to make." Steve smiled. "We'll make an amazing double act, you wait and see."

I hope so, I thought to myself. What had I let myself in for?

Chapter 22

Unfortunately Steve had to catch a ridiculously early flight (five AM) to London the following morning for another book signing, this time in Waterstone's on Charing Cross Road and other London bookshops, so we ended the evening at twelve.

As we waited for the taxi I tried not to worry that he hadn't kissed me all evening, or that he hadn't asked to see me again. After all, we'd talked and laughed all afternoon and evening. I was pretty sure he liked me—maybe. And he'd asked me to illustrate his books—which showed—I wasn't quite sure what it showed but at the very least it meant he thought we'd know each other for a while at least.

As for my own feelings, I really liked him, but I wasn't sure that I could fall in love with him. Jack had been so much more forceful and passionate and manly. I was used to loudness and disagreements. They were par for the course with a man, weren't they? I just wasn't sure that Steve was my type. He was so damn *nice*.

We heard a car pull up outside the house.

"That'll be the taxi," Steve smiled. "I had a great evening, Amy. Thanks." He leaned over and kissed me once on the lips, a lingering, firm kiss. He held me close for several seconds before drawing away. "I'll ring you when I get back on Tuesday."

"OK," I smiled. I was half tempted to give him a big smooch but I decided against it. I didn't want to scare him off.

In the taxi on the way home I thought about Jack. The terrible thing was that I missed him. I missed the excitement, the unpredictability. Or at least I thought I did. It seemed easier and easier to remember the good bits and forget the bad bits. Selective memory.

I had to work the next day so I went straight to bed after saying goodnight to Suzi and Matt, who were sitting in the dark in the living room. Bless them. I could hear the faint tinkle of Suzi giggling from my bedroom. I rolled over and tried to sleep. But the image of Jack's face kept appearing. Jack. Eventually I feel into an exhausted sleep.

"Where were you last night, Amy?" Mum asked as she pottered around the kitchen the next morning, watering the house plants.

"At a friend's house," I said, hoping she'd leave it.

"Anyone I know?" Mum continued. She wasn't going to let it go that easily.

"A children's writer. He wanted some advice on picture-books."

"He?" she smiled. Shit, I should have said she and Mum would have lost interest.

"Is there any more Special K?" I asked, shaking the box. Since the bridesmaid-dress fitting with Suzi I'd tried to make an effort. Although all it had amounted to really was stealing some of Suzi's Special K in the mornings. Still, it was a start. I'd just have to starve myself for a few days before the wedding. Sorry, weddings.

"In the cupboard beside the fridge," Mum said. "Was it that young man from the book signing? Stevie K?"

"Stevie J," I corrected.

At that moment Suzi came in the door. Typical. Was I to get no peace?

"What's that about Steve?" she asked. "Were you out with him, Amy?" she grinned.

"No, I wasn't 'out' with him," I stated firmly. "We were just discussing books, that's all."

"Oh, yes?" Suzi raised her eyebrows. "Is that what they call it these days?"

I'd had enough. I wasn't in the mood. I stood up and pushed the chair into the table with a clunk. Mum looked at me anxiously.

"Are you not going to have some cereal, love?"

"No, I'm running late, I'll get something at work," I replied.

I left the room and collected my bag from the end of the stairs. I could hear Mum telling Suzi to go easy on me as I walked toward the front door.

"Bye, love. See you later." Mum's voice wafted up the hall toward me.

"Bye," I shouted gruffly. And good riddance.

It was a clear enough morning and I walked into work. It was Valentine's Day on Monday and everywhere I looked I was reminded of the fact. Card shops, posters, billboards, bus shelters, they all seemed to have gone Valentine's-mad this year.

I hated Valentine's Day even when I did have a boyfriend. Last year Jack had taken me to an Italian restaurant. He'd left it late to book so we could only get a table for ten o'clock. I hated eating late and I made a bit of a fuss. When we got there the place was teeming with happy couples. There were pink and red helium balloons in the shape of hearts at every table.

From the moment we sat down Jack moaned and complained. The waiter didn't come quickly enough, his garlic bread wasn't hot enough, the white wine wasn't cold enough. Eventually I asked him to stop griping and try to enjoy himself. Then he started laying into me instead.

"It was you who wanted to go out for dinner, not me," he muttered. "I was quite happy to stay in."

I decided it was better to stay quiet. I knew what Jack was like when he was in one of his moods.

"We should have had an early night. God knows it's been long enough." He looked at me accusingly.

"Excuse me? That's unfair!" I spluttered. That was a bit below the belt—literally. "Don't blame me. You've been tired too."

"At least I don't fall asleep the minute my head hits the pillow," he continued. "A man has needs, you know."

I'd had enough. "It's not the time nor the place to have this discussion," I said firmly. "Drop it."

"When are we going to talk about it then?" he asked, an unpleasant sneer on his face. "Maybe I can book an appointment with you sometime, Amy. Because it sure as hell won't get talked about otherwise."

"Jack, it's you who works late all the time, not me," I reminded him.

"But it's you who has to work at the weekends. I've told you to ask Lynn for time off. Or leave the bloody place. It's not as if it's well paid. You're always moaning about it. You're tired all the time, I try and deal with it and you get all moody and snap my head off."

"That's not fair. I like my work!" I said enraged. "And the weekend work won't go on for long. She's asked a student to cover one of the days."

"One of the days!" Jack exclaimed. "We'll still have no time together. It's a shitty job, Amy. I make enough to support us both. Why don't you just leave? I'm sure you'd find part-time work in another shop."

"The Wonderland is not a shop!" I said. My blood was beginning to boil. "It's a bookshop. And I'm not bloody leaving. You leave. Work at home. Lots of architects do."

"Now you're being pathetic," Jack sighed. "I earn a fortune where I am. You're brain-dead sometimes, do you know that?"

"Stop it, Jack," I whispered. I'd had enough. This was supposed to be a romantic dinner not a cat-fight.

"And another thing, I thought you said you'd ring the electrician. My shaving-light still doesn't work."

I stared at him in amazement. "Don't be so petty. Stop picking on me or I'm leaving."

"Yeah, right," he laughed.

That was it. I finally snapped. I stood up, said sorry to the waiter as I brushed abruptly past him and ran out of the restaurant. I began to walk home.

Jack didn't appear until after twelve.

"Where were you?" I asked as he came into the sitting room. I was curled up on the sofa waiting for him. I felt bad. It was Valentine's Day after all and we shouldn't be arguing.

"Having dinner," he said evenly. "And getting some peace."

"You stayed in the restaurant?" I asked in amazement.

"I'm going to bed now," he replied. "I presume you'll sleep down here. Goodnight."

Nice night. One of many similar nice nights.

As I approached The Wonderland I thought about calling into the card shop and buying a card for Steve. But I decided against it.

I knocked on the door and Lynn answered. "Hi, Amy. And how are you this good morning?"

"Fine, thanks," I replied.

"How did your date go yesterday?"

"How did you . . ."

"Steve told me when he rang—that you were going out for coffee."

I smiled. Lynn was as nosy as I was. "It went well, thank you. But I wouldn't exactly call it a date."

"Rendezvous then. We've got a busy day ahead of us. The Puffin and Random House new titles have arrived and they need to be received and priced. And there's a large order to be boxed for Wee Place. Nancy was in yesterday and bought some American picture-books. She said you were a big hit with the kids."

"Did she?" I smiled. "I'll just dump my bag and jacket and I'll get straight into the Puffin order."

"Are you sure?" Lynn asked. "I don't mind doing it."

"No, it's fine." It would mean I was hidden in the back room, far away from any pesky customers.

The day flew by. Lynn was right—there was a lot of work to do. I went home pleasantly exhausted.

The next day—Sunday—Steve rang.

"How's my favorite artist?" he said.

"Where are you?" I asked.

"In The Mayfair Hotel. I though I'd give you a ring and see how you're doing."

"How are the signings going?"

"Really well, I think. I did the two big Waterstone's yesterday and I'm in Borders and Ottakers in the Science Museum today."

"Sounds hectic," I said.

"It is a little," Steve said. "But I've a few more shops tomorrow and then I'm back home."

"Home?" I asked. Was he staying in London?

"Dublin," he replied.

"You call Dublin home?"

"At the moment. You know what they say: 'Home Is Where the Heart Is.' " Steve laughed. "Listen, I have to go. I'll ring you when I get back."

"I look forward to it," I said.

On Monday morning my life fell apart—again.

Chapter 23

I woke up on Monday morning with a feeling of dread. Valentine's Day. God knows what Suzi and Matt would be like, and Beth and Tony, and Mum and Dad, and Jodie and . . . I tried not to think about it.

There were no cards for me on the hall floor—surprise, surprise. I had, however, received a mobile-phone bill, a credit-card bill and a junk mail flyer advertising thermal underwear. Great!

I went into the kitchen, and I was just in time to catch Mum and Dad exchanging cards and kisses. I said my hellos and goodbyes and left their post on the kitchen table.

Suzi and Matt were still in their beds. Or bed, I should say. Although they ostensibly had separate rooms they weren't fooling anyone. At first they'd been discreet about it but you could still hear Suzi's light creeping footsteps most evenings as she made her way into Matt's room. It was all for appearances. We all knew damn well they were not exactly saving themselves for their wedding night.

I showered, pulled on a pair of clean combats, my favorite cream fleece with the hood, and smeared some Clinique Almost Make-Up on my face, to protect my cheeks from getting any redder than they already were. Red cheeks and broken veins ran in the family, unfortunately. Mum had luckily made Suzi and me wear protection on our faces, even in the winter. So we were saved from the ignominy of looking like Noddy every day.

It was another clear day so I decided to walk to work. I pulled on a jacket and a fleece hat as it looked cold enough outside.

I was right, there was a nippy breeze, cutting into my face and chilling my hands which I thrust into my pockets. As I made my way into Blackrock I tried to think about nice things—Steve, *Den 2* . . . that's all I could think of. But it was a start.

As I crossed the street to buy a bottle of water before I went into the bookshop a large billboard caught my eye. What really caught my eye was the small crowd of punters who were congregated under the billboard, looking up, pointing and laughing. It was not even nine o'clock in the morning. What the hell were they doing? I bought my bottle of Ballygowan and walked down the street toward the crowd. As I grew nearer I could see what looked like a radio crew gathered on the path. A young man held a tape recorder and another appeared to be talking into a microphone. A young woman was interviewing a large, aproned woman who I recognized as one of the sandwich-makers from Sam's Sandwiches.

And then I read the billboard. Written in huge letters at least ten foot high were the immortal and heart-crushing words—

Jodie R, I Love You. Will You Marry Me? Jack D

The blood drained from my face and I felt sick. I began to shake.

"Amy? Are you all right?" Lynn appeared beside me. She put her arm around my shoulders.

I looked at her. I was dumbstruck. Large tears began to pour down my face.

"Come with me," she said gently, leading me away. She brought me into The Wonderland, up the stairs and sat me down at the kitchen table.

"I'll just go and put a notice on the door. I'll be back in a second."

I nodded. I sat statue-still until she returned.

"You've had a bit of a shock," she soothed. "I'll make you a cup of tea."

I would have protested that tea wasn't going to help me but I didn't have the energy to open my mouth, I felt completely drained.

"Did you have any idea about . . . about a possible engagement?"

Lynn asked eventually. She was sitting at the table opposite me, with a look of concern on her face.

"No," I mumbled.

"I'm sorry, Amy, but I'll have to open the shop. Would you like to go home?"

"No," I decided. I wiped my eyes on the sleeve of my fleece. Lynn jumped up, tore a piece of kitchen roll from the dispenser on the counter and handed it to me.

"Thanks," I said. "If it's OK with you I'll stay. I don't really want to go home. Mum will be there and . . . I'd only think about it too much."

"I understand," Lynn said. "Come down whenever you're ready." She went downstairs. After a few minutes I heard the door-bell tinkle—our first customer of the day.

My mobile rang in my bag. I looked at the screen. It was Beth.

"Amy, I was listening to Gerry Ryan and they were talking about this billboard in Blackrock. And then I realized. Oh, love, I'm so sorry. Are you all right?"

"I'm not sure," I said honestly. I'd stopped crying and I just felt numb.

"Is there anything I can do? Where are you?"

"In work."

"Will I come and collect you?"

Beth was such a sweetheart but I couldn't drag her out of work again. "No. Maybe you could call over this evening."

"Of course," Beth said. "But I have a better idea. Why don't I collect you from work and make you dinner?"

"Won't Tony mind?" I asked quietly.

"Na," she insisted. "I'll send him over to Jed's. He won't mind." I hoped she wasn't crossing her fingers. Tony must be getting really fed up with me by now. "I'll see you around quarter to six."

"Thanks," I said again. I didn't deserve her. She was too good to me.

I checked my eyes in the mirror on the back of the kitchen door. They were a little red but nothing too vampirish. I took a deep breath and went downstairs.

Lynn was talking to Gwen, who worked in the Blackrock library.

"I was just asking Lynn had she seen the billboard down the road. Some guy called Jack was proposing to . . ."

"Yes, we both saw it on our way in," Lynn interrupted. She put her hand under Gwen's elbow. "Now, which Roald Dahls did you need to replace? And did you want hardbacks or paperbacks?"

Soon the two women were firmly ensconced in the fiction room, leaving me blissfully alone. I realized that everyone in Dublin would have seen or heard about the billboard by the end of the day and I had better get used to it. In fact I was surprised that Mum or Suzi hadn't . . .

My mobile rang in my pocket. It was Mum. I turned the phone onto messages and put it on the shelf under the till.

I threw myself into tidying the picture-book stands. They were always in a state after the weekend. There were large colorful books scattered on the floor in front of the stands and nothing seemed to be in its proper alphabetical order anymore. I pulled every single book out of the stand and placed them in piles around me on the floor. Then I began the tedious job of re-alphabetizing them. Usually I dreaded doing this, but today the laborious job helped keep my mind off Jack and Jodie.

I tried not to admit it to myself but the reason I was so upset was that I was jealous. I didn't want to marry Jack myself but I sure as hell didn't want him to be happy with anyone else. And especially my ex-best friend. I wanted to be happy. I wanted a man who loved *me* enough to proclaim it to the whole world.

I kept myself very busy all morning doing jobs that Lynn and I had put off forever. Taking the stock, taking stickers off the top shelves, taking the blu-tack off the ceiling, dusting the mobiles, cleaning the windows.

Just after twelve the bell rang at the door. I looked up from the computer screen where I'd been checking on an overdue order. It was Steve. My heart sank. I should have been pleased to see him but I was so tired and so emotional I didn't think I could bear talking to him.

"Hi, Amy," he beamed. "I'm back!"

"So I can see," I said evenly.

He leaned over the desk and planted a kiss on my cheek. I tried not to wince. Why today? Why couldn't he have called in tomorrow or in a few days when I was in better form?

"Is everything all right?" he asked carefully.

"Of course, why wouldn't it be?" I replied.

"I just thought . . . never mind. Are you free for lunch?"

"No, sorry." Which was the truth. Lynn had gone to the art shop to pick up some supplies for a new window display and wouldn't be back for ages.

"How about this evening?" he asked.

"I'm having dinner at Beth's."

He seemed disappointed. "Are you sure there's nothing wrong?" he asked again. "Have *I* done anything wrong?"

Why didn't I tell him—about the billboard, about how upset I was, that I really wanted to see him but just not today or tonight? I don't know. I guess I wanted to forget about it all. And I certainly didn't want to break down in tears in front of him—again!

"No, of course not. I'm sorry . . ." I shook my head.

He looked at me for a couple of seconds, as if deciding whether to pursue the conversation. "I'll go then. Bye." And he walked toward the door without looking back.

I know. I should have gone after him and apologized and explained that it wasn't anything to do with him. But I'm stupid and I didn't. I just watched him leave and got back to my work. It was only later that I realized what I'd done.

"You let him leave?" Beth asked after dinner when I told her about Steve's visit. "He's going to think you're mad!" She paused for a second. "Sorry, I didn't mean . . ."

"It's OK. You're right. My behavior isn't exactly sane at the moment. Poor Steve." It was beginning to sink in that he'd never, never want to go out with me again. And as for illustrating his book . . .

Beth looked at me and smiled gently. "But you're doing well, Amy. Do you remember the last time, when I had to collect you from the Martello tower?"

I nodded.

"You're dealing with this really well."

I was pleased. Beth was right. I know I'd had a bit of a weep in the shop but I had got a terrible shock. And it still hurt—a lot. But at least I hadn't taken to my bed this time. Maybe I was getting stronger. And maybe I was finally getting over Jack.

"Thanks," I smiled. "I don't feel great but I also don't feel suicidal." Beth grimaced.

"Sorry," I said. "But what am I going to do about Steve?"

"You'll have to apologize to him and try to explain," she replied.

"I suppose so," I said warily. But perhaps it would be easier to just leave it. After all, men were a lot of trouble. And the last thing I needed right now was trouble.

On Thursday evening I met Stella outside the Powerscourt Town-house Centre to look for bridesmaids' dresses. I hadn't heard from Steve all week and I wasn't exactly surprised. I hadn't rung him either and I was trying to banish him from my mind.

Beth had told me that Jodie had said yes to Jack. She had hated being the bearer of bad news but thought I'd prefer to hear it from her than someone else. The "happy couple" had set their date for—get this—the second week in June. A month after Suzi and Beth's weddings! It was just as well we were no longer speaking to each other. Think of it—I might almost have had to be a bridesmaid three times in one summer. Lucky escape if you ask me! At least Jodie hadn't had the audacity to ask me regardless. She wasn't that thoughtless.

Stella was standing outside French Connection as I approached the center. She was wearing her bottle-green Loreto school uniform but she still managed to look stunning. She waved as I approached.

"Hi, Amy. Good to see you." She gave me a hug. "Isn't this exciting?"

"Um," I said. "Where will we start?"

Stella overlooked my lack of enthusiasm. "There're some great dresses in Karen Millen I want to show you first. Or we could try Brown Thomas's or Pia Bang. I had a look around earlier, I hope you don't mind."

"No, that's fine," I said. The sooner this was all over the better. I wasn't a big shopping fan at the best of times. I never had any money. When I lived with Jack he had liked to buy me nice clothes. But I hadn't bought myself anything really since then.

"Is Beth coming in?" Stella asked as we walked in the entrance of the center.

"No," I replied. "She said to put aside anything we liked and she'd come in and pay for it."

"Sounds like my kind of shopping!" Stella laughed.

"Do you not have a rich boyfriend to buy you things?" I asked acidly.

Stella looked at me carefully. "I don't like accepting presents from James. Especially not clothes. He's always trying to buy me smart little suits and dresses. I'm more comfortable in combats and runners."

"I'm sorry," I said contritely. "I didn't mean . . ."

"That's all right," Stella said. "Everyone presumes I'm with James for the money and the parties and everything. But when we first met I had no idea who he was. He treated me like an adult and he listened to me."

"And now?" I asked, noticing the past tense.

"Things have changed. I've become some sort of accessory that he hangs on his arm when it suits him. We never seem to spend any time alone together. We're always going out and I'm getting a bit sick of it."

"What do you want?" I asked. Maybe Stella's life wasn't so perfect after all. "Someone fun, who makes me laugh," Stella explained. "And someone I can stay in and watch videos with."

I smiled. "Don't we all?"

As we walked into Karen Millen's Stella pointed to a bright blue dress.

"What do you think?"

I unhooked the coat hanger and held the dress in front of me. It was long and slinky, with tiny shoe-string straps. Heavy lace hung over shimmering lycra.

"It might be a bit clingy on me," I said nervously. "I'm not exactly a size ten."

"I think it would look great," Stella said encouragingly. "Try it on and see. I'll try one on too."

She grabbed what I presumed was a size eight and we headed to the changing rooms. I gently pulled the dress up over my hips in the generously sized cubicle and was pleasantly surprised when it didn't get stuck. I wiggled the dress around to zip it up and pulled it into place again. I looked in the mirror.

"What do you think?" Stella's disembodied voice asked.

The dress hugged my curves and accentuated my chest. I wasn't exactly huge—a size 36C—but the bodice gave me a great cleavage. And my hips didn't look that huge. My stomach curved worryingly though—I really would have to diet very soon. The Special K alone didn't seem to be doing the trick.

"It looks OK, I think," I replied.

"Can I see?" she asked.

"Sure."

She pulled back the curtain. "Wow, I wish I had your cleavage! I'll have to wear a Wonder Bra."

I smiled. "You look great. The color really suits you."

"Thanks," Stella said. "Do you think Beth will like them?" She turned in the mirror and surveyed her tiny bottom. "They're quite tight."

"I'm not sure. Why don't we put them on hold and she can come in. We can have a look in BT's and Pia Bang's and see if there's anything we like more."

"Good idea," Stella agreed.

Two hours later we were sharing a pizza in Gotham City. We'd tried the other shops but hadn't seen anything we both liked.

"God, I'm exhausted," Stella said, sipping her Diet Coke. "And I have school tomorrow."

I laughed. "I keep forgetting you're still in school."

"Thanks," she smiled. "I take that as a compliment."

We chatted about Beth's wedding for a while. Stella was debating whether to ask James or not. He hadn't exactly been all that interested when she'd mentioned it to him.

"There's this boy, David, who works in the video shop. I've met him in the pub a couple of times and he seems really nice," she said. "He asked me out once a few months ago but I was mad about James at the time. I was thinking I might ask him. Who are you bringing?"

Good question. I hadn't thought of that. "No one," I said lightly. "I broke up with someone a while ago and there hasn't been anyone since, not really." Steve's face briefly flitted thorough my mind but I brushed it away.

"You know," Stella said thoughtfully, "I think you're right. I don't think I'll bring anyone. Two single, attractive bridesmaids could have great fun, couldn't they?" She raised her eyebrows.

"Dead right," I agreed. I'd changed my mind—Stella was great, it wasn't her fault she was so good-looking.

Chapter 24

The family had tactfully decided not to mention the billboard, ever. Suzi and Mum had both briefly questioned me about it but I assured them both that I was, if not exactly fine, dealing with it. So I guess I couldn't blame Mum too much for letting Jodie in. I mean, how was she to know?

"Amy," Mum called up to me on Sunday morning, "there's someone here to see you."

I looked up from the large, furry St. Patrick's Day hat I was making for Damien. I'd decided Damien, Socky and Dustin would look great in green hats that matched the *Den 2* set.

"Send them up," I yelled, assuming it was Beth. I stood up and opened the door.

And there to my horror was Jodie. Her hair had grown since I'd last seen her and I hate to say it but she looked really well.

"What do you want?" I asked nastily, rooted to the spot.

"Can I come in?" she asked gingerly.

"I suppose," I muttered. "It's a free country."

"I know things between us have been a little . . . strained," she began.

I snorted.

She ignored me and continued. "But I really want you to be OK with me and Jack."

"And why do you think I give a shit?" I spat. "It's not as if I know either of you. It's not as if you're my friend or anything."

She winced.

"Amy, this is all really upsetting me. I don't want to lose you . . ."

"You should have thought of that before you stole my boyfriend!" I exclaimed.

"That's not fair," Jodie said, raising her voice. "You'd broken up. You weren't right for each other. You said it yourself at the time. You didn't want him."

"That's not the point," I shouted. "You were supposed to be my friend. Friends don't marry your ex-fiancé."

"Amy, you're being ridiculous," Jodie said in exasperation. "You're not being logical."

"Life isn't logical," I retorted. "Love isn't logical."

"I guess I'm wasting my time then," Jodie sighed loudly. "I thought that maybe you'd cooled off."

"After that bloody billboard rubbing my nose in it?" I sneered. "What do you expect?"

"That wasn't my idea," Jodie said defensively, putting her hands on her hips. "And it's not my fault if you're jealous . . ."

"Jealous," I screamed. "Of what? Jack is bad news, Jodie. Don't come running to me when he chews you up and spits you out."

Jodie went deathly silent. I could hear Mum calling up the stairs. "Are you all right, girls?" As we had stopped shouting I presume she'd figured it was safe to let us get on with it.

"Jack Daly is a good man. He treated you well, Amy, and you know it. Although I wouldn't have blamed him if he hadn't. You're a complete bitch. I don't know how he put up with you for so long."

I listened to her with my mouth open.

"We've been friends for nearly fifteen years now," Jodie said. "I thought that might mean something. I'm sorry I hurt you. I really am. But I've had enough of this 'poor me' shit. I'm going now."

Tears streamed down my face as I listened to her walk down the stairs and bang the front door behind her.

Suzi walked in. "I was in my bedroom. I heard the shouting. Are you OK?"

"I don't know," I cried. "I don't know."

*   *   *

Early March went by in a blur of wedding details. Final dress fittings, wording for invitations, guest lists, missals for the service, booking string quartets and bands. I hadn't realized there was so much to do. I tried to keep well out of it, but with both Beth and Suzi quite obsessed it was hard. Mum was the worst. She wanted to get every detail right. Because the reception was being held in our house, well, in a marquee in the garden, she'd had painters, tilers and gardeners in to make the place look perfect. We now had a newly terracotta-tiled floor in the washroom which was to be the men's toilet, yellow instead of cream walls in the hall and ready-grown shrubs and flowering plants would be planted in the garden at the end of April. Dad, like myself, was trying to keep a low profile. He'd had to clear the garden of all his "bits" as Mum had disparagingly called his architectural salvage. Every fireplace, Victorian brick, marble statue and iron fender had been hauled off to a friend's workshop in Thomas Street. It had been quite a job and the garden hadn't looked so neat and tidy for years.

He'd also been to Woodie's more times than he cared to remember to pick up garden lanterns, garden candles, varnish for the garden furniture, grouting for the downstairs bathroom—you name it—he'd bought it.

Beth was holding her wedding in West Cork. She'd decided to limit it to family and close friends only. Her mother was from Cork and all her aunts, uncles and cousins lived there. The venues she liked in Dublin were all booked out so she'd decided on the South instead. Tony didn't mind. He was happy to marry Beth wherever she wanted. In fact he was quite relieved that the wedding was going to be a small affair. He didn't fancy the world and his wife seeing him in the morning gear which he'd reluctantly agreed to wear. Jed was to be his best man but I was trying not to think about that too much.

I hadn't heard from Steve at all and I was too embarrassed to ring him. And as for Jodie, according to Beth she was really upset but had resigned herself to the fact that I wouldn't be attending her wedding!

I'd finished the new *Den 2* set and helped Helen set it up. The boys loved their Paddy's Day hats. Helen had asked me to design the Easter set. In fact she'd asked if RTE could keep me on a retainer. I was delighted.

My birthday was getting nearer and nearer and I was so glad I was going away with Beth. Whenever anyone asked me was I having a party I could tell them that I'd be in Rome! Lynn had given me the *Rough Guide to Rome* and I'd spent countless evenings poring over it, deciding where to go. There was so much to see—St. Peter's, the Colosseum, hundreds of cool churches, the Pantheon, the stone mouth thingy that Audrey Hepburn had put her hand in with the very attractive Gregory Peck by her side . . .

The days dragged a little but finally it was holiday D-Day. Tony very kindly dropped us to Dublin airport.

Poor pet, our flight was at seven in the morning which meant collecting me at five. Lovely! But he was very good-tempered about it. I think he was secretly looking forward to ten days without any wedding talk. He and Jed could immerse themselves in their own geeky world of digital cameras, mini-disks and sound cards or whatever new gadgets they could get their hands on.

Beth and I had decided on ten days. We could sandwich our holiday in between Good Friday and the weekend before Suzi's hen night, which obviously we couldn't miss. Suzi had arranged the entire thing herself—holiday chalets, pony trekking, dinner, dancing, local farmers . . . only joking! We were going to stay in a holiday complex just outside Arklow, eleven of us—Suzi, me, Beth, Stella (my suggestion as Beth had decided not to have a hen), Martha and Jan, old school friends, Siobhan and Deirdre who used to work with Suzi in Tiny Tots Crèche, Julie Lowan, and Amber and Polly (our unfeasibly good-looking and incredibly posh English cousins). Suzi had decided to have the hen nice and early so we'd all have lots of time to recover. Knowing Suzi and some of her friends it wasn't a bad idea—it could easily take a month! Beth wasn't having a hen so the Rome trip would be special for her too—her last holiday as a single woman.

From the moment Tony dropped us off at the set-down area I was buzzing with excitement. I hadn't been away on a proper holiday for ages. During college we'd spent each summer working away from home: first year—London; second year—Paris; third year—New York. The last time I'd been on an airplane was with Jack. We'd spent a weekend in London. He never wanted to go on holidays— the most I could ever tempt him away from the office for was three or four days. He thought he was indispensable.

As Tony and Beth smooched beside the car, I looked around. There were people everywhere. Brown people coming out the heavy glass doors and white people going in.

"Bye, Amy," Tony kissed me on the cheek. "Have a good time."

"I'll try," I smiled. "And I'll keep the Italian men away from Beth."

Beth giggled and elbowed me in the ribs. Tony shuffled on his feet nervously.

"Only joking," I said quickly. "It's a man-free holiday!"

Beth laughed. "That's not what you told me."

"Ah, but it's different for me, I'm young, free and single."

"Bye, love," Beth kissed Tony again. "See you on Sunday week."

As soon as Tony's car had driven down the ramp we turned toward each other.

"Dark-haired Romeos, here I come!" I grinned.

We picked up our bags and headed in the glass doors. The place was hopping. We took the lift to the Departures Hall and located the Aer Lingus check-in desk.

"This place is like a madhouse," Beth said. "I can't believe it's so busy—it's not even six yet!"

We waited in line behind an immaculately dressed woman. She was wearing a jet-black suit with a tiny skirt, and dangerously high heels. Gucci sunglasses were perched on the top of her chignoned dark brown head.

"Italian women always make you feel so underdressed," Beth whispered.

"Look at her luggage." I pointed at the matching Gucci brown leather case, vanity bag and handbag.

We watched in awe as the woman hoisted the case onto the conveyor belt and handed the ground steward her ticket.

"An aisle seat please," she said clearly in a strong Galway accent.

"Jeez, she's Irish," I whispered to Beth.

"I know," Beth groaned. "That really puts us to shame."

When we'd checked in our luggage we made our way to the Hughes and Hughes Bookshop and browsed.

"This looks interesting," Beth said, holding up a book with a serious-looking female face on the cover. " 'The latest book by this award-winning author,' " she read aloud from the blurb on the back of the book. " 'An epic love story set in contemporary Ireland, the tale of two women and their tragic lives.' "

"Very cheery," I interrupted. Beth put the book back on the table. "How about this one." I held up a bright green book with the picture of a smiling woman on the cover. " 'Molly is fed up. She's tired of her job in a stuffy insurance company and she longs for some excitement. But when Arthur Dillon comes on the scene, with his sexy smile and his immense fortune, things begin to look up.' Now that sounds more like it."

Beth took the book from me and looked inside the front cover. "It says here that the author is from Dublin and used to work in a bookshop. OK, I think I'll get this one. What about you?"

I scanned the bestsellers table for something that stood out. Finally I settled on the new Marian Keyes and the latest copy of *Cosmopolitan*—purely because it had an article on living without men in it. I needed all the help I could get.

"I hate the boarding area," Beth complained. We were sitting at our gate, waiting to be whisked away to warmer climes. "The seats are so bloody uncomfortable." She wiggled around on the dark-blue upholstery. "Why do they make them so hard?"

"Maybe it's to stop people from falling asleep," I mused. I took a glug of my Ballygowan and flicked through my magazine. An article on sexual positions caught my attention.

"Have you ever tried that?" I asked Beth, pointing at an illustration on one of the glossy pages.

"Amy," she hissed, "stop trying to embarrass me."

"I'm not," I replied. "It was a genuine question." I tried to figure out how the woman had leaned back so far while in that position.

Surely her legs would snap or at the very least she'd strain a muscle or two? I turned the page upside down. That way it looked a little more feasible.

Beth looked over my shoulder.

"I thought you weren't interested," I said.

She smiled. "I guess I might pick up a few tips before my wedding night."

"How about that one?" We studied a position called the "Cosmo Angel." It involved a lot of stretching and exertion. "Maybe not," I continued. "Looks exhausting. What about the 'Starfish'? Now I could see Tony liking that."

"Stop it!" Beth shrieked. "If he only knew what you were saying about him."

"He'd be delighted," I assured her.

"Ladies and gentlemen, we are now boarding the E121 flight to Rome. Please have your tickets ready."

We jumped up and joined the queue.

"Thanks, Beth," I said as we waited.

"For what?" Beth asked.

"For this," I smiled. "For everything."

She squeezed my arm. "You're welcome."

Nearly two hours later we stepped off the airplane and into hot, balmy sun. And it was only ten o'clock local time.

As our feet touched *terra firma* Beth turned her face to the sun. She smiled languorously. "Bliss," she purred.

Lucia and Olivia were standing waiting for us in the arrivals hall. Both had dark-brown hair and warm, chocolate-brown eyes.

"Olivia, you've grown," Beth smiled, kissing her on both cheeks. "You're taller than me!"

Olivia laughed. "You won't be able to call me 'Little Olivia' anymore."

"Beth, Amy, welcome to Rome," Lucia said. "We are so happy to see you."

"Thank you for having us to stay, Lucia," Beth said.

"It's our pleasure," Lucia smiled, her eyes full of kindness. "Your Mamma was so good to me. I'm happy to be able to repay her."

Lucia drove us to their apartment in the suburbs. I stared out the window while Beth filled them in on all the wedding details. Soon we pulled up outside a white apartment building which was surrounded by trees. Hundreds of white and gray birds perched in the branches and the warm air was filled with their gentle chirping.

Olivia showed us to our quarters, a deliriously cool room with a white marble floor and two beds with matching light-blue duvets and insisted we made ourselves at home. A slatted wooden blind hung on the large window. We dumped our bags and collapsed on the beds.

"I love Rome already," I smiled.

Chapter 25

After a light lunch of delicious Italian bread, salad and fruit (very healthy—I felt more full of vitamins than I had for ages!) Olivia took us to the Spanish Steps which led down to the Piazza di Spagna.

"It's so beautiful!" Beth exclaimed as we stood at the top of the steps. At either side of the steps were pots of bright pink flowers. It was a bright, clear day and the sun shone gently.

I pulled out my camera.

"I'll take a photo of you both," Olivia said smiling.

"I have a better idea," I said, looking around for someone to take a shot.

Olivia frowned. "Be careful. Don't give your camera to an Italian."

"Why?" I asked with interest. "Are they lousy photographers?"

Olivia laughed, her brown eyes dancing in the sunlight. "No, silly. There are a lot of thieves around. They offer to take photos and run off with your camera."

I chose an innocent-enough-looking English tourist, a woman in her late fifties, who was happy to oblige.

"How old are these steps?" Beth asked Olivia.

The young girl shrugged. "I think they were built in the eighteenth century sometime. But you'd have to ask Mamma."

We began to walk down the steps, trying to avoid the hordes of other tourists who threatened to trip us up. The place was packed; everywhere we looked there were Japanese tourists with tiny digital cameras. They traveled in packs and each group had a "leader" who held an open umbrella in the air so he or she could be seen. It was quite a sight, crocodiles of tourists following along like the rats after the Pied Piper.

"This is the Fontana della Barcaccia," Olivia said as we passed an oval fountain. We continued along the street and turned right. "And this is the Via Condotti. Shopping heaven!"

"Dangerous," Beth said as we spotted an Armani store. "Better lock up my credit card this week I think. Or else the wedding won't be paid for."

I smiled. At least Beth could still use her credit card. Mine was hovering precariously just under its limit. I hoped I didn't have to use it—there was nothing worse than your card being refused in a shop. The assistant always looked at you with such an accusing air, as if you were a jewel thief or a pickpocket. Believe me, I know.

Beth bought a simple but stunning cream top in Armani, which set her back a bit but she explained that it was "an investment," and we spent several happy hours browsing in the other shops, guided by the ever-patient Olivia.

"So, girls," Lucia asked as we walked in the door of the apartment into the cool, white hall, "how was your day? You must show me what you've bought."

Beth opened the smart black paper bag and held up her new top.

"Che carina!" Lucia said, feeling the soft, luxurious material. "Tell me about your day." She showed us into the kitchen and we sat down at the table. Olivia poured us all welcome glasses of water from the fridge and kicked off her runners.

"Olivia, put your runners in your room," Lucia scolded. The teenager picked up her shoes and pretended to frown.

We told Lucia all about our window shopping, browsing and eating (there had been one or two pit stops for ice cream along the way).

"Olivia was so kind to show us around," I smiled. Olivia was now sprawled on the sofa in the adjoining sitting room, listening to U2.

"She's a good girl," Lucia said, "and it's nice for her to have you both here. I think she'd have liked a sister, but . . ." she paused for a second, "Pat and I were only blessed with one."

"Do I hear my name being mentioned?" A tall, dark-haired man walked into the room. He was dressed in a dark suit, with a crisp, white shirt. He looked more Italian than an Italian. "What have I done now?"

Lucia jumped up and kissed him on the cheek. "*Ciao*, Pat, I didn't hear you come in. This is Amy and you know Beth."

"Beth, how nice to see you again! My girls have been so excited about your visit." He smiled at his wife and at Olivia, who had just come back into the kitchen. He leaned down and kissed his daughter on the forehead. Beth stood up and he hugged her warmly. "I'll leave the kisses," he laughed. "We are Irish after all. And Amy," he shook my hand warmly, "lovely to meet you."

"Thanks for having us," Beth said as we sat back down at the table.

"And now," Lucia smiled, "Beth, tell us all about the great wedding. Every detail."

I groaned inwardly. I couldn't get away from it, even in Rome.

That evening we went to a pizza restaurant in the center of town. Rome at night was bright, lively and exciting. Like a warm, exotic Temple Bar without the stag and hen parties. Everywhere you looked people were zipping around on scooters, weaving in and out of the fast, excitable traffic. Teenagers loitered on the streets, chatting and laughing. Although it was only March, the air was blissfully warm.

The restaurant was brightly lit, with long wooden tables and simple, functional glasses and cutlery. Pat told us that it was family-run and that Lucia's family had been coming here for generations.

"What are you having?" Pat asked, as I read my way through the blackboard on which the menu was clearly listed—in Italian. "Can I help?"

"Please," I smiled.

"I could do with some help too," Beth laughed. "We Irish are so un-lingual. You guys put us to shame."

I nodded. "In Ireland your average seventeen-year-old has maybe a little French or Spanish. A few are fluent but only if they have been abroad while they were at school. Olivia, your English is amazing."

"Thank you," Olivia said, "but you must remember that I'm in an International School and some of our classes are taught in English. And of course Papa is Irish."

"That helps!" Pat laughed. "Now let's order."

An elderly waiter, wearing a black suit and a voluminous white apron, stood patiently by our table while Pat and Lucia deciphered the dishes for me and Beth. As we waited for the food, Pat asked us about Ireland, the recent political scandals, the "Celtic Tiger," and, of course, the house prices.

I looked around the room and my eyes settled on a young couple in the corner who were feeding each other pizza. Jack and I had always meant to visit Rome. In fact we had always meant to visit a lot of places but his work always got in the way.

"Amy," Lucia asked, "were you the *margherita* with mushrooms and pepperoni, or with spinach?"

"Mushrooms and pepperoni," I replied, taking the huge plate from the waiter. I bit into the first slice. It was incredible. Nothing like the pizza at home. The cheese was rich and tasty, the tomato sauce zinged with flavor and the base was deliciously thin and light. "Delicious!" I exclaimed.

Pat smiled. "We try not to eat here too much," he patted his belly, "but it's difficult. I'm a total pizza addict."

"That's why he married me," Lucia quipped. "I make good pizza."

That evening I slept more soundly than I had for a long, long time.

"Amy?" Beth had whispered, just before I'd fallen asleep.

"Yes?"

"Do you feel like a child here or is it just me? You know—being looked after so well, and being taken out and shown around, and having a sleepover with your best friend?"

I thought for a second. "I do a bit." I smiled in the dark. "But, you know, I kind of like it."

"Me too," Beth said. "In fact, I like it a lot."

*   *   *

The week flew by in a blur of sightseeing, shopping (Beth), browsing in bookshops (me), eating, drinking, talking and laughing. I toyed with the idea of looking for an Italian man—searching the bars and nightclubs for worthy specimens but after the first two days the idea no longer had any appeal. I was having too much fun spending "quality time" with Beth and with Pat and his family.

I tried not to think about my fast approaching thirtieth birthday—after all it was no big deal, not really. Who am I kidding—of course it was a big deal, it was a huge, all-encompassing big deal. By thirty you were supposed to have life all mapped out—your mate firmly bagged and ringed, one or two doting children, a blistering career and an involvement in a children's charity, your children's school's PTA or both. Leaving your carefree, live-life-to-the-full twenties is not easy.

I'd considered shifting the goalposts a little. As Oscar Wilde once said "No woman should ever be quite accurate about her age. It looks so calculating." Maybe I'd stay twenty-eight forever. And in my late forties fix my "age" at thirty-four. I'd have to get Beth in on the act. At least I no longer had to deal with Jodie's resolute single-minded determination to tell everyone her exact age at every opportunity. She didn't believe in growing old gracefully. She turned thirty last autumn and made sure everyone knew about it. Beth, on the other hand, was a little ambiguous about the whole age thing—like me her thirtieth birthday did not fill her with relish. At least she had another few precious months of twenty-something denial. Her birthday wasn't until September.

Lucia mothered us constantly and we loved it. Olivia was delighted—it meant her mother didn't notice her as much, and she managed to avoid the usual interrogation before leaving the house. She was on her Easter school break, so spent a lot of time alternating between showing us around and sneaking off to meet her "older" boyfriend who her mother didn't approve of.

I wasn't surprised that Lucia didn't approve of Flavio—he was a shifty-looking character, with a fine red scooter and a pierced eyebrow. But he turned out to be a sweetie and even offered to introduce me to his older brother, Emilio. Surprisingly, I declined the kind offer.

There was one major problem with Rome. The weddings.

There was no getting away from weddings in Rome. Everywhere you looked there were young, attractive dark-skinned couples fawning over each other—in full wedding attire, black suits, whiter than white dresses, veils, the works. The Trevi Fountain was the worst. It was positively riddled with happy couples. Apparently it's a Roman tradition to be photographed in your full garb at the fountain. And photographed they were. By the official photographer, friends, relations and passing tourists.

And don't get me wrong, as settings go it's pretty spectacular— cascading water, dramatic white sculptures of Neptune and Tritons (information kindly supplied by Lucia). Beats the feebly foliated arch in the local Irish hotel any day. But I'd hoped to get away from weddings and instead they seemed to be following me.

Of course Beth squealed with delight when she saw her first Italian newly-wed couple. She turned toward Lucia. "Lucia, is it OK to take a picture do you think?"

Lucia smiled broadly. "Of course, in Italy the bride and groom love being the center of attention. In fact, it's considered very good luck to kiss the bridegroom."

"I dare you, Beth," Olivia said wickedly. "Go on. He's very cute."

Beth blushed. I had a good look at the bridegroom. "Olivia's right. He is cute," I smiled. "Go on, Beth, I won't tell Tony. I promise."

"I couldn't," Beth sighed. "I'd be too embarrassed." She stared at me. "But there's nothing stopping you. I double-dare you."

"So do I," Olivia encouraged.

Lucia laughed. "They say if you kiss the bridegroom you'll meet the man of your dreams within the year."

"In that case," I smiled, "it's worth a try. I feel like we're on a school tour. I haven't been double-dared for years."

"What about the New Year's Eve before last?" Beth giggled. "Do you not remember the chandelier incident?"

I grinned. I had forgotten that.

"Tell us, Beth," Olivia begged.

Beth continued. "Amy decided she could swing from our friend Jodie's chandelier. So I dared her and she managed to pull it out of the ceiling. It smashed onto the tile floor and our friend wasn't impressed."

"I'll never forget her face," I smiled. "Poor Jodie, she loved that chandelier."

"Kissing that nice young man is easy compared to that," Lucia said. "You'd better hurry. They are getting ready to leave." The couple had been sitting at the edge of the fountain and were now picking up the bride's long, flowing train. I took a deep breath and made my way through the crowds toward them. The groom was taller than I'd expected. I gulped.

"Mi scusi?" I asked in my best evening-class Italian. *"Posso?"* I raised my eyebrows and pursed my lips. He turned toward his bride who smiled and nodded. He then kissed me gently on the cheek.

"Tanti auguri," he whispered.

I felt a warm glow spread from my tingling lips right down to my toes. In that split second the thought went through my head that maybe finding love was possible, even for me.

I floated back to the others.

"Well done, Amy," Beth said, beaming. "I have it all on camera."

I smiled. "Great," I said sarcastically. "What does *tanti augun* mean?" I asked Olivia.

"Tanti auguri," Olivia grinned. "Good luck. Maybe I should try," she said.

Lucia put her hand on the young girl's shoulder. "Not so fast, Olivia."

We watched the bridal party leave and sat on the edge of the fountain watching the water. I dipped my fingers into the clear, blue water. It was pleasantly cool.

"Penny for them," Beth said, as I moved my fingers through the water.

I looked up at her. "Weddings," I replied honestly. "I was thinking about weddings."

That evening I dreamt that I was at the altar in a huge, white stone church. All around me were unfamiliar faces, all dressed in black, with dark-skinned, Mediterranean faces. The young man from the fountain was at my side.

"Don't worry," he whispered in my ear. "You'll find him soon."

Chapter 26:

On Friday morning I woke up with a deep-rooted feeling of
dread. I knew I should be worried or wary of something,
but I couldn't quite remember what that something was. I lay in bed
staring at the ceiling. Suddenly it hit me with a bang. I was now officially thirty. I gently fingered the skin around my eyes. No new
crows' feet had etched themselves into my skin during the night.
Not yet anyway. I did, however, feel a brand new spot bumping up
the skin under my left eyebrow. It was throbbing a little and I cursed
plucking my eyebrows last night. I'd obviously poisoned my follicle
and caused a new spot. I wondered absently would it turn into a
whitehead and would I have to pop it? I quite enjoyed popping spots
sometimes. It gave me a certain sense of control.

When I turned eighteen I thought in my innocence that my spots
would clear up. Then I thought they'd disappear on my twenty-first
birthday. But slowly I began to realize in horror that I was destined
to have the offending blemishes forever. And now, in my thirties, I
had spots and wrinkles to beat the band. My weight would start to
pile on next and I'd . . .

"Amy?" Beth interrupted my gloomy thoughts. "Happy birthday, love." She sat up and smiled. "So how does it feel being thirty?"

I moaned. "Don't remind me. I was just pondering on the unfairness of having spots and wrinkles at the same time."

Beth laughed. "You don't have either."

I pointed to my newly acquired lump. "What's this then?"

Beth surveyed my eyebrow. "An eyebrow?" she suggested helpfully.

"No, the thing under it," I said, in exasperation.

"Amy, that's tiny, hardly a spot at all. And anyway, in a few years
when we all have real wrinkles you'll be thanking your lucky stars
for your skin. Mine's so dry I'll definitely get mega-wrinkles."

"You have lovely skin and you know it," I said. "Don't give me
that."

Beth reached down beside her bed and pulled out a small pack-
age. She got up, sat down on my bed and handed it to me.

"Happy birthday," she said, kissing me on the head. I sat up and
smiled.

"Thanks." I ripped off the bright-red wrapping paper. Inside
was a small black box. "Is it jewelry?" I asked with interest.

"Open it and see," she said.

I opened the velvet-covered box. Inside was a small silver angel
brooch. It had a long body embossed with stars and hearts. On the
angel's head was a delicate crown.

"It's beautiful, Beth," I whispered. "I love it, thanks." I took it
out of the box. On the back was engraved "May this angel watch
over you and keep you safe."

"So, birthday girl, what would you like to do today?" Beth asked.

"I'm not sure. There's so much more to see. But I guess the
Colosseum would be top of my list."

"Perfect," Beth smiled. "And I think Pat and Lucia have something organized for tonight, just to warn you."

"Tell me," I begged. "What have they planned?"

"No way," Beth was adamant. "I shouldn't have told you anything. I just didn't want you to think we weren't celebrating tonight,
that's all."

I let her get away with it. After we'd both showered I sat by the
dressingtable as Beth put her hair up. "Beth?" I asked.

"Yes?"

"Are you sure about your hen? That you don't want one, I
mean."

"Positive," she said. "It's not really my kind of thing. I'm happy to spend this time here with you and I can have a few drinks at Suzi's hen."

"If you're sure," I said doubtfully. I felt bad. As bridesmaid I felt honor bound to get Beth very drunk and wearing a plastic "willy" hat and veil. I'd spoken to Stella about it and she'd been disappointed too. But Beth had made up her mind.

"Honestly," Beth looked me in the eye. "I'm not into all that chocolate willy and silly clothes business, or streeling around the pubs and clubs blind drunk."

I winced. Maybe it was just as well I'd abandoned the "willy" hat idea then. "If you're sure."

"Yes!" Beth exclaimed. "Absolutely sure. OK?"

I decided to drop the subject.

We joined Lucia and Olivia for brunch. Pat had left earlier for work at one of the banks where he was in charge of the IT department.

"Hi, girls," Lucia beamed as we sat down at the table. Gentle sun shone in through the window, throwing shafts of light into the room. "How did you both sleep?"

"Very well, thanks," Beth said.

Olivia passed me a long black box which was decorated with a bright yellow ribbon and an envelope. "For your birthday," she smiled.

I was touched. "You shouldn't have," I stammered. "It's really kind of you."

"Open it," Olivia insisted. "I chose it."

I slid off the ribbon and opened the box. Inside was a pink Swatch with tiny gold angels on the straps and watch face. "It's lovely," I said. "Really lovely." I placed the watch on my left wrist and fastened the strap. "You won't believe this, but Beth gave me an angel brooch." I pointed at my T-shirt on which I'd pinned the silver angel.

Lucia whistled. "Must be fate," she said. "Your guardian angel is sending you a message."

I opened the card. It was a picture of David by Michelangelo. On the front was a red arrow which pointed to David's tackle. "Wow, David!" It read.

Lucia laughed. "Olivia chose the card too!"

"I thought so," I said. "Thank you both."

"What would you like to see today?" Olivia asked.

"The Colosseum," Beth said.

"Cool," Olivia said. "I'll come with you. Mamma's shopping and meeting Dad for lunch, I think." She looked over and her mum nodded. "So it's just the girls."

"I nearly forgot," Lucia said. "Your Mum rang. I didn't want to wake you."

"Is it OK to ring her back?" I asked.

"Of course," Lucia said, "I'll write down the codes for you." She handed me a scrap of paper and I punched the numbers into the phone followed by my own number.

Mum answered the phone. It was nice to hear her voice.

"Hi, Mum, it's Amy."

"Amy, love, happy birthday. Are you having a nice day?"

I smiled. "Yes, really nice. Lucia's family are being so kind and we've seen so much. We're off to the Colosseum today."

"Your Dad wants to say hi," Mum said.

"Amy, happy birthday. How does it feel being thirty?" Dad asked.

"Twenty-eight!" I pointed out.

Dad laughed. "I see. Twenty-eight again. Your Mother was thirty-five for years. It must run in the family. Anyway have a great day. Suzi and Matt send their love."

"Thanks, Dad," I said. "See you on Sunday."

Walking toward the bus stop from the apartment after lunch, Olivia turned toward us.

"I told Flavio to meet us there. I hope that's OK."

"Of course," I smiled.

"How long have you two been together?" Beth asked.

"Nearly three months," Olivia replied proudly.

I was impressed. At seventeen that was quite an achievement.

A warm breeze rustled through the trees which lined the small suburban street. It was another deeply pleasant day, weather-wise.

"I wonder what Irish people would be like if they had nicer weather," I pondered aloud.

"What do you mean?" Olivia asked.

I tried to explain. "It's always raining in Ireland. And if it's not raining it's gray and overcast."

Olivia looked at Beth quizzically.

"It's true," Beth assured her. "But we do get the odd nice day."

"In May," I said. "Or September. And we never get more than two or three days on the trot. In fact, it can be sunny in the morning during the summer and pouring from the heavens in the afternoon. It plays havoc with your wardrobe. Some days you just don't know what to wear."

Olivia laughed. "Sounds terrible. I don't remember it raining when I was in Dublin." She paused for a second. "Not all the time. Maybe sometimes."

"See!" I said. "Anyway, I think that if we had a bit more sun and general brightness Irish people might be in better humor most of the time."

Beth smiled. "Gerry Ryan thinks the weather affects our feelings too."

"It's a proven scientific fact." I was on a roll now. "There's a name for it—SADD, I think."

"That's right," Beth nodded. "Now that you mention it, I remember reading about it somewhere. Seasonal adjustment something."

Olivia laughed. "OK, I believe you both."

"Sorry," I grinned. "The weather or lack of it is a bit of an Irish preoccupation."

"That and Man United," Beth added.

The bus was very like an Irish single-decker bus, except it was blue instead of green. We settled into our seats, letting Olivia deal with the driver. She had the right number of tickets in her pocket which had to be bought before you stepped onto the bus. She plonked herself down on a seat in front of Beth and me and began to tell us about Flavio.

"It's so nice to be able to talk about him," she explained, her brown eyes shining. "He used to go out with one of my best friends, Maria, and I haven't told her about us yet, so I can't talk about him with anyone really."

"What does he do?" Beth asked. "Is he in college?"

"No," Olivia replied. "He's in a band with his brother and a few friends. They're called *Eco Eco* after an Italian writer."

"Umberto Eco," I interrupted.

Beth raised her eyebrows. "Aren't we the intellectual?"

I laughed. "He wrote a film Christian Slater was in called *The Name of the Rose*. Stop slagging me."

"Amy works in a bookshop," Beth explained. "And she's a movie freak."

"Less of the freak, thank you very much," I smiled. "A movie fan."

"So am I," Olivia enthused. "I love films. My favorite is *The Sixth Sense* with Bruce Willis. Did you see it? It come out a few years ago."

"Sure did," I said. "I brought Beth and she spent the whole time clinging onto my arm. When the ghosts appeared she wouldn't look. She missed half the film."

"It was bloody terrifying!" Beth exclaimed. "Thinking about it still gives me the shivers."

"We're here," Olivia said, jumping down from her seat. "Come on, you two. Watch your step, Granny Amy."

I glared at her. "I'm not dead yet, Olivia."

We crossed the busy road, avoiding the mad Roman drivers. And in front of us was the famous Colosseum.

"Holy cow," Beth exclaimed as we drew closer. "It's huge!"

"There's Flavio." Olivia waved at her boyfriend who was leaning against the outside wall of the Colosseum, smoking, one leg propped against the weathered red wall. He was wearing immaculate-looking denims, a white T-shirt and a black leather jacket, doing his best James Dean. He threw his cigarette to the ground as we approached him, grinding it into the ground with the heel of his black leather boot.

"*Ciao, bella.*" He swung Olivia in the air and kissed her on the lips.

"Put me down," she giggled. He placed her carefully on the ground beside him.

"Hi, Beth and Amy." He cocked his head to the side and smiled. "How are you pretty girls today?"

"Fine, thanks," I said, delighted that he'd called me a girl.

"Ready to see the mighty Colosseum?" he asked. Just then a tall boy dressed in similar garb walked toward us.

"Ah," Flavio said. "This is Emilio, my brother." Emilio smiled, showing his beautifully white and even teeth. He had a wonderfully cheeky smile. My heart lurched.

"Emilio, this is Amy and Beth—Olivia's friends from Ireland," Flavio said.

"Ireland, I love Ireland. U2, Van Morrison, yes?" Emilio asked, cocking his head.

I smiled. "That's right."

He kissed both our hands. I could feel the blood rush to my face as I felt his cool lips against my skin. He then turned to talk to Flavio.

"This could be interesting," Beth whispered in my ear. "He even looks a bit like your man from *Gladiator*. Imagine what he'd look like in that leather tunic thingy."

"If I get lost later, send him to rescue me, will you?" I asked.

"Absolutely," Beth smiled.

As we wandered around the ancient amphitheatre I was overcome by the sheer scale of the building, the mammoth columns and arches. Flavio and Olivia disappeared early on, leaving Emilio as our tour guide. He didn't seem to mind too much.

"The Colosseum was built by the Emperor," he explained, as we explored an internal corridor behind the tiered stadium of the amphitheatre. "They had wild animal fights here and gladiators."

Beth nudged me. "Gladiators," she grinned.

"Which emperor?" I asked with interest, ignoring her.

"I'm not sure," Emilio answered truthfully.

Beth flicked through the pages of her travel guide. "Here it is. 'Rome's Colosseum was commissioned by Emperor Vespasian in 72 AD. At the first games in 80 AD over 9,000 wild animals were killed. The immense building could seat over 55,000 people,'" she read.

Emilio smiled. "We'd better find my brother and Olivia now. I'll ring him." He pulled out a stylish chrome mobile.

Everyone in Rome seemed to have a mobile, from young children to old grannies. They talked on them incessantly, yabbering away, while they were walking, riding their scooters or eating. It was quite a sight.

Emilio talked for a few seconds, and then turned toward Beth and me.

"They will meet us in the Café Vesta," he said. "Let's go."

"Can I take a picture before we leave?" Beth asked. "Of yourself and Amy."

I stared at her. What was she up to?

"You make a lovely couple," she continued.

I could have killed her. "Beth . . ." I began murderously.

Emilio didn't seem to mind. He grinned and put his arm around me. "Smile, Amy," he insisted, holding me closely. I could feel the leathery coolness of his jacket against the bare skin of my arms. It reminded me of Steve.

"Amy," Beth commanded, "smile!"

She clicked the shutter. "One more," she said, clicking it again. "That's great. Thanks Emilio."

"My pleasure," he said, looking me in the eye. He left his arm draped around my shoulder. I wiggled free and strode toward the entrance. Beth caught up with me.

"What's the matter with you?" she asked in confusion.

"Stop trying to push me at Emilio," I hissed.

"It's only a bit of fun," she whispered back. "Anyway, I think he likes you."

"Yeah, right," I muttered.

"I'm serious," she said. "He's been watching you all afternoon."

"Really?" I asked, beginning to be interested.

"Wait for me," I heard his voice behind us. "You girls walk so quickly. Take your time."

He was nice, and maybe Beth was right. He did seem to be smiling at me a lot.

"The café is on the Piazza del Colosseo. Follow me," he said.

We left the building and followed Emilio as he wound his way through the traffic and stopped outside a restaurant. Olivia and Flavio were sitting at a table outside, holding hands and gazing into each other's eyes. They hadn't noticed us—yet.

Emilio put his fingers in his mouth and gave an earth-shattering whistle, startling the star-crossed lovers as well as myself and Beth.

"Emilio!" I laughed, punching him on the arm.

He grinned and held my clenched fist. "You have quite a punch." He unfolded my fist and brought my hand to his lips. He kissed my fingers, lingering over each digit.

I shivered deliciously.

"Emilio," Flavio's voice drifted toward us. I looked over and realized that Olivia, Flavio and Beth were watching us with interest.

"Stop flirting, Emilio, and join us," Olivia laughed. I blushed.

Minutes later we were sitting at the table, watching the world go by. I was sipping a large cappuccino and Beth and Olivia were sharing mineral water. The boys were tucking into large plates of gnocchi with relish, washed down with large glasses of red wine.

"Did you like the Colosseum?" Olivia asked, as the boys rattled away in Italian about some football match.

"It was amazing," Beth enthused. "You could almost see and smell the people and the gladiators. It's so steeped in history."

Olivia nodded. "I love it. I've been so many times but I still can't get enough. And Amy? Did you like it?"

"Oh, yes," I assured her. "It was a real experience."

Olivia leaned over toward me and whispered. "And Emilio, what do you think?"

I raised my eyebrows. "He's very nice, Olivia."

"No, I mean . . ." she continued. Beth leaned her head down and listened.

"I know what you mean," I said.

"Well?" Olivia asked again.

"She likes him," Beth interjected.

"Beth," I hissed.

"What are you girls talking about?" Flavio asked.

"Nothing," Olivia said.

"*Tanti auguri a te,*" the strong singing voices of the Italian waiters drifted toward us from inside the restaurant. The singing grew nearer and nearer.

"Must be someone's birthday," Olivia smiled. "How nice."

We watched as the waiters came outside. They made their way toward our table, one of them holding in his hands a small, chocolate-covered cake on which birthday candles flickered. They stood at our table and continued to sing.

"Happy birthday, Amy," Olivia giggled, her eyes sparkling.

The cake was placed reverently in front of me and each leaned over and kissed me on the cheek. I was mortified but delighted.

When they had stopped singing the whole restaurant clapped and said "*Buon compleanno.*"

"They're all wishing you a happy birthday," Olivia explained.

"Thanks, Olivia," I smiled, when the commotion had stopped. I was embarrassed but delighted. "Now who would like cake?"

Chapter 27

"I don't know what to wear," I moaned. I was standing in our bedroom in my underwear, a growing pile of discarded clothes on my bed. We were back at the apartment and Beth was sitting on the other bed, watching me. It had taken about ten minutes for her to get dressed, fix her hair and put on some make-up.

Beth, Olivia and Lucia still refused to tell me where we were eating. We were meeting Flavio and Emilio afterward, although we couldn't tell Lucia and Pat.

Just before leaving the restaurant earlier, Emilio had kissed my cheek and said "Until later, bella Amy." And I hated to admit it but I was really looking forward to seeing him again. I kicked myself for not agreeing to meet him earlier in the week.

"How about your red dress?" Beth suggested. We'd already ruled out trousers.

I held it up in front of me and stared at my reflection in the full-length mirror. "I don't think so. It's too long."

"The turquoise then," she said.

I pulled it out of the large, white wardrobe. Another dress caught my eye. "What about this one?" I held a white dress up for her attention.

"How many dresses did you bring?" she asked in amusement.

"It's best to be prepared," I said. I stepped into the white dress and looked critically in the mirror.

"I prefer the turquoise," Beth said. "That one's a bit . . . boring."

"Thanks," I said, sarcastically.

"You want me to be honest, don't you," she replied.

"I suppose," I said doubtfully. I tried on the turquoise lycra dress. It clung to every lump and bump and made me feel very self-conscious. "I look fat in this," I said, twisting my head to look at my backside.

"No, you don't," Beth sighed.

"It's hopeless," I cried, flopping down on the bed on top of my rejected outfits. "I've nothing to wear."

Beth was well used to my histrionics. "Why don't you wear this? I'll find something else," she gestured at the black dress she was wearing.

"I couldn't," I stammered. I loved the dress, it was one of Louise's. Perfectly cut in black linen, it was a dream to wear—I knew 'cos I'd borrowed it more than once.

"Go on," Beth cajoled, unzipping it. "I don't mind. It's a good excuse to wear my new Armani top."

"Are you sure?" I asked.

She handed the dress to me. "Yes. If you'll let me borrow your black trousers."

I put her dress on. It was still slightly warm from her body heat. It looked great. I threw a dark pink cardigan over my shoulders and slipped my feet into my dark pink mules. "What do you think?" I asked her.

"Stunning," she smiled.

"You look great too," I said. Her new purchase shimmered in the light. "That top is beautiful."

There was a gentle knock at the door. Olivia popped her head in. "Are you ready?" she asked.

"Nearly," I replied.

"Papa's home," she explained. "We'll be going in a few minutes."

"Are you going to tell me where?" I said.

"You never give up!" Olivia asked. "You'll find out soon enough." She looked at me carefully. "I love the dress, Amy. It really suits you."

"Thanks," I smiled. "It's Beth's."

Minutes later we were all piling into Pat's car. I felt like a child being taken on a trip by Mum and Dad. It was a warm evening and Pat opened the sunroof to let some air in.

"You all look beautiful," he smiled. "I'm a lucky man." Olivia and Lucia had also dressed up for the occasion—Olivia in a tiny white top and matching skirt and her mother in an elegant navy linen dress with a cut-away back.

We drove toward the city and Pat parked the car and insisted on holding the doors while we all got out.

"We're nearly there," he assured me, looking with concern at my kitten heels. "Just around the corner."

It was nearly eight o'clock and the light had faded, leaving the sky a dusky dark blue. As we walked through the small twisting streets, I could hear the strains of music coming from the near distance.

"This way," Pat said, leading us around an old building.

As we walked around the building, Beth and I went ahead. And before us was one of the most spectacular sights I'd ever seen. I caught my breath.

"Wow!" Beth exclaimed.

We had stepped into a wonderland of huge, artificially-lit fountains which threw white water into the sky, a long *piazza* of monumental buildings, churches and buzzing restaurants, ice-cream parlors and cafés. There were people everywhere, tourists, street entertainers—mime-artists, puppeteers, singers, actors, and all kinds of Italians, young and old, enjoying themselves. It was quite a sight.

Pat led us through the throngs. He stopped outside a restaurant about halfway down the piazza.

"Here we are," he smiled. "The *Navona*. One of our favorite places to eat."

The waiter led us to our outside table. There was a large outside brazier to keep the chill out of the air and above our heads was a white cotton umbrella. Tiny pink roses grew on a trellis over the door of the restaurant. It was heavenly.

"It's lovely," Beth said, smiling. A mime artist was entertaining the crowds and the diners just in front of us.

The waiter handed out menus and Lucia ordered the wine.

"Red and white, I think," she smiled. "And water for Olivia."

"Mamma," Olivia complained.

"Maybe one glass of wine," her mother said kindly.

There were so many delicious dishes on the menu it was hard to choose. Eventually, with the help of Olivia, I decided on suppli di rosa, fried rice croquettes stuffed with cheese, and spaghetti alla carbonara.

As we waited for our food we watched the mime artist.

"What did you see today?" Pat asked, munching on some crispy bread-sticks.

"The Colosseum," Beth said. "It was amazing."

"Tomorrow we'll visit St. Peter's," Pat smiled. "It's a pity you don't have more time. There's so much more to see."

"How long have you lived in Rome, Pat?" I asked.

He thought for a second. "Let's see, Olivia's seventeen and we moved here when she was one. We'd been living with Lucia's parents just outside Naples. So nearly sixteen years."

"Pat moved over when he was nineteen to be with me," Lucia smiled, squeezing his arm. "He couldn't live without me."

"I never thought I'd end up living here," Pat said. "But now I wouldn't live anywhere else. I love it."

The waiter arrived with the starters. We tucked in with relish.

"What's that?" I asked Beth, who was licking her lips.

"Focaccia," she replied, "with olives and tomato. It's delicious, try some."

I pulled off a piece, covering my fingers in warm olive oil. She was right, it was delicious. "Try one of these," I said, cutting one of my rice balls in half, spearing the half with my fork and placing it on her plate.

"Thanks," she said.

"How are the antipasti?" Lucia asked.

Beth looked at me quizzically. "The starters are great, thanks," I replied.

We sipped our wine and listened to a young man singing to a guitar. He was sitting on the side of the main fountain, right under one of Bernini's river sculptures.

"What's he singing?" Beth asked. "It sounds familiar."

"It's called 'Nel Blu Dipinto di Blu,' " he said. "Which means 'In the Blue Painted in Blue'—not a very catchy title. Most people call it 'Volare.' "

"It's lovely," I smiled. I looked at the singer. He looked very like Flavio.

The singer then launched into "That's Amore." Olivia kicked me under the table and winked.

As Pat and Lucia ordered more wine, Olivia whispered "It's Flavio. He sings here some nights to make money. Emilio will be here later too."

I smiled. And Olivia was proved right. Halfway through eating our main courses, Flavio was joined by his brother and they launched into a version of Chris De Burgh's "Lady in Red." Emilio was an excellent singer, even if his choice of music was a little suspect. "Take My Breath Away" was next, followed by several Frank Sinatra croons.

"Is it OK if Olivia shows us around later?" I asked, after we ordered ice cream or *il gelato* all around. "I promise we won't keep her up too late."

"Well, I'm not sure . . ." Pat began.

"*Papa,*" Olivia interrupted, "it's their last night. Please? I have my phone and I can book a taxi on your company's account."

Pat smiled despite himself. "Oh, you can, can you?"

Olivia grinned at her father. "You know it's the only way to get a cab in this city, Papa."

"I suppose it would be all right," Pat began.

"They're big girls," Lucia assured her husband. "They'll be fine. There's no need to worry."

"You're right," Pat said. "But home before one, Olivia. Understand."

"Yes, Papa," she smiled, delighted with herself. "I promise."

Later, as we said our goodbyes, Pat still looked a little apprehensive. It was obvious that Olivia was his little princess and he was very protective of her. I felt a little guilty that we were hoodwinking him and Lucia. But Flavio was a nice young man and Emilio . . . Emilio was also a nice young man, very nice indeed.

The two brothers were still singing by the fountain and we made our way over. They broke into another rendition of "That's Amore," Flavio getting down on one knee, holding Olivia's hand and gazing up at her.

Beth and I laughed. Olivia was blushing furiously but enjoying her boyfriend's attention. As he finished the song the crowd clapped and cheered. Coins jingled into Flavio's open guitar case.

We listened to the boys for almost an hour. Now and again one of them would sing alone and the other would come and talk to us, taking a cigarette break at the same time.

"What do you think?" Emilio asked on one such break. "As good as U2?"

"Better," I stated. "Much more romantic." The wine was beginning to go to my head.

"I will sing a song for you next, my bella Amy," he promised, taking one long last drag from his cigarette. He kissed me on the cheek and returned to Flavio.

"The next song," Emilio told the crowd, "is for a beautiful Irish girl. *Buon compleanno*, Amy." They began to strum their guitars and the opening strains of U2's "With or Without You" rang out.

Beth turned toward me. "It's your favorite song," she smiled. "Did you ask him to play it?"

"No," I whispered back. "No, I didn't."

Beth put her arm around my shoulder and we swayed together to the music.

Olivia joined in. Soon other voices from the crowd did too.

I looked around me. Lots of happy, smiling faces enjoying the music. Emilio winked at me and blew a kiss when the song had finished. I couldn't remember ever feeling quite so relaxed and content.

The boys had to play two "encores" before the crowd would let them stop. When their audience had finally dispersed we approached them.

"That was amazing," Olivia smiled. "You're going to be a big star, Flavio."

He kissed her on the forehead. "Thank you, Olivia," he said genuinely.

"I think she's right," I smiled. "You were both brilliant." I turned to Emilio. "Thanks for the U2 song."

"*Niente,*" he said, grinning. "Would you like to go for a walk, Amy? There's something I'd like to show you."

Oh yeah? I thought to myself cynically.

"Well?" he asked, cocking his head to one side. "Will you come?"

I looked at Beth. She shrugged and smiled. "Go," she said. "I'll stay with Olivia and see she gets home OK."

"And I'll look after both of these beautiful girls," Flavio promised.

"*Benissimo,*" Emilio smiled, offering me his arm. "This way, Amy."

I put my arm in his and let him lead me away.

"See you later," I called to the others, but they were already locked in conversation. Flavio had an arm around each of the girls. He was in his element.

Emilio's guitar was slung over his back and it bumped gently against me as we walked.

"Where are we going?" I asked nervously. My feet were killing me.

"You'll see," he said. "It's only around the corner."

We walked for a few minutes talking about Flavio and Emilio's band and their hopes of breaking into the music scene in Rome. The road became steeper and we took it slowly, Emilio pulling me along.

"Come on," he encouraged. "We're nearly there."

"It better be worth it," I said.

"It will be," he said, his eyes twinkling. He stoppd outside two large, pale-blue gates. "Here we are. We'll have to climb in, I think."

I looked at the high gates and surrounding railings. "You're joking."

"Don't worry. It's easy," he assured me. He swung the guitar off his back and hung it carefully over the railings, dangling down on the far side. He then placed one foot firmly in the grid of the railings beside the gate and hauled himself up. He straddled the railings— precariously as there were long spikes along the top.

"Careful," I said in alarm.

"It's fine," he smiled. "Now put your foot there and give me your arm." He pointed to the side of the gate where there was a flat horizontal bar.

I took a deep breath and did as he said. He grabbed my waist.

"You'll have to lift up your skirt," he grinned, "or you might rip it."

Unfortunately he was right. Beth wouldn't be too pleased if I ruined her good dress. I hitched it up.

"That's better," he said. "Now move your other foot over the railings here." He helped me as I swung my leg over the top of the railings. "Now put your other foot here and lean on me." I moved my other foot over and placed it safely over the spikes. I was now safe.

"Well done," he congratulated me. "Now wait and I'll lift you down." He jumped down onto the grass and held out his arms to help me. I fell into them gratefully. He held me against him and I breathed in his warm, musky scent.

I looked up and smiled. "Thank you," I whispered.

"*Fa niente,*" he whispered, gazing into my eyes. My stomach lurched. I was surprisingly nervous. I knew he liked me and I wanted him to kiss me. But something was holding me back.

He seemed to sense my unease and loosened his embrace. "Follow me," he said, leading me along a rough, pebbled path. We were in a small park which was long and narrow and led toward a waist-high wall. As we approached the wall I began to see why he had brought me here.

Over the wall, stretched out in front of us as far as the eye could see were hundreds and hundreds of lights. We were on top of a hill looking down on the city which sparkled and twinkled beneath us. It was quite a sight.

"It's beautiful," I said, beaming.

"It's my favorite place," Emilio explained, "especially at night. I often come here and just watch the lights."

"I can see why," I said. He put his arm gently around my shoulder and drew me toward him.

"May I kiss you, Amy?" he asked softly.

"Yes," I whispered, my stomach knotting in anticipation.

He brushed my hair off my face and kissed my forehead. Then he kissed my eyelids, delicate, butterfly kisses and made his way down my face, kissing the tip of my nose. My mouth was crying out for him and I closed my eyes and sighed happily. I felt his cool, firm lips on mine and we kissed slowly, savoring the sensation. Our lips and tongues moved together, exploring each other's mouths. He nipped my top lip playfully and whispered *"Amy bella"* in my ear. He nuzzled my neck and kissed my earlobes.

After what seemed like a delicious eternity he pulled back. "Can I sing for you?" he asked, smiling.

"Yes," I smiled shyly back.

He began strumming the guitar softly. I looked out over Rome and listened as Emilio played Italian love songs. It was the perfect end to a perfect birthday.

We didn't talk much for the rest of the evening. We kissed and he sang and played his guitar.

Emilio was the perfect gentleman and just after one o'clock he insisted on bringing me back to the apartment on the back of his scooter which he had left at the Piazza Navona.

"I must bring you home now or Olivia's father will worry," he smiled as I protested half-heartedly. "Flavio tells me Pat worries a lot."

"You're right," I sighed. "I'd better go back."

He pulled a spare helmet out from under the seat of the silver Vespa and handed it to me.

"To keep you safe," he smiled. He pulled his own helmet over his dark hair and smiled broadly at me. "I won't go too fast, I promise."

I hopped on the back and he started the engine. It purred loudly and soon we were zipping along the Roman backstreets. The fresh, invigorating air brushed past my face. I clung onto Emilio, my arms wrapped tightly around his waist.

All too soon we chugged up the familiar road to Pat and Lucia's apartment.

"Come on, *piccola*," Emilio encouraged his Vespa which didn't seem to like inclines. He pulled up outside the apartment. "Home," he smiled, hopping off the scooter and helping me down. He flicked the stand and the scooter stood by itself. He held me against his chest and kissed me firmly.

"It's been a wonderful night," he said. "I will never forget you, Amy. If only you lived in Rome . . ." he sighed.

I smiled. I knew it was probably just a line but it was nice to hear anyway. "I know," I said. "But it's been lovely. Thank you." We kissed for several more minutes. The stars were shining in the sky above us and in the distance I could hear the sounds of the city.

It had been a magical night. I didn't want it to end. Eventually I pulled away from him. "I'll have to go now. I'm sorry. Bye."

He smiled and blew me a kiss as I waved from the doorstep. Then I realized I'd have to wake the family to get in. Oops.

I rang the bell nervously. Olivia answered the door smiling. "We've just got in," she said. "We told Papa that you were in the garden, looking at the stars."

"Did he believe you?" I asked.

"I'm not sure." Olivia waved at Emilio. *"Ciao, Emilio,"* she said. He started up his scooter and rode away.

I watched his back disappear down the road.

Pat's voice startled us. "What are you two doing?" he asked sleepily.

"Watching the stars," I lied. "It's a beautiful night."

He looked out. "It certainly is," he said. "Now I'm going back to bed!"

Chapter 28

The next day Lucia and Pat brought us to St. Peter's. They'd wanted us to visit it last. Beth and I were both tired and a little hungover but we wanted to make the most of our last full day in Rome. Olivia had managed to wangle her way out of it and planned to meet Flavio in town. I told her to say "hi" to Emilio.

"What happened last night?" Beth had asked as we dressed that morning. "You should have woken me up."

"You were sleeping like a baby," I smiled. "It seemed cruel."

"Well, go on," Beth cajoled. "What's Emilio like?"

"You've met him," I stalled. "You know him too."

"But not intimately," Beth laughed.

I raised my eyebrows. "It wasn't like that," I assured her. "He was a real gentleman, very sweet. We walked to this park at the top of a hill. It was beautiful, Beth. You could see the whole of Rome from there, all lit up like fairyland."

"Sounds romantic," Beth said. "Did you kiss him?"

"Of course I did," I smiled. "He's a good-looking guy and I'm on my holidays. I'm not that stupid!"

Beth laughed. "It's nice that he's Flavio's brother. It makes him sort of safe, if you know what I mean. You couldn't go for a walk with an Italian man you'd just met otherwise. It wouldn't be right."

I smiled. "You're always so practical, Beth. But I suppose you have a point."

"Are you going to keep in touch?" Beth asked.

"No, I wouldn't think so," I sighed. "He's a lot younger than me and, to be honest, I much prefer Irish guys. The Italians are too good-looking. It makes me nervous."

"Nervous?" Beth asked.

"You know," I began to explain. "They might go off with someone else or decide I didn't tan quickly enough."

"You're talking rubbish," Beth giggled. "What about English men then? They tend to equal Irish men in the non-good-looking stakes." I knew she was referring to Steve.

"I'm sure they'd all be delighted to hear you say that," I laughed. I tried to change the subject. "Will we give Lucia and Pat their present today or tomorrow?" I asked. "And we should get Olivia a present too."

Beth thought for a second. "Tomorrow morning, I think. I bought a necklace for Stella but I know Olivia would love it. Why don't we give her that and I'll buy Stella some perfume at the airport?"

"Sounds good," I replied.

"You'll see why I told you to leave St. Peter's till last when you step inside," Pat said as we approached the cathedral. "The sheer scale of it is out of this world."

Lucia smiled. "Pat loves St. Peter's. He'll give you all the statistics if you let him." She put on her best tour-guide voice. "The dome is one hundred and ten meters high. It was designed by Michaelangelo, but he died before it was completed."

"Stop making fun of me," Pat laughed. "Lucia's right, I do tend to bore her and Olivia with the details. The dome is one hundred and thirty-six meters wide, by the way."

Beth laughed. "Don't worry. I'm used to it. Dad's the same. He just loves all those details."

We made our way up the steps of the huge church and walked past the black-suited security guards.

"They stop anyone whose shoulders aren't covered," Pat explained. "Or anyone in shorts."

"Heavens!" Beth exclaimed as we stood just inside the doorway. "It's massive. I had no idea."

"This is the Pietà that was damaged in 1972," Pat explained. "Some hooligan took a hammer to it and now it's kept behind glass."

"It's by Michelangelo too," Lucia added.

"Are you girls on for a bit of a climb?" Pat asked. "The view from the top of the dome is amazing."

"How many steps?" I inquired, trying to sound casual.

"Five hundred and thirty-seven," Pat smiled. "But we'll take it slowly."

He was right, the view from the top was spectacular. But getting up there wasn't.

"Think of it as penance," Lucia said as we puffed and panted our way up each step. The walls and the steps got narrower and narrower as we ascended. I felt distinctly light-headed when we reached the top.

Stretched out in front of us was the whole city.

"Over there are the Vatican gardens," Pat explained, pointing to an expanse of green. Small fountains were surrounded by perfectly kept hedges, trees and shrubs.

"The colors of the buildings are so different from Ireland," Beth commented. "We're so used to gray, and here they are all warm reds or oranges, even the roofs."

"Over there is the Vatican Museum and the Sistine Chapel," Pat continued. "The queues for the chapel are unbelievable. You can be waiting for more than three hours to get in."

"I think we'll give it a miss then," Beth said. "I hate queuing. I have no patience. Unless Amy wants to go."

"No," I said. "I hate queuing too. I'd prefer not to if that's OK. Life's too short. We can see them next time we're here. I'm definitely coming back."

"Me too!" Beth exclaimed.

"But there is something you must do," Lucia said firmly. "If you dare."

"What's that?" Beth asked with interest.

" 'Bocca della Verità,' " Lucia said cryptically.

"Mouth of something," I translated. My Italian was a little sketchy.

"You'll see," Pat smiled.

* * *

"Are you sure you want to go through with this?" I asked Beth in a serious voice. "You know it's supposed to bite off the hand of liars?"

We stood in front of the huge stone medallion, the "Bocca della Verità," or mouth of truth. It was in the portico entrance of a small church and it was the sculpture we both knew from the Audrey Hepburn and Gregory Peck film.

Pat and Lucia were standing behind us.

"Go on, Beth," Pat encouraged. "We can always sew it back on."

Beth scrunched up her eyes tightly and shoved her hand into the mouth.

"*Phew!*" she said, drawing it out quickly. "Now you, Amy."

I felt a little nervous. I knew it was only an ancient superstition, but still. I needed my hands, both of them. I shook myself, I was being silly. I took a deep breath and plunged my hand into the gap. The mouth was cool and worn smooth from the millions of hands which had rubbed past its lips. I pulled it out again.

"Well done, girls," Lucia smiled. Pat put his arm around his wife and we all walked back to his car.

"They're a lovely couple," I whispered, as they walked on ahead.

"I know," Beth replied. "I hope Tony and I are as happy together."

"Of course you will be," I assured her. "Sure, aren't you happy now?"

"Yes, I know," Beth said, "but they say marriage changes everything."

"Only if you let it," I replied.

"I guess you're right," Beth smiled. "I guess I'm just nervous about the whole thing."

"Marriage?" I asked.

"Marriage, the wedding, the future . . ." Beth sighed. "It's a big step."

"Beth," I said gently, "you and Tony were meant for each other. He's a great guy and he makes you happy. How long have we known each other?"

"Forever," Beth replied.

"Exactly. I know you inside out. And I genuinely think that Tony is perfect for you. So stop worrying."

"Thanks," Beth smiled gratefully.

"You're more than welcome," I smiled and gave her a little hug. "And I for one am really looking forward to the wedding," I lied. "It's all going to be perfect."

"I hope so," Beth said.

Getting up at seven AM on Sunday morning to catch our flight was a killer. Luckily we'd all had an early night as exhaustion had started to finally kick in after the previous busy day.

We'd spent all week lying in, pottering around the house in the morning, relaxing and taking our time. It would be hard to get back to life in the real world. At breakfast we gave Lucia and Pat a small marble statue, a copy of a Bernini, an Italian sculptor whom they both admired, for the garden.

"Oh, you shouldn't have," Lucia said, unwrapping the white tissue from around the statue. We were sitting at the kitchen table for our last breakfast in Rome. "It's perfect."

"You've been so kind to us," Beth said. "We've had a lovely time."

"We've enjoyed having you," Pat smiled. "And Olivia has too." Olivia was still in bed, her door ajar. Moments later she popped her head around the door. Her hair was ruffled and she smiled sleepily. "Bye, Beth. Bye, Amy," she kissed us both on the cheek. "Safe trip home."

We handed her the present. She opened it eagerly.

"It's beautiful!" she exclaimed, placing the necklace around her slender neck. The silver glistened against her sallow skin. She fastened the clasp expertly. "What do you think, Papa?" she asked.

"*Bellissima,*" Pat said.

Olivia kissed us both again. "It's been fun. I really enjoyed having you both here." There was a twinkle in her eye. As she kissed me she whispered in my ear. "Emilio said he had a wonderful night and to thank you, his beautiful Irish girl."

I smiled to myself. Emilio—what a nice memory.

* * *

Pat drove us to the airport. I stared listlessly out the window while he and Beth talked about Tony's new venture. I really didn't want to leave. We'd had such a chilled-out time. Meeting Emilio had been an added bonus but I knew we wouldn't keep in touch. I hadn't even asked him for his address or number. I was happy to leave it as a glowing Roman memory.

Now it was home to the same old things—to work, to all Suzi's wedding preparations and to Steve. He'd been lingering at the back of my mind all week. Being back in Dublin meant that I'd have to face him again. I'd been so rude and irrational and he deserved an explanation. I wondered if I was brave enough to contact him. Or if he'd even talk to me.

Arriving in Dublin airport, I felt deflated. Tony was waiting in the Arrivals Hall and he'd brought Beth a huge bunch of stargazer lilies, her favorite flowers.

He took my bags off me, slung them onto the luggage trolley and put his arm around Beth's shoulders.

"How are you, Amy?" he asked kindly. "Did you have a nice holiday?"

"Great," I smiled. "Rome is amazing. I definitely want to go back."

"Did Beth behave herself?" Tony asked, only half joking.

"Of course," I smiled. "There was a bit of an incident with a bridegroom but . . ."

"Amy!" Beth interrupted. "That was you!"

"That's your story," I laughed. Beth glared at me. "OK, OK, I admit it—it was me, Tony."

"Sounds interesting," Tony said, relieved. "You can tell me all about it in the car."

"I'd be happy to," I said. "And about Beth and the waiter at my birthday dinner."

Beth scowled at me again.

Tony laughed. "I presume that's another joke," he said uncertainly. "You're certainly in flying form, Amy."

"Um," Beth muttered.

We made our way to the car and Tony slung our bags into the

boot. Men did have their uses after all—slinging bags, not to mention putting out the bins and cutting the grass.

As we drove toward Dun Laoghaire Beth and I told Tony all about Rome—the fountains, the shops, the churches and the food.

"Did you have a good birthday?" Tony asked as we crossed the East-Link Bridge.

"Yes!" I exclaimed. "It was perfect. From start to finish."

"Especially finish," Beth smiled.

Tony looked at me quizzically.

I was more than happy to tell all. "We went to the Colosseum during the day and then to a café and these waiters sang 'Happy Birthday' to me in Italian."

Tony laughed. "You wouldn't get Irish waiters doing that."

"Too right," I said. "We all went out for dinner in the evening in the Piazza Navona and were serenaded by two Italian guys. And then I went for a walk with one of them who showed me Rome by night."

Tony smiled. "Sounds very romantic. And where were you, Beth? I hope you weren't with the other singer."

"No," Beth smiled. "He's Olivia's boyfriend. We all went for a wander around the Piazza and watched the world go by. It was a lovely evening."

Tony whistled. "It's been cold and wet all week. You didn't miss much."

"Did you get much work done?" Beth asked.

"Yeah, loads," Tony assured her. "In fact, I think we may be almost ready to start taking on clients."

"I thought you were going to wait till after the wedding?" Beth asked, a little worried. "We have a lot to organize still—the flowers, the seating plans . . ."

"Beth," Tony interrupted, "once word gets out about what Jed and I are doing we'll lose our jobs. And we can't afford to live on air. If and when it happens, we'll have to move fast."

Beth went silent for a second. "I see," she said. "We'll talk about it later." She stared out the window.

Poor Beth. She had been looking forward to finishing all the wedding plans with Tony's help. Now it looked as if she'd have to bear the brunt of it herself.

I tried to lighten the mood. "I hear Jed's your best man," I said.

"That's right," Tony said carefully.

He obviously hadn't forgotten my behavior at the New Year's party. Oops. Another touchy subject. And as it was my fault he couldn't have Jack, who he'd really wanted, I'm sure I wasn't exactly Tony's favorite person at the moment. "I met Stella, Tony, and we chose our bridesmaids' dresses," I continued, trying to steer myself onto safer ground. "She's great. We're going to have a laugh at the wedding."

"Beth said something about it, all right," Tony said. "What are the dresses like?"

"They're light blue, with heavy lace over lycra," I explained.

"Lycra?" Tony asked. "Is that not the tight, swimsuit material?"

Beth turned to look at me and winked. "The dresses are great, Tony. I went in to see them with Stella. Really tight, with no back and tiny, shoe-string straps. And low-cut at the front. You'll love them."

Tony was bemused. "Are you sure they're suitable, love? Don't bridesmaids usually wear something a little more . . . um . . . traditional?"

"We thought we'd go for something different—a little more racy," I said, enjoying winding Tony up. Wait till you see Beth's red dress. Talk about sexy!"

Tony's eyes widened. "Are you serious?" he asked in a mixture of shock and delight.

Beth laughed. "Don't mind her, Tony. It's not red. But it is very sexy."

"I'm looking forward to it," Tony said, smiling.

Beth asked Tony about the West Cork acccommodation plans. I half-listened. There was a Sunday newspaper on the back seat and I flicked through the Arts supplement. On the Books Review page a familiar face caught my eye. It was Steve. The article was entitled *My Writing Day.* I began to read. "*At the moment, with a new Henry book out and the associated promotional work involved, I am doing* very little actual writing. I recently spent a whole weekend in 'The Wonderland Bookshop' signing copies of the new book and meeting young readers. It was very enjoyable but exhausting . . ." He went on to talk about his new work—a picture-book about a little mouse called Ernie which would be illustrated by Cath Brennan, a young and upcoming Irish artist.

So he'd asked someone else to illustrate his picture book. I can't say I was surprised. I stared at the picture of Steve. It was a professional black and white photograph, very tasteful. Steve stared out, a wry smile playing on his lips. I wondered what was going through his mind as the photographer was snapping away. He looked like he'd been thinking—"Get me out of here!"

I folded up the paper and thought about Steve. I really would have to ring him.

Chapter 29

"Here we are, Amy," Tony said, pulling up outside my house.

"Thanks," I smiled half-heartedly. I reluctantly stepped out of the car, lifting out one of my bags and plonking it on the pavement beside me. Tony lifted my heavy red suitcase out of the boot.

"I'll bring this in for you," he said kindly. Beth got out of the car. She put her arms around me. "It's a bit of an anti-climax being home, isn't it?" she asked. "I'll miss all the late mornings and the pasta."

"I know," I agreed. "It's going to be a killer going back to work tomorrow. But we have the hen next weekend—that'll be a good laugh."

"Yes," Beth smiled uncertainly. I looked at her carefully.

"What's up?"

"I just hope it doesn't get a little out of hand," she explained. "Suzi's friends can be a bit wild."

"Don't you worry," I assured her, mentally crossing my fingers. "I'll take care of you, I promise."

Tony was waiting for us on the doorstep.

"I'll walk you to the door," Beth said.

Tony rang the doorbell and in a few seconds I saw Suzi's shadowy figure approach through the tinted glass. She flung open the door.

"Amy! Welcome home. Did you have a good holiday?" she asked, hugging me warmly.

"Yes, thanks," I grinned. Suzi grabbed the bag I was carrying and bustled me into the hall.

"You look brilliant. Mum and Dad are in the kitchen waiting for you. Go on down," she commanded. "They'd love to see you, Beth. Why don't you and Tony pop down too?"

"Sure," Beth smiled. She turned toward Tony. "Is that OK, love?"

"Of course," Tony replied.

I began to get a little suspicious as I heard loud female laughter coming from the kitchen. Mum's laugh was gentler and less raucous. In fact, it sounded a lot like Eva. I opened the door gingerly.

"Happy birthday!" Dad shouted as I walked into the room. I looked around. Sitting around the table were Mum, Dad, Eva, Matt and Judy, all grinning widely. The table was decorated with a red paper tablecloth with Happy Birthday emblazoned on it in huge yellow letters. There were balloons hanging from the light-fittings, streamers wall to wall and a pile of wrapped presents in the center of the table.

I laughed. "What are you all like?" I asked. I was embarrassed but strangely touched.

"You didn't think we'd forget to celebrate your birthday?" Mum asked. "Sit here, Amy. And over here, Beth and Tony."

"Beth," I spluttered, "did you know about this?"

"Yes," she said, sheepishly. "Your Mum made me promise not to say anything."

"I'll kill you," I hissed.

"Amy," Mum interrupted, "would you like to open your presents while I serve? Frank, can you carve?"

Suzi jumped up with a bottle of wine in each hand. "I'll pour the wine," she offered, splashing generous amounts into the newcomers' glasses. She winked at me as she filled my glass to the very brim.

Eva pulled her present out of the bundle and handed it to me. It was a slightly plump envelope. More M&S vouchers, I figured.

"Happy birthday, Amy," she smiled. "You look so well. Rome must have agreed with you."

"Thanks, Eva," I said, accepting her present. "You're right, I loved Rome."

"I was there in my twenties," Judy joined in. "Such a beautiful city. Did you see the Trevi Fountain? Isn't it spectacular?"

"Sure is," Beth agreed.

I pulled a teddy-bear card out of the envelope and opened it. Inside was a gift voucher for Susan Bunting's exclusive lingerie shop on Dawson Street.

"Thanks, Eva," I grinned. "I've always wanted some La Perla and maybe now I'll be able to get it." I jumped up and planted a kiss on her cheek.

She blushed. "I thought I'd get you something different. It is your thirtieth after all."

"Help yourselves to dips while you're waiting," Mum said, plonking two large plates at either end of the table. Colorful strips of red and yellow peppers, carrots and celery were arranged around small terracotta bowls of garlic and herb cheese dip. We tucked in eagerly, loading the vegetables with as much of the high cholesterol dip as gravity allowed.

Judy passed me another wrapped present and I opened it eagerly. It was a set of Lancôme beauty products—anti-aging cream, fine-line cream for around the eyes and firming cream for the thighs. I wasn't sure whether to be insulted or delighted.

"Thanks, Judy," I smiled, kissing my fingers and blowing the kiss across the table.

Lynn had dropped in a cream silk dressing-gown; Suzi and Matt had given me a silver bracelet and Mum and Dad a gift voucher for Station House Beauty and Health Farm. I was overwhelmed. They had all put so much thought into my presents.

"Thanks, everyone," I smiled, lifting my presents off the table and putting them on top of the kitchen counter.

Mum and Dad passed out plates laden with chicken.

"Help yourselves to vegetables," she said. "There's gravy and butter in the middle of the table."

"This is delicious, Denise," Matt said, loading his fork with potato, carrots and chicken.

Mum smiled. "Thanks, Matt. Anyone for extra stuffing?" Matt and Tony nodded eagerly.

"How does it feel being thirty?" Suzi asked me.

I glared at her.

"Amy's still only twenty-eight," Dad interjected. "Didn't you know?"

"Sorry," Suzi said to me, contrite. "I was only slagging you."

"I know," I muttered. "And that smile will be on the other side of your face in a few years."

"Tell us about St. Peter's," Mum said hastily.

We talked about Rome and Italy for the remainder of the lunch. It was a safe subject and no one wanted to upset me.

"How are the plans for next weekend?" Judy asked as Dad and Suzi cleared away the plates.

"Good," Suzi grinned, a dangerous glint in her eyes. "It's going to be a crazy few days."

I glanced at Beth whose eyes were getting wider.

"Any male strippers?" Eva giggled.

"No," Suzi said. Beth looked relieved. "But we've lots of other things planned."

"I thought the bridesmaid was supposed to organize the hen?" Dad asked, confused.

"I'm helping," I assured him. "Suzi wanted to organize some of it herself," I explained.

"So what's planned?" Matt asked nervously.

"That would be telling," Suzi winked at him.

Tony shifted nervously in his seat. Beth turned to him and smiled reassuringly.

"And what do you have planned, Matt?" Dad asked him.

"Just a few drinks with the Clontarf lads," he smiled. "A quiet night really."

I snorted. "Quiet! The Clontarf rugby team, I don't think so! How about you, Tony?"

"I'm off to Amsterdam with the lads the weekend after next," he smiled. "Jed organized it."

"Is he your best man?" Suzi asked feigning innocence.

"Yes."

"Amy, that means you have to kiss Jed. It's traditional—bridesmaid and best man."

Her comment was met with stony silence as I glared at her. She knew all about New Year's Eve—I'd told her myself.

Beth stepped in. "Maybe Stella will take to Jed, you never know," she said diplomatically. "What are you wearing to Suzi's wedding, Eva?"

Eva and Judy described their planned outfits while I kicked Suzi under the table. "I'll kill you," I hissed under my breath.

"Sorry," she mouthed back. "Couldn't resist it."

"Um," I muttered darkly. I was dreading the whole bridesmaid thing enough without the whole world knowing myself and Jed's short and ignominious history.

Mum carried over an ice-cream cake covered in tiny pink candles. "Happy birthday, love," she smiled, placing it in front of me.

"Happy birthday to you," the table sang as I cringed. *"Happy birthday to you, Happy birthday, dear Amy, Happy birthday to you."*

I felt six years old. I blew out the candles and made a wish. And sad female that I was, before I could stop myself I wished for a boyfriend. Talk about wasting your wishes.

After lunch we retired to the sitting room. Judy and Eva interrogated Suzi about the hen but she was staying mum.

"There's some post for you," Mum said. "A few cards, I think. And Lynn dropped in a letter for you which had been sent to the shop." She handed me an assortment of envelopes—the usual clear-windowed bills, junk mail and two handwritten ones.

"Thanks," I smiled, putting the bills aside. I opened the first handwritten envelope which had a Canadian stamp. It was a card from "The Canadians" and a gift check. I smiled. I really was getting great presents this year. The other envelope, addressed to me at The Wonderland, had a British stamp. I pulled out a typed letter and began to read.

Marra International Press
2 Kew House
Moss Garden
London, SW2 9PE

16 March 2001

Dear Ms. O'Sullivan,

Steve Jones asked me to contact you regarding picture-book illus-
tration. We are always looking for new illustrators and would be
happy to put your portfolio on file. Steve tells me that you have
great talent and we are especially interested in young Irish au-
thors and illustrators for our children's list.

Please read the following guidelines regarding portfolios carefully.

Kind regards,
Serena Rudd
Children's Editor

I put the letter back in its envelope. Steve had contacted his publishers for me, after all my batty behavior. I didn't know what to
think. He'd found someone else to illustrate his own book—so he
obviously didn't want to work with me himself. But he'd told his
publishers that I had talent and he hadn't even seen my work. Apart
from windows and display bits and banners at The Wonderland, but
they hardly counted.

"Are you all right?" Beth asked, sitting down beside me. She nodded at the letter. "Bad news?"

"No, not exactly," I said. I handed her the letter. "Read it."

She scanned the letter and placed it back in the envelope. "But
that's brilliant. They want to see your work. Hey, you could be famous one day. My friend, the illustrator."

I winced. "You don't think I'm sending them anything, do you?"
I asked incredulously.

"Of course," Beth said. "Why ever not?"

"Because," I said slowly, "I'm not good enough."

Beth stared at me. "You've always been brilliant at art. Give it a try anyway. The worst that can happen is that they'll send it back."

"Maybe," I said doubtfully.

"And the *Den 2* sets have been amazing. RTE are hardly paying you if they don't like your work, are they?"

"I suppose not," I said reluctantly.

"Why don't you give it a go?" Beth encouraged. "Show Lynn some of your work and see what she says."

"No way!" I said emphatically.

"Why?" Beth asked gently.

"She'd be too honest," I explained, "and I don't think I could cope with that."

"Amy," Beth began, her face looking serious, "one day you'll wake up and regret not taking every opportunity you were offered. By then it may be too late. You have to seize the day."

I smiled. Beth was off on her *Dead Poets' Society* kick again. But perhaps she was right. Maybe I should take life by the reins and see what happened. Starting tomorrow.

I stood outside The Wonderland and stared. Lynn had changed the window in the last week—it now had a wedding theme. Lots of pink net, dolls dressed in tiny wedding dresses and books celebrating love and marriage. As if I hadn't been getting enough at home. I put my hand over my eyes and looked in through the rain-splattered glass on the door. Lynn was behind the till, the end of a biro in her mouth. I knocked on the door. She looked up and smiled.

"Hi, Amy," she said opening the door. "Come in out of the elements. How was your holiday?"

"Brilliant," I smiled. "What's with the window?" I stuck my umbrella in the stand beside the door and ran my fingers through my damp matted hair. I'd washed it that morning but the hairdryer was on the blink. So I was destined to have mad, windswept hair all day.

"Do you like it?" she asked, smiling. "It was that or yellow spring chicks," she explained. "I couldn't think of another spring theme."

"Right," I said noncommittally. "It's different anyway."

We walked upstairs and Lynn poured me a large mug of fresh coffee.

"Get this inside you," she said. "It's so wet and damp today. I hope the weather improves for your sister's wedding."

"It's not for a few weeks." I said, "Hopefully it will have cleared up by then. Has it been busy?"

"On and off," Lynn said. "There were a few big school orders last week and Saturday was manic. I hope you're ready to get stuck in. The picture-books are in dire need of some attention. Mrs. Potter from Blackrock National School cleared us out of Babette Coles."

"Lynn," I began. I was going to ask her if she would have a look at some of my illustrations but I chickened out.

"Yes?" she asked.

"Nothing," I said. "I'll get stuck into the picture-book order."

I brought up the ordering program on the computer and punched in the code for the picture-books—PICT. I winced as the screen brought up over two hundred titles, all of which had been sold and had gone out of stock since I'd gone away. I began to key in the re-order quantities, three copies of *Can't You Sleep, Little Bear!*, two of *Dogger,* five of *Princess Smartypants.* I continued down the screen until the order was finished. While I worked, Lynn served a few rain-dripping customers.

I jumped up from the desk at one stage to check how many of *The Grumpy Goldfish* were in stock. Walking toward the picture-book stand I had the sudden realization that I'd been doing the same thing every Monday for as long as I could remember. Ordering books on the computer, processing special customer requests and tidying the books—and it was time for a change. I loved the bookshop and I enjoyed working with Lynn but I needed more. And Beth was right—I had to grab the bull by the horns and try and make a go of illustration. I had the *Den 2* money to keep me going. And as I was living at home my costs were minimal.

And working at the bookshop left me open to bumping into Steve again—although, thinking about it, he wasn't likely to come in here again, not after . . . I tried to push him out of my mind, but it was hard when he was the bestselling children's author and every few phone calls were still about his bloody signed books.

On holidays I'd told myself I'd ring him, apologize and try to explain. But as the days went on it became harder and harder. I'd pretty much decided to just leave it at this stage. Put it down to experience, push him out of my mind.

I mulled over things all day. Lynn asked me several times if I was all right. I just smiled and nodded. I'm sure she put it down to post-holiday blues.

After lunch the phone rang. "Hi, Amy, it's Helen from the *Den*."

"Hi, Helen, how are things?"

"Good, thanks. Listen, I know this is a bit sudden but we've got a new children's arts and crafts show for the autumn and I was wondering would you be interested in doing some research for it?"

"Tell me more," I said cautiously. "What would it involve?"

"You'd be working with Darren Shaw, the presenter. Coming up with ideas for shows, making the props, buying the materials, that sort of thing."

"Sounds interesting. How much time is involved?" I asked.

"It would be pretty much full-time, I think," Helen said. "But you could do a lot of the work at home. You'd be on a short-term contract."

"Can I get back to you?" I asked. "I'll have to think about it."

"No problem," Helen said.

"What's the show called?" I asked.

"*Sticky Fingers*," Helen said. "Give me a ring in the next few days. Bye . . ."

I placed the phone back on the receiver and stared at it, biting the skin around my thumb.

"Everything all right?" Lynn asked.

"Fine, thanks," I said.

The afternoon dragged by. I couldn't get Helen's offer out of my mind. I was dying to get home and ring Beth. I needed advice on what to do. I knew it would be risky leaving work for a short-term contract. But it sounded fun, and I knew I could do it. At least I thought I could.

By the time I'd got home I wasn't so sure. I'd tried ringing Beth on the mobile on the way home but hers was powered off.

As I walked in the door Suzi came bounding down the stairs.

"Hi, Amy. Your bridesmaid's dress is ready. I'm going in on Thursday night to collect it. Do you want to come?"

I didn't really. I was hoping the dress would disappear into a puff of smoke at the last minute and I'd have to wear my jeans. "Yes, of course," I lied.

"Excellent. How was your first day back?"

"Fine," I murmured, picking up another mobile-phone bill from the hall table, where they seemed to breed. "See you later," I said, walking up the stairs toward my room, leaving Suzi standing alone in the hall.

"Oh," she said, disappointed. I could tell she wanted a chat but I wasn't in the mood.

I pushed open my bedroom door with my shoulder and sat down on the bed. I tried ringing Beth again. Her mobile was on this time but she wasn't answering it. I left a message and tried her house. No answer.

Suzi's head appeared around the door. She was brave. "Are you really OK? What's up?"

I sighed. I figured I might as well tell her. "I got a call at work today. Helen from RTE offered me a job doing research for a kid's show."

"That's great!" Suzi exclaimed.

"Maybe," I muttered. "I don't know what to do."

"Why?" Suzi asked. "Surely you're going to take it?"

I shrugged my shoulders.

"You'd be mad not to," Suzi said. "And Lynn would understand. In fact I'm sure she'd have you back if it didn't work out. Or you could work part-time for her, just in case."

"I suppose so," I said doubtfully. Maybe Lynn *would* keep my job open. I could always ask her.

"You should have more confidence in yourself," Suzi said. "You're great at art. I wish I had a quarter of your talent."

"Thanks," I said gratefully.

"So you'll take the new job?" she asked. Suzi wasn't one to give up.

"I'll think about it," I smiled.

"Good," she said. "Now I have to talk to you about the weekend. I thought we'd go into Ann Summers after picking up the bridesmaid's dress." She unfolded her costume plans for the weekend.

"What do you think?" she asked. "Is it too much?"

I grinned. "Not at all. It sounds good to me."

"Excellent!" she beamed. "I hope Beth won't mind."

"Don't worry about Beth," I smiled. "I think she'll surprise us all."

I talked to Beth that evening and you'd think herself and Suzi were in cahoots.

"I'm sure Lynn will understand," she assured me. "You've been working for her for years. I'm sure she'll hold your job open for you or let you work part-time or something."

"That's what Suzi said," I smiled. And thinking about it—they were both right.

Chapter 30

The following day I talked to Lynn about Helen's offer. She was scarily blasé about the whole thing.

"You've been a gem, Amy, but it may be time for you to move on," she'd said kindly. "But you know there's always a job here for you if you want it."

"Thanks," I said, genuinely touched.

"I'll ask Jess to work full-time during her holidays and we'll see where we are in September."

I rang Helen. She was delighted that I'd decided to join her team.

"That's cool, Amy," she gushed. "Welcome aboard. When can you start?"

"How about the middle of June?" I asked. The weddings would create havoc with work before then.

"Excellento," she said. "Let's have a meeting before that to sort out the details. I'll talk to Darren and get back to you. And can you start . . . say the fifteenth of June?"

"Perfect," I said. "Thanks, Helen."

Friday came all too quickly. Lynn had kindly given me a half-day as she knew Suzi's hen was in Arklow and we had a party planned for that evening.

Polly and Amber had arrived the previous evening and had terrified us with their plummy accents and designer clothes. They'd brought a huge suitcase and vanity bag each, crammed full of expensive, trendy clothes. They were clothes-obsessed, especially Polly, and insisted on showing myself and Suzi all their gear.

"These are my Manolo Blahniks," Polly purred, holding up a pair of shockingly skyscraper-high pink suede sandals.

"And this is Prada," Amber boasted, pulling out a glorious silk-chiffon dress in chocolate brown.

"I've seen one of the Corrs in that," I said, running the luxurious fabric through my fingers enviously.

"This skirt is fab," Suzi squealed, holding the shimmering silver and blue mermaid-like fabric against her.

"It's Clements Ribeiro," Amber said smugly.

"Last season," Polly added even more smugly.

"You're so lucky," Suzi said enviously. "I'd love some designer clothes."

"Honey," Polly crooned, "you'd look good in anything. When you have hips and thighs like mine you need expensive clothes."

I laughed. Polly was a riot. And she hadn't even had a drink yet.

Amber and Suzi went downstairs to make coffee. "How's work?" I asked Polly as she hung her clothes up in the spare room. Amber and Polly both worked for *Marie Claire* magazine, Polly as Fashion Editor and Amber as Health and Beauty Assistant. They were great fun and visited Ireland at least once a year, usually with their mum. Polly was small and pretty, with a rounded size-sixteen figure (which she never stopped moaning about), and long dark hair which was usually pulled back into some sort of top-knot and secured with the latest accessory—today's being a huge bright-pink silk lily. Amber was tall and blond, white blond—like the Swedish-looking Timotei girl off the ads, bitch.

They were both so painfully stylish that I dreaded to think what they would think of my bridesmaid's dress which I'd collected that very evening. Luckily it was hiding safely on the back of my door in its heavy white plastic wrapping.

"What are you wearing to the wedding?" I asked Polly.

"I'm not sure, really," Polly began. "It's a toss up between my new Pucci in purple and black or a dark-pink and purple-spotted Whistles dress. I haven't quite decided yet."

"Whistles is a bit down-market, darling, isn't it?" Amber said, walking into the room and handing her sister a mug of coffee.

"I know," Polly agreed, "but spots are so now."

Suzi followed her holding what looked like my bridesmaid's dress. I looked closer and cringed: it was my bridesmaid's dress.

"Look what Amy is wearing at the wedding," Amber said, pointing at the frothy pink creation. "Isn't it simply darling?"

Polly stood up and cast her eye over the dress. She handed me her mug, took the dress from Suzi and held it up against me. I dreaded what she was going to say. Polly wasn't a style-guru for nothing.

"Yes," she said thoughtfully. "Gaultier meets the Sugar Plum Fairy, I like it."

"You do?" I asked cautiously.

"Yes!" she replied. "Very now."

I breathed a sigh of relief. Maybe I wouldn't look so tragic after all.

On Friday afternoon I rushed home to join Beth. She was giving Polly and Amber a lift down to Arklow in her Civic. It would be a bit of a squash but we'd persuaded the cousins to decant their clothes into one suitcase. They insisted on bringing the two Gucci leather vanity cases which they perched on their knees. I sat in the front with Beth.

Amber and Polly put on their red-tinted frameless Prada sunglasses and spritzed their faces with water.

"Traveling is so dehydrating," Amber explained as we pulled out of the drive.

Julie was driving Suzi, Stella, Siobhan and Deirdre in her Range Rover Jeep and Martha and Jan were making their own way down on Saturday morning and meeting us there.

"It's like planning a bloody military maneuver," Suzi had said as she waited for Julie at the door. I was talking to her as Beth was loading the car in our drive. Stella was talking to James on her mobile. We could hear snatches of "Of course I won't. What do you think I'm like?" and "It's only two nights. Don't be so bloody selfish" and "James, stop being so stupid."

"Are you ready?" Beth called over when she'd settled the cousins in the back. Trendy dance music was blaring out of the speakers (courtesy of Polly).

"Absolutely," I smiled. I kissed Suzi. "See you down there," I said.

The journey down was a panic. Polly's vanity case turned out to be crammed full with bottles of champagne, small airline style. We glugged the frothy liquid down like it was Coke. All except Beth.

"We'll keep you some, darling," Polly promised as she popped another plastic cork, "I promise."

"That's OK," Beth assured her. "I'm not a big champagne drinker."

"Nonsense," Amber laughed. "Everyone's a champagne drinker."

Every time we passed a good-looking male (and this was a very broad term which encompassed seventeen-year-olds playing football and grampas) we yelled out the window. Polly was unstoppable. Pulling up to traffic lights on the Wicklow road she flirted unmercifully with the man in the Volvo beside us. Unluckily for him, his front passenger's window was open so he could hear everything. He had two baby seats in the back of the estate car, over which a huge golden Labrador was romping freely. He began to redden from his cheeks to the tips of his ears and down his neck as he listened to Polly.

"That's a darling car you have there," Polly purred, sticking her head out Beth's window and nearly strangling herself in the process on the seat belt. "I love estate cars. You must have rather a lot of money and I hear men with estates are awfully well endowed." We all shrieked with laughter at this gem. "And dogs just do it for me, with their big, brown eyes and their warm, lapping tongues and . . ."

Luckily for the Volvo driver the lights changed at this stage. He looked over as he moved away and stared lasciviously at Polly.

"Poor love," Polly smiled as we pulled away from the lights, the Volvo tearing along the road in front of us in a blatant display of male testosterone, "probably doesn't get much at home."

"Speaking of men, how's Arthur?" Amber asked her sister. "Arthur's her latest," she explained to me and Beth.

"Arthur?" Polly asked vaguely. "Oh, Artie! Sorry darling, you lost me there for a moment. Haven't seen Artie for weeks. Got bored of him really. No dress sense for a start and an annoying way of laughing. Frightful job too. Some sort of politician or something. Awfully boring parties."

Amber and Polly went through men like hot dinners. There seemed to be a never-ending supply in London. Amber had been married to a millionaire lord at one stage but it had only lasted a few months. He'd turned out to be incredibly stingy.

"Jazz is the latest. He's a hat designer, terribly talented. Amazingly good with his hands," she smiled wickedly. "Genius with his fingers, in fact."

"Polly!" Amber scolded. "Amy's used to you but Beth . . ."

"It's fine," Beth interrupted, laughing. "I don't mind at all. Tell us more Polly."

"Well," Polly began, "he gives the most amazing massages. He uses some of the feathers from his hats." We all listened, enthralled. "He starts off running the feathers over my back and then cools his hands on ice and traces his fingers over my spine. Then he warms his hands in hot water. It's bliss."

There was deathly silence in the car for a few seconds as we all imagined the sensations.

"Lucky bitch," I said, laughing. "You wouldn't get Irish men doing that kind of thing. It's more wham, bam, thank you ma'am."

"I don't know," Beth said slowly. "Tony can be very inventive when he sets his mind to it."

"Go on," I encouraged.

I looked at Beth smiling. She was blushing. "I couldn't," she stammered.

"Wait till we ply you with some shampoo," Polly assured her. "You can tell us then."

"Go on, ya good thing!" I yelled out the window at an electrician who was halfway up a lamp post, nearly deafening the car.

Beth sighed. "It's going to be a long weekend. I hope I'm able for it."

" 'Course you are," I slurred, the champagne beginning to kick in with a vengeance. "I think that's the roundabout Suzi was talking about. Turn left here."

Beth drove the car up a smaller, windy road. To the right was a sign for the Arklow Holiday Centre.

"We're here," I said, turning my head and looking at Polly and Amber.

"How rural," Amber smiled.

"Very quaint," Polly agreed. "But what's that smell?"

"Silage," Beth smiled.

We pulled up outside a stone-walled cottage with a large wooden reception sign on its wall and Beth and I helped the two girls out of the back of the car. They stood on their heels uncertainly, finding it hard to balance on the gravel.

"Hi, girls," a stocky blond man came out of the building smiling. "The hen party, is it?"

"That's right," Beth nodded.

"None of you look old enough to be getting hitched," he said.

"You charmer," Amber giggled.

"I'm Tim," he explained. "I run the center. I'll be taking you riding . . ."

Polly giggled.

He took a deep breath and continued, "and teaching you archery and shooting."

"Darling," Amber drawled, "we've been shooting since we were tiny."

"Sounds like a challenge to me," he replied grinning.

"I look forward to it," Amber purred. She ran a hand through her hair, flicking it from one side of her perfect face to the other.

"There are definite sparks flying there," I whispered to Beth. Tim was gazing at Amber with undisguised admiration.

"I hope you have some other shoes packed," Tim laughed, staring at Amber and Polly's heels.

"Darling, we have everything packed. Leather catsuits, nurse outfits, the works. We *are* on a hen party." Amber looked him straight in the eye.

Tim stared back for a few seconds in awe before breaking the silence. "Can I join you?" he grinned.

"We'll have to wait and see, won't we," Amber smiled.

Beth coughed. "Can you show us where we're staying?" she asked the distracted man.

"Of course. Sorry. Follow me," he said. "You can park over there, beside your cottage." He pointed at a graveled area beside a yellow-painted bungalow. "I'll help you in with your bags."

Beth parked the car. Amber and Polly tottered toward the cottage, whispering to each other and staring blatantly at Tim's behind as he walked in front of them.

He opened the door, lifted the bags and boxes of drink in from the boot of the car without a word and handed the key to me. "Here you are," he smiled, "Primrose Cottage. If you need anything I live over there." He pointed at the reception building.

"With your family?" Amber asked with interest. I stared at her. How direct could you get? I wish I was that brave.

"No," he smiled, his eyes lingering on her face, "on my own."

As he walked away Amber grinned. "What a darling man."

"He seems quite taken with you," I said.

"Poor misguided soul," Polly beamed.

"Polly," Amber squealed, thumping her sister on the arm.

We made ourselves at home, choosing our beds and jumping up and down on them like children.

Polly took charge of the drinks, whipping up some dynamite vodka and Red Bulls with her "secret ingredient"—tequila.

"Are you trying to kill us?" Beth asked as the strong alcohol hit her stomach.

I lifted a large cardboard box in from the hall. "We'd better get decorating," I said. "Suzi will be here soon." Julie had promised to stall Suzi by stopping for drinks along the way. But we still didn't have long. Not in the state we were in when it would take us twice as long as usual to do anything.

I pulled out the large roll of card. "Beth, you'd better do the photographs." I handed her a brown envelope, some PrittStick and a large black marker. "I'll decorate it when you've finished. And Amber, you can help Beth with the captions." I rummaged in the box and found the streamers and balloons. "Will you help me with these?" I asked Polly.

In less than an hour we had transformed the cottage's living room into a hen's paradise. There were phallic balloons in the shape of large pink willies hanging from the walls and ceilings. Streamers hung wall to wall and willy-candles lit the room, dripping their pink wax suggestively down their stems. Colored and flavored condoms had been placed in a bowl on the mantelpiece above the fireplace, "just in case." One wall was covered with pictures of Suzi, each shot ably captioned by Beth and Amber. *"Our Suze always had her finger on the pulse of fashion,"* one read. Suzi was wearing a very dodgy pair of white leggings, a pink shirt and a wide white leather belt with layers of silver studs on it. *"Her taste in men has improved"* read another, under a picture of poor Gary Simmons, a spotty teenager with gappy teeth and spiky hair, one of Suzi's ex's.

"It's finished," I sighed, collapsing on the sofa. "More drink, Polly." I waved my right hand which held an empty glass.

"Coming up," Polly smiled, bringing over a jug and pouring me a large glass of an orange drink.

"What's this?" Beth asked innocently as Polly handed her a fresh glass.

"Sex on the Beach," Polly grinned. "You'll love it."

Beth giggled. "Sounds good."

"I think that's Suzi," I jumped up, hearing the gravel crunching under tires outside. I looked out the window. "Here they are!"

Beth opened the front door and we spilled onto the gravel, waving our glasses.

"It's the hen," Polly squealed as Suzi staggered out of the jeep.

"I'm plassstered," she slurred. "Those lot were pouring drink into me."

"Well done, girls," I smiled.

"Our pleasure," Julie laughed.

"Hi, Amy, nice to see you again," Siobhan said. She was small and dark-haired, and she and Deirdre looked so alike most people thought they were sisters.

"Are you still in the crèche?" I asked her. Siobhan and Deirdre had worked with Suzi in Tiny Tots Crèche in Foxrock before Suzi had gone to Australia.

"Yes," Siobhan said, "we're both still there." Deirdre walked over. "For our sins," she added.

"How's it going, Amy?" Deirdre smiled. "This is a grand place. We're going to have such a laugh."

Stella plonked a willy hat with a white net veil on Suzi's head. "Suits you," she giggled.

I pushed Suzi in the door and into the living room. "Guys," she exclaimed as she saw the decorations, "you shouldn't have." She looked at the captioned photographs carefully. We all stood behind her, pointing and laughing. "Gary Simmons!" she shrieked. "He was so ugly! You really shouldn't have!" She was laughing so much tears were pouring down her face.

"Love the dress," Siobhan pointed to Suzi's bright blue ruched satin debs dress.

"Do you mind?" Suzi said. "It was the height of fashion."

"Who's that thing beside you?" Deirdre asked.

"Don't be so rude," Suzi grinned. "That's Des. Shit, I can't remember his second name. He was from Blackrock College. Nice guy, shame about the face."

"No kidding," I smiled.

"He was a rugby player," Suzi continued. "He had a great body."

"Always one for the rugby players," Julie laughed.

"Look who's talking!" I exclaimed. "Mrs. Rugby herself!"

"I think I need a drink," Julie said quickly, "or I'm going to be in a lot of trouble."

"What's Brian like in bed?" Polly asked wickedly. She had been told all about Brian by Matt the previous night over dinner.

"Polly!" Amber shouted. "Stop it."

Julie laughed. "Have you ever seen him on the rugby pitch?" she asked.

Polly nodded. "Against England last year."

"Honey, he's twice as good in bed."

We all hooted and clapped.

"Good on you, Julie!" Suzi yelled. "You're well able for them!"

Chapter 31

A lot of drinks later we were sitting around the table, sharing filthy jokes. Julie had kindly offered to provide the food for the weekend and tonight's meal was lasagne and chips.

"This is delicious," I said, dipping a chip into some tomato sauce. "Just what we need to soak up all the alcohol."

"Good girl, Julie," Suzi said. "Toast to Julie."

"To Julie!" we all yelled, clinking our glasses dangerously hard.

"Toast to the hen!" Julie said. "The best girl in the world. Matt's a lucky man."

"To the hen," yelled Siobhan, Julie and me. "To Suzi," yelled Stella, Beth, Amber and Polly. "To Looly," yelled Deirdre, who was the most drunk of us all. We clinked our glasses again, this time spilling lots on the table.

"To the bridesmaids," Suzi shouted, "Amy and Stella."

"To the bridesmaids," we all yelled. The table was by now covered with drink.

"To women," Stella yelled, "without men!"

"To women without men," we all yelled.

"I like men," Amber stated loudly. "That Tim, he's all right. I'm going to snog him."

We all cheered.

"Who's Tim?" Suzi asked.

"The rather hunky guy who runs this place," I explained.

"Tim, Tim, Tim, Tim," the table began to chant.

Amber stood up and clambered onto the table. "Tim, Tim, Tim," she chanted, waving her arms in the air.

Suddenly she jumped down off the table and ran barefoot toward the door. "I'll just go and get him," she shouted.

We all laughed hysterically.

"She's only messing, isn't she?" Stella asked.

Polly smiled. "No, I don't think so."

We watched the door expectantly. There was no sign of Amber.

"Do you think she's OK?" Beth asked, a little less drunk than the rest of us.

"It's Tim we should be worried about," Polly assured us.

"Let's play 'Bunnies,' " Polly shouted. "Everyone get a full drink in front of them and I'll explain the rules."

"Rules?" Siobhan asked. "Is it complicated?"

Polly thought for a bit. "It is a bit. I know, I'll make up a new game. It's called boys' names. You have to think of a boy's name and shout it out when it's your turn. If it's a crap name you have to drink your whole glass. OK?"

"Yes!" everyone yelled.

"What kind of names?" Suzi asked. "Would Matt be good or bad?"

"Good," said Polly definitely.

"What about Tony?" Beth asked a little worried.

"Good!" Polly yelled.

"Cedric?" Siobhan asked.

"Bad!" Polly shouted.

"Kevin?" Deirdre asked.

"Bad!" Polly yelled.

"That's my Dad's name," Stella said.

"Sorry," Polly apologized.

"That's all right," Stella assured her. "I don't like it either."

"Have we started the game?" I asked in confusion.

"No," Polly said, "but we will now. Around the table, Suzi first."

"Matt!" Suzi yelled.

"You already said Matt," I laughed.

"I'm saying it again," Suzi giggled. "I'm the hen. I'm allowed."

"Quite right too," Polly said. "Next!"

"Adam," Stella yelled.

"Good!" Polly said. "Next."

"Brian," Julie shouted.

"Bad!" Polly said.

"Why?" Julie asked, a little perturbed.

"I'm just trying to get you drunk," Polly explained. "It's a nice name really."

"That's OK then," Julie said, knocking back her drink.

We continued yelling out good and bad names, getting more and more drunk. In the middle of the "game" I staggered out to the loo. Hearing a noise outside the house I opened the front door to investigate. It was Amber, her arms draped around Tim's shoulders.

"Hi, Amy," she smiled, "look who I found."

Tim grinned sheepishly. "Hello again."

"I'm not sure you want to go in there," I warned him.

"I'm a big boy," he said. "I'll be fine."

Coming out of the toilet I heard loud shrieks and shouts. As I walked into the living room I saw what all the noise was about. Tim was in the thick of it. All the girls were circling around him trying to pull his jeans down. He was holding onto his denims for dear life.

"Now, girls, stop that," he was shouting ineffectually. "Ow, careful!" They'd already succeeded in removing his fleece and T-shirt which had been thrown onto the floor. Hands pawed at his chest, stroking his six-pack.

"Who's a big boy then?" Polly said.

"Look at those muscles," Julie said admiringly. "Almost as good as my Brian's."

Amber was a little concerned. "Maybe we should leave him alone . . ." she began.

"Why don't we play 'Spin the Bottle'?" Polly suggested.

I giggled. "You can't play with only one man," I said.

"We could kiss each other," Siobhan added helpfully.

"Don't be gross," Suzi said. "I'm not kissing my sister. Or any girl for that matter."

Tim was finally left alone after Polly arrived with another jug of some sort of lethal cocktail.

"What's this one?" Amber asked.

"Don't know," Polly admitted. "I just chucked everything in really. Tastes divine though."

I nearly choked after taking a sip. It was pure rocket fuel. I could taste gin and tequila and after that I didn't want to know.

"Let's have a sing-song," Tim suggested carefully. He was either very brave or very stupid to stay in the room, considering our state. Sitting on the sofa, still bare-chested with one arm resting over Amber's back he obviously had more hormones than sense.

"I nominate 'Two Shy' by Kagagoogo."

"Ya what?" Deirdre asked from the floor where she had raised her head for the first time in several minutes. She really was a little under the weather.

We launched into a bizarre rendition of "Too Shy" followed by an even more dodgy version of "Wherever I Lay My Hat That's My Home," one of Polly's favorites.

At half three I just couldn't take it anymore. My head was spinning, I felt decidedly nauseous and very, very sleepy. I decided to call it a day. I snuck upstairs to my bed and lay down fully clothed on the soft duvet. I was out like a light.

The next morning I woke up to the sounds of music blaring from downstairs. I could also hear laughter and shrieks. I sat up slowly and looked out the window. I hadn't closed the curtains and it was bright outside. Stella was crashed out on the bed beside me, also fully clothed.

I staggered downstairs holding my head in my hands. I needed painkillers and water fast. My temples were throbbing like nobody's business and my stomach felt like a tiny bunch of gremlins were punching the lining from the inside. Not to mention the definite presence of a dead rat in my mouth.

"Hi, Amy," Polly yelled from the sofa. The curtains were drawn and Polly, Siobhan and Deirdre were sprawled on the large sofa covered in duvets. "Wanna drink?"

Were they mad? "No, thanks," I muttered. I stared at them carefully. "How long have you been up?" I looked at my watch. "It's only half eleven."

"Up?" Siobhan giggled. "We haven't been down."

"You stayed up all night?" I asked incredulously. They were barking.

"Yep," Polly stated proudly. She took a long slug of her drink. "Thanks to my amazing cocktails."

The gravel outside crunched and someone knocked on the door. I opened it. Martha and Jan stared at me with a worried expression on their innocent faces.

"Are you OK?" Martha asked. "You look a little ropy."

"I'm fine," I assured them. "Come in. It's good to see you both. Suzi's asleep, I think."

They followed me into the living room.

"Hi, girls," Siobhan shouted from the sofa. "Fancy a drink?"

"It's a bit early, isn't it?" Jan asked.

"Never too early," Polly hiccuped.

At two o'clock Amber arrived at the door barefoot with a grin plastered from ear to ear. Apart from Polly, Siobhan and Deirdre who had taken to their beds for the afternoon, we were all sitting at the table (freshly cleared away and cleaned by Julie or "Mammy" as we'd started calling her, much to her disgust) eating toast and drinking large mugs of coffee.

"Where were you, Amber?" I asked with a grin.

She smiled. "With the lovely Tim, of course."

"Tell us all about it," Stella demanded. "Every little detail."

"To be honest I can't remember much, thanks to my darling sister's cocktails," she laughed, "but he's very sweet. He's on his way up here to bring you all riding."

"I don't think I'd be into that," Suzi winced. "All that up and down motion. I don't think my stomach would survive."

"You're probably right," Julie agreed.

"Then how about shooting?" Amber asked. "That wouldn't affect your stomach."

"It's very noisy though," I muttered. My headache was getting worse.

Amber sighed. "I know," she said brightly. "Archery. That's not noisy."

"Maybe," Stella said. "Is it hard?"

"Not really," Amber said. "It's good fun."

Tim came bounding in the door. "Are you all ready?" he asked.

"Do we look ready?" I asked, glaring at him. He was far too perky for this time of the morning. He stood behind Amber and I could see his hands lingering on her pert buttocks before slotting around her waist.

"I think archery might be the best choice, darling," Amber said, nuzzling his neck.

"Would you two stop that!" Suzi exclaimed. "This is supposed to be my hen weekend. No men allowed."

"Sorry," Amber giggled. "Irish men just do it for me."

"Are you mad?" I asked. Tim glared at me.

"Right, gang," he stated, all gung-ho. "Everyone on their feet. You'll need sensible shoes, no heels please. And bring a jacket. It can get quite cold up by the targets. I'll collect Jasper and meet you outside in two minutes."

"Who's Jasper?" I asked Amber after Tim had left.

"No idea," Amber admitted. "Maybe it's his dog."

We pulled on runners, Nike and Adidas for all of us except Amber who had bright blue Power Girl ones. Jackets and fleece hats followed. Julie had brought spare jackets and hats, bless her.

"Julie, you're too good to us," I smiled as she handed me a gray fleece hat.

"I'm so used to standing on the sidelines I have hundreds of warm jackets and hats," she explained.

Tim smiled as he saw us gathered on the gravel in front of the cottage. "That's better," he said. "This is Jasper," he said, introducing a young man in combats, black fleece and Timberland boots. "He'll be helping me today."

"Cute," Stella whispered in my ear.

"I'll just warn you, this lot are dangerous," he told Jasper. Amber pouted. "Except Amber, of course." The blond woman beamed and blew him a kiss with her perfectly manicured hand. "This is Stella,

Suzi, Amy, Beth, Julie, Martha and Jan," he introduced each of us in turn, delighted that he'd remembered all the names.

"I think I can handle them," Jasper said. He had a deep, throaty voice.

"I wouldn't be too sure," Stella flirted.

"Follow Jasper up to the targets," Tim said. "I'll be there with the bows in a few minutes."

"I'll go with you," Amber trilled.

"This way," Jasper commanded, leading us behind the buildings and toward the top of an open field. In the far corner six large targets came into view, colored circles on heavy straw backgrounds. Each target was the size of a large dustbin lid.

"That doesn't look too bad," Martha said as we approached them. She was a bit of a Sporty Spice—she'd always won everything in school, I remembered. Jan and Beth didn't look too sure.

"Have any of you done archery before?" Jasper asked as we huddled together, waiting for Tim and Amber.

"No," we all chorused.

"There are a few things to keep in mind," he continued. "Firstly, the bows are heavy. You need to hold them firmly and strongly—"

"Oh, yeah?" Stella quipped. Jasper smiled at her.

"As I was saying, hold them firmly. I'll show each of you the correct position when Tim arrives with the bows."

"I wouldn't hold your breath," Suzi laughed.

Jasper looked a little worried. The prospect of entertaining us without bows wasn't too appealing.

"There are two bows and plenty of arrows here," he said, pointing over to a large black box. "So maybe we'll get started with those. "Who would like to go first? I need two of you."

"I will," Martha offered.

"Me too," Julie said.

"Put these on your wrists." He handed them leather pieces with Velcro-fastening straps and helped them secure them. "These are to stop the string catching you."

Jasper then lined them up, facing sideways toward the targets. He handed them a bow each and showed them the correct way to hold them.

"I'll load the arrows for you this time. Next time you'll be doing it yourselves. The green plastic piece needs to be on the top." He slotted the arrow onto the bow. "Now comes the hard part." Stella nudged me in the side. I tried not to giggle. It was great fun being so childish. "Pull back the string, keeping the bow steady. Good, Martha. Stella . . ."

"Julie," she corrected.

"Sorry, Julie, you need to pull back harder. Like this." He stood behind her and helped her pull back the heavy string.

"Now let the string go." Martha's arrow shot toward the target, landing at the edge with a whack. Julie's arrow landed at her feet.

"Oops," she laughed. "I'm not much good at this."

"Not to worry," Jasper said kindly. "It takes a while to get the hang of it."

Julie and Martha had a few more goes before it was Suzi and Stella's turn. I waited nervously with Jan and Beth. I was more than happy to just watch. If Julie couldn't do it I didn't have a hope in hell. I was one of those kids who was always picked last for teams in school. Sport of any kind just wasn't my thing.

Suzi was good. She hit the target every time, several times in the red "bull's eye." Stella wasn't bad either. I'm sure she could have been a lot better but she seemed to like Jasper showing her how to do it.

"Amber's taking her time," Jan said, smiling.

"You should have seen her last night," Julie said, rubbing her upper arm. "She was all over Tim."

"Poor lad," I said, "he was lucky we didn't strip him fully."

"Sounds like I missed a good night," Jan smiled.

"Tonight will be even better," I promised her.

"Here's Amber," Suzi shouted. "Hey, Amber, what were you doing? Your fleece is inside out."

Amber looked at her fleece and giggled. Tim was carrying an armful of bows and handed them out, ignoring our slags.

"Now you have one each. If you've all had a bit of a practice, Jasper will keep the scores. I'll split you into two teams."

"I think I'll just watch," Julie said, rubbing her shoulder. "I'm a bit stiff. Amber can take my place." Julie handed Amber her bow.

"Are you sure?" Amber asked.

"Yes," Julie replied. "You go ahead."

"I'll keep Julie company," Beth said. "There'll be an odd number otherwise."

Amber tested the string on her bow. She looked very professional.

"Have you done this before?" Martha asked.

"A little," Amber said.

Martha was fiercely competitive and didn't like to lose. "You're on my team, so."

"I think I'll pick the teams," Tim decided. "Just to make it interesting. Martha, you take Suzi and Amy, and Amber, you take Jan and Stella."

"OK," Martha agreed. "May the best team win."

Amber turned out to be exceptional. Which was just as well as Jan and Stella were hopeless. But not as hopeless as myself and Suzi who laughed our way through the competition. Much to the annoyance of Martha.

"You could put some effort in," she grumbled. "Concentrate a bit."

We lost spectacularly.

Tim was well impressed with Amber. He gave her a big hug after the competition and lifted her into the air.

"I think we'll have to ban Amber this evening," Suzi grinned. "She'll bring her man and ruin everything."

"Maybe we could invite Tim and Jasper over after dinner," Stella eagerly suggested. She'd taken a liking to the other young instructor.

"After we've dazzled the men of Arklow with our talent, of course," Suzi smiled. "I can't wait to get into my costume."

We trekked back to the cottage, peeled off our fleeces and jackets and collapsed on the sofa and chairs.

"That was fun," Beth said. "Even if I was only watching for most of it. Amber, you're bloody good. Where did you learn archery?"

"One of Polly's ex's was a big archery fan," she explained. "He had a target in his back garden and he taught us both."

"Where's lover-boy?" Stella asked.

"He's gone back to his house," Amber said. "He's going out with Jasper and the riding instructor this evening. I might see him tomorrow but tonight is Suzi's night."

"Damn right!" Suzi exclaimed. "Maybe we can hook up with them later," she said kindly. "I wouldn't mind."

Amber smiled at her warmly. "You always were my fave cousin."

"What about me?" I asked in mock disgust.

"You too," Amber. "You're both my favorite cousins."

At six o'clock, after a few glasses of wine and beer—we'd decided to leave Polly's cocktails till later—we trooped upstairs and changed after waking Polly, Siobhan and Deirdre. The three girls were decidedly chirpy in the circumstances.

"How was your afternoon?" Polly asked, stretching her arms over her head and yawning.

"Great," Suzi said. "We did archery and your sister's team won."

Polly smiled. "Amber's rather super at archery. Now, what are we wearing tonight?"

"We're going for dinner at a local restaurant," Suzi explained. "It also has a nightclub called 'The Copa.' "

"The locals call it the 'cop-a-feel,' " I explained helpfully. "It's a bit of a dive but it'll be a laugh. We have divine costumes for Suzi and Beth that should raise an eyebrow or two."

"And the temperature," Suzi added.

"I'm wearing a skirt and a little top," I said. "And my kitten heels."

"I think it'll be my little pink dress then," Polly said. "Now accessories, let me see . . ."

An hour later we waited in the hall for Suzi and Beth. Everyone looked stunning. Lots of little dresses, skirts and leather trousers. Arklow wouldn't know what hit it. Body jewelry, courtesy of Polly, and the latest sparkly make-up, courtesy of Amber. The second vanity case had been full of sample cosmetics and hair products from all the top trendy companies I'd only ever read about in *OK* and *Now* magazine—Urban Decay Nail Enamel, Philosophy Never

Let Them See You Shine powder, Bumble and Bumble Thickening Hair Spray. We were all in girlie heaven.

"Here we come, girls," Suzi shouted as she appeared at the top of the stairs. "Ready or not."

She was wearing a black latex rubber imitation leather cat-suit that clung unforgivingly to every curve. Luckily Suzi had the figure for it and looked stunning. A little sleazy but amazing none the less. Amber had piled her hair on the top of her head and made up her face to perfection. She was wearing high red sandals.

"Wow," Polly drew her breath. "You look just like Michelle Pfeiffer's Catwoman. Amazing."

"Thanks," she said. "Beth, come down."

"No," Beth wailed. "I look ridiculous."

"Beth," Julie yelled up the stairs. "I'm sure you don't."

"Hen," Polly and Amber shouted.

"Hen, hen," everyone joined in, yelling louder and louder.

"OK, OK," Beth finally shouted. As she stood at the top of the stairs we all gasped.

Chapter 32

I'd never seen Beth look so . . . so . . . well, it just wasn't Beth. She was wearing a red snakeskin printed "leather" bra top which clung to her generous breasts like a second skin. The matching red skirt rested just above her knee but was slashed up the sides to reveal her legs. Black leather high-heeled boots completed the outfit.

"I feel like a porn queen," she complained as she made her way nervously down the stairs.

We were all stunned. Amber had straightened her normally curly hair and used bright, strong colors on her lips and eyes. Her arms and cleavage had been dusted with sparkling bronzer, which danced in the light.

"You look amazing," Polly said admiringly. "You'll stop traffic, darling."

Beth seemed unsure. "Maybe I'll go up and change. They might not let me into the nightclub . . ."

"You're joking," Siobhan said. "They'd definitely let you into any nightclub in the world—even Hollywood looking like that."

"You're any red-blooded male's dream girl," Martha agreed.

"Pamela Anderson eat your heart out," Suzi said.

"I'm not sure," Beth said.

"Grab her, girls," Julie commanded. "We're off!"

"Get off me, you mad things," Beth squealed as we pushed her out the door and into Julie's jeep. Julie was leaving her wheels at the restaurant and would collect them the following day.

We all piled in on top of Beth. It was quite a squeeze but what was a mouthful of hair between friends?

"Are we there yet, Mammy?" Polly asked as we crunched down the gravel drive.

"Stop calling me Mammy," Julie said.

"Yes, Mammy," we all chorused.

We piled out of the jeep and into the "Eden Tree" restaurant. They had quite sensibly given us a large table at the back of the room, looking out onto a brightly lit courtyard.

"Beth and Suzi at the two ends," I said. "And everyone else pile in."

There was much giggling and squeals as we seated ourselves.

"What if I need to go to the loo?" Deirdre asked. "I'm a bit boxed in here."

"You'd better let her sit on the outside," Martha suggested, "just in case."

As Deirdre had shown her lack of staying power the previous evening, Siobhan kindly offered to swap with her.

"I'll crawl under," Siobhan said. "No need for anyone to move." She wriggled down her seat and ducked her head under the table.

"I'll give you these," a young male waiter began, handing out large laminated terracotta-colored menus, "and would you like to order drinks?"

"A 'Flaming Orgasm' for me, mate," came Siobhan's voice from under the table.

The waiter jumped. We all laughed as her head popped up from between Stella and Martha's chairs.

"I'm not sure we have those," the waiter said nervously.

"A 'Sex on the Beach,' so," Siobhan smiled. Deirdre popped out of her seat and began to crawl the opposite way, toward Siobhan's old seat.

"I don't think . . ." the waiter began, staring at Deirdre's disappearing behind in amazement.

"How about a vodka and Red Bull?" she asked.

"Yes," he said, gratefully, "one vodka and Red Bull."

"Me too," said Beth and Suzi in unison.

"Beth!" I exclaimed. "You don't drink spirits."

"It's a special occasion," Beth smiled, "and I think I'm going to need something strong."

"Quite right too, darling," Amber smiled. "Same for me, please."

The waiter came back several minutes later with a tray of eleven vodka and Red Bulls.

"Have you decided on your food yet?" he asked.

"Food?" Deirdre asked vacantly. "Oh, yes, food."

"Come back in a few minutes," Julie said kindly. "We haven't really looked at the menus yet."

"And bring another round," Polly instructed, "same again."

"And three bottles of champagne," Amber said. "No, better make it five. The bubbly's on me."

"Go, Amber," we yelled, waving our arms in the air in true Rikki Lake style. "Go, Amber, go, Amber."

Eventually the waiter managed to extract our order. Garlic bread was the favored starter, except for Stella and Amber who got slagged mightily for ordering melon instead.

"Snoggers," Siobhan shouted, "snoggers, snoggers."

"Do you mind?" Stella asked in mock disgust. "I have a boyfriend."

"Don't let that stop you!" Beth yelled.

"Beth!" I smiled. "I think the drink has gone to your head."

"I think so too," she grinned sloppily. "Iss lovely stuff. *More vodka!* Vodka, vodka," she yelled, banging her knife and fork on the table.

At this stage heads were turning and the waiter scuttled over to us.

"I'm afraid you'll have to keep it down," he insisted. "Other diners are complaining."

"Sorry," Julie said quickly. "We'll behave."

"For now," Polly added, a dangerous glint in her eye.

Luckily our food arrived quickly and soon we were all (except Stella and Amber) tucking into delicious hot garlic bread which was topped with mozzarella cheese and sun-dried tomatoes.

"This is very good," Julie said enthusiastically, licking dripping butter off her fingers. "How's the melon, snoggers?" Polly asked, grinning.

"Very good, thanks, smelly-breath," Stella smiled.

"Will we order wine?" Julie asked, a little anxious at the effect the Red Bull was having on the crew. Even Deirdre was bright-eyed and bushy-tailed. In fact she was very bushy-tailed, her pupils were definitely dilated and she looked a little crazed.

"What happened to the champagne?" Amber asked. We'd forgotten about it.

Just then her question was answered. The waiter carried over two silver buckets, followed by another waiter with a tray of long champagne flutes.

"Sorry about the delay," he said. "We don't get asked for champagne much. I'll bring the other bottles in a minute."

He placed the buckets in the centre of the table and began to pour the sparkling liquid. When all our glasses were filled Amber stood up.

"A toast to the two hens, Suzi and Beth," she said loudly, smiling.

"To the hens," we all clinked our glasses and took a sip.

Suzi jumped up. "To Amber for the champagne," she said.

"To Amber," we toasted.

"Not again," Julie giggled. "This could go on all night. Let's leave the toasts till after the food."

"Good idea," Beth agreed. "Now who's going to give that champagne bottle a blow-job?"

"Beth!" I spluttered, spilling a mouthful of champagne down my silver top.

"I will," Siobhan said, licking her lips. She placed the top of the champagne bottle between her lips and began to slide it in and out of her mouth.

"Go, girl!" Polly said.

Luckily no one appeared to have noticed what we were doing.

"Do you still do that when you're married?" Deirdre asked Julie, pointing at Siobhan.

Julie smiled. "Of course," she said, "and more."

"Tell us," Beth encouraged.

"I will not!" Julie said. "That's between me and the hubby."

"How long have you been married?" I asked, trying to steer the conversation onto safer ground.

"Ten years nearly," Julie smiled. "We met at school."

"Childhood sweethearts," Stella said. "When did you realize that he was, you know, 'the one'?"

"I'm not sure," Julie smiled. "It happened gradually, I suppose."

"How about you, Suzi?" Stella asked. "When did you know you wanted to marry Matt?"

Suzi smiled. "From the moment I saw him, I think. We were at this party and our eyes met across a crowded room. I know it sounds like a cliché but it was like, bang, that was it."

"Once you can be yourself with someone, and they put up with all your funny habits and still love you, that's when you know," Beth smiled.

"You're both so lucky," Amber sighed, "I'd love to be getting married."

"Your turn will come," Julie said. "You never know, Tim might be 'the one.' "

Amber laughed, "I don't think so, but I'm having a good time testing him out."

"Are you really?" Polly said. "And what would that involve, exactly?" she asked.

When the waiter arrived with the food the conversation had taken a downward spiral into the world of favorite sexual positions and the weirdest place anyone had had sex.

"I don't believe you," Suzi was saying as her steak was placed in front of her. "Those airplane toilets are tiny. I thought that was just an urban myth."

"No, honestly, darling," Polly insisted. "It's the most fun."

By the end of the dinner we were all flying on clouds of alcohol and good food.

"Desserts, anyone?" the waiter asked as he cleared away our plates with the help of two other waiters. Polly pinched his bum. He jumped and moved quickly away from her.

"I'd love some ice cream," Amber said.

"Banoffi pie for me," Julie said, handing back the menu.

"Anyone else?" he asked.

There were no other takers.

"Coffee?" he asked.

"No thanks," Beth trilled. "More vodka please."

"Another around of vodka and Red Bull," Polly smiled, "honey." She winked at him and he scuttled away, blushing.

"Are you making a speech, Suzi and Beth?" Amber asked after her ice cream.

"Go on, dolls," Polly smiled. "Speech."

"Speech, speech," we all yelled.

The waiter stared over and we lowered our voices.

Suzi stood up. "Thank you all for coming this evening. It's great to see you all here. Especially Polly and Amber who've traveled a long way to be with us . . ."

"Pleasure, darling," Polly interrupted.

"I'm so excited about getting married. I don't know what to say. I love Matt to bits and I hope all of you find your own Matt."

"Not a doormat, though," Deirdre quipped.

We all groaned.

"That's all really. Oh, and thanks to Amy for being my brides-maid. I know she's not over the moon with the idea but she's been great." She leaned over and gave me a kiss. "So have a good night, everyone."

We clapped and cheered.

"Your turn, Beth," Julie said.

Beth got to her feet. "This is really Suzi's night, I'm just tagging along. So firstly thanks to Suzi for letting me share this evening." Suzi smiled. "And to my bridesmaids, Amy and Stella. Amy is great to do it twice. As most of you know our weddings are only days apart so I really appreciate it."

"You know what they say," I smiled grimly, *"always the brides-maid, never the bride."*

"That won't be true for you," Beth continued. "You're lovely. I'd marry you myself, if I was a boy."

"So would I," Suzi agreed, "if I was a boy and not related to you."

"I would too!" Polly exclaimed.

"We all would," Stella shouted.

I laughed. "Thanks, guys. If any of you ever get a sex change, look me up!"

"That's all I have to say really," Beth finished. "Now have fun!"

Paying the bill was interesting. Julie took charge and split the bill nine ways, paying for Beth and Suzi. Amber covered the champagne which was just as well. Not all of us lived on London salaries.

The doormen at The Copa were very impressed with Suzi and Beth's outfits, as predicted.

"All right, love?" a burly redhead asked Beth. "Doing anything later?"

"Getting married," Beth replied. "First thing in the morning," she lied.

"Bloody hell," he muttered, "the good ones are always feckin' married."

"Hasn't stopped you before, Dirk," another bald bouncer joked.

"True," Dirk answered.

"How about it, sweetheart?" he asked Beth. "I'm off at three."

"No, thanks," Beth laughed. "I appreciate the offer though."

The Copa was very dark inside. The walls were painted matte red, and mirrors and glitter-balls sent broken, reflected light around the room. The dance floor was generously sized and, as we walked in, the dulcet tones of "Come on, Eileen" rang out.

"Excellent," Julie shouted over the noise. "It's an eighties night."

It turned out not to be—the DJ just had very strange taste in music which encompassed the eighties, the nineties and some dodgy modern "hits" from Steps and Billie. He even played slow sets.

We found seats beside the dance floor and settled in. Polly, Amber and Siobhan immediately started dancing to Fatboy Slim, showing a ridiculous amount of energy and enthusiasm.

"Are ya dancing?" a voice beside me asked as I sipped my bottle of Ritz.

"Are ya asking?" I replied, thinking he was joking, looking up at a bum-fluffed cheek. The tall, gangly male in front of me was all of seventeen.

"I am," he said humorlessly, holding out his hand.

"I dare you," Suzi hissed at me.

I glared at her and stood up gingerly, the others giggling and poking each other behind me. I held his clammy palm as he pulled me eagerly onto the dance floor. Just my luck—the music changed and Celine Dion's *Titanic* song bellowed out.

Please don't let him try and kiss me, I thought to myself.

The boy put his arms around me. "What's your name?" he asked.

"Poppy," I lied for some reason.

"Like the flowers?" he asked.

"Yes," I nodded.

"That's nice. I'm Owen," he said resting his head on my bare shoulder.

We shuffled around in circles to the music. It reminded me of school discos. After our one dance the music changed—more eighties this time—he walked me back to my seat, thanked me and walked away.

"Amazing," I said to Stella. "He was the perfect gentleman. Maybe chivalry isn't dead after all."

But Stella was paying me absolutely no attention. Her eyes were fixed on the doorway.

"Look who it is," she said, a smile spreading from ear to ear.

Tim, Jasper and a tall blond man walked in. She jumped down and went over to the threesome. Tim had already stopped Amber on the dance floor and in seconds everyone was waving their arms in the air to "YMCA."

"I love this one!" Julie yelled over the music to me. "Let's dance. Come on, girls, follow us," she said to the others.

We all jumped to our feet except Deirdre who had fallen asleep, her head resting on the table in front of her.

"I'll stay with her," Beth said kindly. "I'll mind the bags."

"Are you sure?" I asked.

"Yes," she smiled. "I'll have fun watching you all making wallies of yourselves."

"Thanks a lot," I grinned.

"This is Justin," Tim yelled over the music, introducing his friend who was dancing beside me. "He works at the center."

"Hi, Justin," I smiled. "I'm Amy."

"Nice name," he smiled back. "You all look like you've been having a good time."

"No kidding," I said loudly.

"And now . . ." the DJ's swarthy voice came over the speakers, "by special request from the Dublin hens for Suzi and Beth—'Like a Virgin' by Madonna."

We all surrounded Suzi and Beth and made them dance in the middle while we clapped and cheered. Jasper and Justin seemed to be entering into the spirit of things with gusto. Tim and Amber had disappeared.

"Where's Tim?" I asked Justin after a while.

"I think he's gone back to the house," he grinned. "He's mad about your friend. He has a bottle of wine in the fridge apparently."

"I see," I smiled. "Lucky Amber."

"Lucky Tim more like," he grinned. "She's a babe."

"She's my cousin," I smiled.

"Must run in the family," he said.

The nightclub closed at three and we were all there till the bitter end. Deirdre slept through most of the night and Julie, Jan and Martha didn't look far off comatose themselves. They were sitting slumped in their seats when the lights came on.

"I hate when they turn on the lights," Justin said to me. "It's such a jolt. Back to the real world."

"And everyone just looks tired," I said. "The girls have mascara-panda eyes and the boys have sweat dripping down their faces."

"You look even better in this light," he smiled, brushing my hair out of my eyes.

My stomach lurched. I realized that Justin was flirting with me. It hadn't occurred to me before—maybe I was too drunk to notice. But now I was just nice drunk, warm and relaxed without feeling out of it. I looked at him. He was very attractive—dark hair cut very short, green eyes and a wide, crooked smile. He looked a little young, twenty-two or -three maybe, but I wasn't going to let that stop me. He was legal after all. I was single and there was no one else to think about, not really. Steve's face briefly flitted through my drunken mind. But that was over, finito.

"We've loads of drink back at the cottage," I smiled, trying to appear cool. "You're welcome to join us."

"Sure," he smiled, "sounds good."

"Hey, Jasper," he shouted over at his friend whose arm was around Stella's waist. "Are you going back to the girls' cottage?"

Jasper looked at Stella who nodded. "Yes!" he exclaimed.

Justin, who was a local, managed to order us three taxis and we arrived back at the cottage within twenty minutes.

"Where do you live?" I asked him.

"Down the road from here, with Jasper. And you're from Dublin, I presume."

"Yes," I said. "Blackrock." I didn't feel like going into any details, to be honest. He was cute and nice but I was really only after his body.

Chapter 33

When we arrived at the cottage the lights were on and music was playing. Not just music—Abba's "Dancing Queen," Suzi's favorite song.

Amber and Tim met us on the doorstep. "I found *Abba's Greatest Hits*," she shouted over the music.

Suzi jumped out of the taxi and ran inside. "Let's dance, girls," she yelled. "Follow me."

Within minutes everyone, including Deirdre who had woken up, was dancing. Justin, Tim and Jasper included.

"Everyone off the floor," Suzi commanded, as the strains of "Waterloo" hit the air.

"Sorry?" Justin asked. He watched in amazement as we all scrambled onto chairs, the sofa, the table and kitchen chairs.

"Come on, boys," Suzi yelled. "Off the floor."

Justin climbed onto one of the windowsills, Tim sat on the top of the fridge and Jasper joined Stella on one of the armchairs.

"You're all mad!" Tim yelled over the music. "I'm not supposed to allow any noise after twelve." He grinned. "Luckily there's no one in the other cottages this weekend as they're being painted."

"So we can make noise all night," Beth shouted.

After three more Abba songs I was exhausted. I hadn't had so much exercise for years. I staggered out into the hall and plonked myself down on the stairs.

"Are you OK?" Justin asked, following me out and handing me a glass.

"What's this?" I asked, sniffing the glass suspiciously.

"I'm not sure," he smiled. "Polly gave it to me. It tastes sweet though. Try it."

He took a sip and handed it to me. I stared at his moist lips. I took the glass from him and placed it on the stair above me. "I think I'll taste yours," I smiled. I leaned over and ran my tongue over his lips seductively. "Umm, nice," I smiled.

He took a sip of the drink, put his hand behind my head and pressed his lips firmly to mine. As my mouth opened he allowed the sweet, warm liquid to trickle into my mouth. He then started kissing me, gently at first, brushing my lips with his, softly and slowly. I began to caress his tongue with mine. He responded immediately, taking my lead. Soon our bodies were entwined on the stairs, the carpeted edges jutting into our backs.

"Let's go upstairs," I suggested. He followed me without a word, holding my hand tightly. We fell onto my bed, kissing passionately.

"You're amazing," Justin whispered in my ear as he nuzzled my neck. His cool, firm hands moved over my bare shoulders and across my back. I pulled his shirt out of his trousers and ran my fingers up and down his spine. He pulled his shirt over his head, ignoring the buttons, and threw it on the floor. His hairless, muscular chest shone in the moonlight.

"What age *are* you?" I asked him, coming up for air as his hands caressed my back.

"Does it matter?" he smiled, kissing me.

"Not really, I was just wondering," I said.

"I'm nearly twenty," he replied.

Bloody hell, I thought to myself. What the feck am I doing? I could be his mother—well, not quite, but almost.

"What's wrong?" Justin asked. "You've gone very quiet."

"What age do you think I am?" I whispered.

He sat up. "I don't know, twenty-four, twenty-five? But don't worry, I like older women."

Yes! I thought. He thinks I'm twenty-four. Yes!

"What age are you?" he asked.

"Twenty-four," I lied.

He smiled and kissed me gently. "Shut up and come here, gorgeous."

He rolled over, pinning me under his body. He carefully pulled my top over my head and removed my bra. I was glad I'd worn my fairly new, pink lacy bra. Shit, I muttered to myself, am I wearing the matching knickers? Amy, I thought as he kissed my breasts, are you seriously thinking of sleeping with this guy? But what harm would it do?

At this stage I should explain that I'd never, ever had a one-night stand. In fact the nearest I'd come to it was the unfortunate Branigan New Year's Eve debacle and you know how that turned out. I'd had sex exactly twice before Jack. Once with a guy called Martin Bowler when I was nineteen. We'd been together for nearly three months and I was mad about him. I was also dying to lose my virginity—it was like an albatross around my late-teenage neck. The sex was mediocre to say the least.

Number two was Ryan Ahearne, my first "real" long-term boyfriend. I'd just broken up with Martin (he went off with Kelly, the local bicycle, who he kept telling me was "mad for it," unlike myself apparently) and I met Ryan in town outside the William Tell pub. We were together for years, literally. Almost four. And the sex was good, but not very good. With Jack it was different. I was older and I had oodles more confidence. I liked my body enough to let him see me naked in semi-darkness (never daylight!) and it made me feel close to him.

So, as you see, one-night stands hadn't really come into it until tonight. Sure, Justin was young, very young. But it was uncomplicated and, feck it, fun.

Justin sat up and looked at me. "You seems miles away," he said with concern. "Do you want me to stop?"

"No," I said, "I just don't normally do this . . ." I shrugged.

"You're on your holidays," Justin smiled. "Relax. We won't do anything you don't want to do."

"How did you get to be so nice?" I asked.

"Practice," he grinned. He began kissing me again, concentrating on my lips and neck and then running his lips down toward my breasts. I revelled in the sensations and began to relax. I moved my hands down over his back toward his pert buttocks. I started to unbuckle his belt using both hands. He sat up slightly, allowing me to unbutton his jeans and slide them down his thighs. He kicked off his shoes and deftly removed his socks with either foot. He then helped me pull his jeans down his legs and pushed them off the bed onto the floor.

He began kissing me again, his hands moving my knee-length skirt toward my waist. As his fingers skimmed over the lacy top of my hold-ups, I moaned. He teased me through the material of my knickers and my body began to respond to his touch. His fingers danced at the edge of the lace, skimming my skin and sending darts of pleasure up and down my spine.

I ran my hand up and down his hardness. He breathed heavily. "I really want you, Amy," he groaned.

"Do you have any . . . you know?" I asked. The word "condom" just wouldn't come out of my mouth.

"Shit, no," he muttered. "Sorry."

"Wait there," I whispered, remembering the stash on the mantelpiece. I pulled down my skirt, threw my top back on and ran down the stairs. Luckily everyone was too drunk or too asleep to notice me helping myself to a handful of Durex. Stella and Jasper were lying asleep on the couch, her head on his knee. Polly, Siobhan, Martha, Jan and Beth were dancing, still to *Abba's Greatest Hits.* Beth, Julie and Suzi were sitting at the table talking, about husbands and weddings no doubt. Deirdre was asleep on an armchair and snoring loudly. Amber waved over to me from the sofa.

"Hi, Amy, bet you're regretting that garlic bread now," she said.

"Justin doesn't seem to mind," I smiled and went back upstairs. Justin was lying on the bed in all his naked glory. He beamed at me as I opened the door.

"Hi, princess," he said. "Any luck?"

I held out my hand.

"Well done," he smiled. I sat down on the bed. He rolled over and bit my bum through my skirt.

"Hey," I squealed, dropping the condoms on the floor.

He picked one up. "What have we here?" he read the wrapper. "Strawberry—my favorite. Will you do the honors or will I?"

I blushed. "You," I whispered. I watched open-eyed as he opened the packet carefully with his teeth, spitting out the edge of the foil onto the floor. He removed the latex sheath and began to roll it on. I'd never seen a guy putting on a condom before. They'd usually done it under the covers or I'd shut my eyes tightly. With Jack I was on the pill so the process hadn't come up. So to speak.

"I hope you like strawberry," he grinned, pulling me toward him.

"I do," I smiled, "and mint."

"Are there mint ones?" he asked.

"There are," I assured him.

"We'll try one of those next, then," he said.

Thank you, God, for younger men, I prayed. Thank you.

When I woke up the following morning I felt remarkably fine considering the copious amounts of alcohol I'd poured into myself. Justin was lying on his back beside me, snoring gently. Julie and Suzi had diplomatically slept downstairs I presumed, as their beds were empty. It was gray outside and fat raindrops were running down the windowpane. I'd forgotten to draw the curtains again.

Justin opened his eyes and looked over at me. "Morning," he smiled. He kissed my cheek gently. "How are you this morning?"

"Good," I smiled.

He looked and his watch and groaned. "Damn, I have to go now. I have to take a group of American tourists trekking." He stared out the window in dismay. "Typical, rain. Can I call in and see you later?"

"Sure," I smiled. It would be nice to see him but I wasn't too bothered one way or another. Which was good. No—which was bloody excellent. We'd had great sex, a real laugh and I was happy to leave it at that. Love them and leave them—it was a strange new feeling to me.

He jumped up and threw on his clothes. He leaned over and kissed me again. "Thanks, I had a great night."

"My pleasure," I smiled, meaning it.

As soon as I heard the door slam, Suzi and Beth bounded into the room.

"I don't believe you did that," Beth giggled. "He's only nineteen."

"Nearly twenty," I grinned.

We spent the day lolling around the house. Tim called in and suggested a hike and we laughed at him. He ended up sitting with us all afternoon watching bad television and eating junk food. Hangover city. Deirdre was quite chipper as she'd slept most of it off in the nightclub—everyone else was dying.

"I thought this was supposed to be a healthy, outdoorsy weekend," Tim smiled. "Lots of fresh air and exercise."

"But some of us *have* had lots of exercise," Polly insisted, grinning at myself and Amber.

"How was the weekend?" Mum asked as Suzi and I staggered in the door on Sunday evening.

"Great," Suzi said, dumping her bag in the hallway.

"Brilliant," I agreed.

"Matt's in bed," Mum said. "He didn't get in till nine this morning. He had a shower, he was covered in shaving-cream and lipstick."

"I don't want to know," Suzi smiled.

"Lipstick writing," Mum insisted. "Not lip marks."

"I think I'll join him," Suzi said, yawning. "I'm bushed."

"Me too," I said, putting my head on my sister's shoulder.

"You can tell me all about it tomorrow then," Mum smiled. "I'll bring your bags up." She swung the bags onto her shoulders.

"I'll help you, Mum," I said, taking my bag off her.

"We'll tell you some of it," Suzi said, winking at me. "Not all."

"There are some things even a mother doesn't need to know," Mum smiled.

Chapter 34

"How many steps?" I asked Suzi. "Three or four?"

She bit her lip. "Four, I'm not used to walking in such a long dress. We'll have to go slowly."

"Did you hear that, Dad?" I asked, "four steps to the end of the aisle from the door, not three, OK?"

"Sure, love," he said distractedly. He was listening to RTE 1 on his Walkman.

We'd been in the church for almost an hour now and he was getting a little bored. Katie and Simon, Julie's children—the flower girl and pageboy—were getting a little twitchy too. But Suzi wanted to get everything just right.

The last few weeks since the hen had flown by. I couldn't believe that Suzi's wedding was in two days. She and Mum had been up to ninety getting all the last-minute details organized. The marquee had been erected the day before as it needed some time to "settle" into the ground according to the company. It was magnificent—a huge white rectangle with pink and white striped awnings inside. The roof was covered with white chiffon and huge imitation crystal chandeliers hung from the ceiling. The wooden floor had been covered with a green carpet except for the dance area which had been left bare. There was a small catering tent to the back and a side tent, opening onto the main tent, for the bar. The fold-up tables and chairs were stacked on the floor, waiting to be erected.

"What music are you using for the procession?" I asked Suzi as we waited while Father Lucas talked to Matt and his brother, Luke, who was his best man. Matt's family had arrived from Perth that morning and poor Luke was looking a little shattered as he'd come straight from the airport.

Luke was tall and well built, like his brother, with a shock of blond hair, blue eyes and a wide, toothy smile. Your average Australian hard body. He was also just twenty-two, which after Arklow didn't seem all that young anymore. Tragic, aren't I?

" 'The Trumpet Tune' by Purcell," Suzi said. "Matt chose it. He originally wanted 'Sympathy for the Devil' . . ."

"The Rolling Stones' song?" I asked incredulously.

"Yes," Suzi smiled. "It's his favorite."

I laughed. "What did Father Lucas say?"

"He didn't think it was appropriate in the circumstances."

"Quite right too," I smiled. "They use it as the funeral song in *The Big Chill*."

"I'd forgotten about that," Suzi mused. She smiled. "But I don't think that was what he meant. Anyway Matt settled for trumpets instead."

"Ladies," Father Lucas said loudly from the front of the church, "ready to proceed?"

"Yes, Father," Suzi smiled.

"And one," Father Lucas began, "two . . . keep your head up, Amy. Mr. O'Sullivan, full attention, please. Simon, hands out of pockets, please."

"Sorry," Dad mumbled, taking the earphones off his head and slipping them into his pocket. Simon took his hands out of his jeans and clasped them in front of him.

We walked up the aisle, slowly and remarkably together.

"Suzi, you stand beside Matt," Father Lucas instructed as we reached the altar, "Amy drop back behind her with Katie and Simon by your side. Matt and Luke stay put. Good, good. That's perfect."

"Can we go now?" Dad whispered to me. I smiled.

"Mr. O'Sullivan, hand your daughter over, good, good, and take your place in the pew. Perfect." Father Lucas beamed. "Nicely done. I think that's it until Saturday. There will be two ushers though?"

"That's right," Matt nodded. "They're playing in a rugby match today, but they'll be here on Saturday."

"Unless there's another bloody rugby match," Suzi muttered under her breath. "Can we practice the readings?" Suzi asked Father Lucas. "Luke's here, he's reading the poem and Siobhan is doing the Mark Chapter Ten one. She's not here though."

Luke butted in. "It'll be all right, mate. I don't need to practice." He was dying to get to the pub with Matt and catch up. Another minute in the church would do his head in. He'd said he couldn't remember the last time he'd been in one.

Suzi seemed doubtful. "I suppose, if you're sure . . ."

"That's it then," Matt grinned. "Who's coming to Fitzie's?" Fitzgerald's Pub was just down the road.

"Matt," Suzi began, "we have to talk to the girl from Mad Flowers and help Dad with the garden."

Matt looked distraught. "But Luke wants to see a real Irish pub, don't you, Luke?" He elbowed his brother in the ribs.

"Please, Suzi," Luke said imploringly, "we'll only stay for one, I promise."

I tried not to laugh.

Suzi's face softened. "OK, but I want you back in one hour, do you hear me?"

Matt nodded.

I had a brainwave. "Why don't I go with them, Suzi, to keep an eye on them?"

"Good one, Amy," Luke smiled. I sensed trouble.

"As long as you're back later to finish the seating plan," Suzi said. "Promise?"

"Of course," I said. "Anyway it's nearly done, I just have to stick the leaves on and spray it again."

"And the place names?" Suzi asked.

Yikes, I thought. I'd forgotten all about those.

"I'll do them tomorrow. How many people are there exactly?" I asked, trying not to appear nervous.

"A hundred and thirty-two."

I whistled. "That many," I said. "I'd better get a few more gold pens."

I'd decided to write each guest's name on a gold-sprayed real leaf. The table plan would also be gold, with each table's names on a separate large leaf—these ones were fake. It was taking rather longer than I'd originally planned. I'd have to get up early and start writing the names on leaves—all one hundred and thirty-two of them!

"Are you married, Amy?" Luke asked as we walked down the road toward the pub.

I spluttered. "Married! Me? No way!"

He smiled. "But you're so pretty—I can't believe no one's snapped you up yet."

"Mate!" Matt interrupted. "Stop flirting with my sister-in-law."

Luke grinned. "Can't help myself, sorry."

"Luke's the womanizer of the family," Matt explained. "Pay no attention to him."

But I intended to pay attention to him, lots and lots of it. He was just what I needed, more good-looking distraction. After Justin I was hooked.

As we walked into Fitzgerald's my heart suddenly lifted and then sank lead-balloon-like to the floor. In the corner, chatting animatedly, was Steve. Beside him was a dark-haired woman in a flamboyant black and purple dress. I tried to peel my eyes away from them but I couldn't. They were smiling and laughing. When Steve took her hand in his and kissed it, I decided I'd had enough.

"Let's go," I said hurriedly to Matt and Luke who were standing at the bar by now. "I'd forgotten how much I disliked this pub."

"Are you joking?" Luke asked, looking around. "It's great."

"We've already ordered," Matt said levelly.

"Right," I said, moodily. "I'll find somewhere to sit."

"We can go if you like, Amy," Luke said kindly.

"No, it's fine," I said quietly. "Ignore me. I'm being stupid." I sat down at the far end of the pub, making sure I couldn't see Steve and he couldn't see me.

Stupid, stupid, stupid. What did I expect—that Steve still held a torch for me? That we were "soul-mates"? That he'd notice me over here, run over and declare undying love? I wasn't living in a Mills and Boon romance. I'd be lucky if he even said hello to me . . .

"Hello, Amy."

I raised my head. Steve was smiling down at me uncertainly.

"How are you?" he asked. "I thought I saw you come in."

"Fine," I snapped. You know what they say—attack is the best form of defense.

He stared at me for a few seconds. "Can I sit down?" he asked.

"It's a free country," I said.

"Is there something wrong?" he asked gently. "You seem . . ."

"How would you know how I seem?" I asked.

"If you're going to be like that," he stood up.

"Steve," I began. I took a deep breath, "I'm sorry, sit down, please."

He sighed. "Listen, don't worry about it. I only wanted to . . ."

"Steve," a voice trilled down from above our heads, "Are you ready?"

Steve stood up. "Amy, this is Ella—Ella, Amy."

"Hello," I said stiffly. Ella? My mind went into overdrive. The ex. It was obvious. They were back together. Maybe they'd been together all along. I was such an idiot. My eyes rested on her left hand. She was wearing a bloody huge hulking diamond on her ring-finger. It was impossible to miss it. As Hugh Grant would say : fuck, fuckity, fuck.

"Amy works in the children's bookshop I was telling you about," Steve explained.

I stood up. I couldn't take this anymore.

"I'm sorry, I must join my friends," I smiled falsely. "Please excuse me." I walked over to the bar where Matt and Luke were talking to the barman.

"Hi, guys," I smiled, putting my arm around Luke's back and holding him close to me.

Luke smiled. "Here's your drink, Amy." He passed me a pint of lager. I turned my head to see if Steve was watching. He was standing by the door of the toilets, his eyes fixed on me. His fiancée was nowhere to be seen.

I held Luke tighter.

"I like the Irish hospitality," Luke beamed at me. "Very welcoming."

Suddenly I felt a tap on my shoulder. "Amy, can I talk to you for a minute?"

Steve was standing beside us, glaring at me.

"She's all yours," Luke said, unraveling himself from my arms and picking up his pint.

I was caught. I didn't want to appear rude in front of Luke so I nodded. "Let's go outside," I suggested.

"Fine," Steve muttered.

We walked out of the bar and into the sunlight. It was a warm and bright day and I wished I'd brought my sunglasses.

"What's wrong with you?" Steve asked again.

"What do you mean?" I asked innocently.

"That was really rude in there. Ella doesn't know what to think," Steve began.

I sighed. I wasn't in the mood for this. I wanted to get back to my uncomplicated Aussie and my pint.

"Well," Steve continued, "an apology would be nice."

"Sorry," I mumbled. "Can I go?"

Steve stared at me and the edges of his mouth began to curl.

"What?" I muttered. "Are you laughing at me?"

"Might be," Steve grinned. "You're just so impossible. You're like a petulant child."

"I beg your pardon?" I asked.

"You heard me," he said.

I scowled.

"Anyway, I wanted to tell you that I'm moving to Bath in a little while, that's all," he said calmly.

This information took a few seconds to sink in.

"Bath?" I asked. "Why Bath?"

"I have friends there," he began. "And it's easier for work, nearer London."

"Fine," I said. "You've told me now." I turned away from him, toward the door. I didn't know how to feel so I blocked everything out and concentrated on Luke and pints. Luke and pints.

"Amy," Steve grabbing my arm and stopping me, "you really are impossible. Do you have nothing to say?"

I'd had enough. "What the hell do you want from me?" I asked loudly. "You're engaged to your ex and about to move back to England!"

Steve began to laugh. "I'm not getting married," he stated. "Ella is though. She came over from London to tell me. But that has nothing to do with me moving back to England. And anyway, I haven't definitely decided to go."

"Why did you say it then?" I asked. And he was calling me mad.

"I was trying to get a reaction, I suppose," he shrugged.

"I don't care where you go or what you do," I said firmly. "So goodbye."

"Amy," Steve said, exasperated, "I also wanted to say I'm sorry about Jack and Jodie."

I narrowed my eyes. "What?"

"I saw the billboard . . . and I put two and two together."

"You and the rest of the world," I muttered.

"I know it must be hard on you. I found out about Ella the same week."

"Really?" I asked.

"Yes," he sighed. "It was a real blow. I didn't want her back or anything, I just didn't want her to move on before me, I guess. I understand how upset you must have been. I was going to ring, but as the days went by I didn't know what to say."

I softened. He was being so nice. And he really did seem to understand. "I'm sorry for being rude that day . . ." I began.

"Valentine's Day," he grinned.

"Um," I nodded. I decided to be brutally honest for once in my life. I had nothing to lose. "I didn't want you to see me cry. I was in bits. I didn't know how to deal with it."

"Bad timing," he smiled.

"Sorry?" I asked.

"You and me," he said gently. "Bad timing."

"Yes," I smiled.

"Steve," Ella pushed the door open and walked toward us. "There you are. I thought you'd done a Houdini on me."

"Hi again," I said. "Sorry for rushing away earlier."

"That's OK, chuck," she smiled. "No hard feelings. Steve, I have to find a phone and ring Earl and then I'll be back out to you, love."

"You can use my mobile," I offered.

"That's all right," she smiled, "I have loads of change I have to use up. Thanks anyway." She went inside again.

"Earl?" I asked. "Who's he when he's at home?"

Steve grinned. "Earl's her fiancé. He's a musician."

I smiled. "Where were we?"

"You were apologizing," he said.

"I'd finished that," I said, raising my eyebrows. "So what next?"

"Who was the tanned guy in the bar," Steve began, "the one you had your arm around?"

"That's Luke," I said, "Matt's brother. From Australia."

"Over for your sister's wedding?" Steve asked. He had a good memory, I thought.

"Yes," I said. "He's the best man. The wedding's the day after to-morrow."

"Pity," Steve said.

"Why?" I asked.

"I was going to ask you out."

"Again?" I asked in amazement. "Are you serious?"

"Yes," he smiled. "Third time lucky. I haven't stopped thinking about you."

I began to blush. "I thought you were moving back to England," I said.

"Not yet," he said. "How about later in the week?"

"For moving back or a date?" I quipped.

"A date," he said.

"I'm sorry, but I have Beth's wedding then," I said.

"That'll be fun," he smiled. "Busy week for you then. I'll give you a ring."

"Tell you what," I smiled. "I'll ring you." I leaned over and gave him a kiss on the cheek. He put his arms around me and held me gently. "I'd better go," I mumbled, relishing the hug. "Bye."

"Bye, Amy," he smiled, releasing his arms.

I joined Matt and Luke at the bar.

"What kept you?" Luke asked. "Who was that man? We were about to send out a search party."

"He's a friend," I said softly, "from work." I picked up my pint. "Now where were we?"

I regretted the pints the following morning while sprawled on the floor of my bedroom writing each guest's name onto a leaf. Suzi had killed me for bringing Matt and Luke back half-cut, but when I'd told her about Steve she'd mellowed a bit.

My gold pens were acting up, clogging and blotting something terrible and some of the leaves had crumpled overnight, forcing me to spray some more replacements.

My mobile rang and I swore as I noticed that I'd misspelled Siobhan's name. Another leaf bit the dust.

"Amy, it's Beth."

"Hi, love, how are things?"

"Fine, I was just checking things for Tuesday—you know—the wedding practice."

"Stella and I are driving down in her Mum's car and we'll get there around lunchtime," I said.

"What time are you leaving?" Beth asked.

"As close to six AM as we can," I grimaced. The things I did for my friends.

"I'll arrange the practice for three," Beth said, relieved. "That should give us plenty of time."

"Perfect," I smiled. "And Beth?" I was going to tell her about Steve. And ask her about Jack and Jodie.

"Yes?"

"Nothing," I said, deciding I didn't have the energy to talk about either. "I'll see you tomorrow."

I clicked the phone off and sat back on my heels. That morning Mum had told me she'd heard on the grapevine that Jack and Jodie's wedding had been postponed indefinitely. I wanted to ask Beth about it so much that it hurt.

My mobile rang again.

"Amy, it's Beth again."

"Everything OK?" I asked.

"You were going to ask me about Jack and Jodie, weren't you?" she asked.

"How did you . . . ?" I began.

"Because," she said, "I know you. Basically it was a mutual decision. Jodie rang me yesterday but she wouldn't talk about it. She sounded upset."

"Really?" I whispered. This wasn't quite what I expected.

"They're coming, by the way," Beth added.

"To what?" I asked in confusion. This was turning into a strange morning indeed.

"To the wedding," Beth continued.

"Your wedding?" I asked. I was in total shock now.

"Yes," Beth said, a little confused. "My wedding. You know I invited them. I think they could do with a weekend away together, to be honest."

"But I thought . . ." I couldn't finish my sentence. I was upset, angry and tired all rolled into one.

"I know," she said. "They changed their minds. I don't know what to say."

"Tell them not to come," I said, my voice dangerously loud. "I'm the bridesmaid. Tell them to fuck off!"

Beth sighed. "If you really want me to, I will. But you know how long Tony's known Jack."

"You'd tell them to fuck off?" I asked in astonishment.

"Not exactly," Beth replied. I could hear her stifle a laugh. "I'd use different words. Why don't you think about it and ring me back?"

"OK," I mumbled.

I put down the phone and sat staring into space. Jack and Jodie had postponed their wedding. What did this mean? With Suzi's wedding on the near horizon I didn't have time to think about it. Which was probably just as well, all things considered.

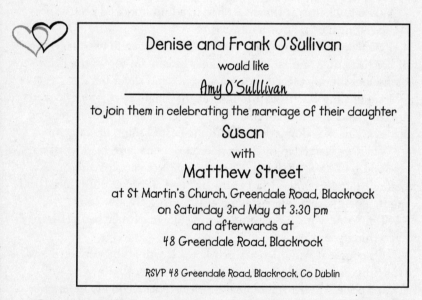

Chapter 35

Denise and Frank O'Sullivan
would like

Amy O'Sulllivan

to join them in celebrating the marriage of their daughter

Susan

with

Matthew Street

at St Martin's Church, Greendale Road, Blackrock
on Saturday 3rd May at 3:30 pm
and afterwards at
48 Greendale Road, Blackrock

RSVP 48 Greendale Road, Blackrock, Co Dublin

"Can you pass me the hairclips, Amy?" Jenny, the hairdresser, asked, "one by one."

"Sure," I smiled. I watched as she took small handfuls of hair in her fingers and twisted them expertly, securing each section with a hairclip. When she had finished the front of my head she tucked pink and white feathers into the twists.

"Suzi," she called over to my sister, who was waiting patiently at the basin, flicking through magazines nervously, "what do you think?"

Suzi jumped up, putting down the tatty old copy of *Hello* on the black leather seat and stood behind me looking in the mirror.

"Perfect," she beamed.

"I'm going to put the back up too," Jenny said, "or would you prefer it down?"

"No, up is good," Suzi said thoughtfully. "But maybe pull down a few tendrils to soften the effect around her face."

I felt like a prize heifer on show.

"Good idea," Jenny smiled. "I'll be finished in five minutes. Martine," she said to the junior who was picking the skin around her nails at the till, "could you wash Suzi's hair, please?"

When my hair was finished I had to admit it looked pretty spectacular. One hair-do down, one to go.

I waited while Jenny dried Suzi's hair and began to twist it on top of her head, in a similar style to mine. Finally on top of the bride's blond locks Jenny placed the delicate pink and silver tiara.

I caught my breath as I looked at the final effect—Suzi looked amazing and she didn't even have a scrap of make-up on yet. Jenny's sister, Ciara, was doing that next in the beauty salon upstairs.

When we walked in the front door two hours later Dad whistled.

"You both look amazing," he smiled. "Now go upstairs quickly before Matt sees you." Matt and Luke had stayed at our house last night. Their parents were staying at Blackrock Castle Hotel.

"I'm so nervous," Suzi said, sitting down on her bed. "I hope everything goes OK."

"Of course it will," I reassured her. "It will all be perfect. Now let's get you dressed."

Suzi peeled off her tracksuit and revealed her wedding underwear.

"What do you think?" she asked, surveying herself in the full-length mirror which had been borrowed from Mum and Dad's room for the day. The white balconet bra and briefs were deliciously lacy and frivolous. Suzi picked up a matching suspender-belt from the dresser and began to roll pale white stockings over her slim legs.

"I can never do these clippy things," she complained, catching her fingers in the small metal hoops.

"Let me do it," I smiled. I clicked the clips into place over the stockings. "There you go."

I then helped her as she stepped into her wedding dress. I fastened her up and straightened the seam. Tears came to my eyes as I looked at the final effect.

"You look beautiful, Suzi," I said. "Just beautiful."

Mum knocked on the door. "The flowers are here, love. Can I come in?"

"Sure," Suzi said.

As Mum walked into the room she gasped. She put the bouquets on the bed and put her hands to her mouth. "My little girl," she smiled. "You look like a princess. Frank," she called, "come here."

Dad walked in the door and stared at Suzi. "I don't believe it," he said in his best Victor Meldrew voice. He kissed Suzi on the forehead. "I can see the dress was worth every penny, Suzi. It's lovely."

"Thanks," Suzi beamed. I felt a little left out. I took my dress off the back of the door and unzipped it from its plastic cover.

Hearing a car pull up outside, Mum and Dad went back downstairs to dispatch Matt and Luke to the church.

I stepped into my dress and Suzi did me up.

I looked in the mirror and was pleasantly surprised. I looked all right. My hair really suited the dress and Ciara had done a bloody good job with the old slap. Amazing what make-up can do these days. We both slipped on our shoes.

"Give us a hand with the ribbons, will you?" Suzi asked. She was finding it hard to bend down in her dress. I wound the white ribbons of her ballet-type slippers around her ankles and tied them carefully in two small bows.

Suzi picked up the bouquets from the bed and handed me the two smaller ones. One for me and one for Katie, Julie's daughter, who we were meeting at the church. The bouquets were made up of white and pink flowers including roses and lilies.

Suzi kissed me on the cheek. "Thanks for being my bridesmaid, Amy," she said.

"It's a pleasure," I smiled back. "I'll just see if it's safe to go downstairs now." I poked my head out the door. "Mum," I shouted, "are the guys here?"

"No," she shouted back, "they've just gone. They're meeting Eamon and Andrew at the church." Eamon and Andrew were the two ushers, friends of Matt's from rugby.

"Are you ready?" I asked.

Suzi took a deep breath. "I think so," she smiled nervously.

Mum, Dad, Suzi and me arrived at the church in a cream vintage car. Suzi had insisted on being driven around the block a few times—just to get the whole wedding experience, car and all. Pulling up outside St. Martin's, Suzi grabbed my hand and squeezed it tightly. She looked anxious.

"You're fine," I whispered. "Matt is waiting for you."

"Yes, you're right," she smiled.

We waited outside the church for a few minutes, arranging Suzi's dress and veil and composing ourselves. It was a bright day and the sun was threatening to shine through the clouds very soon. Julie rushed toward us dragging Simon and Katie by the hands. Simon was wearing a black morning suit with a cream silk waistcoat, which looked sweet on his small, slim frame. Katie's dress was white with tiny pink roses embroidered on the bodice and on the hem and the edges of the sleeves.

"Sorry we're late," Julie gushed. She tried to flatten Simon's cowlick with her hand. Brian Lowan followed behind her, walking at a slower pace. He took his wife's hand.

"Leave the kids with Suzi and Amy," he smiled, "and come inside." He leaned over and kissed Suzi on the cheek. "You look lovely," he smiled. "Good luck."

"Thanks," Suzi said. "Now take your places, Katie and Simon," she said kindly. "Katie, you hold Amy's hand until we get in, OK?"

Dad popped his head inside the church. "That's us," he said. "Eamon gave me the nod."

He took Suzi's arm and I stood behind her holding Simon's and Katie's hands. We began to walk inside. Simon dropped behind us and Katie walked beside me, looking at her feet carefully, determined to get it right.

"Head up," I whispered to her. She smiled at me a little anxiously. "I won't let you trip," I assured her. "I promise."

I was incredibly nervous as we made our way up the aisle. I could see Matt's back, resplendent in a dark cream silk morning suit. It looked amazing against his sallow skin. Luke, Eamon and Andrew were wearing black morning suits with cream waistcoats, like Simon's. I kept my head up and tried to look straight ahead. It was hard not to glance at the guests though.

"Amy," I heard Beth's voice whisper. I turned my head and saw her beaming at me from one of the pews near the front. I smiled. There were tears in her eyes—she was such an old softie. Tony wasn't coming until later, so she was sitting with Judy and Eva.

The service flew by. One minute we were "gathered here today" and the next minute Suzi and Matt were "I do-ing." As we retired to sign the register in a small room to the side of the altar, Suzi let out a huge sigh.

"What a relief," she smiled. She and Matt sat down at the desk and signed the huge black leather-bound register. Followed by myself and Luke as witnesses. As I leaned over him in the cramped room to sign the book, Luke placed his hand on the small of my back. My skin tingled deliriously. Temptation.

"Now it's legal," Father Lucas smiled. We all cheered.

Suzi and Matt beamed. Matt grabbed Suzi and kissed her passionately. Father Lucas cleared his throat.

"Everyone looking this way," the photographer commanded. "Say sausages."

"Sausages," we chorused.

Mum and Dad and Matt's parents squeezed into the room, obstructing the photographer. "Careful," he complained, as Mum knocked his arm with her elbow.

"Sorry," she beamed.

He softened and smiled. "One more. Flower girl and pageboy—look this way please. Best man, eyes front, please. Stop checking out the bridesmaid!"

We all laughed. Warm waves of anticipation slithered up and down my spine. Then I thought of Steve and how kind he had been. Maybe I'd . . .

"Amy," Suzi said, "you need to move so we can get out."

"Sorry," I mumbled, moving toward the door and taking Katie's hand. As we came out the heavy wooden door the guests all began to clap and cheer. Suzi and Matt led the way down the aisle, smiling broadly. It seemed to take forever to walk back down the aisle. I had to pay attention or I'd end up on top of Suzi. Luke walked beside me. Eamon and Andrew brought up the rear with Katie and Simon.

The sun had broken through the clouds outside and was beaming down. Mum handed Simon and Katie plastic bottles of bubbles in the shape of white churches as soon as we got outside, and they began to fill the air with tiny transparent spheres which drifted in the gentle breeze.

Beth joined me outside. "That was a beautiful service," she smiled. "You look lovely. And that Luke's a bit of a hunk."

"No kidding," I grinned. "But wait till you hear about Fitzie's. I completely forgot to tell you. You'll never guess who I bumped into. Go on, guess."

"Um, oh, I don't know, tell me," she squealed impatiently.

"Steve," I grinned again.

"No!" she exclaimed. "What happened?"

"Well," I began, "first of all I thought he was engaged—he was with his ex . . ."

"The English girl?" Beth interrupted.

"Yes, Ella," I continued. "Then he said he was moving back to England, and then he said he thought about me all the time and we kind of made up."

"Really?" Beth asked. "That's great. But I thought you were rude to him . . ."

"Amy!" Matt shouted over at me. He was standing under a tree with Luke and staring over at me expectantly.

"I'll fill you in on the details later," I promised, touching her arm gently. "Right now I have a date with a photographer."

We left the church after the photographs. Luke and I shared a taxi with his parents. I was dying for a drink, but stopping at a pub was out of the question. This bridesmaid lark wasn't the best for one's enjoyment quota.

I perked up when Luke reminded me that we could lay into the champagne early. He was dead right. I just hoped he could open bottles—I hated the bang they made and always refused to do it.

The balloon man had visited the house while we were at the church and the outside of the house was covered in clumps of huge white balloons.

"Looks like Disneyland," Luke quipped as we made our way under a balloon arch and into the house.

"I'll be back in one second," I promised as I nipped upstairs. I checked my appearance in Suzi's room. My hair was still in place, my make-up hadn't run and I had nothing stuck in between my teeth—perfect.

"Here you go," Luke handed me a still fizzing glass of champagne as I joined him in the garden. The string quartet had begun to play and the guests were beginning to arrive. Suzi and Matt had decided to make the most of the vintage car and had gone on a short drive around the neighborhood.

Siobhan and Deirdre bounded over to me. "Hi, Amy," Siobhan smiled. "How are you? You look great!"

"Thanks," I smiled. "This is Luke, Matt's brother."

"Hi, Luke," the girls smiled, giving him appreciative looks.

"Have you both recovered from the other weekend yet?" I asked.

"Just about," Deirdre said. "It was great though. And how's that young man—Joseph, was it?"

"Justin," I corrected her.

"Have you seen him since?" Siobhan asked. Luke was listening with interest.

"No," I said, anxious to change the subject. I didn't want Luke to think I was that sort of girl. Not that I was and, to be honest, in the circumstances I was sure "that sort of girl" was probably exactly what he was looking for. "Here come Suzi and Matt," I said, grateful for the distraction. We all watched them step into the garden, Matt with his arm protectively around his new wife's waist.

"Don't they look sweet together?" Deirdre asked.

I was whisked away from the girls for another round of posed photographs, "The O'Sullivan Family," "The Wedding Party,"

"The Bride and Bridesmaid," "The Bride, Bridesmaid and Flower Girl" . . . I hoped my smile wasn't too lopsided.

The photographs seemed to go on forever and ever. "Smile," "Say cheese," "Sausages." Finally we were allowed to escape. Matt and Suzi weren't so lucky—the photographer took them further into the garden for some romantic shots.

"See you all tomorrow," Suzi laughed as they walked away.

"Amy," I heard my name shouted across the crowd.

Chapter 36:

It was Polly, standing with Amber in the shade of the large cherry tree. I made my way over, squeezing through the guests carefully. As I drew closer I noticed a familiar face beside Amber.

"Hi, girls," I smiled, "hi, Tim. I didn't know you were coming."

Amber blushed slightly under her golden St. Tropez fake tan. "I rang Suzi. She said it was all right."

"Oh, sorry," I apologized, realizing that I'd made her feel awkward, "I didn't mean it that way—it's a nice surprise, that's all."

"Justin was asking for you," Tim grinned. "He's quite taken with you, poor lad. Amber told him what age you really are . . ."

Amber dug him in the ribs. "Hey," he complained. "What was that for? Anyway, Justin didn't seem to mind. In fact he thinks it's way cool. Real Mrs. Robinson stuff."

"And who is Mrs. Robinson?" I heard Luke's voice ask from behind me.

"Amy's been seducing toyboys," Polly laughed.

"This is Luke, Matt's brother," I introduced the grinning man.

"Nice to meet you," he beamed, his gaze lingering on Polly's cleavage. I felt a dagger of jealousy shoot through my bones.

"This is Amber and Polly, they're my cousins, and this is Tim . . ."

"My Irish boyfriend," Amber piped in.

"Amy," Mum's voice rang out across the guests' heads from the back door of the house.

"Coming, Mum," I shouted back. "Have to go, guys," I said reluctantly. "A bridesmaid's work is never done. See you all later."

"And where are you staying?" I heard Polly ask Luke as I walked toward the house.

"Take these," Mum said, a tone of urgency in her voice. She handed me the box of leaves. "The waitresses said they'll help you put them out."

"But I thought the caterers were doing that . . ." I began.

Mum put her hands up in exasperation. "Don't ask. They said they couldn't find them. Please, Amy?"

"Sure, Mum," I smiled. Poor Mum—she looked rather frazzled. "I'll do it right now, OK?"

"Thanks, love," she said gratefully. "Now I have to ring the electrician. The electricity in the tent is on the blink."

I walked around the edge of the garden, waving to friends and relations and trying not to get caught up in any conversations.

"Is there anything we can do?" Judy asked as I passed her and Eva. "You look very busy."

"That would be great," I smiled. "Follow me."

In less then twenty minutes we had managed to put out most of the place names successfully. I'd managed to tweak Suzi and Mum's seating plan a little so that Polly was sitting in between Andrew and Eamon (both single and real charmers)—just in case she'd taken a shine to Luke.

I sat down at the top table and rested my head on my arms. Judy handed me a large glass of champagne which she'd procured from the bar.

"Thanks," I smiled gratefully.

"It's hot out there," Eva said, "noisy too. Not that I'm complaining of course. It's nice and peaceful in here."

The caterers buzzed around us, putting out the starters.

"It looks like the breakfast will be soon," Judy said.

"Breakfast?" I asked confused. "Surely this would be lunch or dinner or something."

"The wedding food is traditionally called breakfast," Eva explained.

"Eating breakfast in morning suits," I laughed. "Makes sense. Here comes the crowd." We watched the guests piling into the marquee, making a beeline for their seats and plonking themselves down. My seating plan was outside the tent and seemed to be doing the trick. I moved to my correct seat, beside Luke, and waited in anticipation.

Luke walked into the tent with the ushers and beamed as he saw me.

"Hi, Amy," he said, "I was looking for you."

"I've been in here for a little while," I explained. "Come and sit down." I patted his seat with my hand.

"Beside you?" he asked. I smiled. "Excellent, this gets better and better."

"I hope you have your speech ready," I said, raising my eyebrows.

"Absolutely," he grinned, patting his breast pocket. "Safe and sound."

"I look forward to it," I said.

"I'll just announce Matt and Suzi," he said, standing up and removing the microphone from its stand in front of him. He switched it on and tapped it lightly with his forefinger. "Ladies and gentlemen, please welcome the bride and groom . . ."

The guests stood up and clapped as the happy couple entered the tent and sat down.

Luke continued. "And now I'd like to ask Father Lucas to say grace. Father?"

Luke handed the priest the microphone.

Halfway through the main course of salmon, new potatoes and salad, Luke asked me about Justin.

"So you like younger men?" he said, his eyes lighting up.

The champagne was beginning to take effect so I was watching what I said. "That depends," I replied, hedging my bets, "on the young man in question."

"I see," Luke beamed. He speared a sliver of salmon on his fork and brought it up to my lips.

"Luke," I chastised. "Behave!"

"Oh, behave," he said in his best Austin Powers voice. He put his hand on my thigh under the table and I jumped.

"Stop," I said. "I'm serious."

"I will," he promised with a twinkle in his eye, "for now."

I looked up and saw Beth watching me with interest. She had a bemused expression on her face. I shrugged my shoulders and continued eating.

Suzi and Matt cut their French-style profiterole cake and the waitresses handed the gooey chocolate and cream-filled pastries to each guest. I tucked into the deliciously sweet concoction with relish. Luckily between eating and reading over his speech Luke was too busy to accost my legs again.

As the coffee was being poured, Luke stood up.

"Here goes," he whispered at me, smiling. "I'd like to introduce my new sister-in-law, Suzi Street." Everyone clapped.

Suzi stood up, smiling nervously. "When Matt asked me to many him I had one major decision to make," she began. "And that was whether to take his name or not. After all, Suzi Street does sound a little funny—like Easy Street or something. But I got over it and I hope you all will too." Everyone laughed gently. She was right— Suzi Street did sound a bit twee. I thought of Beth and Tony—Beth was keeping her own name so there wouldn't be any problems there. And Jack and Jodie, maybe that would never happen . . . I concentrated on what my sister was saying. "I'd like to thank you all for coming today. It means a lot to both Matt and me to see so many of our friends and relations here. Special thanks to Matt's parents Molly and Dan, and to the rest of the Aussies for making the long trip."

"Hear, hear," yelled my Dad who was certainly getting into the spirit, spirit being the operative word. He was on large brandies at this stage—ostensibly to calm his stage nerves.

"I'd like to thank my parents—Denise and Frank," Suzi continued, "for making this day so special and for letting us use the garden. Mum and Dad have been wonderful parents and have always supported me in everything I do. I love them very much." Suzi sniffed and wiped a tear away from her left eye with the back of her hand. "Sorry," she smiled. Mum was crying too and I was just about holding back the tears—what a family! "Amy, thank you for being my bridesmaid and for being a great sister. And thanks Katie and Simon, my wonderful flower girl and pageboy. And finally to Matt." Suzi turned toward Matt who was gazing up at her in open admiration. "Matt, you've made me so happy today—thank you. I look forward to all the years we'll spend together." She sat down and kissed him firmly on the lips. We all clapped and cheered.

Luke jumped to his feet again. "Father of the Bride—Mr. Frank O'Sullivan."

Dad cleared his throat and stood up. "I'm not a man for public speaking," he began, "so you'll have to be kind to me. I count myself lucky to have three beautiful and talented women in my life, my wife, Denise, and my two daughters, Amy and Suzi. When Suzi came back from Perth with Matt and broke the news of the engagement to us we were shocked but overjoyed. She seemed so happy and we knew that Matt was the right man for her. Matt is everything a man could want in a son-in-law—he's strong and fit, perfect for all those jobs around the house and garden I don't want to do." Everyone laughed. "He plays and follows rugby, so we'll never run out of conversation. And finally, he loves my daughter more than anything in the world and that's good enough for me."

"Aah," I sighed.

Luke smiled at me. "Bit of a softie is your dad."

"I know," I agreed.

"Suzi has brought Denise and me years of joy," Dad went on. "I'm delighted to welcome Matt and the Streets into our family." He raised his glass. "To Matt and Suzi Street. May they always live on easy street."

I stood up along with the rest of the marquee and raised my glass. "To Matt and Suzi." Luke clinked his glass against mine. "To the O'Sullivan girls," he whispered.

Luke stayed standing. "I'd now like to introduce the groom."

Matt stood up and took the microphone from his brother. He looked very nervous. Tiny beads of perspiration had formed on his temples.

"I've never done this before," he began, his voice faltering, "spoken in public, I mean. So you'll have to bear with me. Laugh at my jokes and stuff." Everyone laughed gently. Matt turned to face Suzi. "When I first met Suzi in The Irish Bar in Perth I couldn't talk. She was so pretty it took my breath away. So she did most of the talking that evening. I can't believe I'm here today, married!" Matt looked around at the guests, beaming. Everyone clapped and cheered. "I don't know what to say. I suppose I should thank my Mum and Dad and my rellies for being here. And Luke for being my best man. And everyone involved in making today cool—Father Lucas, the caterers, Mad Flowers, Denise and Frank. And anyone else I've forgotten. Oh, and thanks for all the great presents. And thanks to anyone who planted a Child of Prague in their garden. For the Aussies here, that's a little religious statue that's supposed to keep the rain away. As you can see it worked!" Everyone laughed.

"I don't think you plant them, Matt," Dad shouted. "They're not flowers."

Matt grinned sheepishly. "That's about it, then." Matt gazed at Suzi again. "I love you, Suzi. And I'll make you the happiest woman in the world, I promise. I'll look after you and love you till I die. You're my world." He leaned over, kissed her forehead and sat down.

There wasn't a dry eye in the house at this stage. Who would have thought that Matt was such a sentimental old rugby player?

Luke jumped to his feet. "My brother, the big romantic," he began, smiling. "Who would have thought? Married at his young age. In his prime you might say. What would Rosie O'Grady say?" Luke looked around the room, grinning. "Who was Rosie, I hear you ask?" The crowd hooted and cheered. "OK, OK, I'll tell you. Rosie was Matt's first girlfriend. And it was very serious. In fact, I believe he asked her to marry him? Isn't that right, mate?"

Matt smiled. "Yes, but we were only six!" he insisted. The guests clapped and laughed.

"Next there was Hannah," Luke continued.

Matt groaned.

"Matt was obsessed with Hannah. He followed her around

everywhere. He bought her treats. Talked about her incessantly. But there was an age issue. She was ten years older than him."

I stared at Matt. Who was this? Matt was smiling. "She was my baby-sitter. And he's right, I was mad about her when I was seven."

"But I'll stop there," Luke said. "Because although there were a few more girlfriends they all pale into insignificance beside Suzi."

Luke tapped his watch. "Table Ten, how am I on time?" He smiled over at one of the tables which was full of Clontarf rugby players and their partners. "Am I over or under? They're timing my speech," he explained.

"You're under," Andrew yelled. "Keep going."

"Right," Luke said. "What can I say about Suzi?" Suzi covered her face with her hands and squealed. "The first time I met her was at a barbie at Matt's house. She'd had a few tinnies too many and she was lying on her back in the garden looking up at the stars."

"You can stop there, Luke," Suzi shrieked. "No one wants to hear this."

"Yes, we do," I shouted. This sounded interesting.

Luke grinned wickedly. "Suzi looked up at me, bleary-eyed, and said 'You're cute. If things don't work out with my boyfriend I'll have you. What's your name?' So I sat down beside her and said 'Luke, Luke Street.'" Everyone laughed. "She looked at me and said 'That's funny, my Matt's name is Street too. Is that a common name in Australia?' And then Matt came over and introduced me as his brother. Suzi was mortified."

"I can't believe you told them that," Suzi giggled. Luckily she had a good sense of humor.

"So, if things hadn't worked out," Luke continued, "this could have been me and Suzi's wedding!"

Everyone clapped.

"But I don't think I'd be able for her," Luke admitted. "Irish girls are a real handful." I thumped him on the leg. "Thanks, Amy," he smiled down at me. "There's no need for violence, love. But seriously, I think Matt is the luckiest man in the world. Suzi is wonderful and they are obviously madly in love. And I wish them years and years of happiness together." He raised his glass. "To the bride and groom," he toasted.

"The bride and groom," the guests joined in.

"Now how am I on time?" Luke asked. "I'm officially finished."

"Turbo O'Hara won," Andrew shouted. "Four minutes, thirty seconds." A large man sitting to Andrew's right jumped up and cheered. Turbo, I assumed.

"Enjoy the evening, everyone," Luke said, sitting down and clicking off the microphone. A hum of conversation and laughter took over the room.

"I'm glad that's over," Luke smiled, putting his hand on mine. "I can concentrate on other things."

"Luke," Polly trilled, making her way past the tables, her eyes firmly fixed on the Australian prize, "you were wonderful. Well done." She leaned over and kissed him on the cheek.

I gave my cousin a dirty look but it was wasted on her.

"A touch of indigestion, Amy?" she asked sweetly.

"No," I muttered. I gave up and decided to leave her to it. "I'm just going to find Beth." I stood up and felt a little dizzy. The champagne and wine must have gone to my head.

"Are you OK?" Luke asked with concern. "Maybe I should come with you."

"I'm fine," I assured him. "Thanks anyway."

I decided to get some air.

"Amy," Matt called as I walked past him. Suzi was nowhere to be seen. "Join me."

"Where's Mrs. Street?" I grinned, making my way around the table, excusing myself past Father Lucas and sitting down beside Matt.

"Simon and Katie dragged her outside," he smiled. "They wanted to talk to her apparently. I think they're a bit worried that she won't be going back to looking after them, now she's married."

"She is though, isn't she?" I asked suspiciously. I hoped Matt wasn't so neanderthal as to suggest his wife couldn't work.

"Of course," he beamed. "She loves it and the Lowans are really good to her."

"That's all right, then," I said, relieved. "I liked your speech, well done."

"Thanks," he said, gratefully. "You don't think it was a bit short?"

"No," I said honestly. "You said everything you needed to say. Luke was good too. Must run in the family."

"Um," Matt murmured. An anxious look darted across his face.

"What?" I asked.

"Nothing," he said, trying to cover up.

"There's something on your mind," I prompted.

"It's Luke," he said quietly.

Chapter 37

"What about Luke?" I asked with interest.

"I just thought you should know," Matt said, "he has a girlfriend at home—Finn. They've been together nearly three years now."

"A girlfriend?" I asked in amazement. This was the guy whose hand had been on my leg a little while ago and who had been flirting with me shamelessly for the last two days?

"Yes," Matt said. "I'm not sure what kind of relationship they have, to be honest," he said gently. "I just don't want to see you get hurt. I know he's my brother and everything but you're my sister now. Kind of."

"Thanks," I whispered. Typical, bloody typical. Justin probably had a girlfriend too—a slip of a thing—all of eighteen or nineteen. Not that I cared, of course. What the hell was I doing?

"Amy?" Matt asked. "Are you OK?"

"Sure," I said. "Just a little disillusioned with men. Don't worry about it."

But Matt, bless him, did look a little worried. "We're not all like Luke," he said earnestly. "Some of us meet the right woman, fall in love and devote our lives to her. Look at me."

I could have hugged him. All along I thought he was, well, a bit dim to tell the truth. But he wasn't. He was a kind, decent, loving guy. And bloody good-looking, of course. The type of guy I'd like to love me and to take care of me. Sure, I'd take care of him too, but you know what I mean. I wanted hugs when I'd stubbed my toe getting out of the bath, understanding when I was pre-menstrual and crying at *Eastenders* . . .

"Amy," Matt smiled, interrupting my musings, "Suzi told me about that writer guy. He's nice, isn't he?"

I looked at him carefully. "What did Suzi tell you exactly?" I hadn't realized my private life was not so private after all.

"Everything," he said sheepishly. He paused for a few seconds when I hadn't said anything. "I'm sorry," he said, looking at me carefully. "Maybe I shouldn't have mentioned it. He just sounded like a good bloke, that's all."

"It's fine," I replied. "Don't worry about it." I thought for a second. "You know, you're right. He's nice. Bloody nice. Excuse me." I jumped up and walked quickly toward the house.

I walked in the kitchen door, past the caterers and ran up the stairs as fast as my dress would allow me. I picked up my mobile from my dressingtable and searched for the saved number.

"Hi, Steve," I said, "it's Amy."

"So what made you ring?" Steve and I were sitting in the garden, behind the marquee on a wooden bench. The band inside the tent were giving it wellies—their own rendition of favorite Abba songs as requested by Suzi, and Doors and Rolling Stones songs as requested by Matt. It made an interesting mix. "Light My Fire" followed by "Momma Mia."

Steve's arm was draped around my back and we were sharing a bottle of champagne.

"It was my new brother-in-law, I guess," I smiled. "Suzi had told him the whole story and he said you sounded nice."

"Nice?" Steve asked with disgust. "I'm not sure I like that."

"There's nothing wrong with nice," I insisted. "It's a hell of a lot better than nasty, dishonest or violent. And anyway, I'm not so sure you are all that nice."

"Hey you," Steve pinched my arm playfully and then studied my face. "You've been badly burnt along the line, haven't you?" he asked gently.

I nodded.

"But we're not all like that," he continued.

"That's what Matt said," I interjected.

"He's right," Steve stroked my hand. "Let's just be very, very nice to each other and see what happens." He kissed me on each eyelid, his warm lips sending a shiver down my spine.

"Suits me," I whispered as his lips found mine. His tongue gently but firmly explored my mouth, teasing my senses and warming my whole body. His fingers caressed the nape of my bare neck, feather-like and sensuous.

"Amy," he whispered into my ear, his soft breath tingling my earlobe, "in case I've forgotten to say it—you look beautiful."

We kissed for what seemed forever before we parted and he held me close to him, his fingers running up and down my arms in light, hair-raising movements.

"I'd better go inside," I sighed. "Suzi will be wondering where I am. I'm sure I was supposed to dance with the best man at some stage."

"Your sister will understand," Steve assured me, "and Matt sounds like a decent chap. I'd like to meet him."

"I'll introduce him," I smiled. The strains of "Knowing Me, Knowing You" came thundering through the tent. "I love this," I squealed. "Let's dance."

"An Abba freak!" Steve grinned. "What have I let myself in for?"

As we walked inside I caught my breath. Polly and Luke were sitting just inside the door, Polly balancing precariously on his knee. One of his hands was halfway up her Gucci skirt and they were eating the face off each other energetically.

"Charming!" Steve laughed.

"That's the best man," I grinned, glad that I felt nothing. After all, up to a few hours ago I had been harboring feelings for him—of lust perhaps, but they were still feelings.

"You're kidding?" Steve raised his eyebrows.

"No," I smiled, "that's Luke and the girl is Polly, my English cousin."

"Those English people," Steve joked, "no sense of decorum."

I pulled him toward the dance floor. The chairs and tables had been moved toward the back of the tent and the "walls," leaving plenty of room for dancing.

"Amy!" I heard my sister's voice yelling from beside the band. We made our way toward her. "Where were you? I was looking for you. Polly had to dance the first dance with Luke instead of you."

"Sorry," I said contrite. I leaned over and whispered in her ear— loudly as the music was deafening. "I was outside with Steve."

Suzi beamed. "In that case, I forgive you. But don't let it happen again." She grabbed my hand in hers and started to dance.

"Come on," she shouted to Steve. "Shake a leg." Steve took her in his arms and spun her around, flipping her into the air like she was as light as a feather and swinging her from side to side.

"This one can dance," Suzi exclaimed when he finally put her down.

Matt came lumbering over, looking a little worse for wear.

"Hi, mate," Steve shook his hand, "you must be Matt. I'm Steve."

"Nice to meet you, Steve," Matt grinned, putting his arm around Suzi's waist.

The band began to play "Dancing Queen" and we all threw ourselves around the dance floor. Mum and Dad, Beth and Tony, Eva and Judy, Eamon and Andrew, and Julie and Brian joined us, as well as some of the Street family. Luke and Polly had disappeared.

"I was going to ask you where you've been," Beth shouted at me while we were dancing together, "before I spotted Steve, that is."

I grinned guiltily.

"Good on you, Amy," she laughed. "You only live once."

Steve swept me away and held me in his arms.

It was a night to remember.

At two o'clock Dad reluctantly asked the band to stop playing. He didn't want to upset the neighbors, although he and Mum had invited them all to the afters to smooth over the waters. If they hadn't, our deadline would have been more like twelve o'clock.

"What are you doing now?" Steve asked as we made our way to a table at the side of the tent and sat down.

"I'm going to bed, I'm afraid," I said. "It's been a hell of a long day and I'm knackered."

"I'm sure you are," he said, taking my hand in his. "Can I see you tomorrow? I know you'll be busy clearing up but . . ."

"I'd love to," I interrupted. "Why don't I ring you at lunchtime? It would be nice to get away from the demolition site." I gestured toward the garden. The tent was staying till Monday but I'd promised to help tidy up tomorrow. Black-plastic-bag-land—here I come.

Steve stood up. "I think I'll get going."

I was disappointed. I was hoping he'd stay for a little while. But maybe it was just as well. I really was knackered. Suzi and Matt had already left for Blackrock Castle where they were spending the night before flying to Paris for a week the next day. I hadn't really seen Beth all night, let alone Siobhan, Deirdre and the rest of the girls from the hen. But it didn't really bother me. I'd had an amazing night. The best for a long, long time.

The following morning I felt remarkably fine, considering. I woke up with a smile on my face and I found it hard to stifle it. I was full of happy beans.

I could hear noise from outside and I padded toward the window and opened the curtains. Mum, Dad and Matt's parents were sitting outside, drinking coffee and laughing amiably. Luke wasn't with them, thank goodness. The sun was shining down gently and reflected off the white tent, making my eyes squint in the intense light.

I had a quick shower, threw on a T-shirt and shorts and joined them, making sure to bring my sunglasses.

"Morning, Amy," Dad smiled as I walked through the kitchen door, past the leftovers which adorned every available surface. "Would you like a glass of Buck's Fizz?"

My stomach lurched. "No, thanks, Dad. I'll have the orange though, on its own."

He poured me a glass and passed it to me.

"How are you this morning?" Molly Street asked.

"Fine, thanks, Mrs. Street," I said.

"Please call me Molly," she laughed. "We're family now, after all."

"And I'm Dan," Mr. Street smiled.

"So tell us," Molly continued, "who was that nice young man with you last night?"

"Yes, do tell us," Mum smiled wickedly.

I could feel myself blush. "He's a friend from work," I said quickly. "Um, who caught the bouquet by the way? I missed that bit."

"Stop trying to change the subject," my Mum said cruelly. "What's his name?"

"Steve," I muttered.

"Not that Stevie J guy?" Mum gasped.

"Yes, Mum," I said. "Now, drop it."

"That name sounds familiar," Molly mused. "Was he in the papers recently?"

"That's right!" Dan exclaimed. "You're right. He was. He's some sort of children's writer who's made a fortune on witch books."

"Wizard books," I corrected. "Now I really must be going." I jumped up. There was no way I was going to be put through the grinder today.

"But you haven't finished your juice," Dad said. "And I want to hear all about this Steve."

"See you all later," I said. I rushed up the stairs and grabbed my phone.

"Steve, it's Amy. Come and save me."

Chapter 38

Stella sang along with James Taylor's "Carolina in My Mind" which was playing on the radio.

"You've a great voice," I said when she'd finished crooning away.

"Thanks," she said. "I love singing. So tell me all about your sister's wedding, I want to know all the gory details."

"I don't know where to start," I smiled. We were sharing the driving and I was taking the second shift as I knew the directions. Getting to Cork wasn't a problem, the roads were mostly quite reasonable and clearly signposted. But finding Castlehaven was more of a problem. It was only sixty miles west of Cork City but the roads were small and narrow. Stella's mum had very kindly (and a little foolishly I thought) lent us her black convertible Golf. As it was only just after seven in the morning we hadn't put the top down—yet.

Stella turned off the M50 and onto the Cork road. "Start at the hairdresser's."

"Are you sure?" I asked.

"We have hours to fill," Stella laughed, "and I want to find out everything about being a bridesmaid from the expert."

"Thanks," I said glumly.

"Have I said something wrong?" Stella asked with concern.

"No," I said. "I'm just a bit paranoid about being the bridesmaid all the time."

"Twice!" Stella giggled. "Hardly all the time, you nutter." She bit her lip as she overtook a lumbering tractor.

I smiled. A few months ago I would have picked up on the word "nutter" and wondered did she really mean it. Now I knew that she was only slagging me. I felt a whole lot better and stronger in myself. I knew that it could be a temporary thing—that any day now I might feel bad again. But I'd started to recognize the signs—feeling tired and run down, getting upset over insignificant things, obsessive behavior. At the end of the day, I was bloody lucky and I was starting to recognize it and not curse the day I was born every time something went wrong. Although maybe last night's phone call was, in some ways, putting storm clouds on my horizon again. I'd have to wait and see.

"Amy?" Stella interrupted my musings. "Left or straight on, do you think?"

I recognized the road straight away. "Straight on," I said. We'd spent many summers in Schull as children and the drive was still familiar to me.

"So," Stella insisted, "you said you'd tell me everything. Go on."

"OK," I laughed, "OK. We got our hair done in Blackrock." I described our "up-styles" (Jenny had told us this was the official hairdressing name for putting hair up) and our make-up.

"The feathers sound wicked!" Stella grinned, pulling out slightly to avoid a cyclist. "Do you have any photos with you?"

"Give us a chance," I laughed. "It's all been a tad busy at chez O'Sullivan!"

"Sorry!" Stella said. "And then you got dressed."

"Correct," I smiled. "I helped Suzi put on her dress and then we went to the church. It was all quite exciting really."

"I'm really excited," Stella bubbled. "I've never been to a wedding before."

"You must have," I said incredulously.

"Honestly," Stella said. "This is my first. I have no idea what happens."

"Beth has told you about the breaking of the glasses and the plates after the meal?" I asked, keeping a deadly straight face.

"No," Stella replied doubtfully. "Is that not in Greece or Italy or something?"

"It's optional at any wedding," I continued, warming to the subject. "And after the speeches the bridesmaids are carried around the tables by the best man and ushers and any single man can kiss them. But they have to throw a few pounds into a bridesmaids' kitty."

"No!" Stella said, her eyes widening.

"It's true," I insisted. "And at the end of the evening the man who has put the most money into the kitty gets to go home with the bridesmaid of his choice."

"Amy!" Stella laughed. "You're making this up."

"I can't believe you took me seriously," I smiled.

"What's the best man like, anyway?" she asked. "Jed. I've met him once or twice, but I've never really talked to him."

"Why," I said, "are you interested?"

"Might be," she replied. "Depends."

I thought for a minute. "He's quiet," I began.

"And," she said.

"Nice-looking, I guess," I continued. "Tallish, a bit skinny. He wears glasses. Twenty-five, I think. A bit old for you."

"You're not making him sound very attractive," she said. "Maybe you're after him yourself."

"Jed?" I laughed. "I've already . . ." I stopped suddenly.

"You've what?" she asked. "Kissed him?"

I shouldn't have opened my big, fat mouth. Typical. "Yes," I admitted. "Briefly, on New Year's Eve. So it doesn't really count."

"Was he a good snog?" Stella asked with interest.

"He was, I suppose," I grinned. "Very tender and kind. I just wasn't ready for kind at that stage."

"Well, I am!" Stella stated firmly. "I've finally broken up with James."

"Oh, I'm sorry," I said.

"Don't be," Stella insisted. "He was a selfish creep. He didn't deserve me."

"Good attitude." I said. "What about Jasper?"

"He was just my transitional man," she said airily. I looked at her face. She was smiling. We both burst out laughing.

As we drove I told her about the wedding service, the food and the speeches. She listened in rapt attention. It was nice to have a captive audience.

I took over the driving at Cashel. Before we swapped front seats we decided to take the roof down.

"May as well make the most of the wheels," Stella grinned. "Might pick up a few hard-bodies along the way too. Like in *Thelma and Louise*."

"We're unlikely to find Brad Pitt on the side of the road in Ireland," I giggled. "More like Anto Pitted, knowing our luck, but we can give it a go."

With a bit of puffing and panting as it was rather stiff, not to mention awkward, we managed to take down the roof and fold it away.

"I thought you pressed a button and the roof put itself away," I moaned, sucking the top of my finger which one of the metal roof hinges had caught. I hoped it wouldn't turn black—Beth would kill me. She hardly wanted an incapacitated bridesmaid.

Stella looked at my finger, unimpressed. "You'll live, you big baby," she smiled. "And I think you've been in one or two Porsches too many, my love! Not too many roofs do that in real life."

"Hardly," I smiled. "I've been watching too many American soap operas."

Stella laughed.

We buckled ourselves in and I put my foot down on the accelerator. The Golf moved off smoothly, purring like a kitten. It was a joy to drive, responsive and nippy.

"Slow down, Amy," Stella said loudly as we took a corner a little too fast. I glanced over at her. She was holding onto the side-door handle for dear life.

"Sorry," I said. I reduced speed and prayed for an open road and a sleeping Stella. I fancied myself as Eddie Irvine, burning rubber in Monaco, hordes of babes at my beck and call (male ones for me, of course).

Stella reached into the back and pulled a CD case out of her bag. "What do you fancy?" she asked.

"Something poppy," I smiled. "Something we can sing along to."

"How about some early Madonna?"

"Perfect," I said.

Stella pulled out *The Immaculate Collection*. " 'Holiday' is first," she said, "then 'Lucky Star.' "

"Is 'Like a Prayer' on it?" I asked hopefully.

"It most certainly is," Stella confirmed. She slipped in the CD and we began to sing along.

"This is great!" I laughed as we tore down the road. Although we were only doing just over sixty it seemed much faster.

In no time we had reached the outskirts of Cork City and decided to stop for sandwiches at a roadside pub. Luckily we could park the car right outside so we didn't have to grapple with the hood again.

"Did you meet anyone new at the wedding?" Stella asked as she bit into her roll. We were sitting on wooden picnic benches outside.

"Not exactly," I smiled, pulling a large piece of red onion out of my sandwich and putting it on my plate.

"What do you mean?" she asked with interest.

"Have I told you about Steve?" I asked.

"No."

"Well, Steve is an English guy who writes children's books. You might have heard of him—Stevie J?"

"I don't think so," Stella admitted.

"Henry and the Master Wizard?"

"Oh, yes!" she exclaimed. "There was an article about the film in *Empire*."

"That's Steve's book," I continued. "Anyway I met him when he came into the bookshop I work in to do a signing."

"And?" Stella said.

"We kind of hit it off and we went out a couple of times," I skipped over the embarrassing messy bit in the middle. Although Stella was only seventeen I still wanted her to think I was reasonably "cool" and together. Not a complete moron. "And he was at the wedding."

"And you kissed him?" Stella asked with interest.

"Um," I nodded, my mouth full.

"Are you seeing him again?" she asked.

"I think so," I began, taking a sip of my Fanta. "But things have changed a little in the last few days. So, to be honest, I'm not sure now."

"Why not? What things?" Stella said. "Do you like him?"

"It's not as simple as that," I said. "There are other factors involved."

"Like what? Someone else?"

"Not exactly," I said hesitantly. "Well, maybe. I'm bit confused."

"You're confused!" Stella laughed. "I'm baffled. You're being very cryptic."

"Sorry," I said. "I'm not really sure I want to talk about it."

Stella looked at the traffic passing by. After a minute she turned back. "That's OK. I understand. I get like that myself sometimes." She smiled. "Tell me about the band at the wedding. Were they good?"

We talked about Suzi's wedding for a few more minutes before returning to the car. In just under two hours we pulled into Castlehaven. We pulled in outside Trudi's and climbed out of the car.

"I'm so stiff," Stella complained, stretching her arms above her head and yawning at the same time.

"Me too," I said.

"Amy, Stella," Beth came running out of the pub and gave me a huge hug. "It's so good to see you. You're early."

"Amy's a nippy driver," Stella smiled.

"Come inside," Beth said. "Tony and Jed are in the garden at the back. We're about to have lunch. Have you eaten?"

"Not really," Stella said, "we just had a sandwich on the way. I could definitely eat again."

"It's OK for you," I moaned. "You don't have a problem with your stomach sticking out. If I don't stop stuffing myself, I'll look like a pregnant bridesmaid tomorrow!"

"Don't be silly," Beth laughed. "You'll both look great. And the food here is lovely—loads of fresh seafood and salads."

"Well, maybe I could have a salad," I said doubtfully.

Beth led us inside, through the pub and into the garden.

"This place is amazing," Stella enthused. "I love all the low beams and the old wood bar."

Beth smiled. "We were lucky to find it," she admitted. "It's owned by friends of Mum's who retired down here a few years ago. They don't normally do weddings but they made an exception for us."

Tony and Jed stood up as we approached. "Hi, girls," Tony smiled. He kissed us both on the cheek. "Good to see you. Stella, this is Jed, my best man. You've met before."

Jed smiled shyly at Stella. "Only briefly. Hi, Stella." He held out his hand politely.

"Nice to finally meet you properly," Stella smiled.

"And you know Amy," Tony said wryly.

"Um, yes," Jed stammered.

"Hi, Jed," I smiled. I decided to be nice to him. He was a decent bloke and anyway, I didn't want to cause any hassle today of all days. Beth's wedding was only a day away after all.

We sat down and looked at the menus which were on the white metal table in front of us.

"Can I take your order?" a waitress with an American accent asked us.

"I'll have the steak sandwich with chips," Tony said. "And another pint of Guinness."

Beth gave Tony a disapproving look. "What?" he asked.

"It's not even one o'clock," Beth pointed out.

Tony reached over and took Beth's hand in his. "We're on our holidays, love," he smiled. "And I'm only keeping Jed company."

"Don't blame me," Jed said quickly.

"Do you not want another pint?" Tony asked.

"Of course I do," Jed assured him.

"Well then, point proven," Tony said.

We all laughed.

"I'll have the same," Jed smiled at the waitress.

"Scampi for me," Beth said, "and a glass of cider."

"And me," Stella piped up. "But make mine a pint."

"And yourself?" the waitress asked me. I studied the menu carefully. "A Caesar salad," I replied, "and a pint of cider."

"Good on you," Tony smiled.

Beth seemed a little worried. "We have the practice at three. I don't want the wedding party half-cut, thank you very much."

"We'll be fine," Stella assured her. "A couple of drinks won't do us any harm. And we don't have to drive again today, do we?"

"No," Beth said, "I suppose not. Your guest house is across the road."

"Are you staying there too?" I asked.

"Yes and no," Beth said. "Tony's staying there tonight and I'm here. And tomorrow we're both staying here. They have a little guest house which is a converted stables. It's lovely. We're going to stay down for a few days after the wedding to recoup. Then Tony has to get back to work."

"We'll take a proper honeymoon in the New Year," Tony said, "when work's a little less frantic."

"How's it going?" I asked. Tony and Jed's computer company had been up and running for over a month now.

"Really well," Tony said. "We've more work than we can handle right now. We may need to take on another person soon."

"That's great," I smiled.

"What do you do, Stella?" Tony asked quietly.

"I'm studying at the moment," Stella told him. "I mean, I was. I've just finished my Leaving Cert. I'm hoping to get into college this year. I'd like to study computers."

"Really?" Jed asked. He and Tony began to discuss the various college courses with her.

I put my head on Beth's shoulder and sighed. "Computers mean nothing to me," I said. "I can just about use the re-order program at work. And send e-mails. That's about it."

"I know what you mean," Beth said. "At least you don't have to live with a computer nerd," she whispered.

I lifted my head. "When are the other guests arriving?" I asked, trying to sound casual.

Beth looked at me carefully. "Most of them are arriving this evening. Tony's mum and dad are here already. They went into Skibbereen with my parents for lunch. They're all staying in the Skibbereen Grand Hotel. They'll be back for the rehearsal."

"How about your friends?" I asked.

"You know about Jack. I believe you were talking to him," she raised her eyebrows.

"Last night," I mumbled.

"And there aren't that many others really," Beth continued, pretending not to notice my awkwardness. "Just Owen and Gloria, Louise and Hal, and Eithne, Joe and Colm. They're all staying in Skib, I think." Owen, Joe and Colm were friends of Tony's from school and college. Gloria was Owen's wife, and Eithne was a school friend of Beth's.

Beth and Tony had decided to have a tiny wedding—best friends and direct family only. And Louise, Beth's boss who she was very fond of, and her partner Hal who owned a chain of clothes shops.

Neither Beth nor Tony were into big occasions and they wanted their day to be spent with the people they loved the most.

And, as one of Tony's oldest friends, Jack was going. Because last night, on the phone, I had told him to.

Chapter 39

"Amy?" I nearly dropped dead at the vividly familiar voice. I was out of breath as I'd been racing around my room packing for Beth's wedding. Myself and Stella were leaving in the wee hours of the following morning, I had no clean underwear to my name and I couldn't find my wallet.

"Jack?" I faltered. I sat down on the floor. My head was racing. Why was he ringing?

"I'm sorry," he began slowly, "is this a bad time? Will I ring you back?"

"No, no," I said, "it's fine. I'm just packing for Beth's wedding."

"That's why I'm ringing you," he said.

"Oh?" I asked.

"Beth called in. She asked us not to go to the wedding. She said it would cause too much trouble."

I smiled broadly. I knew it was awful but I'd asked Beth to talk to them. After mulling it over I'd told Beth that I was her best friend, not Jodie, and that if she loved me at all she'd ask them not to go to the wedding because it would hurt me too much. Talk about giving someone a guilt trip.

"She told me," I said. Isn't it great? I wanted to say. Beth likes me more than Jodie. It's me she chose. Me, me, me. But I wasn't that stupid. He went silent. I decided to tread carefully. "I'm sorry," I lied, "but it had nothing to do with me."

"Beth said it was her decision and that Tony had reluctantly gone along with it. I don't want to spoil her day. Or your day, I suppose," he added.

"Um, thanks," I murmured. I was beginning to feel a little awkward. Then it hit me. Of course I didn't want *them* there, rubbing my nose in it, but Jack on his own—now that was a different matter. I could show him how great I looked, tell him all about Steve, and Suzi's wedding. Let him know how much better my life was without him. If nothing else it would make *me* feel better.

I could hear the cogs turning over in his brain. "Amy, did you ask Beth to talk to us?"

"No!" I lied shamefully. "I wouldn't do that."

"Sorry," he apologized. "I shouldn't have said that." He didn't sound all that sure.

"Jack," I sighed deeply and audibly, "listen, why don't *you* go, Tony would want you to be there. You've know each other forever."

"On my own, without Jodie?" he asked quietly.

"Yes," I whispered.

"No, I don't think so," he replied, "and anyway, things are a bit difficult at present." He fell silent for a moment. "Actually, you know, that might not be a bad idea. Are you sure you wouldn't mind?"

I gulped a breath. My heart was pounding faster than ever. I tried to keep my voice level. "No," I said. "It would be fine." I gulped. "Fine."

"Really?" he asked doubtfully. After all, the last time we'd seen each other I'd told him where to go in no uncertain terms in front of everyone.

"Jack," I replied, "I'm seeing someone else now. And even if I wasn't it would be all right, honestly."

"But you still haven't spoken to Jodie," he said levelly.

"No," I agreed, "I haven't. But I will."

"When?" he asked.

"Soon."

"Um," he mumbled, sounding unconvinced. "Who's this new bloke anyway?"

I smiled. So he'd heard. "Oh, just a writer," I said nonchalantly. "No one you'd know."

"Is he going to the wedding?" Jack asked.

"No," I said. This was all very strange.

"I have to go now, Amy," Jack said. "I'll ring Beth and check if it's OK with her and Tony."

"Wait," I said.

"Yes?"

"I just wanted to say that I was sorry to hear about you and Jodie, you know, the wedding and everything . . ." I trailed off lamely.

Jack coughed nervously. "Thanks," he murmured.

"Are you all right?" I asked.

"Me?" Jack asked. "Yes, I'm grand. It's . . ." He went silent for a few seconds. "Listen," he whispered, "I'd really like to talk to you about it. That's why I rang really. Maybe we can talk at the wedding."

"Right," I said in astonishment. "I'll see you in Cork."

I held the phone to my ear for several seconds after he'd clicked off his phone. Jack wanted to talk to me. Alone. And his wedding had been practically cancelled.

It suddenly dawned on me—he wanted me back. Yes, that must be it.

I wasn't sure how I felt about this. I sat down on the side of my bed and thought it over. Images of the past came rushing back to haunt me—myself and Jack walking on Brittas beach, myself and Jack painting the spare bedroom and covering each other in light-blue emulsion before sharing a bath and washing the paint out of each other's hair . . . it would be so familiar and so easy.

I decided that it would be simple to sweep all the bad things about our previous relationship under the carpet. Better the devil you know, as Kylie once said. I'd tried to push Jack out of my mind but he'd always been there lurking in the subconscious depths.

I'd had enough of being on my own. I was finally ready to marry Jack.

I had meant to ring Steve that evening but my mind was so full of Jack that I'd forgotten. I'd spent the last few days with Steve and we'd been getting on famously. But now everything had changed.

I sang to myself tunelessly as I threw some jeans into my suitcase. This was going to be one hell of a wedding.

"This is the most beautiful church I've ever seen," Stella said in a reverential whisper. Stella and Jed and I were standing at the entrance of the church looking toward the altar. "It's so quiet." Beth and Tony had gone on ahead while we'd finished up our drinks.

We stepped inside, practically tiptoeing into the cool, still interior. The walls of the simple, rectangular church were painted stark white and the well-worn mahogany wood of the pews and the altar looked hundreds of years old. The floor, which felt cold under my feet even though I had shoes on, was covered with dark copper-colored tiles, and huge brass chandeliers hung from the high wooden-beamed ceiling. The sun shone in through delicately blue and dark-pink colored glass windows which showed scenes from the Nativity and three tall, willowy saints.

"You're right," I agreed.

Beth and Tony were sitting silently in one of the pews to the left of us. They turned and smiled when they saw us.

"Hi, girls," Beth said in a low voice. "Reverend Elmes will be with us in a few minutes. And Mum and Dad are on their way."

I shimmied into the pew beside Beth. "It's so peaceful in here," I smiled.

"Isn't it lovely?" Beth asked. Trudi suggested it. The church was five minutes down the road from the bar which was very handy. "I haven't met Reverend Elmes though," she continued. "I hope he's nice. We did our preparation with Reverend Howe from the local church in Dun Laoghaire but he was taken ill at the last minute and couldn't travel down, unfortunately. He arranged Reverend Elmes for us."

"Welcome, welcome," a loud voice boomed from the back of the church. Myself and Beth jumped. A large woman with short dark hair was making her way toward us, arms outstretched. "Which of you are Beth and Tony?"

We all stared at the woman in astonishment. She was wearing a green T-shirt and a billowing flowery skirt.

"Is this the woman who's doing the flowers?" I whispered to Beth. Beth looked worried. "I'm not sure . . ." she began.

"I'm Clare Elmes, or Reverend Elmes," the woman introduced herself. "This is my parish."

I started to giggle. I couldn't help it. It must have been the cider. I set Stella off too. Beth glared at us before seeing the funny side.

"Sorry, Reverend Elmes," she said, trying not to laugh, "We thought you were a man. I'm Beth."

"Not at all," the smiling woman said. "I'm used to it. And call me Clare. I'm delighted to meet you."

"I'm Tony," Tony stood up and held out his hand. And this is Jed, my best man, and Amy and Stella, the two bridesmaids." We all said hello.

"I'm delighted to see everyone in such good spirits," Clare said. "A wedding is a glorious occasion and certainly one to enjoy. My own wedding was many years ago, of course, but it was a splendid day."

Jed looked at her in astonishment. "Is that allowed?" he whispered to me.

"It is in the Church of Ireland," I smiled.

"That's great!" Stella said quietly. "Getting married by a woman and a married one at that. How cool!"

Beth's dad walked in the door, followed by her mum and Tony's parents.

Beth walked toward them before they had the chance to ask any questions about Clare.

"Hi, everyone, this is Reverend Elmes, or Clare as she's asked to be called. She's the Rector here."

Tony's parents looked a little shocked but took it well. Everyone introduced themselves.

The practice went swimmingly. Clare was a panic and made us all collapse around the church laughing several times. In fact I was looking forward to the ceremony—Beth and Tony had chosen all the readings and music themselves and it would be a very personal service. And a little too interactive for my liking. I wasn't used to singing out loud!

"Did she just say we all had to sing?" Stella whispered. "Is that normal?"

"I think so," I smiled. "Don't worry. At least you have a nice voice." I'd been to a few Church of Ireland weddings and the congregation liked to belt out the hymns like there was no tomorrow. "Onward Christian Soldiers" and all that.

"Have you seen *Four Weddings and a Funeral*?" Jed asked Stella. "There's lots of singing in that. Some hymn about 'Old England.' "

"Oh, yes!" Stella said. "I do remember now."

After the practice we went back to Trudi's. Owen and Gloria had arrived and were sitting outside enjoying the sunshine with their young son, Milo.

"Hi, guys," I said as I approached their table. "Beth and Tony are inside. They'll be out in a second."

"Nice to see you again, Amy," Gloria said. Milo pulled out of my skirt and stared up at me. He had white-blond hair, huge blue eyes and sallow skin.

"Hi, Milo," I smiled. "What age are you?"

"He's not really talking much yet," Owen explained as I sat down beside them. Milo was still hanging onto my skirt. "He's only eighteen months."

"And he's a bit shy," Gloria said. "But he seems to have taken a bit of a liking to you."

"Mook," Milo said. "Choo-choo." He handed me a book with a train on the cover.

"I know this one," I beamed. "*The Little Engine That Could*. Would you like me to read it to you, Milo?"

"Mook!" Milo nodded. "Read mook!"

"He calls books 'mooks,' " Gloria laughed. "He'd love a story but don't feel you have to. It's not a busman's holiday."

"I don't mind," I said honestly. "It's one of my favorites." I lifted Milo onto my knee and began to read the familiar story.

Halfway through the second animated rendition of "*I think I can, I think I can*" I felt a hand on my shoulder.

"Hi, Amy."

I glanced up. It was Jack. My stomach lurched. I could feel my face reddening. Typical, I was pretending to be a steam-train, with my cheeks puffed out and my eyes open wide. Talk about timing!

"Hi, Jack," I said. "How was the drive?" He looked really well. He was wearing a white T-shirt and light blue denims. He had gained a little weight and his jowls had got jowlier but it suited him in a "not-a-little-boy-anymore" sort of way.

"Not too bad, thanks," he smiled. I tried to hold his gaze but he turned toward Owen and Gloria. "Milo's huge! The last time I saw him he was tiny. He must have been only a few months old."

"Has it been that long?" Gloria asked thoughtfully. "I suppose it has. Where have you been hiding yourself? You and Amy haven't been around these days." Owen glared at his wife. "Oh, sorry . . ." Gloria faltered, embarrassed.

"It's OK, Gloria," I said, trying to smooth things over. "It's fine. Jack and I are the best of friends now, aren't we, Jack?"

Jack seemed unsure how to deal with this comment. He decided to nod and move away. "Just going to ask Tony something . . ." he mumbled and went back inside. I was disappointed he hadn't stayed to talk to me but there was all weekend to catch up, after all.

Owen was restless. He was dying to go inside and join "the lads" at the bar. Tony, Jed and now Jack were all watching *Baywatch* on satellite. Or "Babe watch" as Tony liked to call it. Much as Owen loved his wife and son he had a craving for a few snatched lads-only minutes. "Drinks, Amy, Gloria?" He stood up.

"I'm fine, thanks," Gloria beamed, "for now." I shook my head. He disappeared swiftly.

"I'm sorry, Amy," Gloria said as soon as he'd left. "I didn't mean to . . ."

"Honestly, I'm OK about it. Please don't worry," I assured her. "We're both with other people now." I thought for a second. It wasn't strictly true on my part but it sounded better than admitting that I was on my own. It was easier, I suppose. "And you know Jack and Jodie are together?" I asked, stroking Milo's silky head. But not for long, I thought to myself.

"I'd heard," Gloria said. "Beth told me. That must have been hard."

"It was," I agreed. Bloody, devastatingly hard.

"And tell me about your new man," Gloria said. "Beth hasn't filled me in on that one yet."

"Did I hear my name being mentioned?" Beth smiled. "The boys are all watching *Baywatch* and the bikini and swimsuit comments are getting to me. I thought I'd come out and join the normal mortals." She sat down at our table. "Hi, Milo," she kissed him on the top of his head. "He's being very good," she said.

"Don't speak too soon," Gloria replied. "He's bound to break a couple of glasses and terrorize the cat in a few minutes." Trudi's big, fat tabby was sunning itself on the wall beside us and sure enough, Milo's eyes were fixed on the sleeping moggy. "I was just saying you hadn't told me about Amy's new man," Gloria continued.

"New man?" Beth asked in confusion. "Emilio?"

"Steve," I interrupted, staring pointedly at Beth.

"Oh, that new man," she said. "Because he's new on the scene I wasn't sure if Amy wanted people to know about him, that's all." She smiled at me. "He was at Suzi's wedding. Lovely guy. Seemed a little preoccupied that night though, I didn't really get to talk to him."

I kicked her under the table.

"So tell me," Gloria asked. "What does he do? Have you a photo? You know I rely on these things to make my suburban life more interesting."

"Suburban life, my ass," Beth giggled. "Jeez, you have the life of Reilly. Having the day to yourself with only a few nappies to change. Get a grip."

"It's not easy being at home all day," Gloria insisted. "Milo's a real handful. And it's a bit boring to be honest. Most of my friends are out at work all day. And I'm getting a bit tired of *Barney* and *Bear in the Big Blue House* to tell the truth."

"Isn't Milo going to playschool in September?" Beth asked.

"That's right," Gloria said. "I was thinking of going back to work part-time after that. In a shop or something."

"You were in publishing before, weren't you?" I asked.

"Yes," Gloria nodded. "I was in the editorial department of Puffin Books in London, before we moved back. I was in charge of the children's picture-book list."

"You know," I said slowly. "I just might have the right job for you. Lynn is always looking for good part-time help. How would you like working in The Wonderland?"

Gloria smiled. "That sounds perfect. Do you think Lynn would hire me?" she asked hopefully.

"Without a doubt," I said. "With your experience. Are you joking? Picture-books are her big thing. I'll talk to her next week."

"Thanks, Amy," Gloria said gratefully. "You may have just saved my sanity."

"I can't believe we've been here all day," Beth giggled, sipping on a glass of red wine.

"All day and all night more like," Stella smiled. "It's nearly twelve."

"No way!" Beth squealed, plonking her glass down on the table in front of her. "I'm getting married tomorrow. What am I thinking of? I need my sleep. I have to go. Where's Tony?"

Tony was sitting in the corner of the bar, one arm around Jack and the other holding a pint of Guinness.

"He looks well stuck in," I grinned. "Good luck to you. Where's he staying?"

"In the same guest house as you tonight, remember?"

The whole wedding party, those that had arrived that was, had eaten in the bar. There was a restaurant upstairs but we were leaving that till tomorrow night, as that's where we'd be eating after the wedding. We'd lost count of the wine and after-dinner drinks we'd consumed. Tony's and Beth's parents had retired for the evening, followed by Gloria and Owen, a gently snoring Milo in his arms. Unlike Dublin pubs, Trudi's was supremely child-and-parent-friendly.

"Let him sleep over there," Trudi had told Gloria at nine o'clock. She'd pointed at a small, wide bench beside the back door. The bench was covered in a long, flat cushion and was out of the way of the smoky bar. Gloria had been carrying Milo out the front door.

"I'll get him a rug and he'll be happy as Larry. Means you can stay and enjoy yourself, love."

Gloria had been so grateful she'd nearly cried. "Thank you so much," she'd gushed. "I don't get out much, you see."

"It's a special occasion," Trudi had said gently, "and I know what it's like with small children. I've grandchildren myself."

"Right, come on, you," Beth commanded, standing in front of Tony. "We're off. I'll drop you back to your guesthouse."

"Just a few more minutes, love," Tony insisted, slurring his words slightly. "Have to talk to Jack about . . ."

Beth sighed. "Please, Tony. It's late."

Tony looked up at her and beamed. "For the future Mrs. O'Leary, anything." He got up slowly. "Bye, old friend," he said to Jack. "See you tomorrow."

"Cheers, Tony," Jack grinned. "Get some beauty sleep. You need it!"

My eyes lingered on the seat vacated by Tony. "Excuse me," I said to Stella and Jed, standing up.

Chapter 40

"Amy," Jack said as I sat down beside him. He didn't say any more and we sat in silence for a few minutes. The bar was beginning to thin out and the gentle strains of "Have I Told You Lately" filled the air.

"Van Morrison," Jack said finally. "Every pub in Ireland must have a Van Morrison CD."

I smiled. "Remember this one? We used to dance to it in the kitchen."

"In the early days," Jack murmured.

"What's that supposed to mean?" I asked.

"Forget it," Jack said, running his finger up and down his pint which was sitting on the table in front of him. "I'm just a bit . . . oh, I don't know. Tony and myself were talking about old times, when the four of us used to do things together."

"Do you miss them, the old days, I mean?" I asked slowly.

He looked at me carefully. "I suppose I do," he said, shrugging his shoulders. "But things change. People change."

"I miss those days too," I began, taking a deep breath. "I miss you." There, I'd said it.

Jack put his hand on mine. "I know, Amy," he said gently, "and I miss you too. I hope we can be friends now."

"Friends?" I blurted out. This wasn't quite what I'd expected.

"You're right," Jack said. "It's probably a bit too soon to be friends. I'm sorry."

What the hell was he talking about? I tried again. "What did you want to talk about, Jack?" I asked, trying not to sound impatient, and attempting to make him move quickly to the point. He took his hand off mine.

"Jodie," he said softly.

"Jodie?" I asked. "What about Jodie?"

"She's going to kill me for telling you this."

"What?" I demanded. This "talk" wasn't going as planned.

"Listen, we've both had a few drinks. Let's discuss it tomorrow, OK?"

"No!" I exclaimed, "I want to talk about it right now. You can't start telling me something and then cut off like that. It's not fair. You've broken up, is that it?"

"Sorry?" he asked in confusion. "Whatever gave you that idea?"

"Don't act the innocent with me," I began, raising my voice. "*First* you postpone your wedding, and *then* you ring and tell me you want to talk to me. And *then* you ask me if I'm coming here alone and you show up without Jodie. What in God's name am I supposed to think?"

Jack sighed and put his head in his hands. "I'm sorry," he murmured. "I'm so, so sorry." When he raised his head there were tears in his eyes.

"But you want me back," I whispered. "I know you do."

We sat in silence for several minutes. I could feel tears pricking my eyes and there was a large lump forming in the back of my throat.

"I'm sorry if you got the wrong idea," Jack said finally. "Postponing the wedding has nothing to do with you, honestly."

I stared at him. "But I love you. You love me."

"You're not making sense, Amy," Jack said gently. "Let it go. We'd never have made it to the altar anyway. We weren't right for each other."

"What do you mean?" I asked emotionally. Tears began to roll down my cheeks. Jack handed me a red paper napkin from the table, left over from dinner.

"Here," he said kindly. "Don't cry. You'll be fine."

"Why?" I asked him. "What was wrong?"

"I don't really want to talk about this right now," Jack said, gulping back some of his pint.

"You feel guilty, don't you?" I muttered. "For treating me so badly."

"Guilty!" he spluttered, nearly choking on his drink. "OK, Amy, if you want to talk about it, let's talk about it. Starting with your unbearably moody behavior. Or your obsessive jealousy. Do you remember almost giving me a black eye the evening after Owen and Gloria's party because I'd spent the evening talking to Eithne about computers?"

"I was drunk," I sniffed. "I didn't mean to hurt you. And you were flirting with her!"

"I used to come home from work knackered and you'd be moaning on about your job and how you wanted to do something else. And we'd spend hours talking about your future and then you'd ignore all my advice and stay at that bloody bookshop."

"I've got a new job now," I said defensively. "I'm going to be working for RTE."

"Good!" Jack said, mellowing slightly. "I'm glad, about time too. What will you be doing?"

"Research on a children's art show," I said. "So you see, I have changed, really."

Jack smiled gently. "Amy, I'm not trying to argue with you. But I'm with Jodie now and we're happy."

I gulped back the tears. "But we were happy too."

"I know," he said. "But I couldn't deal with you. You need someone with more patience. Two moody people in one house just doesn't work. I used to get so annoyed and frustrated with you."

"Was I that bad?" I asked.

"Not all the time," he said. He sighed. "Sometimes. And I used to yell at you and I'm sorry for that. But I never treated you badly, Amy. Jodie said . . ."

"I shouldn't have said that to her," I said. "I'm sorry." Tears were pouring down my face. Jack put his arm around me.

"You'll be fine," he said, stroking my head. I breathed in his familiar smell. "It was you who left me, remember?"

"I know," I mumbled. "But that doesn't make it any easier."

"Amy, we've never really discussed this properly," Jack said.

"What?" I asked.

"You, me, breaking up, everything. You just shut me out. We should have talked it through."

"I know," I sniffed. "I just wasn't strong enough and when I found out about you and Jodie . . ."

"We never meant to hurt you," Jack interrupted. "I'm sorry you had to find out like that. It must have been terrible. We wanted to tell you. We were just waiting for the right time."

"I don't think there ever would have been a good time," I frowned. "I felt so betrayed and so bloody stupid."

"I can understand that," Jack said, "but I promise you, nothing happened between myself and Jodie until way after you and I broke up. We met at a work do and the rest is history."

I sighed. I didn't know quite what to say. I still hated them both for putting me through all the heartache but Jack was right—it was time to move on.

"It's in the past now," I said, attempting a smile. "And I'm sorry for telling you to fuck off at New Year's."

"That's OK," Jack grinned. "And maybe I deserved it. I should have just kept quiet."

"No," I grinned back. "In the mood I was in I still would have yelled at you in some form or another. I wasn't exactly the life and the soul of the party that night."

"And now?" Jack asked gently.

"I'm better," I said. "Things have been a little topsy-turvy but they'll sort themselves out."

"Well, you look great," Jack smiled. "But then again, you always did."

I smiled at him gratefully.

I'd painted him as a monster in my mind over the last while—mainly because it was easier that way—but he was a decent guy. "You don't look so bad yourself. Jodie must be feeding you well."

"She is," Jack agreed. "Anyway, tell me about your boyfriend. The writer."

I thought about Steve for a moment. I didn't know him the way I knew Jack, yet Steve seemed to understand me.

"His name is Steve, Steve Jones. He writes children's books," I said.

"Sounds ideal," Jack smiled. "You won't ever run out of things to talk about then."

I smiled. "No."

We listened to Van Morrison sing. I felt tired and emotionally washed out.

"That's Jodie's song," I said finally, " 'Brown-Eyed Girl.' "

"Yes," Jack said softly, looking into space. "There's something I wanted to tell you. Jodie's going to murder me but I don't care."

"What is it?" I asked. Jack's face was ashen-pale.

"I don't really know how to say this." He took a deep breath. "Jodie's mum has cancer. She's quite bad. The doctors don't know how long she has left."

"Oh my God," I whispered in shock. I didn't know what to say. Jane Ryan was a lovely woman, full of life and great energy. "I'm sorry," I began, starting to cry once more. I couldn't believe that I'd been so selfish—worrying about my love life when Jodie was losing her mother.

"It's OK," Jack said, holding my hand. "Jodie wanted to tell you herself, but the way things have been in the last while . . ."

"I've been such a bitch," I cried. "Poor Jodie."

"She's dealing with it really well," Jack said. "But you can see why we postponed the wedding."

"Of course," I whispered.

"The family doesn't want everyone to know. They want to deal with things quietly and in their own time," Jack continued. "Jodie's been staying at home a lot, to help her Mum."

I felt so bad. Whatever had happened she was still one of my oldest friends. "Where is she this weekend, Jack?" I asked softly.

"She's at home. Jane's staying in our house this weekend to get some peace and quiet and some rest."

"I'll ring Jodie first thing in the morning," I said firmly.

"I don't think . . ." Jack began.

"I have to," I told him. "It's about time I apologized. She needs her friends around her now. I hope she'll forgive me."

"She will," Jack said. "She has a big heart. Like yourself."

"Thanks," I smiled through the tears.

"Listen, it's been a long night," Jack said. "Why don't I walk you back to the guesthouse?"

"That would be nice, thanks," I smiled. We stood up and made our way toward Jed and Stella's table.

"I'm walking Amy back," Jack said to the couple.

"We should be joining you," Jed replied. "Big day tomorrow after all."

Jack offered me his arm. "Come on, Amy," he whispered. "Let's be friends. For Beth and Tony."

"And for Jodie," I added.

I slept remarkably well that evening. Talking to Jack must have had a cathartic effect. I'm sure the drink helped too.

Stella and I were sharing a large room in "The Oaks" guesthouse. Jack and Jed had rooms across the hall, and Tony had stayed in another room on the ground floor for the night. Our beds were supremely comfortable, high, brass beds with cool, white linen embroidered quilts. The room was an eclectic mix of the old and the new—an antique dressingtable was furnished with a funky steel mirror, and the wardrobe had been given a lime-green distressed look. Our bridesmaids' dresses hung ready on the back of the door.

I opened my eyes and sighed in relief as a shaft of bright sunlight was visible through the white curtains. I lay, cossetted in the soft warm bed, thinking about Jack, Jodie and our conversation the previous evening. It hurt like hell that he'd moved on but in a strange way it was a relief. Now I knew I had to get on with my own life, without Jack. And as for Jodie, I just hoped that she'd talk to me after all that had happened.

"Penny for them," Stella smiled. She was sitting up in her bed, her hair a messy dark halo around her pretty face.

I smiled. "Forget about me," I said. "What about you and Jed? You were getting on very well last night."

Stella grinned. "He's a nice guy. We were talking about computers. Anyway, I'm sure he thinks I'm a bit young for him."

"You're nearly eighteen," I said, "I wouldn't worry about that. You'll have to make the first move, though. He's very shy."

"You said that before," Stella mused, "but he didn't seem shy to me. We were chatting for hours. He has a great sense of humor."

"Maybe he's just met the right woman," I said.

She threw a pillow at me.

"What's that for?" I squealed.

"Maybe he has. Stop slagging me," she said. "I'm going to use the shower." She jumped up and loped over toward the en-suite bathroom. "See you in a minute. How are we for time, by the way?"

I looked at my watch, which was beside my mobile on the bedside table. "Grand," I said. "It's nearly ten and we have to be over with Beth at twelve."

"Perfect," she beamed, closing the bathroom door behind her.

I picked up my phone and held it for a few minutes before finding the familiar number.

"Amy?"

"Sorry, did I wake you up? It is pretty early."

"Not at all. It's fine. I was up."

"What are you doing today?" I asked.

I made one more phone call before lying back against the pillow and closing my eyes.

Chapter 41

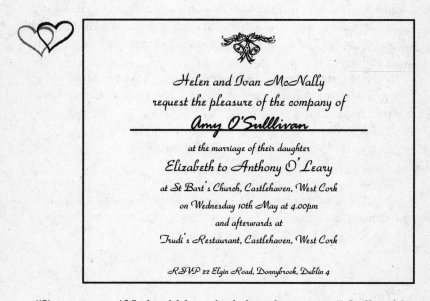

Helen and Ivan McNally
request the pleasure of the company of

Amy O'Sulllivan

at the marriage of their daughter
Elizabeth to Anthony O'Leary
at St Bart's Church, Castlehaven, West Cork
on Wednesday 10th May at 4.00pm
and afterwards at
Trudi's Restaurant, Castlehaven, West Cork

RSVP 22 Elgin Road, Donnybrook, Dublin 4

"I'm not sure if I should have had that champagne," Stella whispered to me.

"You'll be fine," I assured her. "Just think of Jed at the altar."

Stella giggled. "I'm only seventeen. It's a bit early for that, I think."

I laughed. "You know what I mean."

"What are we waiting for?" she asked.

"Beth, you ninny," I whispered. "She'll be here with her Dad in a second."

"Right," she said.

I looked toward the church gate. She'd want to get a move on. She was almost over the obligatory fifteen minutes and Tony would be getting worried.

"Here she is," Stella whispered.

Beth made her way up the church steps toward us, her Dad, Ivan, at her side.

I could feel the waterworks again. Her Dad hadn't been well recently and he was taking the steps slowly. We'd spotted Tony, Jack and Jed this morning having breakfast in "The Oaks" with Tony's parents. The lads had all looked a little worse for wear.

Stella and Beth and I had had a lovely morning getting ready. First a slap-up breakfast with Beth's parents, and then Beth did her own make-up and hair, with my and Stella's "help." Then we lazed around in the huge hotel room and drank champagne.

"Beth," Stella waved excitedly.

"Hi," Beth smiled nervously. "This is it."

"Tony's waiting for you inside," I said.

"Will I give Clare the nod?" Ivan asked.

Beth took a deep breath. "One minute, Dad." She brushed away a tear with the back of her hand. "Oh, my make-up is going to run."

"No, it won't," I said gently. "You have waterproof mascara on, remember? And anyway, what does it matter?"

"I'm just so happy," Beth smiled. She squeezed my hand. "Thanks for being here."

"My pleasure," I said. "Now we really had better get going. Tony will be bricking it."

"OK, Dad," Beth said.

Ivan popped his head inside the door.

"Take my arm, love," he said kindly to his only daughter.

The strains of violins filled the church.

"What's that music?" I asked. "It's beautiful."

"It's Mozart," Beth smiled. "Tony chose it. We weren't mad on the usual 'here comes the bride' stuff."

As we entered the church I looked up the aisle. Louise had arrived and was wearing the most amazing purple hat and matching dress. Her partner, Hal, was resplendent in a cream suit. All eyes turned toward Beth.

And in the pew in front of Louise was Jodie, standing at Jack's side, in a flowing lilac Ghost dress.

"Jodie's here," Beth turned to whisper to me.

"I know," I whispered back. "I rang her and begged her to come."

"Oh, Amy," Beth smiled. "Thank you."

As I walked up the aisle toward Tony and Jed a glowing feeling came over my whole body. It felt such a magical happy day. All the people Beth and Tony loved most in the world were gathered in this special place to wish them well.

When we reached the top of the small church Clare said, "Please be seated."

"We are gathered here," she began, "on this wonderful, sunny day for Beth and Tony's wedding. I would like to begin the service by welcoming you all to St. Bart's. I know you have all traveled to be here today and I'm delighted to share my church with you all, regardless of your religious persuasion. And now we will all sing the first hymn—'All Things Bright and Beautiful.' "

Stella smiled at me as she began to sing, her sweet voice ringing out. Jed, surprisingly, also had a wonderful voice, deep and mellow. I mouthed the words, not wanting to ruin things.

"Please be seated for the first reading," Clare said.

Beth made her way up to the bronze lectern. "This is for Tony," she said.

" 'He Wishes for the Cloths of Heaven' by William Butler Yeats."

As I listened to her voice ringing out softly but clearly in the hushed church a wave of emotion washed over me. There seemed to be a real presence in the air. It was hard to explain. A religious person would say that God was in the church, touching everyone's lives and filling everyone with his divine love. I just felt filled with a sense of calm, wonder and, for the first time in as long as I could remember, peace.

Beth finished, gazing at Tony. His eyes in turn were fixed on hers.

"Thank you, Beth. That was splendid," Clare said. "And now we have a reading from Tony."

Tony approached the lectern and coughed quietly. "Um, this is for Beth," he said nervously.

"This is from the Book of Ruth. *'Wherever you go, I will go; wherever you live, I will live; your people shall be my people and your God will be my God too. Where you die, I will die, and there I shall be buried beside you. We shall be together forever, and our love will be the gift of our lives.'* "

I'd never seen Tony cry but there were definitely tears in his eyes at that moment. Beth was smiling through her own tears. In fact, there wasn't a dry eye in the house.

"Wonderful. Thank you, Tony," Clare said. "And now we'll begin the wedding ceremony.

"Dearly beloved, we are gathered here in the sight of God and in the face of this congregation, to join together this man and this woman in holy matrimony . . ."

As I listened to Tony and Beth exchange their wedding vows I wondered how Suzi and Matt were. I missed my sister already and she'd only been away a few days. But when they moved out of Mum and Dad's I'd have to get used to not seeing her as much. I'd have to start putting together my own new life, new job and all. I was nervous but, as Jack had pointed out last night, it was about time.

Beth's mum read the lesson, all about love and loving one another. And then we all sang "Be Thou My Vision." Stella winked at me as she began to sing.

As we made our way into the side room to sign the register, Stella smiled. "That was so lovely," she sighed. "I never thought it would all be so . . . so emotional."

"They're not all like that," I smiled back. "Some weddings are boring, to be honest. It's different when you're a bridesmaid. You're more involved."

"I suppose you're right," she said. "The voice of the experienced bridesmaid speaks."

I glared at her and began to laugh.

"Did you see the cute blond guy who snuck in after the first hymn?" she asked.

"Amy," Clare interrupted, "can you sign here?" I was ushered toward the long mahogany table before I had a chance to ask Stella what the man looked like. But I knew in my heart who it was.

Outside the church I spotted him immediately. He was wearing a dark blue suit and a white shirt with a lemon yellow tie. It was sunny and he was sporting metal-framed sunglasses that made him look like a movie star. My heart leapt. I made my way toward him.

"Steve," I grinned. He kissed me tenderly on the cheek.

"You look so beautiful," he smiled. "It was a beautiful service too. I loved the Yeats poem."

"Me too," I agreed.

"Sorry I was a bit late," he said, taking my hand. "It's one hell of a drive."

"I know," I said. "It was good of you to come on such short notice." I was overjoyed that he had driven the whole way down here to be with me.

"Thanks for asking me," he beamed, taking my hand in his. "I've never been to an Irish wedding. It's a new experience for me." He brought my hand to his lips and kissed it gently.

"I want to introduce you to a few people," I said, guiding him toward Tony and Beth. "Beth, Tony, this is Steve."

"Great to meet you," Tony shook his hand warmly.

"Steve," Beth smiled, "I've heard so much about you. I'm delighted you could make it." Beth had squealed with delight when I'd told her that morning that I'd asked him. I felt a bit bad as it was supposed to be close friends and family only, but Beth has such a giant-sized heart she didn't mind one bit.

Jodie and Jack joined us. Jack smiled at me gently. Jodie was hopping from one foot to another and seemed very nervous. We looked at each other for a few seconds. And the funny thing was, I didn't feel angry with her anymore. In fact, I missed her. I gave her a hug and whispered, "I'm so sorry" into her ear.

She whispered, "It's OK. I'm sorry too" back.

"We'll catch up later," I promised her, trying not to cry.

"Yes," she smiled. She also looked on the verge of tears.

I knew things could never go back to the way they were, but maybe, in time, we could be close again.

"Jodie, this is Steve, my boyfriend." Steve took my hand, squeezed it and smiled at me.

"This is Jodie," I continued, "one of my oldest friends."

Chapter 42

 Three months later

Jane and Desmond Ryan
request the pleasure of the company of
Amy O'Sullivan & Steve Jones
at the marriage of their daughter
Jodie Ryan to *Jack Daly*
at St Paul's Church, Booterstown
on Saturday 14th August at 3:00pm
and afterwards at Blackrock Castle,
Blackrock, Co Dublin

RSVP 2 The Elms, Rathgar, Co Dublin

"Are you all right?" Steve asked as we sat together in a taxi on our way to Booterstown. "You look a little pale."

"I'm fine," I lied. My stomach was churning and I felt decidedly faint.

"Are you sure you want to go through with this?" he asked. "You don't have to."

"I know," I smiled wanly. "But I want to. Honestly."

He squeezed my hand. "I understand." He looked out the window for a few minutes and then turned toward me. "There's something I wanted to ask you."

"Shoot," I said.

"Will you go to Ella's wedding with me? It's at the end of September."

I smiled. "I'd be honored. Where is it?"

"Southampton," he said. "I'll book a hotel. There's a lovely one down by the sea."

"Sounds nice," I smiled.

"Here we are," the taxi man said, pulling up in front of St. Paul's. Steve paid the fare. He also jumped out of the taxi, held the door for me and helped me out.

I put on my large black hat, which had been resting on my knee in the taxi, and took a deep breath. "Let's go in," I smiled.

Steve gave me his arm and supported some of my weight as I'd insisted on wearing my new black kitten heels which I hadn't really mastered walking in. They looked great, though, and today of all days I wanted to look my best. In my new green dress which Beth had given me for being her bridesmaid (the one I'd loved so much in Khan), black mules and black hat I was pleased with the effect.

It was a sunny day and I popped my sunglasses on, grateful for the opportunity to be somewhat incognito.

"There's Beth," Steve said, pointing to the right side of the church entrance.

"Well spotted," I said. Being tall had its advantages. As a squirt, I knew this only too well.

Beth smiled as we approached. "You're here," she said beaming. "I'm glad. I wasn't sure if you were going to come."

"I wasn't going to," I began, "but Jack and Jodie rang me last night and begged me to come. It's what they both wanted." I squeezed Steve's arm. "And I've Steve here with me for moral support. I'm only going to stay for the ceremony."

"Then I'm taking her away for some stiff drinks," Steve smiled, his blue eyes twinkling.

Beth beamed. "It's great that you're here, Amy. Really, really great."

The guests began to move inside and we followed the crowd. Jack and Jodie's family had already taken their seats toward the top of the church. Jodie's mum looked thin and tired but there was a huge grin plastered on her face. She was a determined woman and she was responding well to the chemotherapy, much to everyone's delight. Jack and Jodie had decided to go ahead with the wedding at her request. So it really was a very special day for her family.

"Let's sit here," I suggested, gesturing toward a pew at the back of the church.

"Do you not want to go a bit further up?" Steve asked gently.

I shook my head.

As I shuffled into my seat I stared at Jack's back. He was wearing a dark red velvet jacket and matching trousers. He looked handsome. As I watched him he turned slowly and caught my eye. He looked at me intently for a long second, smiled and then raised his hand in a small wave. I took a deep breath, smiled and waved back. He turned back toward the altar.

"Penny for them," Steve whispered.

"I was just thinking about myself and Jack. The past, you know," I whispered.

Just then the church went deathly silent and all eyes were glued on the door. The music began, the same trumpet music as was played at Suzi's wedding, and Jodie appeared at the entrance. She looked stunning and very, very happy. Her cream ivory dress suited her to a T, and her elegant bouquet of lilies was simply perfect. Her two sisters, the bridesmaids, were dressed in dark red satin, the same color as Jack's suit.

As she walked slowly in the door on her father's arm, I whispered, "Good luck, Jodie."

She looked over and our eyes met. She smiled fondly. "Thanks," she mouthed. There were tears in her eyes. And in mine.

"Here," Steve said, handing me a huge, clean white linen handkerchief. "I think you'll need this."

One year later

(On RTE's morning television)

"Hi everyone, it's *Den 2* and I'm Amy O'Sullivan, your new presenter."

"Does that mean we have to be nice to you?"

"Yes, Socky. It certainly does."

"Is it a bit like the boys' and girls' first day at school when they're really nervous?"

"That's right, Socky. It's just like that. And before *Scooby Doo* I'd like to say 'hi and welcome' to baby Aran, my little nephew who was born the day before yesterday and his Mummy and Daddy, Suzi and Matt."

"That means he's only two days old!"

"That's right, Socky."

"And who's on Den 2 *later, Amy?"*

"That's a secret, Socky. But here's a clue—he writes magic books."

"Amy. I know, I know. It's Stevie J and he's your boyfriend, isn't he? And I heard you're getting married at Christmas!"

"Socky!!"

"It's true, isn't it, Amy? Amy?"

THE END

AVON TRADE... because every great bag deserves a great book!

SARAH WEBB
For when you are always in the wedding... but never catch the bouquet.

ALWAYS THE BRIDESMAID *A Novel*

Paperback $13.95
ISBN 0-06-057166-7

MICHELLE CUNNAH
32AA
Sixth time sixtine...

Paperback $13.95
($21.95 Can.)
ISBN 0-06-056012-6

playing house
patricia pearson

Paperback $13.95
ISBN 0-06-053437-0

THE **NOT-SO-PERFECT MAN**
Everyone agrees he's all wrong... except for the woman he's right for!
VALERIE FRANKEL
Author of *Smart vs. Pretty* and *The Accidental Virgin*

Paperback $13.95 ($21.95 Can.)
ISBN 0-06-053668-3

KiM WONG KELTNER
"A sumptuous Chinese banquet... The minute you're finished, you'll want to devour it all over again!"
—Carole Matthews

THE DiM SUM OF ALL THiNGS

Paperback $13.95 ($21.95 Can.)
ISBN 0-06-056075-4

#1 *NEW YORK TIMES* BESTSELLING AUTHOR
MEG CABOT
author of *The Princess Diaries* and *The Boy Next Door*

boy meets girl
Life's a game you can win... if the dice roll the right way!

Paperback $13.95 ($21.95 Can.)
ISBN 0-06-008545-2

Don't miss the next book by your favorite author.
Sign up for AuthorTracker by visiting *www.AuthorTracker.com*.

Available wherever books are sold, or call 1-800-331-3761 to order.

ATP 0304